A
Cornish
Maid

A
Cornish
Maid

RACHEL MOORE

POCKET
BOOKS

LONDON • NEW YORK • SYDNEY • TORONTO

First published in Great Britain by Simon & Schuster UK Ltd, 2006
This edition published by Pocket Books, 2006
An imprint of Simon & Schuster UK Ltd
A CBS Company

3 5 7 9 10 8 6 4 2

Simon & Schuster UK Ltd
Africa House
64–78 Kingsway
London WC2B 6AH

www.simonsays.co.uk

Simon & Schuster Australia
Sydney

A CIP catalogue record for this book is available
from the British Library.

ISBN-10: 1-4165-1151-2
ISBN-13: 978-1-4165-1151-9

Typeset in Baskerville by Palimpsest Book Production Ltd,
Polmont, Stirlingshire

Printed and bound in Great Britain by
Cox & Wyman Ltd, Reading, Berkshire

For Geoff and all our family

Chapter One

Old Mrs Penry, known to everyone locally as Granny Pen, eyed her granddaughter warily as she whirled into the cottage on the outskirts of Falmouth, her dark pigtails flying. The girl threw her school bag halfway across the room, her gas mask following with a thud, which probably did it no good at all. Granny Pen tut-tutted, hiding a smile at the familiar display, but she knew that if something had upset Amber, this wouldn't be a good time to give her the news. But when was it ever a good time? Hopefully a supper of the girl's favourite pasty and peas would soften the surprise, Granny Pen thought, more in grim determination than hope.

'I hate boys,' Amber shouted. 'They're smelly pigs, and I hate Luke Gillam most of all.'

'What's he done now?' Granny Pen said, unable to check the smile any longer, and aware that by tomorrow the two of them would be as thick as thieves again. Privately, she had every sympathy for the young boat-builder's son, knowing her granddaughter's flights of temper only too well.

1

'He says there are some more evacuees from London coming to Falmouth, and that we'll probably have to have one of them living here, and it will put my nose out of joint. I told him not to be so stupid, and that there's only room here for you and me, Gran, but he said we'd have to put up with it, same as everybody else, and I hate him.'

If Amber hadn't been seething so much she might have noticed the small silence in the living room, but the smell of the meat and vegetable pasty wafting towards her from the kitchen had begun to make her mouth water, so she found it easy enough to put Luke Gillam out of her mind for the moment.

'Would you have the poor little dabs staying in London to be killed when the Jerries start dropping bombs on them, then?' her grandmother said. 'You take in stray animals, and you're fond enough of your school friends when you're not in a spite with them. We're safe enough down here in Cornwall, so spare a thought for the poor city children who never asked to be targets for the Jerry bombs.'

If ever Amber knew she had a touch of her gran's second sight, she knew she had it now. It didn't need much to guess what was going on. Nor a look in the tea leaves to see what lay ahead, as her gran was partial to doing for anyone who was in need of her gift of fortune-telling. Not that it always worked, but few felt inclined to question it when Granny Pen got one of her 'looks'.

'You've said we'll take one in, haven't you, Gran?' Amber shrieked. 'We're all right as we are, and we

2

haven't got room for anyone else, so where is it supposed to sleep?'

There was only one place, and she knew it. The unknown evacuee, whom she hated already, would be sharing her bedroom. Sharing her meals and her cottage; and sharing her gran . . .

'Now, Amber, we don't know if we'll be having anyone yet. If we do, I've asked for a girl of your own age. It'll be company for you, a special friend to go to school with. You can show her what the country's like and teach her things, and with any luck she can tame you down a bit,' Granny Pen added.

'I've got friends to go to school with!'

'It didn't sound like it when you were grumbling about that nice Gillam boy. Wash your hands and eat your supper before it gets cold,' she said encouragingly.

Amber stared at the steaming golden crust of the pasty on the plate that her gran was putting on the table now. She turned away, not wanting to admit to the tears in her eyes and the sudden feeling that everything was going to change. To be truthful, the name of Hitler hadn't meant much to her until the teachers at school kept saying they would all be part of history, and insisting that this second world war, which was a couple of months old now, was an important and tragic time in their lives.

So far, neither Falmouth nor anywhere else, as far as Amber knew, had seen a German plane or any other sign of war, except for the ugly, rubbery gas masks everyone had been issued with, which they were supposed to carry about with them at all times. The kids at school had soon made a joke of them, painting pictures on the cardboard boxes they were in, to make each one different. They'd had one lot of evacuees in the town very early on, but there were apparently stragglers still to be dumped on them.

She knew she was being uncharitable, but as sure as eggs were eggs the Penrys were going to have one of them living in their cottage, and nothing was ever going to be the same again. Amber was twelve years old, and it felt like the beginning of the end.

'I don't know what you're so worried about,' Luke Gillam said on Saturday morning when the usual crowd of friends had cycled up to the headland where the ancient magnificence of Pendennis Castle stood in sentinel seclusion overlooking the congested little town. From here they could see the harbour and docks on one side, the wide expanse of soft golden sands and elegant hotels on the other.

'I don't want some kid sharing my bedroom, that's what,' Amber said, her eyes full of misery. 'Granny Pen says there's room enough for another bed in my room, but we'll still be squashed in together, and she'll be a stranger.'

'Not for long she won't, if you're that squashed,' Luke said, grinning.

At fourteen he could feel far superior to the crazy kid with the intense blue eyes and the streaming long

4

black hair, freed from her plaits at weekends. His father called her a wild child, and living with her weird grandmother didn't help, which was a sentiment echoed by more than one. Amber was a darned sight livelier than some of the girls at school though, thought Luke. He'd miss her company when he left next year, even though he was itching to work in the family boatyard where the smell of the freshly cut wood and paint always tingled his nostrils. To Luke, seeing a gleaming, varnished boat come to life from a detailed set of plans, or even from no more than an idea in his father's mind, was never less than exciting, sending the blood pulsing around his veins.

Amber tossed her head, aware that her friends were waiting to hear just what she was going to do about this interloper.

'Well, I shall refuse to talk to her. How long are these evacuees expected to stay with us, anyway? A week? A month?'

Luke hooted. 'Don't you ever listen to anything, Amber? Until the war's over, I suppose. For the duration, my dad calls it. He says it could all be over by Christmas, or it could go on for years. The last one lasted four years, didn't it?'

Amber looked at him in horror. 'Four years? I'm not having a strange girl sleeping in my room for four years! I'll be sixteen by then!'

'Then I'll have to marry you and take you away from it all,' Luke taunted, at which the others chanted that Luke Gillam was sweet on Amber

Penry, while she furiously said that she wasn't marrying anyone who could talk so soppy.

Granny Pen was waiting for her when she arrived home, red faced, her clothes awry, her hair blown all ways, and looking more like the wild witch of the west than a normal twelve-year-old schoolgirl. Granny Pen wasn't alone and she had obviously been out somewhere since she was wearing her tidy clothes.

'This is Miss Felixstone, Amber, the billeting officer.'

Amber had never heard of a billeting officer, and she didn't care who the woman was. She was more concerned with the small, poorly dressed girl standing diffidently beside her, looking as if she was about to burst into tears at any minute. A girl whose pale hair and pale skin made her look as though a puff of wind would blow her away.

'Who's this?' Amber said, as if she couldn't guess.

Well, she didn't know the girl's name, but she knew exactly who she was. She was an evacuee. *Their* evacuee, and the very thought of it made Amber smart with anxiety. She knew all about compassion for those less fortunate than themselves, and how they all had to do their best to befriend the city children who had been sent here already, and would be missing their homes and families. They had had it all drummed into them for the past few weeks at school.

Of course she was sorry for anyone who was

about to be bombed out of existence. At school Miss
Dean had got all tearful explaining what being an
evacuee meant, and how they'd been put on trains
to take them away from their parents, even very
young children. They each had to wear a name label
as if they were no more than a piece of luggage,
and they would rely on the good-hearted folk of
Falmouth to show them every kindness.

By the end of that little talk, half the class had
been in tears too, including Amber. But that was
when the first batch came to town, and this was
today. *She* was here, one of the so-called stragglers,
standing in their cottage with her big blue eyes fixed
on Amber's face, and her chin wobbling.

'Amber, this is Dolly Nash from Brixton in
London,' Miss Felixstone said swiftly, 'and she's
going to stay with you and your gran for a while.
She's the same age as you, and I'm sure you two
little maids are going to be great friends.'

'No, we're not!'

The two young voices spoke at the same time,
one tearful and one angry, and Amber wasn't sure
whether to laugh or be astonished or just plain mad
that this city girl could be so ungrateful when she
was being given somewhere to live away from the
Jerry bombs.

Dolly was snivelling now, and Miss Felixstone was
mopping her up while Granny Pen fussed around
her. Amber glared at Dolly and Dolly glared right
back through those swimming blue eyes.

'Miss Felixstone's brother has put an extra bed in

your room while you were out, Amber, so you can take Dolly upstairs and show her where to put her things. She doesn't have very much,' Granny Pen said meaningly, as if to make Amber more aware of how much she had herself.

Amber turned without speaking, knowing that if she said anything she would just explode, and then that prim Miss Felixstone would go back to her billeting committee and tell them how disgracefully the Penry girl was behaving. For a second, Amber paused with her hand on the banister, wondering if she dared to do such a thing anyway, and if it would mean that Dolly Nash would be taken away from such a bad influence.

'I won't be a bother, honest I won't,' she heard Dolly whisper right behind her, and then the moment was gone and Amber marched up the stairs of the cottage, with Dolly right behind her like a little pale ghost. Amber flung open her bedroom door. Her bed had been pushed against one wall, and a second bed was now against the other wall, made up neatly. She sat down on her own, claiming possession, her arms folded tightly, while Dolly put down her small case and her gas mask on the second bed.

'I didn't want you here,' Amber said, to make things crystal clear, and forgetting everything she had been told about extending the hand of friendship.

'I didn't want to come.'

Away from the adults, she answered smartly. Perhaps she wasn't as dumb as she looked, Amber thought uneasily.

8

Rachel Moore

'Why not? Would you rather have stayed in dirty
old London?'

'I'd rather have stayed with my mum and dad,
but they said it wasn't safe. Besides, my dad's joined
up now, and my mum has to work down the market,
so I'd be a bother. Where's your mum and dad, or
is it only your gran who lives here?'

Amber jumped up from the bed and dragged
open a drawer. 'You ask too many questions, and
you can put your stuff in here. I'm going downstairs
and you can come down when you're ready.'

'I'm only trying to be friendly like I'm supposed
to.'

So they had been instructed too, Amber thought.
'Well, somebody's bound to tell you, so if you must
know my mum died when I was born and my dad
was drowned when I was two, so it's just been my
gran and me ever since.'

'Oh. That's why you think I'm pushing in, then.'

Amber flew back downstairs, where Granny Pen
was setting three places at the table. Three plates, three
sets of knives and forks. Three mugs. It said it all.

'Give it time, my dear,' Granny Pen said sympathetically. 'Remember she'll be missing her folks.
We'll all settle down in a day or two.'

Amber nodded without speaking. She knew that
jealousy was a sin, and that it was stupid to feel such
sharpness in her chest whenever she thought of
Dolly Nash's bright fair hair and big blue eyes.

Little Dolly daydream, she thought, just like one
of the pictures on a box of chocolates, so small and

9

dainty, and making her feel like an elephant along-side her. She knew she mustn't be jealous. She mustn't be unkind. She must learn to share Granny Pen if she had to. Lord knew half the town did, anyway, coming to her for advice and a look at the tea leaves or a palm reading, or one of her herbal remedies that did more for coughs and colds than all the doctor's stuff.

She'd even have to share her school friends with Dolly daydream, and Luke Gillam wouldn't want to marry her once he set eyes on *her* . . . Amber drew in her breath, wondering where such a thought had come from. It was almost like one of Granny Pen's revelations, flitting into her head just when she needed them most.

Well, Amber didn't need that kind of revelation, thank you very much. She might be a big girl for her age and starting to develop in all kinds of ways that she didn't fully understand, despite Granny Pen having awkwardly explained it all. But it had nothing to do with boys, she thought disdainfully, no matter how handsome he was with his hair black enough to match her own and his laughing eyes that could tease her enough to drive her mad.

'Where have you gone to now, Amber?' she heard Granny Pen say. 'Have you and Dolly made friends yet? She seems a nice little thing, and I hope you're not going to leave her all by herself.'

'Oh, I'm not going to do that, Gran,' Amber said in a kind of strangled voice. 'I'll keep my eye on her, don't you worry.'

It was funny that she'd begun to call her Dolly daydream, too, Amber thought, since *she* was the one letting daft daydreams start her heart thumping.

That night, after they had blown out their candles and pulled back the blackout curtains a little so that they weren't in complete darkness, Amber lay stiffly in her bed, trying to shut out the unfamiliar sound of someone else's breathing. She was never going to sleep for all the sniffing and snuffling. She buried her head beneath the bedcovers, but it slowly dawned on her that the creaks coming from the other bed were more than the other girl trying to get comfortable on the lumpy and unfamiliar mattress. Amber peered out from the jumble of sheets and blankets, trying to see across the room to where the bulge in the bedclothes was heaving up and down.

'Are you crying?' Amber said hoarsely.

''Course not,' Dolly mumbled.

'Yes you are! What's up?'

The sudden rage in Dolly's voice took her by surprise.

'What the bleedin' hell do you think is up? How would you like to be dragged hundreds of miles away to live with some daft old woman and her bossy kid?'

Amber sat bolt upright. For the moment she ignored the swearing, which would certainly have shocked Granny Pen if she'd heard it.

'Granny Pen's not daft, and I'm not bossy!'

11

'She's an old witch, if you ask me,' Dolly raged again. 'She looks like it, anyway, with her funny clothes and her grey curls that look as if they've been stuck on with glue. I'll be looking for her bleedin' black cat next.'

Amber felt her mouth twitching. 'You'd better not let her hear you talking like that or you'll be for it.'

'What's she going to do – put a spell on me?' Dolly said, full of sarcasm.

The next minute there was a loud tapping on the bedroom wall, and Dolly gave a small scream and leaped across the room and into Amber's bed.

'Get off me,' Amber gasped. 'It's only Gran telling us to go to sleep.'

'I don't like it here,' Dolly said, shivering. 'I want to go home.'

Amber considered. She didn't particularly want the kid clinging to her in a fright. On the other hand, it made her feel superior and sorry for her at the same time. She disentangled Dolly's arms from around her neck.

'Well, you can't, and you'll soon get used to it. Gran's looked after me all my life and she ain't put a spell on me yet, so why would she put one on you – even if she could? Which she can't,' she added hastily. 'Go back to bed and go to sleep.'

Dolly slid out of the bed and stood for a moment, pale and fragile in her nightdress. Then, without a word, she sped back to her own bed and mumbled goodnight.

'And don't let the bed bugs bite,' Amber said automatically. She thought she heard a small giggle, but probably not. In any case she was too fed up to care.

'My dad don't hold with church-going,' Dolly said flatly.

Amber held her breath at such blasphemy as Granny Pen rammed her black church-going hat on top of her rigid grey curls. The Cornishwoman wasn't much taller than Dolly, but as she asserted herself in her Sunday best clothes she seemed to tower above the young girl.

'I never heard such talk, and while you're here, my girl, you'll come to church on Sunday mornings with Amber and me. You'll show some respect for the Lord, and give thanks for your deliverance out of the jaws of evil.'

'Blimey,' Dolly said.

Amber grinned nervously. Granny Pen didn't often go off on a religious tirade, but she had the gift of the gab for any occasion when required. She looked Dolly coolly up and down now.

'I'm sure the good Lord will overlook such language since you're new to our ways, Dolly, so go and tidy yourself.'

'I am tidy.'

'Aren't they the clothes you were wearing yesterday when you arrived with Miss Felixstone?'

'What if they are? What's wrong with them? I ain't got nothing else, so if you're ashamed of me I'll just have to stay indoors, won't I?'

Granny Pen tutted. 'I wasn't thinking, and of

course we're not ashamed of you, my dear. We're glad to have you here, but I think you'll be a bit cold in that blouse, so you can borrow one of Amber's jumpers.'

Amber felt her mouth drop open, and all her sympathy for the evacuee who was being delivered from the jaws of hell, according to Granny Pen, vanished in an instant. Here it was then, the first hint that Granny Pen was going to favour the little squirt over her. No, the *second* hint, because the first one was having to share her bedroom. But she had no option but to fetch one of her jumpers for Dolly to wear. It was too big for her, but she didn't seem to mind that, and ten minutes later the three of them trooped off to church, and Amber had to stand the indignity of having the vicar and the town do-gooders fawning over Dolly and all the other little aliens.

'What's she like then?' she heard Luke Gillam's voice hiss behind her, as people lingered outside the church after the service as usual.

'She's a drip,' Amber snapped. 'Just look at her, making up to everybody like a little waif and stray.'

Luke laughed. 'You're jealous because she's got long blonde hair and baby-blue eyes,' he stated, his eyes dancing with mischief.

'I'm not jealous! Why should I be jealous? She's only staying with us for a little while and then I'll never see her again, and good riddance.'

As if aware that they were talking about her, Dolly glaned their way. The early November sunshine

14

seemed to light up her hair as she half turned, so that for a moment the strands of it were like pure gold. She was pretty, Amber thought, with a stab of fury. She was far too pretty. If they'd had to have an evacuee, why couldn't they have had a younger kid with glasses and rabbit teeth, not one who was going to attract everyone in sight, especially Luke Gillam?

She caught her breath, suddenly aware of the way he was looking at Dolly daydream Nash. She couldn't pretend she had ever thought of him in terms of a boyfriend. She wasn't ready for any of that stuff yet, and Granny Pen would soon put the clappers on it if she was. He was just Luke, part of the group who went tearing up to the headland on their bikes and larked about near Pendennis Castle and explored some of the cliff-side caves. Even though he was fourteen years old and as handsome as any film star at the flicks, he was still one of the gang, and as daft as the rest of them.

But in that split second, she knew that the way he was looking at Dolly now was different from any way Amber had ever seen him look before. She couldn't explain it. It was almost as if he was just waking up from a dream . . . or moving into a dream . . . Dolly daydream . . .

The searing feeling that surged through her took her completely by surprise. It was jealousy, raw and simple. She was jealous of the way Luke was looking at Dolly Nash, in a way he had never looked at Amber. And he was hers, she thought savagely. Her friend, her boy. She snapped into action and yanked at his arm, forcing him to look away from the white-haired wonder.

'How about going up to the castle this afternoon?' she said feverishly. 'We could take a picnic if the others are game, and it may be one of the last chances before the weather turns colder.'

She hadn't actually mentioned it to anyone else yet, but she was confident that the rest of their friends would agree. They usually agreed to whatever Amber Penry wanted to do.

'Good idea. My mum's got an old bike that will do for Dolly if you haven't already got one, and I can bring it over to the cottage when you're ready.'

She stared at him stupidly. Including Dolly hadn't been part of the plan, but she saw now that it would have to be. Everything they did from now on would have to include Dolly. She saw too that Dolly was going to be a novelty. She looked different, she talked differently, in that funny quick accent that they couldn't always follow, and she *was* different. That was the attraction, of course, and once people got used to her and all the other evacuees who were getting all the attention at church that morning, the novelty would fade away.

Amber saw Granny Pen watching them, and she let go of Luke's arm quickly.

'I'll see you this afternoon then. Bring the bikes and some sandwiches.'

Granny Pen had reached them now, and nodded to Luke before he went to join his family.

'I see you've changed your tune, but there's time enough for boys, Amber.'

'He's only a school friend, Gran!' she protested, feeling her face flush.

'And you're growing up fast, and I've got eyes to see and a wise old head on my shoulders.'

'What does that mean?' Amber said crossly as Dolly came skipping across the gravel to join them, her face eager and almost glowing.

'I've just met Miss Dean, Amber, and she says we'll be in the same class at school tomorrow. It makes me feel better already, knowing I've got a friend.'

She linked arms with Amber, just as if she had known her all her life, Amber thought, enraged. Just as if they were sisters or something. Well, that might be the way London folk behaved, in and out of one another's houses and poking their noses into one another's lives, but it wasn't way they did things down here. Not that she really had the faintest idea how London folk behaved, but the plain fact was that she didn't want to know, either. She didn't want Dolly here, and she didn't want another friend. She already had friends.

Across the church gravel they heard the sound of wailing, and Granny Pen made sympathetic noises in her throat.

'Look at those poor little dabs. They can't be more than six or seven years old and they'll be missing their mum and dad something dreadful.'

The two children were obviously twins, clinging to one another with the offensive gas mask boxes

banging against their sides, and apparently incon-
solable as one of the church ladies tried to give them
sweets to calm them down.

'They were on the same train as me,' Dolly said.
'Their teacher tried to make them recite nursery
rhymes, but they couldn't stop crying then, either,
poor little buggers. They'll just have to make the
best of it, same as we all will, I suppose.'

Granny Pen hustled her charges away, clearly
thinking that if Dolly was going to use that kind of
language it had better not be in the vicinity of the
church, and that the sooner it was curbed the better.

But right then Amber couldn't blame her for the
way she spoke. What she said was more important.
It must be heartbreaking to be so small and be taken
away from your parents to somewhere completely
new to live with strangers. Those kids had probably
never even seen a cow or the sea before. She hadn't
really considered it until that moment and it made
her think twice about how unwelcoming she had
been to Dolly. The guilty feeling wouldn't last, and
she knew it wouldn't, but perhaps it was time to
make a gesture, if only to please Granny Pen.

'You can come up to Pendennis Castle with us
this afternoon if you like,' she said grudgingly. 'Luke
can probably borrow his mum's old bike for you
now she doesn't use it any more. I suppose you can
ride one?' she said sarcastically.

'I never even tried before, but I'm willing to try
if Luke will show me how,' Dolly said, with a gleam
in her eyes.

Chapter Two

Amber didn't know much about London, except that it was a city where the king and queen and the two little princesses lived. If she'd thought about it at all, she'd have thought everybody else who lived there was just as posh, and that the evacuees who were sent away to the country for safety would be posh too, though you couldn't really tell from some of the smaller ones. But now there was Dolly Nash, who looked as if she didn't have two halfpennies to rub together and was going to be given some of Amber's clothes to wear in order to look decent. If ever there was a cause for simmering resentment on Amber's part, that was it.

'We've got to be generous and not selfish, Amber,' Granny Pen told her one frosty morning when Dolly had gone scampering down to the lav in the garden. 'I don't think she's got much of a home life, by all accounts, and once the Jerries start bombing in earnest it's a sure thing they'll be aiming for London, so we must do all we can to make Dolly feel at home here.'

'She's not staying for ever, is she?' Amber said in a panic. The sudden vision of the two of them growing older and bigger as the years went by, and filling that tiny bedroom, was too much to bear.

'Of course not. She'll want to go home as soon as possible, but nobody knows when that will be.'

Dolly had appeared back inside the cottage now, shivering with the early morning chill, creeping about and eavesdropping like a perishing little ghost, Amber thought in annoyance.

'My mum says she'll be too busy to see me for Christmas, but she'll try to get down here for my birthday, if she can get the train fare,' she announced.

Amber groaned. 'When's that then?'

'February the eighth. I'll be thirteen then.'

'You can't be. You've been looking at my school rough book.'

'No I haven't. Why can't I be thirteen on February the eighth?'

'Because that's *my* birthday,' Amber said.

Granny Pen banged three dishes on the table for their breakfast porridge.

'Well, if that's not the funniest thing. Sharing a birthday is an omen that you two are meant to be friends.' She ignored the way the two girls were glaring at one another and went on relentlessly. 'The next time you write to your mother, Dolly, you must tell her about the coincidence, and that we hope she'll be able to come to Cornwall for your birthday so we can all have a party.'

'My Dad don't hold with parties,' Dolly said.

'What *does* he hold with?' Amber said. 'He sounds a blooming misery if you ask me.'

Dolly's sudden rage took them both by surprise. 'He's not a misery and you've got no bleedin' right to say that. Anyway, whatever he's like, it's better than not having a dad at all!'

Before Amber's temper could fly up to match hers, Granny Pen intervened.

'It's time we put down a few ground rules if we're all to get along together, Dolly, and one of them is that *we* don't hold with swearing. I'll overlook it this time, but if you do it again you'll go and wash your mouth out with soap.'

Dolly looked at her in astonishment. 'I never swore. When did I swear?'

Granny Pen sighed. If the girl didn't even know she was doing it, what hope did they have in curbing her? Since neither girl was touching the wholesome porridge she had put in front of them now, she tried another tack.

'Get on with your breakfast, both of you. There are starving children in Africa who'd be glad of it.'

She ignored the muttered comment from both girls that they could flipping well have it then, and went on calmly.

'We'll have a birthday party for both of you, whether your mother's here or not, Dolly. It's a special milestone for a girl to reach the age of thirteen.'

Privately, she was thinking again that the poor

little dab couldn't have had much of a life in Brixton if she didn't even have a party on her birthday. Amber might not have a mum and dad, but she didn't want for love and home comforts. She hoped desperately that the two of them would start to get along, but Dolly had been here a month already, and so far there wasn't much sign of it.

'Why don't your dad hold with parties then?' Amber said sullenly as they cycled to school that morning, now that Dolly had mastered the art of it with Luke Gillam's help. 'He's no bible-puncher if you say he don't hold with church-going either.'

Unexpectedly she found her lips starting to twitch. Without warning she had imagined a black-clad figure with horns coming out of his head putting a damper on everything his daughter wanted to do. Not that Dolly had wanted to go to church at first, but she always joined in the singing now in her thin reedy voice.

'What's so funny?' Dolly said, wobbling dangerously on her bike as she glared at Amber.

'You are. Sometimes I don't know what to make of you, Dolly daydream.'

'That's because you don't know me, and you don't want to!' she snapped, and then she shot ahead of Amber, pedalling as fast as her legs would take her.

'Don't go so fast,' Amber shouted.

It was too late. Dolly suddenly swerved to avoid a cat in the road. The cat squealed with fright and Dolly crashed into the kerb and went headlong over the handlebars to land in a bramble hedge. By the time Amber caught up with her she was sitting on the pavement hugging her knee, her eyes brimming.

'You idiot. I told you not to go so fast!'

'I'm bleeding!' Dolly howled. 'I don't like blood.'

Amber prised her hand away from her knee where there was a nasty looking graze and a few scratches from the brambles.

'You should be glad that hedge was there or you'd have banged your head and you might have killed yourself, you idiot,' Amber said again, and then she realised that Dolly was whimpering now.

'Stop calling me that. It really hurts.'

Amber fished a grubby looking plaster from her pocket, then decided it wouldn't cover the graze and discarded it. She spat on her clean hanky to dab away the worst of the blood and grit as gently as she could.

'I'll tie this up for you and then you'd better see if you can still ride your bike. If not, we'll have to walk and tell Miss Dean why we're late.'

'What will she do?'

'Well, she won't kill us. Now, shut up while I see to this.'

When it was done, Dolly spoke humbly. 'I don't really mean to be a bother, Amber. You were good at fixing my knee, and I think you should be a nurse.'

'Good Lord, I did hardly anything at all, you ninny. Now come on, or it won't be worth going to school at all today.'

She wasn't going to admit that Dolly's words had

made her feel quite puffed up. Dolly might be small
and blonde and pretty, but she was afraid of blood,
even from a little scratch. It made Amber feel superior, but not in a bad way, to her surprise. It made
her feel that she could do things that Dolly couldn't.
She could even be a nurse if she wanted to be. If
only she was older she could nurse the poor
wounded soldiers when they came home from the
war, and see the undying love and admiration in
their eyes. She could be a proper little Florence
Nightingale . . . and if only her birthday in February
was going to be her eighteenth instead of her thir-
teenth, she could be doing it right now, she thought,
with her usual impatience.

'Why d'you call me Dolly daydream when it's more
often you who's going off in a trance?' Dolly's voice
came out of the darkness that night in bed.

Amber didn't answer for a minute, still caught up
in the unlikely dream of tending a slightly wounded
Luke Gillam and seeing that look of undying love
and admiration in his eyes. He'd only be very slightly
wounded, of course. She wouldn't want anything
major to happen to him . . .

She gave a start at Dolly's words, annoyed at being
jerked out of her dream.

'I don't know. The words just went together, I
suppose.'

'Well, I wish you wouldn't do it. Why did they
call you Amber, anyway? It's a daft name for a girl.'

'No it's not. It's the name of a semi-precious stone.

Don't you know anything? It's better than Dolly, anyway. Makes you sound like a doll.'

'It's Dorothy, actually.'

'Oh, it is *actually*, is it?'

Granny Pen's tapping on the bedroom wall made them both jump.

'Is there anybody there?' Amber said in a deep, mysterious voice that started Dolly giggling. 'Shut up, or she'll be in here. How's your knee, by the way?'

'It's all right, thanks. 'Night.'

''Night,' Amber said, gazing up at the ceiling and considering.

She supposed it wasn't as bad as she had thought at first, having Dolly around, as long as she knew the rules and kept away from Luke Gillam. Well, not that she could strictly keep away from him, but as long as she understood that Luke was out of bounds in a certain way, they would be all right. It wasn't as if any of them was old enough to have a proper boyfriend, and Granny Pen would soon put a stop to any of that nonsense, but Amber had known Luke far longer, and still had a proprietary right to him.

She turned over in bed, and as she drifted off to sleep the image of an older version of herself in some kind of uniform, leaning over a handsome boy in a hospital bed and saying soothing words to him, wouldn't quite go away.

'Do you believe in visions?' she asked Luke one Saturday morning. They were in his father's boatyard and she had called there after doing some shopping in the town. She leant on her bicycle, the pungent smell of paint in her nostrils as she watched his deft brushstrokes on a boat repair.

He burst out laughing. 'You've gone cuckoo again. You spend too much time with Granny Pen and her fortune-telling, Amber.'

'Well, I can hardly help it, seeing as how I live with her, can I? But I don't mean that. I mean, do you think a vivid dream can foretell the future?'

He put down his paintbrush and looked at her uneasily.

'No idea. I suppose it depends on the dream. I wouldn't pay too much attention to it myself.'

'Do you think I'm cut out to be a nurse then?'

'I think you're potty. Not so long ago you were going to be a hairdresser. What makes you think you'd be any good at being a nurse?'

She shrugged, wishing she'd never said anything. 'Oh, it was just something somebody said, that's all.'

Luke picked up the paintbrush and continued working. 'If you really want to know, I think you could do anything you set out to do.'

'Really?'

'Really. And that's enough flattery for one day. You'd better get out of here before my dad starts accusing me of wasting time.'

She was ready enough to go. She'd left Dolly tidying up their bedroom, since they were now taking it in turns, and she preferred shopping, anyway, with the added incentive of seeing Luke out of school hours. She preened at his having said he thought she could be anything she set out to be. It might be a nurse, or it might be something quite different, she thought breezily. She could be anything she chose.

The sight of a funeral procession going through the town stopped her thoughts abruptly. She knew who it was for. A friend of her gran's had come to the cottage completely distraught, to say that her son's aeroplane had been shot down over the English Channel. He'd managed to bale out but he'd been badly wounded, and he'd died in hospital. As Amber caught sight of his mother, all in black and weeping as she clung to her husband, she knew this must be his funeral.

It sobered her at once. It was easy, sometimes, to forget down here, where nothing much was happening, that there was a war on. Of course, the newspapers were full of it, and Granny Pen listened to the wireless all the time. She told the girls that they should do so too, but it was all too depressing and far away when you were only twelve-going-on-thirteen.

But this wasn't far away at all. This wasn't some distant country where bad things happened. This was here in Falmouth where the sad little procession for Ronnie Hanham's funeral went through the streets to the churchyard. Amber remembered him as a cheerful red-haired chap who'd been mad with excitement about joining up as soon as the war started, and had always wanted to fly. He was only nineteen, and now he was dead, and people were standing respectfully in the street as the procession went by and men were removing their hats, and some of the women were openly weeping.

Amber shuddered wildly, and as soon as she decently could she got back on her bike and rode as hard as she could until she reached home. She flung the bag of shopping on the kitchen table and tore upstairs to her bedroom, slamming the door behind her and flinging herself on her bed, face down.

'Blimey, what's happened?' Dolly said. 'Have you lost a shilling and found a tanner or something?'

'Shut up! Leave me alone!'

'Well, pardon me for breathing,' Dolly said.

When she heard the bedroom door open and shut again, Amber knew she would have gone downstairs to report to Granny Pen how Amber was behaving. She did that, she seethed. She was a sneak. They might be getting on a bit better these days, but Dolly Nash was a sneak. She told on people. She probably always would, if it made her out to be the shining angel.

Granny Pen came upstairs a few minutes later. Her voice was gentle.

'I know what's happened, and I shouldn't have asked you to go into the town today, Amber, on the day they were burying young Ronnie Hanham.'

Amber sat up, her face tear-stained, her hair wild. She didn't ask how Granny Pen knew uncannily that this was the reason she was so upset. Granny Pen could always put two and two together, sometimes even two and one.

'It was awful to see his mum and dad and his little brother, all clinging together and crying. They looked as if they didn't know how to walk along behind the car. It was horrible, and I *hate* the Germans,' she burst out.

Granny Pen stroked her hair. 'I'm afraid that's the price we all pay in a war, my love. I daresay somewhere in Germany there are mothers and fathers crying over their sons as well.'

'That doesn't make it any better.'

'I know. I'm just trying to point out that there are two sides to it all.'

'They started it though, didn't they? They invaded Poland and started it all.'

Shaken as she was by what she had seen that day, Amber was amazed and guiltily pleased that she had taken in this much information. Right there and then, she resolved to be more informed on what was happening in the war. If it went on for years and years, her friends at school might have to join up. Some of them might come home wounded, or never come home at all. It was enough to give her nerves a real attack of the jitters. This wasn't dreaming. This was real.

'Come down and have a cup of tea, Amber. I'll put in one of my herbal powders and it will help to calm you down. You've had a shock, but it's over now, and there's nothing you can do about it. If it's made you more aware of the plight of other people perhaps it's all to the good.'

'You mean I'm a selfish brat, don't you?'

Granny Pen laughed at Amber's frank assessment of herself. 'I wouldn't say that, my love. But you're straightforward and honest, I'll give you that. Come on now, or Dolly will wonder what's wrong with you.'

Oh yes, Dolly. Dolly the sneak, who wasn't as straightforward and honest as Amber was . . . but she knew she should be more tolerant towards her. She didn't particularly want to, and she would have preferred not to. But Dolly's dad had also gone away to fight in the war, and he could die too.

'It's a shame Dolly's mum can't get down to see her at Christmas, isn't it, Gran?' she forced herself to say huskily. (And even take her back to London.)

'We all have to make the best of things now, even at Christmas,' Granny Pen said, and then added, 'especially as it may be the last good one for a while.'

Somehow Ronnie Hanham's funeral, and what it meant, resulted in an uneasy truce between the two girls. Dolly wasn't aware of why Amber had changed a little, but there was no doubt that they began to mellow towards each other.

Now that Amber had got more interested in the war – in a purely academic way, she told her friends airily, which had them all hooting – she was going to save any newspaper articles that intrigued her.

'Oh Lord, she's going to be a journalist now,' Luke said with a mock groan.

'No I'm not. I just think we should be aware of what's happening. Gran says bacon and butter's about to be rationed, so we've all got to pull our horns in, whatever that means.' She lowered her voice so that Dolly wouldn't hear. 'The newspaper said the Jerry planes dropped some mines in the Thames Estuary. That's near London, isn't it?'

'Well, as long as they don't drop them here, you needn't worry too much.'

'No, but Dolly might.'

'Is her dad in the navy?'

'No, the army, I think.'

'Well then,' he said, as casual as you like.

She felt like stamping her foot. Here she was, trying to be all grown up and sensible about what was happening, and he was treating her like a little girl who didn't know what was going on. But she did. She knew it would be the big cities that would be in the worst danger when the bombs fell, as well as the ports like Portsmouth and Plymouth along the south coast. She wasn't a complete idiot. And Plymouth wasn't that far away. She'd already found it on the map.

'Would you join up if the war went on for years and years, Luke?'

He snorted. 'Of course I would. I'd go now if I could. In the last war kids of fourteen joined up, lying about their age.'

'Oh, you'd never do that, would you?' she said in sudden fright.

He laughed. 'My dad would soon haul me back

31

if I tried it. But if the time comes, I'll join the navy like a shot.'

Dolly sauntered across to them in time to hear his last remark.

'I bet you'll look smashing in bell-bottoms, Lukey,' she said archly, at which Amber pretended to throw up, instantly forgetting all about the mines that had been dropped into the Thames Estuary.

They had as good a Christmas as possible, considering that Dolly spent half of it crying and wishing she was back home in what she called 'the smoke', and Granny Pen was bemoaning the fact that sugar and meat were going to be rationed in the new year as well, and soon they'd have nothing in the cupboard to eat at all.

'We must grow our own vegetables,' she declared. 'You girls can help me dig up the back garden and we'll plant seeds. By the summer we'll have a few cabbages and potatoes, if nothing else.'

The girls weren't thrilled by the idea, but in any case a spell of very cold weather stopped all such thoughts as they huddled around the fire during January. According to the newspapers, the river Thames froze over for the first time since 1888, even pushing news about the war aside for a moment.

'Do you think the cold weather will stop my mum coming down for my birthday?' Dolly said anxiously. 'I ain't heard much from her lately.'

'I'm sure she'll get here providing the trains are running, my dear.'

Dolly's mum wasn't a good letter-writer, and Granny Pen had her doubts that she would make the long journey to Cornwall in early February. There was no room for her to stay at the cottage, but a neighbour had promised to let her have a room for a couple of nights. There was always some doubt as to whether or not it was a good thing for the evacuees' families to visit them. Much as they would all be longing to see one another, it could unsettle the children and cause more heartache when they had to part all over again.

'She won't bring me anything if she does come,' Dolly said to Amber that night, during their usual lights-out chat. 'Well, I suppose she might bring me something off the stall, but it won't be much. My dad always says we can't waste money on fripperies.'

'Why doesn't he ever write to you?' Amber said, but she knew at once it was the wrong thing to say. Any minute now and she'd hear the words 'My dad don't hold with giving presents'.

'I told you, he's away in the army. Soldiers don't have time for writing letters. He writes to my mum when he can, and always sends a kiss for me,' Dolly said crossly. Then she gave a great sigh. 'I miss him more than my mum, really.'

Amber was silent. Not having had a mum or a dad to miss – well, not a dad that she could remember – she didn't know how to respond, although she'd have thought a person would miss them equally.

'We sometimes had uncles coming to the house,

see?' Dolly said next in a funny sort of strangled voice. 'Whenever my dad was on night shift at the factory before he joined up we sometimes had uncles coming round, and I never had to say anything about them. My mum always got dressed up for the uncles, and she smelled 'specially nice then, and sometimes the uncles would give me sweets, but I didn't have to tell my dad about that, neither.'

'Why not?' Amber said in astonishment, not understanding any of this.

'Oh, you're so *dumb* sometimes, Amber! They were having it off with my mum, see, although I'm not exactly sure what that means,' she admitted. 'But sometimes I'd hear them giggling and whispering, and it always made me want to cry because my dad wasn't there to join in the fun.'

'Gosh. You poor thing,' Amber said, completely bewildered now.

'Yes, well, you're not to say nothing about it, because it's my secret and I shouldn't have told you at all,' Dolly said fiercely. 'Promise me you won't say nothing, or I'll never speak to you again.'

'Of course I promise! I'd never tell a secret.'

Even as she said it, and meant it, she couldn't help thinking that Dolly would tell, if ever the need for it occurred, but this was a family secret that was somehow serious and solemn, and whoever these uncles were, they must be special to make Dolly's mother so happy. It was a shame that in the process they made Dolly cry. If she dared, she'd ask Luke at a convenient moment what 'having it off' with

somebody meant, being sure not to give anything
away, of course.

He spluttered over the drink of lemonade his
mother had made for them both. It had been an
inspiration to tell Granny Pen she could ask Luke's
dad for a small pot of paint to tidy up the door of
their outside lav before Dolly's mum arrived next
month. Now, armed with the paint, and being left
alone with him for five minutes, she asked the innocent question.

'Who the hell have you been talking to?' he hissed.

'Nobody,' Amber said, feeling her cheeks go hot
at this response. 'Why? What does it mean, anyway?'

'You're too young to know.'

'I'm not too young to ask a perfectly ordinary
question and if you don't tell me, I'll have to ask
somebody else. Your dad, for instance, or Miss Dean!'

She looked so indignant that he started to laugh.
'Oh Amber, you're a girl and a half, you are. Don't
you dare go asking my dad or Miss Dean, or she'll
have a blue fit.'

'Well, what *is* it then? You're always such a know-
all that I was sure you could tell me.'

He studied her thoughtfully. He would be leaving
school soon, and was already thinking he might stop
going around with the school crowd once he started
work properly. They were all such kids, but looking
into Amber Penry's enquiring blue eyes now, he felt
anything but childish feelings towards her. She was
already too knowing, in a way she didn't even

understand, and yet still so innocent, as the blunt question had proved. He wondered where she had heard it. It was the sort of daring language the bigger lads used when they were larking about, yet never having tried it on with a girl, of course, despite all their bragging.

'If you won't tell me, I'm going home,' she said flatly.

'All right, I'll tell you, but not here.' He put his hand over hers and could feel it tremble. Probably with rage, he thought. She was nothing if not passionate about something she wanted to know or do. 'Let's go for a ride.'

They left the boatyard and eventually pushed their bikes down one of the narrow cobbled alleyways to the quay, where they sat on a bench and watched the ships in the harbour. It was too cold to be sitting around for long, and Amber snuggled down into her coat collar, wondering what was so interesting about what Dolly had said that it couldn't be told in Luke's mother's front room.

He explained it simply, fighting down his own embarrassment at realizing he shouldn't be the one to tell her such intimate things. Her eyes grew large as she listened, her hands clasped together. And then she looked at him frankly.

'So if somebody was having it off with somebody they weren't married to, even a relative, that would be wrong, wouldn't it?'

'Good God, Amber, who's put such ideas into your head?

'Nobody. I'm just trying to get it straight. So is that right – what I just said?'

'Yes, it is, but you'd better forget it, because it's not the sort of thing your gran would want you to be talking about.'

'I shan't tell her, then,' she said, slipping off the bench.

Before either of them knew what she was going to do, she leaned forward and planted a kiss on his cold cheek, before grabbing her bike and pushing it back up the cobbled alleyway, and leaving him wondering what the hell had got into her today.

Chapter Three

Dolly's mother arrived on the afternoon of the
birthday, flustered and hot from the long train ride
from Paddington, but still joking about sharing a
compartment with half a dozen cheeky servicemen
who kept her amused on the journey. Gertie Nash
was buxom, as blonde as Dolly, as pert in her talk,
and smelling strongly of ashes of roses. Another
smell wafted about her as well as the cheap scent,
and later Dolly told Amber it came from her fags –
another word for Amber's education.

Amber disliked her on sight. On the other hand,
if Mrs Nash felt like taking Dolly back to London
with her, she wouldn't object. Although, now that
she knew all about Dolly's mother 'having it off'
with various uncles who she wasn't married to,
Amber wasn't sure she was a very nice person and
was a bit sorry for Dolly having to live with her. She
knew her gran would be scandalized if she knew,
but Amber had promised to keep a secret, and she
wouldn't be the one to tell.

'So this is your little friend, is it?' Mrs Nash said,

smiling winningly at Amber. 'I hope you two kids are hitting it off all right, and not causing problems for Amber's old gran here.'

Granny Pen smiled stiffly back as she made cups of tea for them all. She was thankful the woman was staying next door with Win Phillips. She may be a countrywoman herself and not considered as worldly wise as city folk, but she could smell a wrong 'un a mile away, let alone when she was sitting right here in her own parlour.

'Here you are, ducks. This is for your birthday to keep you warm in this God-forsaken place. Your dad sends his regards too,' Mrs Nash said to Dolly.

She tossed the brown paper parcel over to her daughter, completely oblivious of the insult to her new environment. Dolly tore open the wrappings eagerly and thanked her mother for the long knitted scarf and matching bobble hat. Gertie glanced at Amber.

'It's your birthday too, isn't it, kid? I'm sorry I ain't brought you nothing, but the pennies don't run to it when you've got train fares to pay for.'

Considering this was the only time she'd had to pay a train fare and that she probably had her own way of earning a bit of extra cash, thought Granny Pen shrewdly, she probably didn't do too badly.

'I've made a cake for tea,' Granny Pen said, covering her annoyance at the woman. 'You can't celebrate two birthdays without a cake.'

'Good Gawd, our Dolly will think she's landed on her feet and no mistake,' gushed Gertie.

'Do you want to see where I sleep after tea, Mum?' Dolly said. 'Me and Amber have to share a room, but it's not too bad.'

Amber managed to keep a straight face. The nerve of the girl, saying the room she shared with Amber wasn't too bad, and inviting her mother up there without even asking! Her recent mellowing towards Dolly was fading fast.

'How long are you staying, Mum?' Dolly said eagerly now. 'I could show you around the town tomorrow if you like.'

'Sorry, ducks, I've got to go back tomorrow. The market don't run on its own, you know, and two days away will cost me a few bob.'

Dolly was clearly disappointed, and Granny Pen covered the moment by bringing in the cake with its two candles on it, one for each girl, since there was hardly room on it for twenty-six.

'It ain't very big,' Gertie said, 'but it's very nice, I'm sure.'

They were all relieved when the tea-time ritual was over and the candles had been blown out. Dolly took her mother upstairs to show her the room, and then they went out for a walk along the waterfront, since Gertie seemed keen to take a look at the ships in the harbour.

'I wouldn't have thought Dolly's mother was interested in ships,' Granny Pen said with a sniff as she and Amber cleared away the table and did the washing-up.

Amber said nothing. From what Dolly had told

her about her mother, she wondered if it was just the ships that had caught Gertie's interest, or the sailors who frequented the pubs along the quay every night. She wished Dolly had never told her about the 'uncles' who came to their house while her father had been on night shift, then she would never have thought of such a thing. But between them Dolly and Luke had opened her eyes to something she had not been aware of before.

'Never mind, girl, she'll be going home tomorrow,' Granny Pen said calmly, when Amber inadvertently sucked on her teeth. 'We can't like everybody in this world, and that's a fact.'

It was the nearest she came to saying what she thought of Gertie Nash.

'She's like a film star, ain't she?' Dolly said enthusiastically, when they were in bed that night. 'When I grow up I want to be just like her.'

'Do you? Well, I suppose it's natural to want to be like your mother.'

Dolly twisted her head to look towards Amber in the dim light from the window. 'What's that supposed to mean? My mum's very popular down the Dog and Duck of an evening.'

'Is she?' Amber said, having no idea what the Dog and Duck was, but assuming that it was a local pub.

Dolly stretched luxuriously. 'She makes friends wherever she goes. We met a couple of sailors down the quay tonight, and it didn't take long before they was telling Mum and me some ripe old jokes.'

'Is that what you do in London? Go out with your mum, I mean, and talk to strangers and tell jokes?'

'Here, are you bleedin' well getting at me, Amber Penry? There's nothing wrong with being friendly.'

'Of course I'm not getting at you. Go to sleep.'

She turned her face to the wall, remembering that it didn't seem long ago that Dolly was complaining about the uncles who could make her mum whisper and giggle but never included her dad in the fun. And now that she knew what it all meant – even if Dolly said she didn't – it didn't sound very proper at all. It sounded pretty nasty if anybody wanted to know what she thought. Only she wouldn't be so mean as to say as much to Dolly.

'I did want you to like her, Amber,' Dolly said eventually in a muffled voice.

'I do like her,' Amber fibbed. Now go to *sleep*!'

Dolly had the next day off from school so that she could spend the morning with her mother until Gertie had to catch the train back to London. After they had gone to the station, Win Phillips had a morning cuppa and a chat with Granny Pen.

'She was a rum one and no mistake,' Win said. 'A little of her goes a long way, I reckon, and I've practically had to fumigate the room to get rid of the smell of scent and cigarettes. Not my sort at all, Granny Pen.'

'Nor mine, but I suppose they do things differently in London. She may be all powder and paint, but she's got a lot to cope with, what with Dolly down here and her hubby away in the Army.'

'I daresay she manages to keep from being too lonely,' Win said.

Granny Pen sniffed. Some things were best left unsaid, but it was clear they had both got the measure of Gertie Nash in the short time she'd been here.

'Did you read her tea leaves?' Win went on.

'I might have done.'

Win laughed. 'Go on then, what did you see?'

Granny Pen fetched an unwashed breakfast cup from the kitchen, from which she had swirled Gertie's dregs away, leaving a fine display of tea leaves around the base and sides of the cup.

'I don't normally do this unless I'm asked, as you know, but in this case, I thought it might be interesting.'

The two women pored over the cup. Win couldn't make head nor tail of what the patterns made, but Granny Pen frowned and nodded sagely.

'There's no surprises here, Win. The woman's a flighty one, but you could see that just by looking at her. She's the sort who's got the luck of the devil, but there's also sorrow ahead. I couldn't say how or when, but there's definitely something to stop her in her tracks. And that's all I can see.'

Win sometimes thought Granny Pen made half of it up, but neither she nor the women who consulted her from time to time, nor those who came here for their regular card game on Wednesday afternoons would dare to dispute what she said. She had the reputation of being a bit fey, and her herbal powders often did more for a body than any doctor's remedy. Win had no doubt that there was some truth in what she said about Gertie Nash, and the less they saw of her, the better.

Dolly came home from saying goodbye to her mother, awash with tears.

'I wanted to go back with her,' she sobbed. 'There ain't no bad raids in London, and some of the younger kids are going back home, so why can't I?'

'Now then, Dolly, you know you can't go because it's not safe. Make no mistake, when the bombs start to fall, you'll be glad you're out of harm's way,' Granny Pen told her.

'No I won't. Mum says it'll be quite exciting when they have to sleep in the air-raid shelters when the bombs fall, or even down the tubes, like some people are saying they will.'

'It wouldn't be so exciting to come out of there and find your house has been flattened, would it?' Granny Pen said, wondering how any woman could put such ideas into a gullible child's head.

'What's the tube?' Amber asked, mystified.

'Don't you know anything?' Dolly said, the tears miraculously stopping as she proceeded to enlighten her.

'I can't think of anything more horrible,' Amber said to Luke in their school break. 'Dolly's mum said if the worst comes to the worst everybody will start going down the tube together – that's the underground train stations, in case you don't know,' she added, with her new-found knowledge, 'and they'll all be like moles underground, crammed inside with trains hurtling through all night long and babies screaming at the noise—'

'They won't have trains hurtling through all night, you dope. If it happens at all, they'll have stopped them so that people can get some sleep. I read something about it in the paper, but the government says it's far too dangerous, anyway.'

Amber looked at him respectfully. In many ways, not only by a couple of years, Luke was so much older than she was. He read the newspapers and listened to the wireless just like grown-ups did, and he knew a lot more about the war than she did – or wanted to. Contrary to the way she had felt after Ronnie Hanham's funeral, if she had her way now, she'd bury her head in the sand on Gyllyngvase Beach and only come out when the final all-clear sounded. Not that they'd heard one all-clear yet, nor even a air-raid siren, thank goodness.

But by now everybody was saving scrap iron because the government told them to; there were huge barrage balloons in the sky that were supposed to ward off enemy aircraft; pillar boxes had been painted yellow with special stuff that was supposed to repel gas in case of gas attacks; and sandbags were being piled around some shops and public buildings. Name boards from towns and railway stations were painted out, so that if an invasion came, the Germans wouldn't know where they were. All this preparation was being done even more thoroughly in London, according to Dolly's mum, but so far it seemed as if both sides were playing a waiting game. Luke said the newspapers were starting to call it the 'phoney war' because after six months nothing was happening – yet.

'Well, I can tell you, I wouldn't like to have to sleep with hundreds of other people in one of those tube stations,' Amber told him. 'What if you wanted to go to the lav – or do – you know – *married things*?'

Luke grinned. 'I daresay anybody who wanted to do *married things* would find a way beneath the blankets, and as for the lav they'd have to find a way for that, too, unless they wanted to flood the entire underground train system. Imagine London suddenly floating on a rising tide of pee.'

'Or worse,' Amber said, giggling back at his daring. Then, without warning, they were off on a wicked discussion of what it would be like, wading through piles of unmentionables, just like in a sewer . . .

Dolly frowned as she found them in the schoolyard, apparently locked in some hilarious discussion of their own.

'What's so funny? You'd better cross your legs, Amber Penry, or you be wetting yourself in a minute.'

It was an apt comment that had them howling with laughter even more.

'I'm thinking of joining the drama group after school,' Dolly announced a few weeks later, having got over the disappointment of her mother going home and leaving her there.

'I think that's a good idea. You're well suited to it,' Granny Pen said dryly, relieved that she wasn't still moping about.

Dolly stared at her suspiciously, not sure if there was anything in the remark she should question, but decided not to bother.

'I'm joining it too,' Amber said.

Granny paused in preparing their tea and looked at them both in astonishment.

'Well, I'm very glad to see that you two little maids are getting along better at last. It's nice that you want to do things together.'

Amber kept her eyes lowered. She knew very well why Dolly wanted to join the drama group, which was putting on a play for the whole school at the end of term. It was because Luke Gillam had a leading part in it, and Amber had no intention of letting the little sneak steal a march over her.

The initial feelings of jealousy over Dolly being here, sharing her clothes and her room and her gran, were as nothing compared to the jealousy Amber felt whenever Dolly sidled up to Luke with her prettiness and her helplessness.

Amber Penry was in love, she thought grandly,

and if anybody tried to tell her that being in love at thirteen was impossible, and just a crush, she would refer them to Romeo and Juliet. Not that she had any intention of *dying* for love, she amended hastily, just in case God or Somebody Up There was listening.

And if the school play they were doing wasn't exactly Shakespeare, at least it meant that on two days a week they would stay after school and join the exclusive little drama group under the direction of Mr Thomas, who barked at them to stop giggling and behave or he'd throw them out of the stage arena forthwith. He often spoke in heavy Shakespearean terms, having once had aspirations to be an AcTor himself, Luke told them in an aside that made them fight to hold down the laughter at the image of portly old Tommo striding across the stage in some flamboyant Shakespearean costume.

The play, which Tommo had written himself in what he considered a Shakespearean style, was scheduled for the end of June, which was when Luke would be leaving school, and they had plenty of rehearsals to get through before then. Amber and Dolly were both extras, having come in at the last minute when the cast had already been established, and they had to watch Luke and an older girl who was playing the part of Griselda look adoringly into one another's eyes and share a kiss at the last moment.

'For the love of Christendom, Luke,' Mr Thomas thundered at one of the early rehearsals, 'try to look as if you're enjoying it and not as if you're holding a piece of timber at your father's boatyard. The girl's supposed to be your sweetheart, and you're leaving her for ever. Put some oomph into it, boy!'

While they all sniggered behind the teacher's back, Amber looked at Luke, and for a brief moment their glances locked, and she caught her breath. He should be holding *me*, she thought passionately. We'd show you what oomph means . . .

'Your eyes are turning a bright shade of green, Amber,' Dolly whispered behind her back. 'I bet you wish you'd got the part.'

'Me and Luke don't need play-acting,' Amber whipped back, and immediately wished she hadn't, especially as it wasn't strictly true. But it would make Dolly even keener to be her rival from now on. Whatever Amber had, Dolly wanted.

With frightening speed, far more serious events overtook the adolescent rivalries between two young girls in a Cornish town. The British Expeditionary Force had been established in France ever since the beginning of the war, and British troops were moving ever forwards towards Germany. It was inevitable that in due course the Germans would begin to push back, and they did so with a vast army of troops and tanks, relentlessly pushing the British back towards the French coast.

If the government hadn't acted as swiftly as they did, the numbers of men slaughtered would have been catastrophic, but the orders went out for ships of all sizes, however small, to set sail for the French coast in a massive rescue attempt. There would still be many casualties when the troops were brought home, and every town along the south coast was ordered to be ready with bandages and first aid equipment and to give help wherever it was needed.

It seemed as if almost overnight Falmouth's enormous harbour became densely populated with anything that could float, from large ships to small paddle-boats, motor boats and dinghies that almost obliterated the sight of the water.

'Me and dad are going in our motor boat,' Luke informed the drama group. 'We've loaned out a couple of our boats from the yard, but we don't intend to be left behind. So expect to see me when you see me!'

He sounded so brave, just like Sir Galahad, fighting for what was right, Amber thought dreamily. They were due to hold a play rehearsal on the day he left for France. Another boy acted as Luke's understudy and was to take his place, but the time went on, and Mr Thomas failed to turn up after normal lessons. He usually went back to his house for a change of clothes and then returned to the school. After half an hour's fidgeting and cat-calling among the would-be actors, a quivering Miss Dean came into the classroom and called them to order.

'I'm afraid I've got some very upsetting news to tell you. Mr Thomas won't be coming to rehearsals today, and it may be that we abandon his play altogether.'

In the uproar following her words, she shouted at them to be quiet, in a voice quite unlike her usual mild-mannered way.

'Mr Thomas has had a telegram to say that his son has been killed in France. It's a terrible thing to happen at any time, but even more so when he might have been one of the soldiers coming home to Falmouth from Dunkirk.'

She choked on the last words and swallowed hard amid the shocked murmurs among the pupils, and then went on as best she could.

'I want you all to go home as quietly as possible now as a mark of respect. I'm sure none of us feels like continuing today.'

They grabbed their school bags and the obnoxious gas masks which half of the country had abandoned carrying now, and filed out. Some of the girls were crying, others simply couldn't look at one another. It was hard for them to come to terms with the fact that the pompous little man they had so often laughed at behind his back was now a grieving father whose son had been killed somewhere in France. Every one of them was unnerved by the news, so close to home. And Luke Gillam, one of their schoolmates, was on his way to France right now.

'I hate this war,' Amber ground out on the way back to the cottage.

'I bleedin' well hate it more,' Dolly said. 'My dad's in France too.'

'Oh Dolly, are you sure?' Amber said.

She shrugged. 'Well, that's what my mum said, but you never know whether to believe her or not.'

'You can't say things like that about your mother.'

'Why not? She'll say anything if it'll get her what she wants. She wanted me out of the way soon enough when it suited her, and I bet she'll send for me to go back to London when it suits her too.'

Amber didn't know what to say to this bit of news about Dolly's mother. She'd overheard Granny Pen and Mrs Phillips next door refer to Gertie Nash as a flighty piece of goods, but she had been brought up in a God-fearing household, and she found it hard to imagine a grown-up telling lies to suit herself. Dolly wasn't above being a bit devious to get her own way, but Amber thought she fell short of telling outright whoppers.

'Anyway, that's what you want, isn't it?' Amber said encouragingly. 'To go back to London, I mean?'

Dolly leant over the handlebars of her bike as they neared the cottage.

'Well, I did,' she said savagely. 'I'm not so sure now. I never thought I'd say it, but it's not so bad down here, especially if Jerry's going to start bombing. I'd rather be safe than bleedin' well dead.'

'I'd rather you were safe as well,' Amber said reluctantly.

She wouldn't go so far as to say they were friends, because they weren't. Not really. Not close. And yet they could hardly be otherwise, sharing their lives as much as they did. She took a deep breath after that momentous thought.

'You're not too bad, Dolly. I suppose I could have had somebody far worse than you being dumped on gran and me.'

Dolly grinned. 'Well, we ain't exactly Siamese twins, but I suppose I could have been dumped on somebody worse as well.'

They pedalled on towards the cottage, too embarrassed to say anything more. But it was weird how something as tragic as hearing about old Tommo's son, who had been killed in France, and the fact of all those ships, big and small, heroically setting off for France right now to rescue their poor stranded soldiers seemed to mark a shift in the relationship between two very different and unimportant schoolgirls.

People thronged the quays and waterfront between the end of May and beginning of June, watching and waiting for the ships to return with their human cargo. The larger ships found a haven in the deepwater harbour and spilled out hundreds of soldiers, many of whom were wounded, some on stretchers, others on crutches, and all of them exhausted after the struggle to survive, and grateful to their saviours.

The women of the town were on hand with tea and welcome cigarettes, along with the Red Cross and ambulance services, all ready to help out wherever they were needed. The Forces' Club near the harbour was turned into a temporary staging post until the men could be sent back on trains and buses to their homes or to hospital. The entire harbour throbbed with activity on shore and off, and there were boats as far as the eye could see, almost stretching to the horizon, Amber told Dolly excitedly, completely caught up in the thrill of it all now.

'They say some of the little boats have gone back and forth across the Channel several times,' she reported. 'I hope Luke has got home all right.'

They looked at one another. For once, Amber didn't feel jealous of Dolly's blonde hair and china blue eyes, so much lighter than her own. For once, they only had one thought in mind, that Luke Gillam, in his father's motor boat, would return to Falmouth safely.

'I'm going to the boatyard to ask his mother,' Amber said, scrambling off the seat by the jetty where they had been watching all the activity.

'I'm coming as well,' Dolly said, before Amber could protest. What mattered most was knowing that Luke and his father were home.

'Not yet,' his mother said, when they turned up, out of breath and asking the all-important question. 'But I'm not too worried. They're good seamen, both of them, and they've got a good craft beneath them.'

She spoke with all the authority of a seafarer's wife as she smiled at the two young girls, their hair wild and unkempt, chests heaving with the effort of rivalling one another to get there first, and she had a sudden flash of foresight as to which of them might steal her son's heart. She dismissed it at once. They were children, concerned about a school pal, that was all. But their anxiety was no less real, and to calm them down she gave them lemonade and cake and showed them photos of Luke as a baby and a small boy, which made them laugh.

Some time later they heard shouting, and then Luke and his father came into the house. They looked tired and strained, and as unkempt as the girls, and Luke's face and clothes were covered in blood.

Dolly screamed, and Amber snapped at her not to show herself up.

'I'm all right,' Luke said harshly. 'We had as many men as we could cram in the boat and one of them was badly injured. It's his blood, not mine. We got him off the boat and into an ambulance, but I don't give much for his chances. I'm going to get cleaned up, and after a bite to eat me and Dad are going back again.'

'Please don't go back again, it's too dangerous!' Dolly begged, blanched by the sight of his blood-stained clothes and skin.

'Don't be stupid, Dolly,' Amber said, wanting to shake her. 'They can't leave our soldiers over there to get slaughtered, can they? Your dad might be one of them, remember.'

Dolly burst into tears, to be comforted by Luke's mother, while Luke and his father cleared their throats and went upstairs to wash and change their clothes. And Amber thought furiously that if this wasn't just like Dolly daydream. Taking every advantage of the situation to be all soft and fluffy and tearful, while Amber had appeared to be hard and unfeeling, which she bloody well wasn't, she thought, allowing the swear word to creep into her mind. She was as terrified for Luke as anybody. More so, in fact, as she had every right to be. She was the one who loved him, wasn't she?

'You two girls get along home now,' Mrs Gillam said gently, once she had extricated herself from Dolly's clinging arms. 'You've seen that Luke's all right, and I'm sure the worst of the evacuation must be over by now. One more trip will probably be their last,' she added, mentally crossing her fingers as she spoke.

They had no option but to do as they were told. They went back through the town, dodging the crush of people and helpers, and the convoys of vehicles now filling every street that were taking the soldiers to their various destinations. As if by instinct they didn't go back to the cottage yet. Instead, they pedalled their bikes furiously to Pendennis Castle headland, where they could look down at the chaotic scenes below. The harbour was still bursting with the number of boats, the quays swarming with people, and the faint, sickly sweet smell of blood was on the air.

In these last few days the realization of what war could do to people had become frighteningly real to them both. Granny Pen had told them not to go near the quays, but in the first excitement of wanting to see what was happening, some of the sights had filled them with horror. Amber's vague ambitions of

56

being a nurse were being severely questioned now after seeing some of the men with raw and bleeding injuries barely covered by ragged and dirty bandages.

'Sometimes I don't think there's any point in being good if you're just going to end up crippled or killed,' she said in a sudden rage.

'Blimey, that's a turn-up. What's got into you?' Dolly said.

'I'm thinking about all the young chaps around here who joined up as soon as the war broke out, and already some of them aren't coming back. Old Tommo's son, for one. What's the point of being a hero?'

'Like Luke, you mean?'

Amber snorted. That wasn't what she meant at all. She was still thanking God that Luke wasn't old enough to be a proper soldier, or sailor, or whatever he wanted to be.

'Leave Luke out of it,' she said rudely. 'He's different.'

And he's *mine*, she thought passionately.

Chapter Four

Mr Thomas didn't return to the school after his son's death. He was already on the brink of retiring, and the play was abandoned. The pupils had little heart to continue with the drama group without his encouragement, and, as none of the other teachers had Tommo's expertise to direct them, it simply disintegrated. They all seemed to have grown up considerably since that awful day when the war had come right into their classroom, and since it was near the end of term many of them lacked interest in lessons too. It was a situation that couldn't continue, and they were called to account by the headmaster and told that life had to go on, no matter what tragedies befell them.

'It's all right for him to say that,' Amber Penry snapped to anyone who would listen. 'It's not his son who was killed, is it?'

She was restless and frustrated in a way she didn't fully understand. She and Dolly had become closer in a strange way, as if their lives were interlocked regardless of anything they could do about it. They

were even being called the wild Penry girls now, a
term that didn't entirely displease Dolly, even though
she didn't strictly qualify for the name. They had
discovered that singly they irritated one another in
their different ways, but together they were a strong
unit. And this sense of unity had developed into
being disruptive and awkward at school, and a trial
to Granny Pen at home.

'I'm not sure I want them around all day in the
school holidays,' Granny Pen told her group of card
players one Wednesday afternoon. 'I don't know
what's got into them lately. Amber was always
strong-willed, of course, but Dolly was such a sweet
little thing. Now they're like a pair of whirling
dervishes, flying about here, there and everywhere,
and leaving their bedroom in a constant muddle.'

'They're growing up, that's what,' Win Phillips
said sagely. 'You should know what it's like at their
age, if you can remember that far back.'

'I'm not so old that I don't remember what it's
like to be young, thank you, missus,' she replied
smartly. 'But I don't recall being quite as contrary
as those two. Half the time they're as thick as thieves,
and the rest of it they're squabbling over something
petty.'

'Maybe they're fighting over some boy,' one of
the others said. 'If they're mooning about the place,
it's a sure sign of trouble brewing in that direction.
I'm surprised you haven't checked it in their tea
leaves, Granny Pen.'

'Well, I haven't. They're always racing about on

their bikes with that school crowd of theirs, but I don't know as there's one of them singled out now that that nice Luke Gillam has gone out of favour since he started work with his father. So let's forget them for the time being, and get on with more important business,' she said, shuffling the pack of cards determinedly.

If the girls had had to grow up suddenly after recent events, so had Luke Gillam, and far more soberly than they were aware. In the several hazardous trips he and his father had made to Dunkirk, he had seen sights he never wanted to see again, but which he simply couldn't get out of his head. Men with their heads half bashed in, with gaping wounds that were never going to heal, and men only a few years older than himself blinded, or with half their limbs torn away; they were images forever fixed in his consciousness.

The man's blood that had covered him in the boat had spurted out from a bubbling artery, and the shock of it had nearly finished him as well as the soldier concerned. It had changed him. He wasn't the same young boy who had gone out so eagerly that night, but one thing was clearer than ever in his mind.

The minute he was old enough he was going to join up. Now that he had left school behind him that was the only thought in his mind. He wanted to go and fight, like every other red-blooded chap in the country. There was no time for girls. He knew there were couples in the town who had married hastily before the men joined up, but young as he was he thought it was folly to tie yourself up without ever knowing if you would come home again.

There would be time enough for that when the war was over, and without realising the insensitivity of his actions he virtually turned his back on his old gang of friends, who were still such school kids, and concentrated on becoming a craftsman until his time came.

'You might as well face it, Amber. Luke Gillam don't want to be bothered with you no more. It always happens when they leave school and think themselves better than the rest of us,' Dolly taunted her after finding Luke's name written a dozen times on the inside cover of Amber's school rough book.

'Give me that,' Amber said, snatching it from her. 'You don't know what you're talking about.'

'I know you've always been sweet on him.'

'If I have, it's none of your business. Give me my book, anyway.'

They had been given a project about America to do in the school holidays, and tomorrow would be July 4th, American Independence Day. The midsummer day was hot, and they had brought their books up to the headland instead of working indoors. By now, after the efforts of the little ships to bring the troops out of Dunkirk, it was clear that the Germans had control of the French coast, and everyone feared that they would be next. When the horrific news broke that the Channel Islands had been occupied by the Germans, every precaution was taken to protect the coast and the cities on the mainland. In Falmouth, and all along the Cornish coast now, the beaches bristled with barbed wire, and barrage balloons floated high above the docks like prehistoric monsters.

It still seemed unreal to think that the Germans would invade England, but a month ago Mr Churchill had told the nation that they would fight them on the beaches, in the fields, in the streets and in the hills. So since the new Prime Minister had said it they had to believe it, Granny Pen had told the two girls in her care.

'I'm tired of doing this project,' Amber said, her nerves increasingly jangled by the sight of all the preparations for invasion. 'I'm going home.'

She didn't have the kind of premonitions Granny Pen was reputed to have, although lately her gran hadn't said much that anybody couldn't see by reading the newspapers, and it didn't need her tea leaves to know what was coming. But that day it was as if Amber was holding her breath, waiting for she didn't know what. Dolly couldn't see anything amiss, but then Dolly couldn't see beyond the blue sky and grumbling about how the huge barrage balloons blotted out the sun.

The next day, American Independence Day, Falmouth Docks had its first taste of German bombs after the sickening sound of the air-raid siren split the silence of the night. As soon as they heard the dismal whining sound, the girls were bundled into a cupboard under the stairs to try to sleep, while Granny Pen sat beneath the solid kitchen table with her knitting, refusing to go to bed until the all-clear sounded. She had stubbornly resisted having a shelter put up in the garden, which was so small it would have taken all the light from the cottage windows.

'They're building dummy railway stations to fool the Germans,' Granny Pen told them later, with her uncanny way of finding out local news almost before it happened. 'The lights will be turned on in the dummy areas to divert the bombs away from the docks and the town.'

Dolly didn't see the sense of it, but she had another thought on her mind now.

'If the Jerries are dropping bombs here, I might as well go home. I'm writing to my mum to ask her to come and get me,' she announced.

'I don't think that's very wise, Dolly.'

'Well, you can't stop me. It's up to my mum where I stay, not you.'

She wrote the letter that night, and Amber was in two minds whether or not she wanted Dolly to leave. Surprisingly, she knew she would miss her. But before there was any chance for Gertie Nash to make one of her infrequent replies, central London was attacked by German bombers in August, and from September onwards came an onslaught of air raids on the capital, which stopped any more idea of Dolly going home.

'It looks as if I'm stuck here for a bit longer,' Dolly said sulkily as another Christmas and February birthday came and went, and the news from London became increasingly terrifying.

The relentless bombing raids were now being called the Blitz, and among Dolly's mum's erratic letters came one telling Dolly that even Buckingham Palace had been bombed – which everybody knew anyway, since it had been reported with many pictures of bombed-out streets and buildings in London, and photographs of the king and queen walking amongst the rubble. And Queen Elizabeth had made the remark that now that Buckingham Palace had been bombed as well they could look the East End in the face, which cheered everybody up, according to Gertie.

After this important bit of information – although Dolly was never quite sure whether her mother was being sarcastic or not – Gertie also told her daughter not to worry because their own place hadn't been bombed out yet, and somebody called Uncle Joe was seeing that she was all right with extra rations.

'He sounds like a good friend,' Amber said cautiously, although, at fourteen now, she had more than a shrewd idea of how Dolly's mum was paying for her extra rations.

'Friend, my Aunt Fanny,' Dolly said with a sniff. 'More like her fancy man, if you ask me. Oh, don't look so shocked, Amber. I can guess what's been going on, even if I didn't twig it when I was younger.'

'Well, at least she's getting plenty to eat,' Amber said, not knowing what else to say.

'And plenty of something else, too,' Dolly

snapped. 'I ain't no bleedin' saint, but it's not fair that my dad's away fighting while this spiv has his fun with my mum. And in our house, too!'

They all knew what a spiv was by now. A spiv could somehow lay his hands on anything, from extra food rations to petrol coupons or anything else that could be obtained not-quite-legally.

'Mind you,' Dolly went on thoughtfully, her mood abruptly changing, 'I often wonder what it's like, doing that stuff – you *know*. Mum always seemed to be giggling, so it can't be too horrible, can it?'

Amber was quick to catch on. They'd had a brief and sketchy lesson about reproduction at school, mainly to do with rabbits, which told them precisely nothing that they really wanted to hear. Or maybe it might have done, if the boys in the class hadn't been grinning like idiots as the teacher got redder and redder.

'It's for married people, isn't it?' Amber said. 'Me and gran went to a wedding once, and the vicar was going on about marriage being for mutual comfort and the procreation of children. I asked Gran what it meant and she said I'd know when I was older, and I still don't, not really.'

'We could ask her,' Dolly said. 'You could, anyway. She's your gran.'

'She's always *my* gran when something awkward crops up, isn't she?'

'Well, she is. So will you?'

'No,' Amber said crossly.

Somehow she couldn't imagine her gran going

into such details. In any case, she had already asked Luke. At one time she could have asked him anything, even something as personal as this. But she hardly ever saw him now, and the love in her heart remained an unfulfilled and beautiful dream, she thought dramatically.

'But it must be weird, doing it with one person, and then another one,' Dolly persisted now, forgetting it was her mum they had been discussing, her eyes full of curiosity and something that was bordering on excitement.

'Good Lord, Dolly Nash, there's nothing glamorous about it,' Amber said. 'If you're married, it's being unfaithful.'

Dolly went bright red. 'Are you calling my mother unfaithful?'

'Well, isn't she? You said the uncles kept coming to the house when your dad was on night shift, and now your dad's away in the Army there's this Uncle Joe who you've never heard about before.'

'Sometimes I hate you. You're always so perishing clever,' Dolly yelled. 'Just because my mum's friendly to people don't mean she deserves a bad name.'

She looked so comical, standing there with her hands on her hips and glaring so hard she almost had sparks coming out of her eyes, that Amber had to laugh.

'You know I'm right, and, anyway, it's probably quite flattering to have people thinking she's nice and friendly when your dad's away,' she said, as delicately as she could. 'You seemed to think it was exciting a minute ago. You like it when your mum sends you things, and I bet she gets half of it from Uncle Joe.'

Dolly had been receiving the odd parcel lately: a new blouse with no questions asked regarding clothing coupons; a few packets of hair shampoo; a nice brush and comb set; and even a pale pink lipstick since Dolly was growing up now, her mum's letter said, which had caused a huge argument with Granny Pen, and she had been forbidden to use it outside the house. Which only made Dolly slip it into her pocket for her and Amber to apply it as soon as they were out of sight.

Amber had her own thoughts about when the war was over and Dolly's dad would be coming home. Presumably Uncle Joe and all the others would disappear again then, unless her dad went back to his old night shift job. When the war was over was a phrase that was often on people's lips, but as the Blitz in London continued and air raids all along the coast and on the big cities became part of daily life, the end of it seemed as far away as ever. As the danger increased, the children who had gone back to their homes in London during the phoney war came flooding back to all parts of the country in a new wave of evacuees.

Almost to her surprise, Dolly was quite glad now that her mother hadn't given in to her pleas to go home. She was used to it down here in the sticks. She was used to Granny Pen and her funny little ways, even her dire predictions about how it all had to get worse before it got better, and her card-playing afternoons, and her tea-leaf reading and her herbal powders.

She was quaint, Dolly decided, and Amber wasn't bad either. Amber was almost as good as having a sister, even a twin, since their birthdays were on the same day. Not that they looked in the least bit alike. They had both rounded out by now, having bumps that weren't there before, and starting their monthlies, which Granny Pen had managed to explain without too much throat-clearing. Dolly was still small and dainty with that china-doll prettiness that her classmates alternately envied and resented, while Amber was taller, darker, with more dramatic looks that had already made her a beautiful young girl who looked older than her years. Together, they made a striking pair.

The nickname Amber had given Dolly when she first arrived at the cottage wasn't so far wrong; Dolly sometimes daydreamed, too, about what would happen when the war was over. And it had nothing to do with her mother. She wanted to go home, of course she did, but there was a small part of her that wouldn't mind staying in Cornwall for ever, providing she had someone special of her own. Granny Pen was always strictly fair to them both, but she was still Amber's gran. Dolly didn't truly belong properly to anyone here, and the many talks she and Amber often had now about married people and what they did had given her peculiar feelings in her tummy that weren't altogether unpleasant.

She didn't fully understand them, but when she

drifted into one of her dreams about having a special person of her own, the hazy face she dreamed about was that of a handsome boy with dark curly hair and laughing eyes. Sometimes, when Amber was asleep in her own bed, Dolly would retrieve the crumpled photo of a small boy that she had sneaked out of Luke Gillam's house; a photo of a small boy with dark hair and laughing eyes who was growing into a man now . . .

School-leaving age was fourteen, so the girls both thought themselves officially grown up when they were due to leave that summer. Neither of them had any clear idea of what they wanted to do. Amber's ambitions changed like the wind. Her vague idea of being a nurse had faded long ago, and eventually Granny Pen suggested she might think about applying to help at the Forces' Club near the docks.

Dolly had decided that any shop that would employ her would be good enough as long as she was earning a few bob, but the minute she heard about the opportunity at the Forces' Club she changed her mind. Helping to cheer up the many servicemen in the town who frequented it appealed to Dolly. Conversely, Amber immediately decided against it.

They had no choice over sharing their lives, but once schooldays were over Amber didn't want to be thought of as one half of a pair who couldn't bear to be separated. Besides, having become well aware of Dolly's flirtatious nature, Amber wasn't sure she could stand to watch the silly little twerp making

eyes at chaps old enough to be her father. She didn't
particularly want to be handing out cups of tea and
biscuits and washing up after them, either. She could
do all that at home.

But with so many young men away at the war,
even married women were taking over many of the
jobs that had been thought exclusively theirs.
Women became bus conductresses and worked in
munitions factories and drove Army vehicles, and
jobs for girls straight out of school were not quite
so plentiful now.

Dolly had already begun work at the Forces' Club
when one of Granny Pen's cronies at her Knitting
Socks for Soldiers meeting came up with a suggestion for Amber. Mrs Veal owned a little craft shop
off one of the cobbled alleyways leading down to
the quays. It was a moderately successful business,
of especial interest to visiting seamen looking for
souvenirs for their wives or sweethearts. They were
always fascinated by the unique Cornishness of the
wares, whether it was a corn dolly, a crochet mat in
a particular Cornish design, a teapot stand or a piece
of jewellery crafted out of Cornish stone or pebbles
that Mr Veal fashioned in the back room. He could
also turn a piece of driftwood into polished shapes
that resembled animals or fish, and what he called
wooden love-spoons in Celtic designs, and the shop
window was crammed full of such items to intrigue
visitors to the county.

'Go down there and see what you think, Amber,'
said Granny Pen. 'You can't waste your time waiting

for something wonderful to turn up, because it never does. You can't depend on luck, either. You've got to go out and make your luck in this world.'

It was ironic and a bit galling that the very thing Dolly had first wanted to do – work in a shop – was the one opening put in Amber's way now. But because she knew Granny Pen was right, and she didn't want Dolly crowing over her about the wage packet she got at the end of every week now, she reported to Veal's Craft Shop. The minute she stepped inside it she felt as if she was in wonderland.

There was nothing humdrum about this shop. It was full of magic and mystery, and she knew exactly why Granny Pen thought so highly of it. There were packets with strange names on them that sounded and smelled mystically Eastern – Granny Pen probably got half the ingredients for her herbal powders here. There were pendant necklaces with polished stones, and Amber immediately noticed one in particular, a gleaming gold-coloured pendant stone that felt smooth and sensually warm to the touch, and whose colour seemed to go deep inside it for ever.

'I thought that 'ould take your eye, Amber, love,' Mrs Veal said complacently, when the girl had poked around the shelves and displays with the feeling that she wanted to buy every single thing on offer.

'Why? Is it some magic charm?' she said with a grin, thinking Mrs Veal was halfway to being as dotty and mysterious as half the town thought her grandmother.

'It's amber, your stone. Not your birth-stone, your name stone, although amber is also associated with Aquarius, which is your birth sign,' Mrs Veal said. 'In fact, there are many tales about the magical properties of amber, so don't scoff.'

'I'm not scoffing,' Amber said, thinking this was turning into the most intriguing conversation she'd had in ages. She fingered the shimmering stone curiously. 'So what's it supposed to do then?'

'Well, amber pendants, like this one, were once worn to preserve chastity – and that's always a good thing! Amber is also a talisman for good luck and a guard against evil. In fact, many years ago sailors used to burn amber on ships to drive away sea serpents and other perils of the deep.'

'Good Lord!' Amber said, near-mesmerized by all that the woman was saying, and the almost dreamy way she was saying it. She gave a shaky laugh. 'Perhaps the government ought to issue a piece of amber to every sailor who goes to sea during the war then – and the soldiers and airmen, too, to keep them safe.'

She gave a sudden gulp as if she had never really sensed the immense danger all of them were in before now. Or else she hadn't wanted to see it. Even Tommo's son being killed had been remote from her. Sad though it was, it had nothing to do with her. She was fourteen years old, just leaving school behind her, and the war didn't really touch her, and she didn't want it to. As if it was red hot, she put the amber pendant back on the shelf, and her voice cracked when she spoke.

72

'Well, I think it's all a lot of nonsense, although I know you and Granny Pen see all kinds of omens and signs in perfectly ordinary things.'

'Ah, but that's just the point, my dear. Nothing in this world is perfectly ordinary, is it? Now then, come and have a glass of lemonade and tell me if you're going to come and work for me or not. If you do, I'm sure we can come to some arrangement about letting you have the pendant at a reasonable price.'

'I don't want to buy it,' Amber spluttered.

But even as she spoke, she knew she wanted it desperately. Its glowing surface was as bright as the sun, as fathomless as the sea, and she had never wanted anything so much.

'We'll see,' Mrs Veal said. 'Anyway, I'll put it aside for you until you've made up your mind. It's the only one of its kind we have at present.'

Amber watched as the woman removed the pendant again. There was a faint film of dust on the shelf where it had lain. Without thinking, Amber wiped it away with her finger. As she did so, a shadow outside the window caught her eye, and then the shadow became a person with a face, and it was Luke.

She hadn't seen him for some weeks now, and in that time he seemed to have got taller and broader and more serious-looking. Or perhaps the look was because he was surprised at seeing her inside Veal's Craft Shop apparently dusting shelves. And then the look changed to a smile, and seconds later the bell above the door tinkled and he came inside.

'Don't tell me you're a working girl at last?' he greeted her. 'Though I don't know why I should be surprised to see you in here. It's the obvious place for you.'

She found her breath without realizing she had been holding it for those brief seconds. 'Why should it be?'

Luke laughed. 'Well, I never expected you to be doing some ordinary job. It always had to be somewhere among the weird and wonderful, didn't it?'

Amber wanted to rage at him the way she always did when he baited her. But even more she wanted him to finish the sentence by adding a few more words.

Just like you . . . weird and wonderful . . . *just like you*.

He never said it, of course, and then Mrs Veal appeared from behind the bead curtain at the back of the shop again and told Luke he was welcome to join them for some lemonade on this hot day.

'Thanks all the same, and I wish I could, but me and Dad have got a big job on, and I'm just in town to get some supplies,' he said regretfully. 'We're doing war work at the yard now, but it's a bit hush-hush so don't ask me about it.'

'I wasn't going to,' Mrs Veal said with a smile. 'So was there anything in here that you wanted, Luke?'

Only me, thought Amber. *Say it's only me.*

'No, I was just passing and saw Amber in here. I'm glad you've got her working at last, Mrs Veal –

and how about the other one? Is Dolly lurking somewhere behind the scenes as well?'

'No, she's not,' Amber snapped. 'And if you've got errands to do for your dad, hadn't you better get on and do them?'

She turned around and flounced away from him, hearing him mutter something like 'Still the same old temper, then,' before she heard the door bell tinkle again, and he was gone.

'It doesn't always do to wear your heart on your sleeve, Amber love,' Mrs Veal said as Amber followed her through the bead curtain to the rear of the shop. 'When you're a bit older you'll find that being a bit more subtle is far more likely to get results.'

'I don't know what you mean,' Amber said.

But she did. And right there and then she really wished she was older. Wished it hard, even though her gran always said it was wicked to wish time away, and you should cherish what you had. But if only she was older, maybe Luke Gillam would stop thinking of her as a child and think of her as a woman – or a sweetheart, or a – a lover. The word slid into her mind, delicious and wicked. And she felt her face grow hot as Mrs Veal put the cool drink of lemonade in front of her, because despite all her schoolgirl dreaming about him, she had never actually thought of Luke in quite that way before. But she was thinking of it now.

Chapter Five

Dolly sat on her bed with a superior smile, her legs crossed beneath her as she watched Amber put the torturous pipe cleaners in her hair to try and curl it.

'I'm glad I don't need to do all that,' she said.

'So you've told me a hundred times,' Amber retorted.

'It's not even as if it does any good. You end up with a few springy curls for half an hour and then it springs back out again and it's as straight as a ruler. Why go through the pain of sleeping on all those bumps for nothing?'

Amber glared at her. 'I'm training it. The more I do it, the more it'll get used to being curly instead of straight.'

She was never going to admit how much she envied Dolly's natural golden curls, and nor was she going to let on that one night she'd tried fixing the curls with sugar water, and had to spend time the following morning washing it all out before she could get the pipe cleaners out of the sticky mess. It was all the rage at the flicks now, for girls to have waves and curls . . . and Amber wanted to be one of them.

The customers who came into Veal's Craft Shop deserved to see somebody glamorous working in such a glamorous place, however small it was, but she just wasn't glamorous. She easily overlooked her own dramatic dark looks when she thought about the film stars at the flicks. All of them blonde, like Dolly.

'What you staring at now?' Dolly scowled, unravelling her legs and going over to the small mirror to get a look in and fluff up her own hair before bedtime.

'Nothing,' Amber began, and then there was a howl from Dolly as she almost pushed Amber out of the way. 'Here, what did you do that for?'

'I've got a huge spot,' Dolly yelled. 'Right there by the side of my nose. I look hideous, and everybody will laugh at me if it hasn't gone by next month.'

'It'll be long gone by then, and what's happening next month, anyway?' Amber asked suspiciously.

'Didn't I tell you?' Dolly said, studiously inspecting the small red spot and avoiding Amber's eyes. 'There's going to be a dance at the Forces' Club to raise funds for the Dunkirk victims. I'll be serving teas and drinks in the interval.'

'No, you didn't tell me, and has Granny Pen agreed to this?'

'Well, it's my work, isn't it?' Dolly said, her big blue eyes innocent. 'You could have been going if you hadn't wanted to work in a soppy craft shop.'

'It's not soppy, and you're right. That spot on your nose is hideous.'

She was being petty and she knew it, but inside she was raging. Dolly knew very well she hadn't mentioned any dance in October. Neither of them was allowed out late in the evenings unless it was for some special reason. She was surprised Granny Pen thought a dance was a special reason for somebody of Dolly's age. But, of course, she was going to serve teas and drinks in the interval, and she'd be well chaperoned by the older women who worked there. As if that would stop Dolly flirting with any good-looking chap who caught her eye!

'I'm going downstairs to get a drink of water,' Amber said, and whirled out of the room with one side of her hair still long and straight and the other side pipe-curlered up against her head like a porcupine. She found her gran reading the newspaper in the parlour and having a late-night cup of cocoa.

'Dolly says she's going to help out at the Forces' Club dance next month. Can I see if I can go and help too?' she said.

Granny Pen frowned at being suddenly interrupted just as she was reading about the latest German bombing raids on the coastal towns, and the reprisal raids by the RAF, and wondering just how much the government was suppressing about how bad the situation really was. Dunkirk had been both a triumph and a disaster but nothing could take away the fact that the English coast was more accessible to the enemy now, and that invasion was no longer a distant nightmare but a real possibility.

For a moment she couldn't get her mind off the war and the futility of it all, just like the last one, and then she fully registered the girl standing in front of her in that bizarre manner, arms crossed tightly over her nightgown, her eyes blazing.

'Good heavens, Amber, what are you doing down here like this? Do you know what time it is, and what a sketch you look?'

At the sharp sound of her voice, Amber couldn't speak for a moment. Her eyes filled with tears at the injustice of it all, when all she wanted was to look beautiful and glamorous, and to be allowed to do what Dolly was doing.

'You're letting *her* go, so why can't I? You always favour her, just because she's a poor little evacuee,' she mimicked, 'but I'm your granddaughter, not her.'

She was shivering, not so much with cold, even though the fire had dwindled to nothing in the grate now, despite being banked up with old newspapers soaked in tea leaves and then dried and made into brickettes, in the way the government was urging people to do to save coal. She shivered at knowing it was always going to be the same between her and Dolly, and she hadn't wanted to blurt it all out like that, but Dolly's announcement about the dance was just about the last straw.

'Come and sit down, Amber,' Granny Pen said gently. 'Of course it's not true that I always favour Dolly over you, and for goodness' sake let me take those ridiculous pipe cleaners out of your hair.'

'I've only just put them in,' Amber said, jerking away as Granny Pen began to tug at one of the pipe cleaners.

'Well, you look much prettier with your hair straight as nature intended. You shouldn't try to copy someone else, my dear. You should be proud to be yourself. Your mother had hair just like yours and she never felt the need to try and tame it,' she added with a sigh.

'Did she?' Amber said, her thoughts temporarily frozen. It was rare that Granny Pen spoke about either of Amber's parents.

'Oh yes. It was just as long and black and shiny, and your father spent hours brushing it for her when they were first married. It was lovely to watch them together, but I don't suppose you can do that with tight curly hair.'

She continued unwinding the pipe cleaners, speaking quietly but unemotionally, and it was Amber whose throat felt choked, imagining the intimate act between the mother she never knew and the father she couldn't remember. There was only a hazy photograph of them that Granny Pen kept in a frame in her bedroom, and a few that she kept in a cardboard box she called her memory box.

'You're so much like her, Amber. The older you get, the more I see her in you. Don't ever lose that, my dear.'

Amber yanked out the remaining pipe cleaner and gave a sigh of relief. She truly hated sleeping on the horrid things, and she had only been doing it for a couple of months since she started work. The idea had been to make her look older and more sophisticated, but she knew it hadn't worked. Besides, it took her ages to get comfortable in bed, and there and then she decided not to bother any more.

'So can I go to the Forces' Club dance if they'll let me help?' she repeated, remembering what she had come downstairs for.

Five minutes later she crept back up to her bedroom with a triumphant smile on her face. Dolly had blown out the candle now and pulled back the curtains a little, but there was enough light in the room for Amber to get into bed. So who wanted prissy Shirley Temple curls anyway . . . ?

Dolly was already asleep, one arm flung outside her bed. Amber saw that she had dropped something on the floor, and she bent to pick it up. For a moment she stared at it, trying to think who the small boy was in the crumpled photo. She tiptoed across to the window to get a better look, and then she gave a furious gasp as she recognized it. The little sneak had pinched this from Luke Gillam's house when his mum had shown them the photos. Dolly had pinched it and kept it all this time, as if he was *her* boy. Well, she wasn't keeping it any longer.

Shaking with rage now, Amber got into bed with the precious photo beneath her pillow, and fell asleep while she was still deciding what she was going to do about it. But one thing was sure. This was war, just as surely as that other one.

*

It was a certainty that Dolly wasn't going to ask about the photo, and just as certain that Amber wasn't going to tell her she had found it. Let Dolly sweat a bit, wondering if Granny Pen had picked it up when she was cleaning their bedroom. Granny Pen might not recognize who it was in the photo, although Luke hadn't really changed that much, but she wouldn't be too pleased to know Dolly was thinking about boys, either.

Granny Pen hadn't been the one to find it . . . but Dolly didn't know that, and Amber enjoyed watching the little sneak eyeing Granny Pen cautiously, as if wondering when the axe was going to fall, and doing extra little jobs to please her.

She ached to keep the photo herself, but instead she knew it gave her the perfect excuse to go to the boatyard and call on Luke's mother to return the photo, saying it must have accidentally fallen into one of their satchels. She wasn't going to say it was Dolly's, but the fact that Amber was honest enough to return it probably spoke for itself. Dolly wasn't the only one who could be sneaky.

During the time she had been working at the craft shop Amber had become familiar with many of the objects crammed into every space. She loved being surrounded by them, and often found herself weaving stories about them, especially the exotic Eastern smells from the packets of spices and dried herbs. It wasn't a busy shop like a dairy or bakery, and since there were plenty of quiet moments she had watched, fascinated, as Mr Veal fashioned a wooden love-spoon from a piece of driftwood. She had even tried her hand at making some crochet doileys to Mrs Veal's own design and was pathetically pleased with the result.

But now, at the end of Friday afternoon when the shop closed, she had a mission of her own to attend to. She rode her bike through the bustling streets of the town, where there were plenty of uniforms to be seen now, from regular servicemen to ARP wardens, to Civil Defence people, Home Guard and ambulance drivers. Seeing some of the old boys in the town, puffed up with importance in their new roles, Amber thought it must feel good to wear a uniform, but the only one she had ever worn was a Brownie uniform, long discarded.

If the war went on for years and years, though, she supposed the time could still come when she – and Dolly, too – could be called up, and then they'd have to wear them, unless they went into horrible munitions factories. It was a thought that made her wobble on her bike and almost come off as she neared Gillam's boatyard.

'You'd better mind where you're going, or you'll find yourself carted off in one of those things yourself,' she heard a voice say as an ambulance trundled by, and she looked straight up into the eyes of Luke Gillam, just walking into the boatyard ahead of her as the daylight began to fade.

Instead of being thrilled to be in such unexpected closeness with her hero, she was frantically embarrassed. This had seemed like such a good idea, bringing back the photo and letting Mrs Gillam know in a subtle way who had taken it. Now, as she got off her bike and walked along beside Luke with her heart thumping, she felt stupid, wondering how she was going to explain herself when the inevitable question came.

'So what are you doing here, kiddo? Mrs Veal was asking around for any old scraps of wool for picture-making, I think, but I don't know whether Mum has sorted out anything yet.'

Her heart suddenly skipped a beat. He didn't think he'd said anything out of the ordinary, but Amber's spectacular smile lit up her face as if he had. She could almost ignore the fact that he'd called her kiddo as if she was still a child, when all her feelings towards him were definitely grown-up ones, even if he didn't know it. He'd given her the perfect reason for being here.

'Well, of course it's your mum I've come to see. You didn't think I'd come all this way to see you, did you?' she said airily.

'No.' He grinned. 'You're far too busy being a shop girl now.'

'A *craft shop assistant*, if you don't mind. There's far more to it than just serving customers with their weekly newspaper or something. Ours is a creative business,' she added grandly.

He laughed out loud. 'My God, Amber, you do like to put on airs and graces, don't you? And since when did it become *our* business? Are you planning to take it over?'

'I might, one day! I rather fancy having my own business.'

She'd never thought of it before, and she wasn't thinking of it now. She was still hardly out of school. But if it ever happened, it would make her a Somebody in this town, and far more important than a minor somebody who was content to serve tea and sandwiches in a Forces' Club canteen . . . and listening to her own thoughts, fancying herself, she knew she could turn into a right little snob with no bother.

'You need to be better at sums than you ever were at school then,' she heard Luke say with a laugh. 'You hardly knew what two and two made sometimes, if I remember correctly.'

'As long as I know what one and one makes, that's good enough for me,' Amber whipped out, and then blushed as he gave her shoulders a quick hug.

'You kill me sometimes, you really do,' he said, and then he went off whistling, never realizing how her words had been aimed specifically at him.

She gazed after him as he disappeared into one of the huge sheds from where she could hear the sound of hammering and machinery, wondering if he had any idea at all that the only one and one she was thinking about was Luke and Amber . . . Amber and Luke . . . She turned away quickly and walked up to the front door of the Gillam house, adjacent to the boatyard.

'Amber, how nice to see you, dear,' Mrs Gillam said, slightly puzzled as to why the girl should be visiting her at all.

She was growing up, Mrs Gillam reflected. She was nearly as tall as Luke now, and that glorious black hair and those deep blue eyes were going to charm some young man's heart one of these days in the not too distant future.

'I came to bring you something,' Amber said a little awkwardly. 'I think it belongs to you. In fact, I know it does.'

'You'd better come inside then, and have some supper. The men will be in soon, and you're welcome to join us if your gran won't worry about you going home after dark.'

'Oh, I didn't mean to stay,' Amber said, flustered. 'I only came on an – an errand, of sorts.'

'Well, an errand still deserves a cup of tea and a piece of cake, at least, so stop dithering, there's a love, and tell me what it is that's so important.'

Amber followed Luke's mother inside, not knowing quite how to begin. And then it all came out in a rush.

'When we were here before – me and Dolly – and you were showing us photos – I think this one somehow fell into somebody's satchel. We don't use them any more, of course, now that we've left school, but we were emptying them the other day to pass them on to other children – and, well, here it is,' she finished lamely, and handed it over.

Mrs Gillam took the photo from Amber and gave a slight smile as she thanked her for it.

'It's kind of you to return it, but there was no need. I've got plenty of others, and you can keep it if you like, Amber.'

She handed it back, but Amber flinched away from it as if it was poisonous.

'Oh no, I don't want it. It wasn't me. I mean, well, it doesn't belong to me, does it? Gran always says it's important to keep photos because they're part of somebody's life and shouldn't be given away, or you might be giving away a little part of them as well.'

God, where the dickens did all that come from? Amber must have heard it from somewhere, and it was almost certainly Granny Pen who had said it, but she didn't truly remember hearing it. The words just seemed to appear in her mind.

Luke's mother smiled again, but this time the smile was a little strained.

'I'm sure Granny Pen has all sorts of philosophies to pass on to you, Amber, but in the middle of a war I'm not sure anybody wants to hear of taking away a little part of somebody's life.'

'Oh, she didn't mean it like that. Neither did I! I don't really know what I meant!' she said, in real distress now.

'I know you didn't, so let's not talk any more about it. I'll put this old photo back where it belongs and then you can help me set the table for when the men come in.'

'I don't think I can stay, thank you all the same. I forgot I have to be home on time tonight because Gran's going out,' she stammered.

It was already growing dark and there would be no lights for her to make her way home through the town and to the outskirts where they lived. She knew the roads like the back of her hand, but there had been more than one account of people crashing into lamp-posts and stationary vehicles in the blackout, and the whole town had been shocked to hear about an ARP man on night duty who had suffered a serious head injury from just such a blow, which had killed him.

Amber made her escape, knowing it was more than she could bear to be sitting around a table with Luke and his parents, remembering she'd said something far too emotive and simply appalling, about taking away part of a person's life by something as silly as the gift of a photograph. It was completely thoughtless when people were being bombed and losing their lives in air raids . . . Thankfully, Luke's father was too old to go to war, and Luke was too young, but all the same . . . She should never have said it, and she just couldn't stay . . .

She cycled home as the clouds darkened overhead, and a fine warm rain began to fall, cooling her fiery cheeks as she wondered how she could have been so insensitive. And knowing to her shame that it was still the child in her, blurting everything out without thinking, when she was trying so hard to behave like an adult.

She finally arrived home and had to submit to her gran's fussing as she rubbed her hair dry in the parlour and took off her damp jacket and shoes. At last she was allowed to go upstairs to her bedroom and change her clothes and find her slippers. Dolly had already lit their candle and pulled the blackout curtains across the window, and she was now preening this way and that in front of the mirror as she experimented with one of Amber's hair ribbons. It was the final, *final* straw.

'Do you always steal things that don't belong to you?' Amber yelled, almost flying across the room to snatch the ribbon back and fling it on to her bed.

'I wasn't stealing it! I was only seeing how it looked on my hair. The colour looks better on me, anyway,' Dolly said rudely.

'Well, it's mine, and it's still stealing when you take something that doesn't belong to you – or didn't they teach you that in your London school?'

She stared at Dolly unflinchingly, her eyes large and accusing, and Dolly's face went a dull red. The photo of Luke wasn't mentioned, but Amber was pretty sure Dolly knew exactly what she was talking about. She suddenly foraged in one of her allotted drawers and dragged out a pen and a second ribbon and threw them at Amber.

'You'd better have these then. I was only borrowing them, and if you don't know the difference, you don't know much, do you, clever-clogs?'

It was tempting to hurl the accusation back at Dolly, but right on cue, as the night darkened, they heard the moan of an air-raid siren and Granny Pen was shouting at them to come downstairs at once. Dolly's face seemed to change from red to white in an instant, and Amber realized how petrified she really was about being bombed after the graphic details her mother chose to send her.

'Oh come on,' Amber said roughly. 'It's not worth bothering about, providing you promise not to do it again.'

'Well, I'll try not to,' Dolly began, and then felt a yank on her arm as Amber pulled her to the door. 'All *right*, I bleedin' well promise!'

Amber wasn't sure that Dolly was too concerned about keeping promises, but none of it mattered as much as doing what they had been told to do in an air raid.

'Where is it?' Dolly whispered, as Granny Pen bundled them into the cupboard under the stairs, as if the Jerries were going to rain bombs down on them at any minute, when all they could hear was distant gunfire.

'Where's what?'

'You know what.'

'I don't know what you're talking about,' Amber said, and then she yelped as she felt a vicious pinch on her arm. 'If you mean something that didn't belong to you in the first place, it's gone back where it belongs.'

Dolly didn't answer, and Amber felt ridiculously pleased at keeping the little twerp guessing without actually saying anything. Then came a sudden louder burst of gunfire and the drone of aircraft overhead, and Dolly screamed and clung to Amber, whose mood changed at once.

'It's all right, you're safe with us,' she said clumsily. 'The stupid Jerries might be aiming for the docks, but they'll probably go for the decoy place, and they're not going to bother about one little cottage out in the sticks, are they?'

'You don't know that,' Dolly whimpered. 'My mum says they drop their bombs anywhere they like. They don't care how many people they kill.'

'Well, I don't suppose our chaps always hit their targets either, so it's tit for tat, isn't it?'

Not that she liked to think of the RAF chaps killing people just for the sake of it, but war was war, and they all had to do as they were told.

'I wonder what's worse. Being drowned at sea or being blown up on the ground, or being blasted out of the sky by an enemy bomber,' she said conversationally, more to keep Dolly from shaking than anything else, but it was hardly the best topic to choose.

As Dolly gave a little scream and told her she was horrible, Granny Pen spoke sharply from the other side of the cupboard.

'If you two don't keep quiet, we'll never hear the all-clear, and it sounds as if the worst is past already.'

The girls perked up, listening hard and realizing that the drone of aircraft had already stopped and there was no more gunfire. Either the planes had given up, or it had been another hit and run raid, which was happening all too frequently when, according to Granny Pen, the Jerries didn't really know which target to hit and aimed for anything that looked like a large town. That was her theory, anyway.

Sure enough, not long afterwards the all-clear

sounded, and when the girls emerged from the cupboard Granny Pen was putting their supper on the table and telling them to clear it up themselves as she searched for her torch, grumbling that she was already late for her evening meeting.

'You're not going out after that raid, are you?' Dolly squeaked.

'Of course I am. It'll be a long time before a Cornish woman lets a few Jerry planes prevent her from going about her normal business. They were early tonight, but they won't be back now they've done their stuff. You two girls can amuse yourselves without any worries, and I'll be back later.'

She was a stoic, Amber thought, with a surge of affection. She was made of strong stuff, as tough as Cornish granite. She had seen her son die, and her daughter-in-law die in childbirth, and she had never wavered in bringing up Amber as her own, nor at bringing Dolly into her home.

'Good old Gran,' she said softly, at which Granny Pen grimaced.

'Not so much of the old, young lady,' she said, ramming her hat on top of her grey curls. 'We all do what we have to do these days, and it wouldn't hurt you two to do something for the war effort, either. You can both knit, and there's wool and patterns in the sideboard drawer. There's many a soldier who'd be glad of an extra pair of socks. If you can't do that, then get on with unravelling that old grey cardigan of mine. I can wash the wool and use it again. Now, I must get on.'

There was a small silence after she had gone as the girls ate their supper of spam and bread, spread so thinly with butter they could hardly see it.

'She's quite a girl, ain't she?' Dolly said at last. 'Do you think we give her a hard time?'

'Probably,' Amber said.

'She don't deserve it, though, does she?' Dolly persisted. 'I mean, she didn't have to take me in, and you didn't have to share your bedroom with me, did you?'

Amber stared suspiciously. 'What's this, your conscience talking?'

Dolly flushed. 'Perhaps it is. I know I ain't always the easiest person to get on with, and I pinch things without meaning to, well, not always without meaning to, but you always seemed to have everything.'

'I'm not exactly rich, am I!' Amber said.

'No, but you've got a gran who'd do anything for you, and my mum – well, I reckon she was glad to get rid of me when the war started. It wasn't just for my sake that she put me on that train at Paddington.'

She couldn't hide the bitterness in her voice, and it wasn't hard for Amber to follow her thoughts. Her dad away in the army, and all those uncles who came to the house, and now this Uncle Joe who was taking care of her mum. No wonder Dolly could be a nuisance. She looked so abject now that Amber couldn't help feeling sorry for her.

'You can have a bit of my spam if you like,' she offered.

After a startled second, Dolly grinned.

'I'll swop you for half a piece of bread and scrape,' she said.

It was hardly the beginning of a beautiful friendship, but it was a start.

Chapter Six

The Forces' Club dance to raise funds in aid of the Dunkirk victims was open to all.

The more the merrier for our brave servicemen said the slogan outside the place, inviting everyone to come and donate whatever they could spare to the collecting buckets inside. Granny Pen said she might even come herself, which met with a united howl of disapproval from Amber and Dolly.

'Well, at least there's something you two seem to agree about,' she said mildly. 'And thank heaven it's been a bit more harmonious around here lately.'

'We've decided to be more like sisters,' Amber said importantly.

'Sisters that sometimes fight,' Dolly added, 'but on the whole Amber ain't too bad, and I could have done a lot worse.'

'So could I – and a lot better!'

But a minor miracle had occurred since the night when Dolly had revealed how hurt she had felt over her mum abandoning her to the back of beyond in

95

Cornwall, as she put it. They had since forgotten much of their antagonism towards one another, and found it was far easier to confide in each other than to fight.

There was one thing that Amber had no intention of confiding in Dolly about, though, and that was the way she felt about Luke Gillam. They might be sisters of a sort now, but sisters could still be rivals in love, and Dolly had a fine knack of wanting what somebody else had. It probably came from her not having had much of a life in the first place, Amber conceded, but there was no way she was going to share Luke's affection with her! Even if she had it . . .

'Don't worry,' Granny Pen went on, 'I'll give you a donation for the cause, but my dancing days are over. In any case, I don't know how anybody can dance to this fast and noisy music that's on the wireless so often now.'

'It's called jazz music, Gran, as you very well know, and you can't really dance to it, so you just have to jig about on your own,' Amber said, her eyes sparkling as she imagined Granny Pen kicking her legs about with the best of them.

Granny Pen sniffed. 'They had proper dancing in my day, waltzes and foxtrots, and gentlemen were courteous to their partners and held them discreetly, and didn't just prance about by themselves!'

With her inside knowledge of the event, Dolly informed her of what was going to happen. 'There's still going to be plenty of waltzes and foxtrots, Granny Pen, and veletas and military two-steps for old folks as well.'

'Cheeky young madam,' Granny Pen said. 'I suppose you'd put me in that category, would you?'

'I wouldn't dare!' She giggled.

It didn't seem such an imposition for Dolly to joke with her gran any more, Amber thought. She was glad they got along so well, and it was more fun for the two of them to gang up on Granny Pen and tease her when they got the chance than always to be at loggerheads. It was good to have a sister – even a make-believe one.

They were excited about the dance. It would be the first grown-up dance they had been to. They both had their orders to serve the teas and sandwiches during the interval, but after that they would be free to join the rest of the dancers. They might even jig about to the jazz tunes themselves, though there would only be a few of those, despite what they had told Granny Pen. Most of the dances would be the kind that Granny Pen considered respectable.

'My supervisor says they might make some of the old-tyme dances progressive,' Dolly said, as they got ready to go out that evening. They were each wearing a dress that Granny Pen had made for them, using up some of her own precious clothing coupons to buy the material. Amber's was sky blue and Dolly's was apple green. They each admired the other one, and then set about applying a touch of lipstick, and rouged their cheeks as much as they dared.

'What's progressive?' Amber said, wondering if Luke would be there tonight. His parents would probably come too. It wasn't a dance solely for young people. They weren't the ones with the money for the donations, and the whole idea was to raise funds.

Dolly was a bit vague about what progressive dancing meant too, having only just heard about it herself. 'I think it's when all the couples dance in a circle and then the compere tells one partner to move ahead at a certain part of the dance so that you all get a new partner.'

'It sounds smashing!' Amber said excitedly. 'I hope we're doing it when it's progressive, then.'

Dolly glanced at her, and, as if for the first time, she saw how truly beautiful Amber was, with her eyes and her lips glowing. Beside her she felt suddenly pale and dowdy, despite the new apple green dress.

'Well, you'll have to wait until somebody asks you to dance first, dummy,' she said sharply.

'I'd probably die if a boy asked me to dance, with all those old people looking at us, but we can always dance together.'

Dolly shrugged. 'I suppose so.'

This idea didn't exactly appeal to Dolly. She wanted to be swept off her feet by some handsome young man, preferably in uniform, who wanted to dance with her the whole evening – but she knew how unlikely that was. Ladies did dance together, and often had to when there was a shortage of males, but if the dance was progressive, then hopefully one of them should end up with a male partner at some stage of the evening.

*

That night everyone seemed determined to forget there was a war on when they entered the newly decorated Forces' Club, with balloons and banners and flags everywhere. The local band was already playing a background tune, so, providing old Jerry stayed away tonight, everyone was set on having a good time. The Penry girls had to cover their new dresses with work overalls for the first part of the evening, but then each of them was going to emerge like a butterfly from a chrysalis, Amber told Dolly poetically, which made her screech with laughter.

'You are a twerp sometimes, Amber. I ain't no bleedin' butterfly and I ain't one of them whatever it was you said, neither.'

'It's a chrysalis. Didn't you pay attention to *anything* at school?'

Dolly wasn't paying attention now. She was more interested in a group of newcomers who had just entered the Forces' Club. Among them were the old gang of friends who had all left school now, most of whom they hadn't seen for a while. They all looked so grown up, dressed up to the nines for the occasion. Among them was Luke Gillam.

'Look who's just arrived,' Dolly said, then half wished she hadn't drawn Amber's attention to him. He didn't scrub up at all badly, as her mum would have said, and he'd got taller and broader in these past few months.

'Who?' Amber said absently, as if she hadn't known the minute he arrived, and stood up a bit taller and straighter behind the canteen counter because of it. The normal tables and chairs had been pushed to the sides of the room, making a large open space for dancing, and the large open space was rapidly filling with people.

'You bleedin' well know who,' Dolly said with a grin. 'Your bloke.'

Among the people arriving now were Mr and Mrs Veal, and Amber felt obliged to wave back to them as Dolly sniggered.

'I bet old Veal will want a dance with you. I heard him telling you he used to like to trip the light fantastic, whatever the hell that means.'

'It just means dancing, you dope. I hope he doesn't ask me. He sweats a lot.'

They both started giggling, and were told to get on with preparing the spam and scrape sandwiches that would be on offer later, all proceeds for the cause.

Amber hoped Luke would ask her to dance, but she didn't think it was likely. Her main hope was if he and the other younger ones got up to do one of the progressive old-tyme dances, goaded into it by the compere. Although the older people in the canteen were greeting friends and neighbours and chatting together, it seemed as if all the girls her age were huddled together on one side of the room, and all the boys on the other. A fat chance you had of getting to know a chap if he couldn't even be bothered to sit near you or talk to you, Amber thought indignantly.

'Blimey, I thought she said she wasn't coming!' Dolly exclaimed. 'That'll curb your love life, gel.'

Amber gave a start as she saw Granny Pen come into the canteen, dressed in a neat navy blue frock with a string of pearls around her neck. She wasn't ancient by any means, but she had always seemed so in her daytime overall and the rather stern hat she wore for shopping. Now, with her grey hair fluffed up a bit more than usual, she seemed softer, younger. But Amber scowled at Dolly's words.

'I don't have any love life and you know it,' she snapped. 'I'm going over to see if everything's all right.'

She didn't know why it wouldn't be, and her gran didn't look in the least ruffled, but she had to find out. Excusing herself from the spam and scrape preparation, she wove her way between the crowds to where Granny Pen was sitting with several of her cronies.

'You said you weren't coming, Gran. What made you change your mind?' She hoped she didn't sound too accusing.

'Perhaps a little bird told me to keep my eye on my two charges,' Granny Pen replied with a chuckle, and then went on when Amber flushed: 'No, love, I decided that if our boys were brave enough to do their duty for King and Country, then I should be brave enough to risk putting my two left feet on the dance floor.'

'You're not actually going to dance?' Amber squeaked.

The other ladies beside Granny Pen tittered. She gave a little sniff.

'Don't worry, my dear, I shan't show you up. I'll wait until there's a crowd on the dance floor before I add my two-penn'orth.'

One of her friends leaned forward. 'Your gran used to be a nifty dancer many years ago, Amber. She wasn't born old, and she'll show you young maids a thing or two when she gets started.'

Amber groaned. This was a side of her gran she had never seen before. To her knowledge Granny Pen had never been to a dance in Amber's lifetime, but she shouldn't forget that there had been a long life before Amber was born.

'I'd better get back to my sandwich-making,' she said quickly.

She moved away, but not before she had caught Luke Gillam watching her. Oh, why, why, why couldn't she have been suave and sophisticated at that moment, she thought, gliding across the canteen floor in her lovely new dress, instead of scurrying back in her work overall, her face red with embarrassment?

'What did she say then?' Dolly asked without too much interest, while Amber had a horrible vision of changing partners in a progressive old-tyme dance and finding herself trotting around the room with Granny Pen of all people!

The evening got off to a good start, with some lively music and a bit of a sing-song, and the compere urging everyone to dig deep into their pockets to put a few coppers or tanners or whatever they could spare into the collecting buckets. Even the three-penny bits they were saving for the Christmas puds could go in, he boomed. Since there was no dried fruit and few other ingredients to spare for making traditional Christmas puddings any more, it wasn't such a daft idea.

As expected there was the usual mixture of waltzes and foxtrots and old-tyme dances. There were plenty of ladies without male partners who were dancing together, and a few of their braver ex-school friends were already hopping about trying to follow the steps. The old-tyme dances looked the easiest, since all you had to do was follow the couple in front as you moved around the circle, and when the compere bellowed out that the next one would be progressive, all the gentlemen partners dutifully followed orders.

'See what I mean?' Dolly hissed in Amber's ear. 'Once the refreshments are over, we can have a go.'

Amber wondered if it had occurred to her that the gentlemen always danced on the outer ring. This meant that either she or Dolly would have to take the gentleman's part, and the other one would end up dancing with all the ladies in the circle. But she might have known Dolly would have thought of it.

'You'll have to be the man, because you're taller than me. Besides, I don't fancy dancing with some of these old dears.'

'Oh no! We'll take it in turns, otherwise I shall end up only knowing the men's steps and that's not fair,' Amber snapped. 'Everybody changes partners, so it doesn't really matter who we end up with, does it? And don't call them old dears.'

As Dolly grumbled that she supposed it was fair enough, Amber had to concede that there were a lot of old dears here tonight, as well as a good selection of men in uniform, some walking stiffly and a few with bandages around their heads or arms in slings. It was a timely reminder of why they were all here.

But Amber was going to make very sure Dolly stuck to the rules. With any luck, when it was Amber's turn to dance in the inner ring she might end up with Luke – if he bothered to join in at all. Right now he seemed to be deep in conversation with several servicemen, and her heart gave an uncomfortable lurch. He was keen to join up as soon as he could, and it didn't take a genius to know he wanted to find out as much as possible about it.

She turned away as the buxom supervisor told her and Dolly to get a move on as people would be getting thirsty soon after all the dancing activity.

'You little maids take care to be pleasant to the customers,' she said, 'and especially to that couple sitting over in the corner. They may not feel like walking through all these folk to get their tea themselves, and it's brave of them to turn out at all, considering.'

'Considering what?' Amber asked.

'They got some bad news a week or so ago. One of their sons has already been killed in France, and now the other one's being sent to some big hospital in another part of the country where they can deal with his spinal injuries. They don't think he'll ever walk again, and him so young too.'

She said it so matter-of-factly that Amber was shocked. The woman saw how the girl's face paled and she gave her shoulder a squeeze.

'I know I sounded a bit brutal, my dear, but in this job you get to hear a fair few such tales, and you have to steel yourself and not make too much fuss, or you'd just fall apart instead of getting on with the work.'

Amber whispered to Dolly, 'Have you heard this sort of thing before?'

Dolly shrugged. 'Once or twice, but I try not to listen. She's always asking servicemen if they've been at the Front and what it was like. She likes to talk about the gory details, but I just shut my ears to it. If you can't do nothing about it, what's the use of worrying about it?'

'For somebody who looks so sweet and angelic you've got a very hard streak, Dolly.'

'Do you think I look sweet and angelic, then?' Dolly said, preening and ignoring the rest of it.

'I'm not answering that.'

'Too late. You've already said it.'

They were prevented from any more bickering as there was a sudden drumroll from the band, and the compere announced that there would be a half-hour interval for refreshments.

'That's our cue,' the supervisor said to her small team of helpers. 'Be as efficient as you can and see that everyone has what they want. You two young ones,' she said to Amber and Dolly, 'go and see if any of the older ones want to stay sitting down and want anything brought to them. Shoo now.'

Amber felt as if they were being dismissed. They were good enough to do all the donkey work, but now they had to walk around the room to where people were sitting out for reasons of their own.

'Oh no, I don't want to ask them,' she said quickly to Dolly, seeing the middle-aged couple the super-visor had pointed out. The woman was wiping her eyes and the man had his arm around her, his face full of misery.

'Why not? They look as if they could do with a cup of tea. Go on, they won't eat you,' Dolly said, giving her a little push.

While she dithered, Amber saw Granny Pen go across to the couple, sit beside them and take the woman's hand, and she immediately felt ashamed at being afraid to speak to them. It was what people did . . . they turned away from anything embar-rassing, when it was often when people needed them most, and it isolated them even more. She made her feet move forward until she reached them. By now the woman was silently weeping. It was more distressing than if she had been bawling out loud, and Amber's heart thudded sickly. But she couldn't just stand there, saying nothing.

'Can I fetch you both some tea?' she stammered. 'And you too, Gran.'

'I wish I'd never come,' the woman moaned as if

she hadn't heard her. 'Ernest insisted, saying it would take me out of myself, but I knew I'd make a fool of myself if I did. I was all right until the band played that last song – it was one of our Bill's favourites.'

Granny Pen looked at Amber. 'Bill was Mr and Mrs Tremayne's older son, who was killed,' she said quietly. 'It's been an ordeal for her to come here tonight, but it was the right thing to do, not to shut herself away like a leper. You bring that tea for the three of us, Amber, and make it hot and strong.'

Amber almost ran away from them, near to tears herself. It must be a terrible time for the couple. She had never experienced the death of anyone close to her. She hadn't known Mr Thomas's son, but his grief had affected the whole school. All these young men were dying who were little more than boys. It was a thought that frightened her more than anything else so far.

The wail of an air-raid siren broke through the chatter in the canteen. The compere called for quiet for a minute, although everyone knew by now that every time Plymouth had a raid they had the sirens too, and hearing the distant sound of aircraft and gunfire it was assumed that that was the case this time. The man then announced that everyone was at liberty to leave if they chose, but from the sound of it the bombers weren't coming their way. Seconds later everyone was doing exactly what they'd been doing before, chatting and drinking tea and ordering sandwiches.

'The good old British spirit, eh?' The supervisor grinned to one and all. 'It's probably poor old Plymouth getting it tonight, so I hope my sister and her kids have taken to the shelter.'

She spoke brightly, but Amber realized that her hands were shaking. This was a war that affected everyone in one way or another, she thought, and none of them could truly feel safe until it was all over.

'I need three teas, please, hot and strong,' she almost gasped to the helper who was pouring them out.

'You'll get what you're given, miss, and no favouritism,' the woman said, and then glanced across to the trio that Amber had just left. 'Well, just this once.'

Against the background of general chatter and laughter and tears, the distant sound of gunfire and aircraft was an added accompaniment that nobody wanted but most chose to ignore, until at last the all-clear sounded and everyone gave a cheer. But Amber saw the sense in Dolly's philosophy. If you couldn't do anything about it, you might as well not worry about it. Easy to say, not so easy to do. But once the interval was over and the band struck up again, most people were determined to have a good time. It was what they were here for after all.

Once they had helped with the washing-up they could remove their overalls and mingle with the crowd. They joined in one or two of the progressive old-tyme dances, but, as expected, few of the boys left their seats, and Amber had to put up with

Mr Veal's enthusiastic hugging on several circuits of the floor. It was almost preferable to take the man's part, she decided.

Mostly, she and Dolly stayed with their old school friends, some of whom were talking excitedly about having had the chance of dancing with some good-looking soldiers in the progressives. Just their luck! By the time the evening was almost over Amber looked across to where Luke was still talking to the servicemen, as if oblivious to what this evening was all about, or that he had a duty to take part in it. Well, not a duty, exactly, but he could at least look interested!

As if aware of her stare, if not her simmering resentment, he slowly turned his head to look straight at her, and gave her one of his stunning smiles. Her heart stopped and then raced on again. And then she heard the compere announce that the next dance would be a Ladies' Excuse-Me, and that ladies shouldn't be shy about asking the gentleman of their choice to take a turn on the floor.

She was hardly conscious of the fact that her feet had begun to move, or of the screams of laughter behind her as the other girls realized what she was going to do. She didn't pause as she wove between the couples already on the dance floor until she reached Luke's side, because if she had stopped for a moment she knew she would never have had the nerve to do it.

'Can I have the pleasure?' she croaked.

One of the soldiers talking to Luke leered and

gave him a nudge. 'Go on, mate, it looks as if your luck's in tonight.'

Amber wanted to hit him for spoiling the moment, but incredibly it didn't. Luke stood up and took the hand she offered him.

'I'd be honoured, my lady,' he said with admirable dignity, considering they could still hear the hoots and catcalls of their old classmates.

And then they were drifting, stumbling, falling over one another's feet in a crazy, haphazard kind of a waltz, and all the time Luke held her close, knowing that if he didn't they'd probably both end up in a heap on the floor.

'We'll never make a championship pair,' he said with an apologetic laugh when she winced as he trod on her toe for the umpteenth time, and then his voice changed to amazement. 'My God, have you seen Granny Pen?'

Amber looked over his shoulder, and there was her gran in the arms of the local greengrocer, doing as elegant a waltz as you like. Amber giggled.

'I didn't know she had it in her,' she said, stumbling again and leaning heavily into Luke, her arms tightening around him to keep her balance. 'Sorry!'

'Don't be. You don't hear me objecting, do you?'

Amber caught sight of Dolly's furious face with the other girls, and knew that she hadn't had the nerve to do what Amber had done. It made her feel good. It made her feel even better than she did already and that was pretty wonderful.

The music ended, and for one more brief moment she was still in Luke's arms before he released her.

'I've got my dad's car tonight,' he said casually. 'Once the dance is over, we could drive to the top of the hill if you like and see if we can see anything towards Plymouth. I reckon they had it tonight.'

'I don't know,' Amber stammered. 'Gran's here, and so is Dolly.'

'I wasn't asking them. I was asking you. But I can see it's not the best idea I've ever had.'

'Oh, but it is! It's a wonderful idea, but I don't expect I'd be allowed.'

She groaned as she said it, because if ever she felt her lack of years, she felt it now. Why couldn't she be two years older, the same as Luke, instead of not quite fifteen? All the feelings racing around inside her were every bit as adult as his, and she desperately wanted to do as he suggested.

'Well, if you can, let me know,' he said.

They parted company and a few minutes later she saw Granny Pen coming towards her. She composed her face, afraid that she might be giving something away – though she wasn't sure exactly what. But Granny Pen had other plans.

'Amber, I'm leaving now and I'm going to stay with Mr and Mrs Tremayne tonight. The poor soul's in need of some female company and understanding, so you and Dolly get off home when the dance finishes. I shouldn't think there'll be another raid tonight, but if there is you know what to do. I'll be back in the morning in time for church.'

Amber wasn't sure if this was fate or if she had subconsciously wished for something like this to happen. It was horrible to think of that poor woman's misfortune as her own good luck, but all she had to do now was to make sure Dolly didn't get wind of her and Luke going off in his dad's car . . . and the very thought almost made her wet herself with excitement.

Dolly's eyes lit up when she heard what Granny Pen was going to do.

'Some of the girls are going down the quay for a look around, if you know what I mean. I didn't think I dared, but when the cat's away, eh? Are you coming?'

'No thanks, and you'd better be careful, Dolly. You know what *I* mean. There are lots of strangers and foreigners off the ships down there.'

'Oh, don't be so stuffy. Just because you never put a foot wrong!' Dolly said with a sneer, which was a laugh, because that was just what Amber intended to do. It might seem a tame adventure to some, going up the hill in a car with a boy to see if they could see as far as Plymouth, but it all depended on the boy . . .

'I'll see you back at the cottage then, and don't be too late,' Amber warned.

Dolly's eyes narrowed. 'You're not up to something, are you?'

'Of course not. What could I get up to!'

When the evening officially ended people left the Forces' Club in dribs and drabs, some lingering to

112

talk to friends, others anxious to get home. The night was chilly and Amber was glad she and Luke weren't riding their bikes to the top of Pendennis Hill. It was far cosier, and far more sophisticated, to be going there in his dad's car which he had only just learned to drive. Even so, she felt oddly tongue-tied as it chugged up the steep bends of the hill. It was weird, as if they hadn't known one another for years. It was as if they had just met and had to get to know one another for the first time – if only they knew the right words to say.

'That was brave of you tonight, asking me to dance,' he said at last. 'I doubt if I'd have got up at all if you hadn't.'

'You're brave!' she told him. 'If you're going to join up someday, that'll be the bravest thing!'

Had she said those words to him before, or had she merely dreamed of saying them? She was confused, just sitting here beside him. He gave a short laugh.

'Maybe I won't have much choice once I'm of an age to be conscripted, and it won't matter then if I feel brave or not.'

'But you want to go, don't you?' she said, almost accusingly.

The car rounded the last bend at the top of the hill before he turned off the engine and stopped. He turned to her, and in the dim interior his face was very close to hers.

'Of course I do. It's what men do in a war.'

'But you're not a man yet!'

'No, and you're not grown-up yet either, more's the pity, and I'm not about to be arrested for cradle-snatching,' he said, sounding odd.

Amber had thought for one glorious second that he was going to kiss her, but he pulled away from her with those words, which insulted and demoralised her.

'So are we going to get out of this blessed car or are we going to sit here all night?' she snapped.

She opened the door and stepped out, immediately feeling the wind whipping up her hair. She shivered, not so much from the cold, but from the sight that faced them. Plymouth was a long way away, but, as now, when there had been a bad raid it was always possible to see the red glow that hung like a pall over the distant city. Even if she couldn't smell the burning, she could imagine it, taste it, even. Against the glow of the bomb damage, the barrage balloons in the sky hovered even more menacingly than usual.

'Oh my God,' she whispered. She felt Luke's arms go around her from behind, sheltering her from the worst of the wind. Her hair was in his mouth, and he brushed it away. 'It must be like something out of hell. All those poor people – and did you hear about Bill Tremayne?' she said, her thoughts distractedly winging from one terrible event to another.

'I did, and I'm beginning to think it was a mistake to come up here after all, and it's time I took you home,' he said roughly. 'You can't take everybody's tragedy on your own shoulders, Amber. We all have to live with it.'

'I know – and some people have to die with it,' she said, the enormity of it all making her harsh.

Without warning he turned her around so that she was facing him, and he touched her mouth with his in a slow sweet kiss. She could feel every part of herself pressing into him, and it was thrilling and exciting, and a bit scary. She was soft, curving against him, and his body was harder and muscular. The difference had never seemed so acute to her as it did in those breathtaking moments. And then he let her go just as abruptly and turned to get back in the car.

'Grow up soon, Amber,' was all he said in a strangled kind of voice.

Chapter Seven

'*The Yanks are in!*'

Amber almost dropped the tray of knick-knacks she was carrying as Luke burst into the shop early on the morning of December 8th. She had hardly seen him since the night of the dance, and she'd begun to wonder if that kiss had been all in her imagination after all. It was frustrating and infuriating to think that they had been so close in those few moments, and then it seemed as if he was keeping well away from her. Dolly had pumped her endlessly to ask where she had been that night but Amber wasn't telling. Some secrets were too precious to share.

Dolly had become an unexpected source of information, working as she did with older girls who weren't reticent in telling stories of their escapades with the French sailors who were in port from time to time, and some of the Dunkirk refugees that they called 'ready, willing and able'.

'They have to be bleedin' careful, mind,' Dolly said importantly. 'They don't want to get caught.'

'Who's going to catch them?' Amber said, not twigging at first.

Dolly screamed with laughter. 'Caught with a *baby*, you oik. Gladys at work says a bloke can get his whatsit up just by holding a girl too tight, and that's a sure way of heading for trouble. Blokes can't help it, see? It just happens.'

Amber had decided not to question Dolly any more, in case Dolly got suspicious as to why Amber was so interested in a bloke getting his whatsit up, but even though she'd put it so crudely, it explained a lot. Amber knew exactly now why Luke had pulled away from her on that night on Pendennis Hill and why he wished she would grow up soon. It thrilled her and scared her.

And now he was here, and they were face to face for the first time since that night, and she felt so embarrassed with her new-found knowledge of the workings of a bloke's whatsit that she could hardly look at him. All that sniggering stuff at school about rabbits flew out of the window, and her palms were damp.

But she yelled at him now, unnerved at seeing him so unexpectedly in the aromatic intimacy of the little craft shop and not yet understanding what he was shouting about.

'What the heck are you on about? You nearly made me drop this lot!'

'The Yanks! It was on the wireless, and it'll be all over the papers soon. The Japs have bombed a place called Pearl Harbour out in the Pacific, and the

Yanks and Britain have declared war on Japan, so they're *in*!'

As her heartbeats stopped thudding, Amber looked at him coolly, determined not to give away anything about her churning feelings.

'In where? In the Pacific?'

From what she remembered of her sketchy geography lessons, it was so far away from Cornwall she couldn't even picture where the ocean was, let alone some place called Pearl Harbour that she'd never even heard about.

Luke cursed, wanting her excitement to match his.

'Christ Almighty, Amber, sometimes you can be the most infuriating girl in the world. You know damn well what I mean. The Yanks are our allies now, and pretty soon there'll probably be shiploads of them coming over here. That'll please you girls, won't it?'

Mrs Veal pushed through the bead curtain before Amber could think of a suitable reply, her face as animated as Luke's.

'You're quite right, Luke, and it's a great day for us, even though it must have been dreadful for those poor American sailors in the thick of it. Their ships were bombed in that harbour without any warning.'

'Does everybody know about this but me?' Amber demanded.

'Surely your gran heard it on the wireless this morning,' Mrs Veal said. 'It's not like her to miss anything.'

'And even if she hadn't heard it, are you sure she

hasn't seen it coming in the tea leaves or the cards?' Luke said, mocking.

Amber glared at him. 'Well, for your information, our accumulator needs charging, and Gran was going to get it done after I came to work, so we didn't hear anything today. I wondered why so many people were standing about and gossiping in the streets, though. Is it so important that we have these Yanks with us then?'

She wasn't stupid, and she knew damn well how important it was, but she looked at Luke with innocent eyes, waiting for his explosion. She waited, but it didn't come. Instead, he caught her up in his arms and smacked a whopping great kiss on her cheek. It was their second kiss, but a million miles away from the impact of the first one.

'No wonder I love this crazy woman!' He grinned at her. 'You never know where you are with her, and it'll take an even crazier chap to tame her!'

He went out of the shop, whistling, and the shop bell tinkled and echoed for a few seconds after he had gone, while Amber doubted if she had really heard those words. Had Luke Gillam actually said that he *loved* her?

'Close your mouth, Amber, or you'll be catching flies,' Mrs Veal said dryly. 'Come on through and let's see if Father's still twiddling with the wireless.'

She always referred to her husband as Father, Amber thought vaguely, hardly registering anything else but the ecstatic fact that Luke Gillam had said he loved her.

Of course, he hadn't said it in a romantic way. Of course he hadn't really meant it. But he had said it, and Granny Pen always said that once words had been said they no longer belonged to the person saying them but to the person who heard them. Amber had never understood the logic of it, but it suited her to believe it now.

She seemed to have been standing there motionless for so long that her legs jerked into action of their own accord when she heard Mrs Veal calling to her again to come and hear the news. It was all true then. The terrible onslaught of Japanese aircraft over this place called Pearl Harbour in the Hawaiian Islands had been nothing short of premeditated murder. The Americans hadn't been prepared, and no wonder, since Pearl Harbour was simply an American naval base way out in the Pacific Ocean, and they had had no quarrel with the Japanese.

But they did now, and this war, which had once been between Britain and Germany, had all the potential to escalate into a worldwide conflict.

Amber shivered with a huge sense of foreboding, wondering if she had more of her gran's so-called sixth sense than she'd ever wanted. Everyone must feel like that now, but from the shouts and cheering that she could hear in the streets outside, she knew that the overriding feeling was one of jubilation that the Yanks were *in*.

Throughout the day it was impossible not to be drawn into those feelings, and there was huge optimism that with the might of the Americans alongside them, the war would soon be over. It would be the turning point. Even Dolly came dashing into the shop before closing time, her eyes wild with excitement after she had finished her shift at the Forces' Club early.

'Ain't it fantastic?' she shouted. 'Everybody's saying the Yanks will be sure to be sent to Falmouth, what with the docks and all. P'raps we'll get some of them film stars here as well. They'll have to join up, and they've always got lots of dosh, so if the war lasts a bit longer I might find a rich millionaire to take me to America!'

She paused for breath to see Amber and Mrs Veal laughing at her.

'What's so blee— What's so funny?'

'You are!' Amber said. 'You're mad! Even if they do come here, it probably won't be for ages yet, and they're hardly going to look at kids like us, practically straight out of school, are they? I'm not sure I want them looking at me, anyway.'

'That's because you think mister wonderful Lukey-boy is the answer to every girl's dream. You should remember that Cornwall's not the end of the world, even though it perishing well seems like it to some people,' she couldn't resist adding.

'I wonder why you ever stay here then.'

'Got no choice, have I?'

They glowered at one another, and then Amber began to laugh. Now that she had heard the news and realised what wonderful news it was, apart from the disaster at Pearl Harbour, she added hastily, she

121

didn't want to be out of sorts with Dolly. They had been getting along too well of late for that.

'Well, I'm sure you'll catch the eye of some Yank,' she said generously. 'You'll probably remind them of home, looking just like a Hollywood starlet. You'd do well in the flicks.'

Dolly looked at her suspiciously, and then patted her blonde curls, gloriously dishevelled now from the frantic bike ride here.

'You're probably right,' she said with massive self-confidence. 'Anyway, if you've nearly finished here now, I'll wait for you.'

'You might as well go on home, Amber,' Mrs Veal said. 'I doubt that I'd get much more work out of you today.'

'Do people ever buy any of this stuff?' Dolly said, peering around the shop.

'Lots,' Amber told her, 'and I bet when the Yanks come there'll be dozens of them in here buying traditional Cornish souvenirs to send home,' she added sweetly, and was rewarded by a scowl.

It was the only news on anyone's lips over the next days and weeks. The newspapers were full of it, reporters turning into poets over how soon the war was going to be over now that the Americans were joining the allies. There were many copycat headlines such as 'The Yanks Are Coming!' and 'Good Old Uncle Sam', until Granny Pen said sourly that it was a wonder the news rags didn't call it comparable to the Second Coming of Christ.

'Blimey, coming from your churchified gran, that's

blooming blasphemous, ain't it?' Dolly whispered to Amber in bed that night.

'Yes, but Mr Veal told me that older folks still remember how the Yanks were late in the last lot and they're late in this. That's how he put it, but I don't see why people should take offence. It wasn't their war, was it?'

'It is now. I wonder what they'll be like,' Dolly said dreamily, clearly seeing Hollywood and stardom ahead.

'They won't understand your cockney gabble, that's for sure,' Amber said.

'Well, do you think they'll understand you? They'll expect to see hayseeds growing out of the corner of your mouth.'

Amber snorted. 'I'm not rising to that bait, so shut up.'

Dolly leaned up on one elbow and looked across the moonlit room to the other bed.

'I know you've got your sights set on Luke Gillam, but if these Yanks are anything like they look at the flicks, it'll be exciting, won't it?'

'Not *everyone* in America looks like a film star, you twerp. Most of them will be just ordinary. Now shut *up* and go to sleep.'

And let me go on dreaming of that moment when Luke said he loved me, she thought, her heart giving a little leap of happiness at remembering. Until today she hadn't seen anything of him since the Forces' Club dance, but she still cherished the memory of the Ladies' Excuse-Me waltz when they had lurched around the dance floor clutching one another to prevent themselves falling over . . . and then that sweet kiss at the top of Pendennis Hill . . . and now that kiss in the shop.

Collectively, she knew that maybe none of it meant very much to him, but it did to her. Oh yes, it did to her. It meant everything. And when he had asked her to grow up soon, she knew in her heart that it meant he would wait for her to do so.

A few days after Britain and America declared war on Japan, Germany and Italy declared war on America and other nations followed suit. It was almost as if they were choosing their enemies now in a horrible game of tit-for-tat, except that the stakes were far higher and deadlier.

By December 19th all men aged between eighteen and sixty-four in Britain had to register, and those between twenty-two and forty-four were liable for military service. It was a chilling thought, but tempering it was the certainty that in due course thousands of American servicemen would be based in Britain as their jumping-off point for attacks on Europe.

That Christmas was tentatively more joyful than in the past few years, because everyone felt they must be turning the corner in the war. Even though the Jerries were still raining down bombs on the cities, and air-raid warnings were regular occurrences, whether or not the planes came this far west, there was a feeling that it surely couldn't go on for ever.

'I'm glad you're not twenty-two yet,' Amber told Luke when he called at the shop to say hello, as he occasionally did now. They were good friends and always had been. They weren't courting, and since she was still two months short of her fifteenth birthday, Amber knew her gran would put her foot down at any suggestion of the sort, but she also knew in her heart that he was sweet on her, even if he never said so. A girl always knew.

'Why? You know I'd give anything to go right now if I could,' Luke said, in answer to her comment.

'I don't want you to be killed, that's why!'

'Being killed isn't a requirement of joining up, you dope,' he said. 'I'd just like the chance to have a go at whipping the Jerries.'

'Well, it'll all be over long before you're old enough to go.'

'Oh yes. Have you been looking in your gran's crystal ball?'

'No. I just know.'

'You just *wish*, but you don't always get what you wish for, kid.'

I wish you'd take me seriously, she thought. *And don't call me kid.*

For a moment she wondered if she'd said the words out loud, but she knew she couldn't have done, because he'd picked up a small polished piece of amber among a jumble of other semi-precious stones in the tray she'd been sorting through.

'This is nice,' he said.

She answered on impulse. 'If you ever have to join up, I'll buy it for you as a talisman. It's amber, in case you didn't know it, and it's meant to keep sailors safe at sea from the perils of the deep or something,' she said lamely. 'I suppose those awful German U-boats could be called perils of the deep, couldn't they?'

He laughed. 'Cuckoo as ever, I see, but I might take you up on it if it ever happens. And —' he hesitated — 'it could be sooner than you think.'

If he was implying that worse was yet to come, she didn't want to know and wouldn't ask. But when he left the shop she picked up the piece of amber, still warm from his touch, and informed Mrs Veal that she wanted to buy it, and that she could take the money out of her wages. Then she was going to put it away safely, just as she put away all her personal and precious things until such time as they were needed, while praying that in this case it never would be.

Ever since she was little, Amber had listened to her gran making mysterious predictions, saying solemnly that good things always followed bad. It was balance and counterbalance, she'd say, putting the young Amber in awe of her, and making her wonder if her gran had swallowed the dictionary. But that meant it also worked the other way. Even if Granny Pen didn't mean to make the words mysterious, they had always seemed so to Amber, so that she was almost holding her breath at times, waiting for something good to happen, and apprehensive over what would come to counterbalance it.

Her first kiss with Luke had been a good time, and then there had been the bad weeks when she hadn't seen him at all. Then there was that second kiss, but as the time passed and nothing bad had followed she breathed easier again. Of course, she thought guiltily, she shouldn't be thinking only of herself. The wider world had far more disastrous bad things going on, but the Yanks' becoming their allies had surely been a good thing. The best thing. So what was due next, good or bad?

'You pay too much attention to your gran's daft sayings,' Dolly told her. 'She ain't a witch, even if I thought she might be when I first came here,' she added with a grin. 'She likes to be mysterious for her old biddies, because everybody knows that bad things happen in a war. Anyway, I've got a good thing going for me with Eddie now, so I ain't paying attention to what she says.'

'You want to be careful,' Amber said, echoing Dolly's own words.

Eddie Fielding had been in the class above them at school, a thin, spotty youth nobody had paid much attention to at the time. He worked at the docks now, and it was funny how time changed people, because it seemed as if he'd grown broader and better-looking almost overnight, and when Dolly had bumped into him at the Saturday morning pictures, she'd been instantly smitten.

It wouldn't last. Dolly's fads were swift, and

burned out just as swiftly, and if Granny Pen knew she was seeing Eddie every Saturday morning regular now, she'd definitely disapprove.

'We don't *do* anything,' Dolly said. 'Just a bit of necking in the back row.'

Amber covered her ears. 'Don't tell me any more, then there's no danger of me giving you away.'

Dolly sighed. 'That's the difference between you and me, gel. I like playing the field – the *field*, get it – with Eddie Fielding – but it ain't a for ever thing! You want to forget all about Lukey-boy and have some fun.'

'And you want to make sure you don't get *caught*.'

'What – with Eddie? I'm not sure he's even got a you-know-what!' She sniggered. 'But take it from me, gel, your gran just likes to stir things up with her good things-bad things tripe.'

The bad thing came for Amber when Luke came into the shop one Monday morning a month before her birthday. For a moment she felt as if the whole world was jangling around her until she realized it was the previous customer leaving the shop and it was merely the bell above the door.

'You aren't serious, are you, Luke? Tell me this is a joke.'

'It's not a joke. I've volunteered for the navy. I'm leaving tomorrow for a naval training camp in Wales, so you won't see me for the next six weeks.'

He couldn't hide the pride in his voice any more

than Amber could hide her bitterness that he hadn't even waited to be old enough to be called up. He'd simply volunteered. She felt cheated, as if Hitler or God or whoever was pulling the strings in this war was determined to take him away from her. But it was none of those people, wicked or spiritual, of course. It was Luke himself. He couldn't wait to go, to leave Cornwall, to be killed, to be drowned like her father had been drowned. The sea was taking both of them. Her head felt as if it was about to burst with the way her imagination was leaping about inside it.

'Are you all right?' Luke said, and his face came back into focus. 'I'm not going away for ever. Once I've joined a ship I'll get leave, and I'll come home when I can. But I've got to do this. I thought you knew me well enough for that.'

'I don't think I know you at all,' she croaked. 'Luke, don't go. I've got a bad feeling about it.'

He laughed uneasily. 'Don't go all spooky on me, Amber. Leave that for Granny Pen. I daresay if she looks in her cards for me, she'll see that I come back safe and sound.'

'Don't make fun of her. Nor me,' Amber flared. Then she swallowed. 'If you have to do this, then do something for me. Wait here a minute.'

She turned and pushed through the bead curtain to the back of the shop. She stood quite still for a moment, her eyes closed, listening to her own ragged breathing. *Please keep him safe*, she whispered to anyone who was listening. *Please bring him back to me.*

She rummaged in the little box where she kept her personal things at the shop, and then went back to where Luke was waiting.

He was gazing through the shop window, to where they could glimpse the sea, and in his mind she knew that already he had gone away from her to that world of adventure that belonged exclusively to men and boys. She had already lost him.

'I want you to have this,' she said, thrusting a small smooth object into his hand. 'Please keep it with you always, Luke, as a – a talisman. It's a friendship gift.'

She longed to say it was a gift of love, but she didn't dare. If she said such words, she would be in floods of tears, and he wouldn't want that. You didn't send a gladiator off to war with a tearful woman clinging to him. Not that she was quite a woman yet, according to all the rules of nature, but she had never known more womanly feelings for a man than she did right then.

He opened his hand and saw the small shiny piece of amber. Her stone. Her name. His mouth curved into a smile.

'My crazy girl,' he said softly, and then closed his hand around the amber again. 'It'll never leave me, I promise.'

He kissed her for a third time, and wild horses couldn't have stopped her clinging to him then. Just for a moment. For a long, sweet moment that was goodbye. Fifteen wasn't too young to be in love, to want him to stay with her so badly that she was giddy with love. Fifteen was also the start of a rite of passage that told her when to hold her tongue, and to pray for his safe return.

It was only when the bell over the shop door tinkled again after his departure that she ran into the back room and let the tears pour out on Mrs Veal's accommodating shoulder.

Dolly said flatly that she shouldn't let herself get so worked up over a boy.

'There's plenty more fish in the sea, if you'll pardon the pun,' she said.

'You're a bloody cold fish yourself,' Amber raged, unable to resist swearing at her irritatingly calm face. 'Nothing really touches you, does it? One of these days you'll get your comeuppance.'

'And who's been watching too many Hollywood flicks now then? Get my comeuppance indeed,' Dolly mocked. 'I'm expecting my mum and Uncle Joe to send me a postal order for my birthday and that'll be all the comeuppance I need!'

She rarely mentioned her dad any more, thought Amber sourly. This Uncle Joe who had a bit of dosh and was something to do with the Black Market seemed to be favourite now, and since he could get anything they needed from one of his sources, Dolly's mum was apparently queening it among her neighbours.

Dolly's comeuppance came on their fifteenth birthday, and it was nothing like she had expected. She waited eagerly for the postman to arrive and when he handed her the letter with the London postmark, she tore it open.

'You mind you don't tear up that postal order you're expecting as well, my girl,' Granny Pen told her, but Dolly wasn't listening.

Dolly was reading the letter her mum had sent her, and her face was even paler than usual. Her lips shook and her eyes were blurry with tears and shock.

'What's wrong, my dear?' Granny Pen said at once.

Dolly gulped and then managed to gasp out the words. 'It's my dad. He's gone and got himself blown up and killed, and my mum's only just heard about it. She had one of them "missing believed killed" telegrams, and Uncle Joe went and got it confirmed. My dad's dead and he ain't coming home no more.'

'Oh, my love, I'm so sorry,' Granny Pen said, her arms going around the girl at once. 'Come and sit down and take some deep breaths.'

'It's a rotten birthday present, isn't it?' Amber muttered without thinking, and immediately knew it was the very worst thing she could have said.

'That's not all,' Dolly said, choked. Her hands were still shaking as she clutched the letter. 'This happened a month ago, only being my mum she didn't think to tell me 'cos she didn't want to worry me, she said. Too busy enjoying herself, I bet. But now the bleedin' neighbours have got all snooty about Uncle Joe being there so often – well, living in our house is what she means – and she says she ain't going to be targeted as a bleedin' scarlet woman, so although he's just her paying lodger – and if you believe that you'll believe anything – I've got to go back home and work with her down the market to make it all respectable.'

Amber gasped. 'She can't force you to go back to London where the bombs are falling. You live here with us! You're my sister – well, sort of!'

'Dolly was only ever here as a temporary arrangement, Amber,' Granny Pen said, seeing the distress on her granddaughter's face. 'If her mother wants her back, then I'm afraid she'll have to do as she's told.'

'Do you *want* to go?' Amber demanded.

Dolly was still shaking. 'Of course I bleedin' well don't. I never wanted to come here in the first place, but I'm sort of used to it now. But she's sent the postal order for my train fare, and she says I've got to go back next Saturday.'

Amber didn't know what to say. It was the worst birthday either of them had ever known, and in the middle of it all was Dolly's grief over her dad, though it wasn't too much in evidence right now. The next minute her anger was obvious.

'Why did my dad have to bleedin' well go and get killed, the silly bugger! He was never much of a hero, and I bet he just lay down and let some Jerry bugger blast him to kingdom come!'

Granny Pen couldn't let this go on any longer.

'Dolly, you're understandably upset, and we all say things we don't mean at such times, but this is a Christian house and I can't tolerate this sort of language any longer. I suggest we all close our eyes for a few moments and think kindly of your dad, and how he died for his country. There are more ways of being a hero than going into battle with all guns blazing.'

'Where'd you hear that? At the flicks?' Dolly muttered, and then had the grace to do as the others were doing and sit with her head bowed. As she did so, the tears began to slide down her face, an angry few at first, and then a torrent.

Amber threw her arms around her and held her tight. It had all happened so fast that it was only just dawning on her that Dolly was leaving. She had lost Luke, and now she was losing Dolly. And it was all the fault of that bloody, bloody war.

'We mustn't lose touch,' she said fiercely into Dolly's tangle of hair. 'We must write to one another all the time and then we'll feel as close as we do now.'

Dolly pushed her away, lashing out at those nearest to her.

'P'raps I don't want to feel close to you Cornish hayseeds any longer. P'raps I'm glad to be going back where I belong!'

The bravado lasted all of ten seconds, and then she was sobbing and pulling Amber back to her and promising to write all the time, sharing their secrets as they had begun to do lately.

Granny Pen cleared her throat, trying to lighten the gloom.

'So, seeing as how this is a birthday, why don't you girls help me see if there's anything in the larder to make a cake for tea?'

Chapter Eight

On Saturday morning the train station bustled with civilians and servicemen, some coming, some going. Most of them had grim faces except for the lucky ones who were greeting a loved one returning home. Dolly had said goodbye to her workmates at the Forces' Club and done the rounds of the people she knew, the old school friends, the church ladies and Granny Pen's cronies. By now Dolly had assumed the role of a martyr, alternately infuriating and amusing Amber. But now that the moment of parting was almost here, there was nothing artificial about the misery in both girls' eyes. What had begun nearly three years ago as a necessary annoyance in both their lives had turned into the best kind of friendship, the kind that survived, despite, or because of, knowing each other's faults.

'I'll miss you like mad,' Amber gulped, hugging her for a last moment.

'Soppy date,' Dolly said, her chin wobbling. 'You can have that bedroom all to yourself now, and you won't miss me at all.'

'Yes I will.'

'Come on now, you two,' Granny Pen said, before an argument started that neither could win. 'It's time to go, Dolly.'

Granny Pen was only given to hugging and kissing in exceptional circumstances, so she was startled when Dolly threw her arms around her and planted a smacker on the old woman's cheek.

'You ain't been so bad,' Dolly told her, reverting to type, and then she gathered up her bags and gas mask and boarded the train, pushing past some soldiers in the corridor to get into a compartment and squeeze into a window seat, disregarding the grumbles of everyone else. By the time the train pulled out, sparking on the tracks and sending clouds of steam into the air, Dolly was also sharing a saucy laugh with a young soldier in the same compartment. Whatever else happened in this war, Amber had to agree that Dolly would almost certainly come up smelling of roses.

After so long, the cottage felt strange without her. Amber felt lost in a different way from the way she felt lost over Luke's departure. Dolly had had no choice but to do as her mother asked, and eventually Amber knew she had come to terms with that, even looking forward to the nightly dash for the tube station when the sirens went, as a big adventure.

But Luke didn't have to go at all. He wasn't eighteen yet, so he wasn't old enough to be conscripted, and he didn't have to go and volunteer for the navy. She knew he must have lied about his age, and Amber was furious at the stupidity of boys wanting to be heroes who went away to war before they needed to.

After church on Sunday she came face to face with Luke's mother. Like Granny Pen, Mrs Gillam was a God-fearing woman, and always spoke her mind.

'I hear you've lost your little friend, Amber, and we've lost our Luke, so I hope you paid special attention when the vicar told us to pray for all our brave men and women, girls and boys, who are working hard to bring us to victory.'

Amber's temper flared in an instant. It wasn't the place and it wasn't the time, but she had never heard anything so damn stupid in her life.

'I'd hardly call what Dolly Nash is doing "bringing us to victory",' she mimicked. 'She's gone back to London because her mother wants her to help on some market stall, and Luke didn't have to volunteer, did he? I thought he was supposed to be doing something hush-hush with Mr Gillam at the boatyard that was all-important to the war effort!'

Amber was all too aware of her gran bearing down on her at that moment, and she desperately hoped she hadn't overheard her caustic remark.

'I know you're upset over Luke volunteering, Amber, but his father and I are very proud of him,' Luke's mother said quietly. 'But in Dolly's case, I think you're forgetting that her father has just been killed, and I'm sure it will be a traumatic homecoming for her. Her mother will need her now, and we must all learn the meaning of compassion in these difficult times.'

Recklessly, Amber opened her mouth to say just what she thought about Dolly's mother needing her now. Whether she really would have blurted it all out about the Black Market, Uncle Joe or Dolly's mother's late-in-the-day need to appear respectable she didn't know, because the iron grip of Granny Pen's hand on her wrist effectively stopped her.

'We're all feeling a little overwrought these days, Mrs Gillam, and it's harder for the young,' Granny Pen said. 'They haven't been through it all before the way we older ones have, and there's a lesson in tolerance to be learned for all of us.'

Amber squirmed as her gran made excuses for her, while wondering if Mrs Gillam would think the words were intended as a bit of a slight on herself. Apparently she didn't, because she smiled at Amber.

'Your gran's a wise woman, Amber. You'll be missing Dolly of course, and I know you and Luke were great chums too, so how would you like to come and have some tea with me tomorrow afternoon when you finish work?'

'That would be nice, thank you,' Amber said, taken unawares by the request, and not sure if this was a sop or not. As for her and Luke being 'great chums', well, she supposed that in everyone else's eyes that's what they were. Great lovers they certainly were not. Not even sweethearts. Just great chums. She supposed the words were intended to please her, she thought, as the Gillams moved away, but they just filled her with added misery. If she wasn't careful, she'd be wallowing in it soon. It was better to keep the anger uppermost than to keep feeling sorry for herself.

'I won't say what I thought of you back there, Amber,' her gran said, striding ahead of her so fast that Amber had a job to keep up.

At this rate, she'd be having a heart attack soon, Amber thought uncharitably, and immediately willed the thought away, because Granny Pen's demise was too frightening to be contemplated.

'I'm sorry,' she said. 'I wasn't thinking, and the words just came out.'

Granny Pen slowed down a little as they left the church grounds and reached the road. 'You shouldn't think too much about this Gillam boy, Amber. You're far too young to have your head filled with any romantic nonsense.'

'Luke's almost eighteen,' she said defensively.

Granny Pen looked at her sharply, noting the flushed face and the slender, curving shape of her, so aggressive now. She was like a mother defending her young, except that this was no maternal feeling her granddaughter was experiencing, Granny Pen thought in alarm. This was first love, raw and painful.

Where have I been all this time, she asked herself angrily? *For one supposedly so far-seeing, I seem to have missed what was right under my nose.* First love could be powerful and intense. It usually faded in time – but sometimes it never did.

'You should see some of your old school friends again, my dear,' she told Amber, gentler now. 'You and Dolly relied far too much on one another's company. I daresay she'll remember to write to you now and then, but don't bank on it.'

'Well, I know she will, and I'll write to her, too. I'll write to her this very night, and get her to tell me everything about what it's like in London. You never know, I might want to go and visit her there one day.'

'You might, but you won't stay. People always come back to Cornwall. It has a special pull on them. It has to do with the land and the sea and the old Celtic ways, and the fact that we taper down to the ocean at Land's End, as if there's no need for anything more except the traditional living of good Cornish folk.'

'Good Lord, no wonder people say you have some weird ideas, Gran!' Amber said, but she was starting to grin in spite of herself, and she tucked her arm inside her grandmother's as they began to walk more slowly.

'Don't scoff. Don't you think Luke Gillam will come back to Cornwall once he's gone to sea and seen the world? Don't you think there's a strong enough pull here for him?'

Amber flushed. 'You said all that mysterious stuff deliberately, didn't you?'

'What if I did? Whatever anybody says, you should always try to take the truth out of it for whatever suits you, and discard the rest. If you believe in something strongly enough, it will happen.'

There was a time when Amber was a young child when she loved listening to Granny Pen's deliciously mysterious tales of old tin miners and the cheeky underground gnomes who teased or tormented them; the tales of pirates and smugglers and caves; the mysteries of the ancient standing stones and stone circles, the quoits and menhirs, where wishes were made and trysts were kept. She hadn't known what half the words meant then but they had charmed her all the same.

But she was no longer a young child, agog at all these ancient tales, and she wasn't prepared to accept that if you believed in something it would happen. She had foolishly believed that, because of his age, Luke would be safe for years yet, and look where that had got her. But as Granny Pen stumbled over the rough ground and clung a little more tightly to Amber, she was adult enough to hold her tongue.

To her surprise, Dolly became an avid letter-writer. She had got over her dad's death surprisingly quickly, Amber thought cynically, but that was Dolly, never at a loss at making the best of things. She'd eventually made the best of living in Cornwall, but London was home and it was obvious that she was glad to be back there, and that Uncle Joe was now the kingpin in her life.

'He ain't so bad,' Dolly wrote. 'He brings stuff home for Mum and me that we ain't supposed to brag about, if you know what I mean. He don't worry me no more, and he's good to us. Working down the market is a lark too. Of course it ain't so good when the Jerry planes come over and we have to make a dash for the tube, but they usually come of a night. It's a bit scary in the daytime when you hear the planes coming over though, and a couple of stalls at the other end of the market got a direct hit, which put the frighteners up Mum and me for a bit, but so far we're OK.

'Oh yes, and the street next to us has had it and old Mr Hannah the jew-boy and his sons who ran a clothes shop near us all got killed. But Uncle Joe managed to get some of their stock for our stall, no questions asked, and so-say bomb-damaged goods, see? It's an ill wind, as they say, so we're still smiling.

'It's a bit of fun down the tube sometimes. We've all got our places for sleeping now, and we go down there of a night more often that not. You know how we was once wondering how people would all get on doing married things. Well, they just get on and do it, those that ain't shit-scared of being bombed in mid-flow, if you see what I mean! There's so much noise with families all crammed together and the screaming kids and yapping dogs that nobody takes no notice.

'We're always glad to get out of there in the morning, mind, to breathe a bit of fresh air after some of the stinks down there, even though you can hardly call it fresh air by then. The streets are always full of smoke and smells of burning and dust and blood and dead bodies. Am I making you puke yet?

When Uncle Joe was grubbing around in the bomb rubble one morning, he found somebody's arm. Can you imagine that? Just an arm. How can you identify just an arm?

'Anyway, you'd better not let Granny Pen read this, or she'll be reaching for the smelling-salts. How is the old girl, by the way? And have you heard anything from Lukey-boy? Remember me to one and all.

'Your pal, Dolly'

Amber was always exhausted by the time she came to the end of one of Dolly's letters. She read out the bits that she thought would interest Granny Pen, but wisely didn't hand them over for her to read. She thought the underground shelters sounded like sheer hell, and the horrific and matter-of-fact way Dolly spoke about Uncle Joe finding just an arm made her retch. She didn't want to think about what he might be looking for, grubbing about in the bomb rubble, either.

Dolly's letters made her realize how lucky she was to be living in Cornwall. Because of the docks, Falmouth had its share of raids, but nothing like the worst onslaught of the German bombers, and she really wished Dolly hadn't had to go back to London. Being apart had somehow made the bond between them stronger than before, and she tried to make her own letters cheerful and full of local incidents to make Dolly smile.

'I had one letter from Luke, not long after he

went away,' she wrote. 'He said he was sorry he'd got me all upset, but he felt it was his duty to do what he could. He's still doing square-bashing, so he's not exactly playing the big hero, being stuck in some Welsh training camp for six weeks. When he does get on a ship, though, he may be away for much longer and he won't even be allowed to tell me where it's going. Does he think I'm a German spy or something? That's a joke, haha.'

She nearly tore that up and started again. It sounded mean and petty and stupid, but that was because right then she was feeling mean and petty, because Luke hadn't even ended his letter in the way she would have liked. It was just signed 'Luke', and not even a kiss at the end. The only thing that had made her heart leap for a moment was the PS he had added.

'I'm keeping my amber safe, like I promised.'

She would dearly have loved to read something into that, but she was being so damn pernickety now, telling herself it was probably deliberate that he had written 'amber' and not 'Amber', to keep her in her place as a friend and nothing more. But she wasn't going to care. If he didn't want her she wouldn't want him.

She continued her letter to Dolly. 'I may join a drama group again, a proper one this time. It's one evening a week, and they're putting on a play that somebody local has written. I've been once, but I'm still making up my mind whether I really want to do it. It's supposed to poke fun at Hitler, but some

of the lines are so feeble nobody's going to find them
funny. They're even worse than old Tommo's. I wish
you were here to liven things up!'

She'd only gone to the drama group to stop
Granny Pen telling her she was moping too much
and she might not even go again. She paused again,
thinking that this whole letter sounded feeble
compared with the daring and dangerous life Dolly
was living now. Racing to get to the underground
shelter at night before the bombs fell and sharing a
house with her mum and the dodgy-sounding Uncle
Joe was a world away from sharing the cottage with
Granny Pen, where nothing much happened.
Sometimes Amber knew exactly why Luke had
wanted to *do* something. Sometimes she wished she
was old enough to volunteer to do something useful
for the war effort as well, instead of being a perishing
assistant in a craft shop. It was hardly saving the
world.

The wireless and newspapers were so full of reports
of the war that the ordinary lives of people sometimes seemed to fade into the background. Luke
came home briefly after his six weeks' training,
looking older and smarter in his uniform and itching
to board his ship in Portsmouth. Late in April the
German bombers struck the towns of Exeter and
Bath heavily, followed by vicious attacks on Norwich
and York. Although the raids were obviously aimed
at key towns and cities, they were so indiscriminate
that nowhere seemed safe any more. Many people

lost their lives and homes were flattened. It was becoming a frighteningly familiar story.

Everyone was unnerved, wondering who was going to be hit next. The papers screamed out that the German raids were retaliation for the way the RAF had devastated the Baltic port of Lubeck in March, which sounded as alien as the moon to most British people, and most said it simply proved the senseless futility of war.

'Pray to God they don't get this far west too often,' Granny Pen commented. 'The docks ought to be a prime target, but so far we've been let off lightly compared with Portsmouth and Plymouth.'

Amber hated it when her gran got all serious like this, but how could she help it? How could anyone help it, even a fifteen-year-old, when the only thing people seemed to talk about was death and destruction, and gloomy faces were all that you saw in the streets now? Even these Americans who were supposed to be their allies were off fighting the Japanese in the Pacific now, instead of being over here, but that was understandable considering it was the Japs who first got them into the war.

What with the letters from Dolly and the lack of letters from Luke, Amber felt constantly on edge, wondering if anything was ever going to be normal again. She wondered where Luke was, and if he was safe. She couldn't bear the news that British ships were being sunk by these terrible German U-boats. Submarines must be the worst and most wicked enemy of all, she thought, gliding silently beneath the waves, ready to strike at any moment. But submarines had been blown out of the water too, and everyone inside them would have been drowned. She shuddered. Because of her father, the thought of drowning petrified her, and the very idea of the sea crushing the sailors to death in a submarine made her feel tight in her chest as if she couldn't breathe. As if she was drowning too . . .

One particular April morning she pedalled to work in a furious temper, willing such morbid thoughts away, while raging in her heart against the stupid bureaucracies who had made all this happen. She'd been caught out in a sharp April shower, and she was damp and chilled by the time she reached the shop, only to find that it was locked and silent. Mrs Porter from the chandlery nearby was looking out for her, and she appeared as soon as Amber had leaned her bicycle against a side wall, red and flustered. Mrs Porter was a busybody as well as a panicky sort, and Amber sighed impatiently as she saw her wringing her hands like a bad actress.

'Oh lovey, I'm glad you're here. I've been waiting to give you the news.'

'What is it today, Mrs Porter?'

More gossip about the war, she supposed. It must be something big, if Mrs Veal hadn't bothered to open the shop yet.

The woman's voice was shrill. 'It's poor Mr Veal. He was rushed off to hospital in the ambulance in the middle of the night. They say it's a heart attack, but Mrs Veal hasn't come back yet, so we don't know how bad it is. She left the key for you to open up as usual,' the woman added, her eyes like dinner plates as she waited for Amber's reaction.

It was hard for Amber to take in. The weight of the war news had been so oppressive lately that something as ordinary as a perfectly nice elderly man being rushed off in the middle of the night with a heart attack was almost ludicrous.

As the shameful thought flashed in and out of her mind, she knew it wasn't ludicrous at all. It was awful, and her thoughts were all at sixes and sevens as Mrs Porter thrust the key into her hand, hot and sweaty from where she had been clutching it for so long.

'She wants me to open up the shop as usual?' Amber stammered. 'Are you sure that's what I'm supposed to do?'

'Well, as far as we know, the poor old dab hasn't gone yet, so it's best to do as she says, my dear.'

'Gone? Gone where?' Amber said, not understanding for a moment. And then she gasped. 'You don't mean he's going to *die*?'

The woman gave an exaggerated shrug, her eyes rolling. 'His mouth looked a fair shade of blue when they took him out, so it don't look too good.'

She would have noted everything, of course, and passed it around to anybody who was willing to listen. Right then Amber hated her.

'I'd better do as Mrs Veal wanted and open up,' she said, wanting to get away from the woman as quickly as possible as she fumbled to get the key in the door. Once inside, she slammed it behind her, effectively keeping everybody else out for the moment. The shop bell jangled, echoing in the silent shop now, and Amber felt her own heart beating rapidly in a way she had never been aware of before. It was drumming in her ears . . . and then she realized the drumming was the sound of someone rapping on the shop door behind her. She was tempted to push the bolt across, but Mrs Porter knew she was in there and would probably just keep hammering until she answered it. She moved away from the door and then it opened.

'My goodness,' said a familiar voice. 'I thought I was being shut out of my own shop for a minute and I can't abide these blessed April showers – oh, Amber love, don't take on so. Everything's all right, truly it is.'

'Mrs Veal! I didn't expect to see you yet,' she gasped, almost hysterical.

The woman gave a faint smile. 'You expected to see me in widow's weeds already, did you? No, Father's made of tougher stuff than that, my dear, and he'll be around for a long time yet, God willing.'

'But Mrs Porter said—'

'Mrs Porter means well, but she's an old scaremonger. I've put her right, so she won't go around asking the neighbours for a wreath just yet.'

'So Mr Veal isn't – I mean, is he going to be all right?'

'It was just a bit of a warning, that's all,' his wife said briskly. 'The old fool decided to have a feast with

149

his cheese ration and mine too. I told him it was too late at night, but would he listen? Do they ever? No, they don't, so then of course he got terrible indigestion and convinced himself he was having a heart attack and insisted that I sent for the ambulance.'

She was prattling on much faster than usual, which told Amber that Mr Veal hadn't been the only one to have a scare during the night.

'Shall I make us a cup of tea?' she asked tentatively.

'That would be nice, Amber love. And while you put the kettle on I'll go upstairs and take off my hat and coat and have a little cry, and by the time I come down again I'll be as right as rain.'

Amber watched her go with something like awe. Mrs Veal was made of the same stern stuff as her gran, as strong as Cornish granite, coping with everything that came her way. It wasn't right to think of old folks as being past their day. It was young ones, like herself, who had to learn to cope, she thought, still shaking as she filled the kettle from the tap and flinched as the sting of ice-cold water splashed over her hands. But not all young ones were weak. Some were like Dolly, living among the bombs in London; and Luke, wherever he was now, had more guts than a lot of others too. There and then, she vowed to try to be more like them.

Mr Veal was only in hospital for a couple of days. The beds were needed for more important cases than one old man who'd brought this on himself, a nurse told him cheerfully, while pressing his hand as she did so to show there were no hard feelings. Amber asked to go and see him with Mrs Veal that evening, just to satisfy herself that he really was going to be all right. He looked older and more frail in the hospital bed, but was perky enough to give his wife back as good as she gave him.

'Silly old fool! All this upset for the sake of a bit of cheese!' she scolded.

'And you'd do the same for a bit of chocolate, old girl, so don't harp on.'

Despite the good-hearted bickering, it wasn't hard to see the affection between them, even though they never expressed it in a sloppy way, and Amber found herself wondering if her own mum and dad would have been like this, if things had been different.

It brought a lump to her throat, because she would never know. She busied herself in looking around the ward instead, and immediately wished she hadn't, because apart from one or two older ones like Mr Veal, there were so many young men, heavily bandaged or hooked up to machines, who were clearly casualties of the war. Somehow it seemed to bring it all together. The young fighting men who were wounded in battle, lying amongst those who had almost lived their lives and were subjected to the normal process of just getting old.

'I thought about being a nurse once,' she said without thinking, 'but it didn't last long. I don't think I could deal with the blood and stuff, and all the things they have to do.'

She shuddered, unable to get the thought of Uncle Joe out of her head at that moment, and the horrific imagery of him finding an arm among the rubble of what had once been someone's house.

'You could do anything you set your heart on, Amber,' Mr Veal said. 'Although I'd much rather you stayed and worked for us, if that's not being selfish.'

'It's not,' she said quickly, 'but it does make me feel a bit useless, seeing these nurses rushing about and saving lives.'

One of the nurses, attending the patient at the next bed, straightened up and paused at Mr Veal's bedside.

'If you really want to help, you can always come in on Sundays,' she said. 'We always need help in winding bandages and making teas for the patients and all the extra things that take our time. Go and see Matron if you're interested.'

It had been said on a whim, no more, but Amber almost felt that she had no option now, if she didn't want to appear as a scaredy-cat kid. It wasn't what she had planned, but by the time she and Mrs Veal left the hospital, with the assurance that Mr Veal could go home tomorrow and a warning to keep off the cheese, even if they could get any, it was all settled.

Chapter Nine

'Well, I must say this has been quite a day,' Granny Pen said at last, when Amber finally reached home that evening. 'I thought you had gone to that drama group again after work. I certainly didn't expect this news about Mr Veal, but I'm glad to hear he's going to be all right. I'm a bit surprised that you're going to work at the hospital on Sundays, though.'

'Do you mind, Gran?' Amber asked anxiously. 'I'd forgotten all about going to church in the mornings when I said I'd do it.'

'I daresay the Good Lord will think this is just as important as you turning up at His house once a week. I'm proud of you, my dear.'

'Are you?' she said, flushing. 'I don't know why. I nearly fell to pieces when I heard Mr Veal had had a heart attack – even if it didn't turn out to be one – so I don't know yet how I'll cope if I have to see anything bad in the wards. And don't think I'm thinking seriously about being a nurse, because I'm definitely *not*!'

She knew she was babbling a bit, but the reality

of it was only just dawning on her, and she couldn't back out now. She had too much pride for that. She meant what she said though. She was definitely not going to be a proper nurse. But if Dolly could face all those terrible sights on the London streets every day, then she could do a Sunday job, and she *would* do it. It was funny how the thought of Dolly kept cropping up, as if she was using her as a yardstick. Little Dolly daydream, who wasn't as drippy as Amber had at first thought.

'You're my granddaughter,' Granny Pen went on. 'And no granddaughter of mine is going to flinch from a bit of blood. What you must do is always to think of the person inside the bandages, my dear, and remember that he won't particularly want to see his blood outside his body, either, instead of inside it where it belongs!'

Amber started to laugh. 'You always put things so well, Gran!'

And if she could cheer up even one of those poor wounded men on the ward on Sunday, she supposed she could be a sort of Florence Nightingale. Matron had said some of the wounded soldiers whose hands were burned wanted somebody to write letters home for them, and she had volunteered for that at once. It was something special to tell Dolly in her letter that night.

'Poor old Vealy has to keep off the cheese in future,' she wrote, 'but it gave us all a scare. Anyway, I'm going to work at the hospital on Sundays now, rolling bandages and making teas and writing letters for the wounded soldiers. I won't have to do anything *medical*, thank goodness. Even seeing some of the blokes with blood seeping out of their bandages gave me the willies. Gran's quite pleased with me, though, and you've got to do what you can, haven't you?'

She read it back, groaning as she realized how damn pompous she sounded, when really she was starting to get nervous about what she had promised to do. It was all very well to be determined to be brave and patriotic, but why couldn't she have thought of something else, like working in a factory making munitions or something? Or joining the Womens' Land Army? She'd never even thought about that, and she was too young, anyway. But she was fond of animals and she could always work on a farm.

She had to admit it wasn't something that really appealed to her, even though there were farms not far from the outskirts of Falmouth in easy distance of cycling home every night. It was just an idea to tuck away in her mind if the Sunday hospital work became too much. She knew she should feel guilty, because the real nurses had far worse jobs to do than making tea and rolling bandages, including the horror of changing the dressings on some of the festering wounds that she had been unfortunate enough to see. Not everybody could deal with pain and suffering, but there had to be other ways of being useful, especially when you were only fifteen.

Because she and Dolly were supposed to be sharing their thoughts and secrets, she decided to tell her all about the idea of maybe working on a farm. It wasn't a secret, anyway. It was just a passing thought. If she decided to work on a farm or anywhere else where she could be doing useful war work, she'd have to give up the craft shop. That would be a blow, but the Veals could manage very well without her. She finished her letter to Dolly with a flourish.

'So that's what's been happening down here in the sticks. By the way, how's life on the market stall? Met any passing Yanks who are going to make you a Hollywood star yet?

'Your friend, Amber'

It was a bit sarky and she knew it, but that was the way she and Dolly had always been. And after relating all her own ideas about the hospital and then the farm possibility, well, working on a market stall and selling dreary bomb-damaged goods that were obviously a bit dodgy was the tamest thing she could imagine.

She wrote a similar letter to Luke. His ship was called HMS *Tigress* – but with only the vaguest address to send letters to she had to restrain herself from writing too often. Her feelings for him hadn't diminished in the slightest though, and she knew they never would.

She began work at the hospital on the very next Sunday, remembering to tie her hair up neatly. She was so nervous she could have wet herself, but the first job she was given was rolling bandages well out of sight of the wards, and it was such a boring and repetitive task that she gradually relaxed. Teas were the next thing on the agenda, and all she had to do was to hand them to the patients alongside the nurse with the trolley. The only time she faltered was when she tried to offer a cup of tea to a man with heavily bandaged hands and realized she had to offer it to him for him to sip. She was so terrified it was going to be too hot that she slopped it down his hospital gown and caused the older nurse to tut-tut loudly.

'Leave the girl alone, nursie,' the man said. 'A bit of a spill never hurt anybody, and it's a treat to see a pretty young lass on the ward for a change.'

'You're not from around here, are you?' Amber said, noting the way he had called her lass. A Cornishman would have called her a pretty young maid.

'Yorkshire, born and bred, and missing the wife and bairns. I'd show you a photo of 'em if I didn't have these blasted stumps to deal with.' He held up the heavy bandages, and Amber realized with horror that there were probably no hands there at all, only what was left of them.

'Come along, Amber,' the nurse said briskly, seeing her face. 'There are more patients on the ward waiting for their tea.'

'Come back and see me again,' the man called after her.

There were more patients in a similar state to that one, and more embarrassments, but thankfully the teas were eventually finished. Amber was left with collecting the cups and clearing everything away, and her hands still shook as she did so.

'You can write a letter home for me if you like, lass,' the man she had spoken to before told her. 'They said there might be somebody who could do it.'

'I'll ask,' she said with a gasp, thinking this was going to be her salvation. Otherwise, she knew she couldn't do this after all. The nurses were mostly cheerful even if they seemed hard and unfeeling to Amber, but she realized they had to keep their emotions in check because of the things they were expected to do. But she wasn't hard. She wasn't used to any of this, and she was almost in tears as some of the patients with scarred and disfigured faces and bodies, some without limbs, tried to mouth their requests and to drink the tea that was clearly scalding their throats, however weak it was. And it was truly what Granny Pen would have called ditch water, Amber thought, with a catch in her throat. There wouldn't be many tea leaves left for her to juggle with in these empty cups. She was sure that some of the patients would prefer not to have their fortunes told, anyway, and the future for one or two of them looked horribly bleak.

But at least Amber could write letters. After that first eye-opening morning she went to Matron and asked if she could have paper and envelopes to do it for anyone who requested it. She stared at Matron unblinkingly, only the slight trembling in her hands giving her feelings away. But Matron's eyes were keen enough to notice the signs.

'That's a good idea, and you know, my dear, not everyone is suited to hospital work,' she said. 'I want you to think of today as a trial period, that's all, and if you find it's not to your choosing, then you are perfectly free to say so.'

'I don't want to let you down,' Amber mumbled. 'It's just that sometimes the smells and the groaning in the wards make me feel as if I'm suffocating. I know I'm being a coward, but I can't help it.'

'You're not being a coward at all. It's braver of you to say exactly how you feel. But please do as I suggest, Amber, and try it just for today. Nobody will think badly of you if you decided not to carry on. In the meantime, I'll organize the paper and envelopes for the patients' letters. They'll really appreciate that.'

'She was very kind,' Amber told Granny Pen that night when she went home, more exhausted than she had expected. 'She looks a bit of an old harridan, but she's not really. It was better when I spent the afternoon writing letters for some of the patients, although even that was difficult when one or two wanted me to put in quite personal things. I don't know which of us was more embarrassed, them or me, but I tried to imagine I was writing lines in a play, and then it was a bit easier.'

'So are you going back next week?'

Amber avoided her eyes. 'I'm not sure. Probably.

Today was a trial period. I need to decide if I feel really suited to it – and if they still want me.'

'Just remember there's no disgrace in changing your mind. You're very young to be working in a hospital and seeing the kinds of things no young girl should have to see.'

Amber was filled with sudden passion. 'Some of those patients aren't much older than me, Gran, and they didn't ask to see those things, either, nor to have their arms or legs blown off or to lose their sight, did they? I don't want to feel like a failure, so I'll have to see how I feel about it next Sunday.'

During the following week the decision was made for her. Amber and Mrs Veal were chatting amiably in the shop when there was an almighty crash from the back room. They rushed through the bead curtain to find that Mr Veal had collapsed on the floor. A large pool of blood was seeping out from an angry gash on his head where he must have caught it on the edge of the table when he fell. The blood was already matting his white hair, his face a greyish, parchment-like hue to match it.

The doctor eventually said that it wasn't the blow to his head that killed him. This time it was a genuine and massive heart attack, and he could never have reached the hospital in time for them to do anything. In fact, he was almost certainly dead before he reached the floor.

The shock of finding the man in such a state almost paralysed Amber, but not nearly as much as

the wailing and keening from Mrs Veal. She was
covered in her husband's blood by the time she went
to the hospital with him in the ambulance, even
though it was obvious they could do nothing for him
except to confirm that death had occurred. Amber
was left to clean up the back room, scrubbing the
floor as best she could, while the hot, sweet stench
of fresh blood made her stomach heave almost
uncontrollably. Such an intimate act for the two
people who had been so kind to her made up her
mind about her future instantly, although her head
was in such a crazy muddle she couldn't formulate
the thought properly.

She didn't know how long she had been on her
knees, near to sobbing as she did the gruesome task,
and she had no idea that someone had sent for her
gran until she heard the shop bell tinkle. She yelled
out angrily that they were closed, having forgotten
to shoot the bolt when the others had left. The next
moment Granny Pen had pushed the bead curtain
aside and gathered Amber up in her arms.

'My poor little maid,' Granny Pen said roughly.
'You shouldn't have to do this. There's surely one
of the men hereabouts who would have come and
done it.'

'It's my job, Gran' she said shrilly. 'It's where I
work, and I couldn't let Mrs Veal come back and
see it, could I?'

She looked down to where the soap and hot water
had made an impression on the bloodstains now,
but in her mind's eye she knew she would always

see them there, probably even more than Mrs Veal would. This was the least she could do for her. It was the only thing – except to be here when she returned home. Her eyes moved to her hands, red raw now both with scrubbing and blood, and she felt the hysteria rising as she babbled.

'Oh Gran, it was the worst thing! Not so much for poor Mr Veal, because he wasn't feeling anything any more, and the doctor said he wouldn't have known what was happening. It was so much worse for *her*, for poor Mrs Veal, and I couldn't do anything to comfort her. But it made me realize I couldn't face seeing any of the soldiers' wives and families coming to the hospital and having to be told that their men had died. I couldn't bear seeing them and hearing them and feeling as helpless and useless as I did today.'

Granny Pen held her tight until the shaking began to ease a little.

'You've had a bad shock, my dear, and now you're going to sit down while I make us both a strong cup of tea and then we'll clear all this up together so that it's all nice and tidy for when Mrs Veal gets back. My old bones aren't so creaky that I can't get down and do a bit of scrubbing, although you've already done the worst of it. Go and wash your hands now, and splash your face with cold water, and then you'll feel a lot better.'

Amber doubted that she'd ever feel better again. She might get the stains off her hands but the smell was still in her nostrils, and the memories were in her head, and she was still trembling when Granny Pen thrust a hot cup of tea in her hands.

'I can't go back to the hospital any more, Gran,' she whimpered. 'I *can't*.'

'Then you won't go. There's no need.'

'But won't you think badly of me?'

Granny Pen spoke solemnly. 'I couldn't think more highly of you than for what you've been doing here today, my love. I think you'd be doing a Christian duty in calling in on Mrs Veal on a Sunday afternoon for a few weeks, and doing a good turn for a neighbour. She'll be needing to see a cheerful face that she knows, just as much as those poor casualties at the hospital who've got plenty of nurses to take care of them. Things always seem so much worse to deal with at your age, love, but you'll get over it, I promise, and so will Mrs Veal, given time.'

Somehow she managed to take away all the shame of it, thought Amber. Even though Amber had only spent one day at the hospital, there was no hint of censure from her gran that she wasn't going back there. She'd only been on trial, after all, but Granny Pen was the saint, not her. She'd tried, but she'd failed, and in her own mind she would always know it, no matter what anybody said.

There were practical things to be done before some kind person brought Mrs Veal back home. The back-room floor had eventually begun to dry and to look less of a slaughterhouse, and Amber had put a sign in the craft shop window to say that owing to a bereavement it would be closed until further notice. The news would probably have spread already, and she wouldn't have detailed it more personally without Mrs Veal's permission.

Granny Pen took the ashen-faced widow upstairs for a lie-down, while Amber remained in the shop itself, pretending to be busy, dusting things that didn't need dusting, and wishing all the time that she wasn't aware of the murmur of voices from upstairs and the frequent sound of weeping.

Nothing was as bad as this, she thought fiercely. She had felt desperately sorry for those poor patients in the hospital, but they were strangers. They hadn't been close to her, the way this was close. This was personal. It was almost like losing one of her own family, and she hardly knew how to stop crying herself.

Granny Pen came downstairs a while later and told Amber that Mrs Veal was sleeping with the help of one of her sedatives. She had a piece of paper in her hand.

'Apparently, there's a daughter living about five miles from here on the Redruth road,' Granny Pen said. 'She doesn't know what's happened yet, of course, and it's bound to be a shock. From what I can gather she and her father hadn't spoken for years, but Mrs Veal thinks she may come and stay for a week or two until the funeral's over. I've got the address, so we must find someone to go there and break the news.'

'I'll go,' Amber said at once. 'I can easily cycle there.'

Anything was better than staying here and not knowing what to do. Not that she knew how to tell a stranger that she had just lost her father. Oh God . . .

'You're a good girl, Amber. Well then, I'll stay here and see what I can find in the cupboard to make a stew or something for later. They won't feel like eating, but they'll need to keep up their strength.'

Any hope that her gran might say it was too far for her to cycle or that it would be better to send someone older was dashed at once. Besides, she had cycled far longer distances than this many times, and she just hoped she would find the right words to say once she reached the daughter's house. She'd never heard Mrs Veal mention a daughter, though it probably explained the photo on the mantelpiece in the back room.

It was almost a surprise to be out in the fresh air and to find that the day was still bright, the birds still singing, the docks full of ships and sailors, and the town still going about its usual business. It was as if Amber had expected everything to have stopped, held in some kind of suspension, just because one middle-aged man had died. She bent low over the handlebars, not wanting anyone to stop her and greet her, expecting her to make small-talk as if nothing had happened to shake the daylights out of her on this lovely summer's day.

She found the house she sought without any trouble. It was a bit rundown, with different coloured curtains upstairs from downstairs. Sloppy, Granny

Pen would have said, but it was explained by the woman who answered the door, who told Amber that Miss Veal lived in the upper part of the house, before showing her up the stairs.

Amber knocked on the door tentatively. She knew at once that this was Mr Veal's daughter, by her likeness to him. She was about forty years old, plain-faced and suspicious at seeing a young stranger at her door.

'What is it? I'm not buying anything,' she said.

Amber swallowed. 'I'm sorry. I've been sent by your mother with a message.'

'My *mother*?' Myra Veal couldn't have looked more surprised if Amber had said the Virgin Mary had sent her. 'I can't think what she wants with me, but I suppose you'd better come in.'

Amber went inside. The room was stuffy and cluttered, the way an old person's room sometimes was. But Myra wasn't old, just faded and a bit dreary looking. Amber took a deep breath.

'I'm very sorry to bring you bad news, but I'm afraid your father had a heart attack this morning. He – he – died,' she added, hardly able to say the word.

For a moment Myra said nothing, and then to Amber's horror she started laughing. 'So the old bugger's gone, has he? And good riddance too!'

Amber was too shocked to speak at first, and then she burst out angrily, 'Didn't you hear what I said? Your father's dead, and your mother needs you.'

'Well, I'm not sure she can have me, although I

had no quarrel with her. It was him, the mean old bugger. We haven't spoken for years, so don't expect me to mourn him now.'

'But your mother's so upset!' Amber felt close to tears herself.

'What's it to you, anyway?'

'I work at the craft shop in Falmouth. Please say you'll go and see her. I don't know what happened between you all and I don't want to. I just know that if I had the chance to see my mum and dad again, I'd go like a shot.'

Myra stared at her for a long moment, and then nodded slowly.

'You're probably right, even if you are just a kid. You can tell my mother I'll be along this evening, as soon as I can get a neighbour to take me. But there's no way I'm going to see *him* again.'

Amber cycled back with her thoughts in a whirl. All families had secrets and it was none of her business what had gone on in the Veal family. She would never ask Mrs Veal, but she wondered if her gran knew. When she reached the shop again there was a lovely smell of stew coming from the kitchen. Mrs Veal was red-eyed, but calmer now, and trying to eat a little of the stew along with Granny Pen.

'Is she coming?' Mrs Veal said at once.

Amber told her Myra would be here later that evening, and then she was invited to join the older women in some supper. She was surprisingly hungry after all that had gone on that day, but she didn't want to be there when Myra Veal arrived, and as soon as she had eaten she tentatively asked her gran if she could go on home.

'You go, love, and I'll stay for the company until Myra arrives. It don't need all of us as a welcoming committee.'

Amber was thankful to get away, thinking what a weird family they must be. There had never been any hint of it before, but then she had never known that Myra existed. There must have been some terrible row for them to have effectively shut her out of their lives. But whatever it was it was going to remain their secret, Granny Pen told her later, and Mrs Veal was like the proverbial clam when it came to discussing family matters. All Granny Pen could say was that the two women had hugged and kissed and wept when they met, and that Myra had dumped a large suitcase on the floor and announced that she was staying.

Chapter Ten

'You wouldn't believe it,' Amber complained in her letter to Dolly a month later. 'Myra's taken over in the shop now, and she treats me as little more than a hired help, when I almost had the run of the place before. Now that the funeral's over, Mrs Veal's gone away for a few days, but she's decided to take a back seat in the shop when she comes back, and Myra's now the boss. She's left the place where she lived and moved in permanently. I can see what's coming. She's making sure the shop and the flat upstairs is left to her when Mrs Veal pops it as well.

'I'm not too pleased, as you can tell. But something more exciting has happened lately. The Yanks are coming. There's a camp somewhere outside the town and people say there will be loads and loads of them here. It's very exciting, especially for the girls! They're called GIs, but I expect you knew that. The old chaps who remember them from the last war say they always make a fuss of the little kids, and that some of them are sure to turn up at church on Sundays, which will please a few of the local fuddy-duddies who turn up their nose at them. Apart from their big new camp some of them are going to be billeted with local people, but we don't have any room for them, worse luck.

'More important than all that is that when I saw Luke's mother recently, she said he's hoping he'll get some leave by the end of the summer. I wish he'd told me, but never mind. I can't wait to see him again. So apart from the gloom in the shop and Myra forever sniping at me, things aren't looking too bad. By the way, how's the great romance with your mum and Uncle Joe – or aren't I supposed to ask?

'Your friend,
Amber'

A visitor arrived at the cottage one evening in late September. Granny Pen was out at one of her meetings, and although the woman looked vaguely familiar, Amber couldn't place her, and then she remembered her manners and invited her inside.

'You're from the Forces' Club, aren't you?'

'That's right. I'm Jennie Tandy, the assistant supervisor. Your friend Dolly worked for us for a time until she went back to London. How is she, by the way?'

'She's all right. I hear from her quite often. Is that why you're here, to talk about Dolly?'

'No. It's to talk about you, actually.'

'Me?' Amber said. 'What do you want with me?'

'I'm here to offer you a job, if you're interested.

You had the right attitude when you came for the evening with Dolly, and now that we're expanding our activities with the influx of GIs and so on, we've got a few vacancies. A couple of our girls have decided to join the ATS, and before we start advertising for more staff we thought of you straight away. Are you interested?'

Amber didn't know what to say for a minute. It had taken longer than she'd thought it would to get over the trauma of working at the hospital for that single day, and then the sadness of dealing with Mr Veal's death, and now having to listen to Myra's sniping in the craft shop every day.

But this didn't take longer than a minute . . .

'I say *yes*! I'll have to give my notice to Mrs Veal, but now that her daughter's working for her as well, I don't think that will be any trouble.'

Amber was suddenly elated. She'd rather looked down on Dolly at first, serving teas in a glorified canteen, but having worked there on the evening of the dance and seen what a social place it could be, she had quickly changed her mind about it. Especially now, if there were going to be so many GIs coming and going, she thought gleefully, thinking how jealous that would make Dolly when she got to hear of it. Not that she would be interested in them herself, Amber thought hastily, not when she already had a boy – sort of.

'You'll have to see what your gran thinks as well, of course,' Jennie went on. 'But I don't think she'll object. Dolly never came to any harm and there are plenty of us older ones to keep an eye on you, if you see what I mean – or maybe we'll all have to keep an eye on one another when the Yanks are about,' she added with a conspiratorial wink.

Amber felt a little glow of pleasure, realizing that she was being treated as an adult. She would be working in an adult world at the Forces' Club, and when Jennie went on to tell her how much they were expanding the premises and planning to hold a regular monthly dance soon, all her recent restlessness seemed to fall away. She might be not quite sixteen years old, and it wasn't the same as making munitions or joining the ATS, but it was useful war work all the same.

By the time Jennie left, Amber was in high spirits. She couldn't wait for Granny Pen to come home so she could tell her the news. She was quite sure she wouldn't object. How could she, when she had encouraged Dolly to work there? She was impatient to tell her what had happened, but it seemed ages before she heard footsteps crunching on the gravel outside, and she flung open the front door excitedly.

'Well, this is a nice way to greet anybody, nearly knocking me over before I've even got through the door,' said a laughing voice.

'*Luke!*' Amber almost shrieked. 'What are you doing here?'

Her head swam so much at the unexpected sight of him in his naval uniform that she could only gape for a few seconds.

'I've come to see you, so are you going to let me

in, or are we going to stand here like idiots all night? Didn't my mother tell you I was having some leave?'

'Yes she did, but I didn't know when.'

She felt suddenly awkward as she stood aside for him to come into the cottage. Once the door had closed behind him and they were alone, she thought how much larger he seemed than before he joined up. Larger and broader and older in his dark uniform. And she felt so much younger and sillier because of her reaction . . . but then she saw that he was looking at her in a different way too, and it wasn't because she was young and silly at all.

'You've grown up since I've been away,' he stated. 'You're taller, and rounder and – somehow different.'

'And it's been such a long time, hasn't it!' she taunted.

But her breath was ragged in her throat, because it *was* a long time. Even one day would have seemed a long time, and right now it seemed like an eternity since she had seen him and talked to him, and been with him.

'Give us a kiss then,' Luke said.

She giggled nervously. But before she could make some daft and typically Amber comment, Luke had pulled her into his arms, and his mouth was hard and demanding on hers.

Again, this was a proper kiss, a grown-up kiss, and her arms were wrapped tightly around him, and she could feel herself pressing into every part of him, as he was into her. She could feel the texture of his skin against her face, so different from her own soft skin. She could breathe his scent, warm and deeply masculine, and if she'd ever thought herself in love before, it was nothing compared with this overwhelming feeling.

'Well,' Luke said in a husky voice, when they finally broke away. 'You've definitely grown up, and it's probably just as well I came back to stake my claim before these Yanks get a good look at you.'

'You've got a nerve,' she said, trying to be flippant and to slow down the hammering of her heart. 'Stake your claim indeed. What do you think I am, some kind of gold mine?'

'No. Just my crazy Amber. You *are* my Amber, aren't you?'

'If you want me,' she said, unknowingly provocative.

He broke away properly as they heard sounds outside the cottage.

'You'll never know how much,' he muttered, just before the door opened and Granny Pen came inside and greeted Luke in surprise.

But then she took a good look at the two of them, both with flushed cheeks and breathing faster than usual, and she dumped her hat and bag on the sofa, effectively putting a small barrier between any two people who wanted to share it.

'Time for a cold drink, I think. You two look as if you could do with it, and I certainly could. Have you been here long, Luke?'

'Hardly any time at all,' he said.

He looked at Amber and saw the small smile

curving around her mouth, the soft, generous mouth that he had so recently kissed. Instinctively, he knew their thoughts were the same at that moment. He had been here hardly any time at all in terms of minutes and seconds, but in their hearts and minds they had covered a great distance. The moment was so intense that Amber had to turn away before she gave away too much of her feelings in her eyes.

'Gran, I've got some news for you,' she called out to Granny Pen in the kitchen. 'I had another visitor just before Luke arrived, and I've been offered a job at the Forces' Club. They're expanding the place now that the Yanks are here, and are going to have a regular monthly dance there too.'

'You didn't tell me anything about that!' Luke said.

'I've hardly had a chance, have I?'

Granny Pen came back into the room and put three glasses of lemonade on the table. There was a distinct change of atmosphere between the other two now, and she hid a small smile, remembering how volatile young love could be – if young love was what she was witnessing now. She sat down firmly on one end of the sofa and took a long cool drink before she replied to Amber.

'So what makes you think this new job will suit you? I thought you were settled at the craft shop, and not so long ago you thought you'd like to work at the hospital. You can't spend your life chopping and changing, my dear.'

Amber stared at her. Her new-found happiness,

partly from the job offer, but mostly because of Luke, began to ebb away.

'Why are you looking so cross?' she burst out. 'You know how much I hate working with Myra, and I thought you understood my feelings about the hospital. I haven't done anything wrong, as far as I know, so what else has upset you?'

Luke drained his glass of lemonade in one swallow, sensing a battle of wills to come. 'I think I'd better go and leave you two to sort out your problems. If you fancy it, we can go to the pictures tomorrow night, Amber. I'm only home for three days, so I'll look in at the shop tomorrow to fix it up.'

'All right,' she said, wishing she dared say goodbye with a kiss, and knowing she had better not. In any case, the decision was taken away from her when he turned abruptly and left the cottage.

Amber railed at her gran, her eyes bright with anger.

'Why did you have to go and say all that? Just as me and Luke were getting along fine, you made me sound like an idiot who couldn't make up her mind about anything.'

'He's taking you to the pictures tomorrow night, isn't he? I'd say you were still getting along fine. Perhaps a bit too fine.'

'What's that supposed to mean?' Amber said, aware that her heart was thudding for a different reason now.

'My love, it's easy to see when a pretty girl's just been kissed by a lusty young man, and I'm not so old that I don't remember how easily a young maid can have her head turned, either.'

'Is that what you think of me then? That I'm just a silly young maid who's had her head turned because a boy has kissed her? Me and Luke have known one another all our lives, Gran; and he's always been my friend.'

Granny Pen's eyebrows arched. 'Oh, really? It doesn't seem so long ago that you frequently came storming in here telling me you hated all boys, and Luke Gillam in particular. I seem to recall that he could always rub you up the wrong way, and I'm sure you were nothing more than a thorn in his flesh at times too.'

'I was just a kid then.'

'You're still a baby in my eyes, my love.'

Amber folded her arms tightly around herself, as if only by doing so could she stop herself exploding with rage. But this wasn't the time. This was a time for keeping as calm as possible and not resorting to childish tantrums.

'But I'm not a baby, am I, Gran? I'll be sixteen in a few months' time, and that's quite old enough to have deep feelings about – well, about somebody, or anybody.'

'And do you have deep feelings about a particular somebody already?'

Amber felt her face grow hot. 'I think you know I do.'

She felt suddenly deflated as she sat down on the sofa, pushing her gran's hat and bag aside.

177

'Gran, you don't really believe that going on sixteen is too young to have proper grown-up feelings for somebody, do you?'

To her surprise Granny Pen leaned forward and kissed her cheek.

'Of course I don't, but nor do I think they're going to be the last feelings you'll ever have, either. They might, but it's unlikely. Call it first love or puppy love, or any other fancy name you like. The fact is, it doesn't usually last, my dear, so it's unwise to get too intense about it.'

'So how do you help it?' Amber asked. 'If you're going to say that me and Luke shouldn't see too much of each other, well, the war's going to see to that. We've always seen a lot of each other, so I don't see why that should change now. Anyway, I don't want to talk about it any more, so what about this job at the Forces' Club? You still haven't told me what you think about it.'

'Would it make any difference if I did?' Granny Pen said dryly. 'You've got a strong will and a mind of your own, Amber, and if it's what you want to do, I think you'll do it.'

'But I want to know what you *think*,' Amber said crossly.

'I think you'll do whatever you want to do, but if it means so much to you, then you have my blessing. Perhaps mixing with other people in a social atmosphere instead of being in a small shop all day long will be a good thing, anyway.'

It might even take her mind off Luke Gillam, too,

Granny Pen thought. Not that she had any objections
to the boy. She liked him a good deal, but in those
few moments when she had come home she had seen
him as a man and not a boy. And Amber wasn't ready
for an adult relationship yet, whatever she might think.

Amber could read her gran's mind very well. In local
circles Granny Pen might be considered a wise
woman with a sixth sense, and a teller of fortunes,
but for once, she was wrong, Amber thought passionately. That evening Granny Pen wasn't the only one
who had seen Luke as a man and not a boy. And
the feelings racing around Amber's body as she got
ready for bed that evening were far from the childish
ones she used to have when they argued and fought
and teased one another. She was thinking of him
now as her young man, her lover . . . the seduc-
tively beautiful word crept into her mind and made
her catch her breath.

For once, she didn't feel inclined to grab her pen
and paper and write down details of the whole
evening to Dolly. Some things were too private to
share at once, if at all. Maybe she would tell her in
time . . . well, all right, of course she would tell her,
she amended. She was in love, and it was an always
and for ever kind of love, despite what Granny Pen
might think it, and she wouldn't be able to keep
such a momentous event to herself for ever. But
tonight, instead of writing to Dolly, there would be
a single, dignified entry in her diary, and no other
words were necessary.

'Luke's home. Tonight, he kissed me again.'

Just reading the words in black and white gave her a thrill, and she touched her fingers to her mouth, remembering the sensation when Luke had kissed it. Remembering how every part of his body had pressed into hers, and being very aware that his feelings for her were far from childish ones too. She gave a shiver as she snuggled into bed, because although the feelings were so new and exciting, she wasn't exactly sure what to do with them – or what he might expect of her now.

She found out that things were not as rose-coloured as she might have imagined when he strode into the craft shop the following morning. By then she had had what her gran would have called 'words' with Myra Veal, who had been scathing over her decision to work at the Forces' Club, her normally pasty face turning an ugly puce colour as Amber snapped at her.

'You want to mind what you say, miss,' Myra snapped back. 'You don't know what sort of blokes you'll come into contact with at that place, though maybe that's what you're hoping for. Young girls like you get their heads turned far too easily these days, what with all the riff-raff coming off the ships, and now these Yanks invading us with their easy talk and easier money.'

'*Invading* us? Are you stupid? They're not the enemy! And just because you were never able to attract a man, don't put us all in the same boat!' Amber hadn't meant to be so personal, but the words were out before she could stop them.

'That's enough of your insolence. If you can't keep a civil tongue in your head, you can leave right now. There's no need to work out your notice.'

Amber gasped. 'You can't tell me to leave. You're not my employer.'

'I can do what I like on my mother's behalf, and I don't want her worried by any of your nonsense. I'll sort out what's owing to you and you can call in another time to collect it. It doesn't take two of us here to run this little place.'

'Well, that sounds to me as if you've just been waiting for an excuse to sack me, but I was going, anyway, and the sooner the better.'

That was when the shop door opened and Luke appeared. He took one look at the two angry faces inside, and shrugged.

'Still antagonizing people, I see,' he said to Amber. 'If you can be spared for ten minutes, come for a walk with me to cool off.'

'I can be spared for more than ten minutes,' Amber said, furious at his remark when he had no idea what had been going on. 'I'm leaving here for good, and I *might* think about taking a walk with you.'

She bit her lip, angry that it was trembling now. After last night, the last thing she wanted to do was to seem so infantile in front of Luke, or to be bickering with him. It wasn't his row, but somehow she had made it so. She couldn't think why he looked so mad, but he certainly did. In a moment, it seemed, they were back to their squabbling schooldays, when last night she had felt so grown-up and sophisticated, and really believed they were on the brink of courting properly.

'What's up?' she said, as she tried to keep up with his long legs. She was tall, but he was taller, and she was exhausted by the time they finally sat down on a wooden seat along the quay. It was hardly the weather for it. It was a dank morning, which added to the downbeat mood.

'Are you sure you want to take this job at the Forces' Club?'

'Why shouldn't I? You're not jealous, are you? You don't think I'm going to get carried away by the first handsome Yank I see, do you? That's more up Dolly's street, not mine.'

'Maybe, but they'd be far more attracted to you.'

'You *are* jealous!' Amber was unsure whether to be flattered or astonished.

'Don't be ridiculous. I'm just concerned about you, that's all. You're not exactly the most worldly person, are you?'

'I'm not an idiot, either. Why would I be interested in anybody else when I have you?'

She felt her heart begin to thud, and she wished she hadn't blurted out such a stupid thing. She was as good as telling him she wanted to be his girl, and he hadn't actually asked her yet, not in so many words, anyway. It was all in her head. If he wasn't even the tiniest bit jealous that she'd be in contact with the glamorous GIs, it seemed to say it all.

'Amber, you're only fifteen—'

Rachel Moore

'I'll be sixteen in a few months' time!'

'And God knows where I'll be by then, probably on some God-forsaken ocean nobody's ever heard of. If this war goes on much longer, there's always a chance I may not even come back at all.'

She was suddenly frightened. 'You shouldn't say such things. It's bad luck. It's all right for me to be nervous, but now that you've said it, you've got to take it back at once. Say you know you're coming back. Say it out loud. I mean it, Luke! If you care for me at all, don't frighten me.'

He laughed. 'My God, you're definitely Granny Pen's granddaughter, aren't you, with your weird omens and superstitions? All right, if it means so much to you, then of course I'm coming back. I've got my piece of amber to keep me safe, you cuckoo, and I seem to remember when we were kids I said I was going to marry you to keep you under control. I'll have to come back for that, won't I?'

Amber caught her breath. From the sparkle in his eyes she knew he was only teasing. But he'd said the words, and she stored them away in her heart. She knew it would be a mistake to make some soppy comment and spoil the moment. Instead she spoke airily as if a long-ago childish remark meant nothing to her, when in reality it meant everything.

'That's all right then, so are we still going to the pictures tonight or not?'

'Of course we are. I'll meet you outside. Now I'm off to see some old mates.'

He squeezed her hand and strode off along the

quay. Watching him walk away from her, she knew he was going to show off in his uniform, more like! He wasn't totally hers. She felt at a complete loss for a few moments. She had just given up her job at the craft shop and she wasn't due to start at the Forces' Club for another week. The day was grey and miserable and within minutes it had begun to drizzle with a fine rain. She shivered as she looked out to where the sea almost met the sky in greyness.

Falmouth Bay was practically clogged with ships of every description now, and the quays constantly teemed with men in uniform. Nothing emphasised these dangerous times more. The days when they would come down here as children and watch the ferries come and go, and the little sailing boats putting to sea at the weekends in a glorious cluster of coloured sails, were long gone. People still did those things; they still fell in love, got married and had babies, but nothing was so relaxed any more, and there was anxiety in everything nowadays. It was easy not to think about such things when you were little, but impossible to ignore them now.

Amber found herself gazing upwards, into a sombre, wintry sky where there was no sign of enemy planes right now, but where the hovering barrage balloons gave a constant reminder of their threat. It had been relatively quiet of late, but that only added to the tension of wondering when the next air raid would come, and what the result of it would be.

'Hey there, you'd better mind where you're going, little lady. You nearly walked right into us.'

Amber felt her heart jolt. She had been walking aimlessly ever since Luke had left her. She was quite aware of the water's edge, and she'd been along here enough times to walk blindfold without any mishap. It was almost second nature to dodge anyone coming her way, but she had been so busy looking upward that she hadn't noticed the three laughing young men in smart uniforms until one of them caught hold of her by the shoulders to stop her blundering right into him.

She registered the unfamiliar accent seconds after she recognized the fact that these weren't British soldiers, nor sailors off the ships. They were Americans; Yanks; GIs; and since she had not met any of them yet, she was too flustered to say anything until the one who had spoken let her go and looked anxious.

'Say, miss, I didn't hurt you when I grabbed hold of you, did I? I was afraid you were daydreaming there and you might have gone into the drink.'

She replied quickly then, lest they should think her a country bumpkin.

'No, you didn't hurt me. It was my fault for not looking where I was going. I'm perfectly all right, thank you.'

'That's OK then. It wouldn't do to get on the wrong side of the locals before we've hardly arrived in town, would it, guys? I'm Will, by the way, and these two are Gary and Chuck.'

'Oh – uh – I'm Amber,' she said unthinkingly, though what her gran would have said about her being so free and easy with three strangers she couldn't think.

'Well, then, hope to see you around, Amber, since we'll be in the neighbourhood for a spell,' Will said breezily, and then they seemed to separate and move away from her in one swift movement.

She was still taking all this in as the rain began to fall more persistently, and she bolted back to the shop to fetch her bicycle and pelted on home. Once indoors she yelled out loudly to her gran that she'd left the craft shop and miserable Myra for good, and that she had just met some Yanks, and that they didn't seem foreign after all.

'They're just like us, really,' she finished. 'They talk funny, of course, but I daresay we talk funny to them as well.'

'What did you expect? Creatures from Mars?' Granny Pen said.

Amber giggled, suddenly realizing that the encounter had been quite exciting, even if she'd been too startled to notice it at the time. It was certainly something to tell Dolly next time she wrote. And it was funny how the Yanks, well, Will, had sort of teased her about daydreaming, when she had always used that word to describe Dolly. It must mean something, but right now she couldn't think what.

Chapter Eleven

Luke was waiting outside the cinema when she arrived that evening. The rain had stopped and it was a cool evening, with pale glimpses of moonlight now and then. Just the sort of night for enemy planes to take advantage of the shifting clouds, Amber thought, and immediately wished it had never come into her head.

'Cheer up,' Luke said. 'I thought you'd be in a good mood tonight, having chucked in one job and got another one without even trying.'

'I am in a good mood. I'm just hoping we don't have an air raid tonight, that's all.'

'They'll probably be too busy bombing some other poor devils to bother with us down here in the sticks. Forget them and enjoy the picture.'

She probably did, but afterwards she could hardly remember what it was about. She was all too conscious that they were sitting in the back row, and that after a little while Luke's arm slid around her shoulders, and she snuggled into him. Even when the usherette's torch shone briefly on them as she showed other people to their seats, he didn't take his arm away, and it made her feel special and elated.

They came out of the cinema to calmer skies, and he tucked her arm in his as he walked her home and she had never felt so happy. They were definitely walking out together now, she thought. They paused at the gate of the cottage, and he put his arms around her as she waited eagerly for his kiss. She had wondered if she should ask him inside for a drink or something, but thought better of it. It would be a bit of an anticlimax to the evening to have Granny Pen sitting there playing gooseberry.

'There's something I want to tell you, Amber.'

She blinked, because he sounded so serious, without a hint of romance in his voice. 'Something good, I hope.'

But it wouldn't be. She knew it wouldn't be. How many senses did it take to know you were about to hear something you didn't want to hear?

'Something sensible,' he said.

She groaned inwardly, but tried to be flippant. 'I hate it when somebody says that. It always means they're going to tell me something I don't want to hear, so if it's all the same to you, Luke, I'd rather you didn't say it.'

'I have to say it, sweetheart.'

Amber caught her breath. It must be serious if he was actually calling her sweetheart instead of cuckoo or idiot or crackpot . . . and she knew instinctively that it was going to break her heart.

He raised her hand to his lips in a sweet, old-fashioned gesture, but she snatched her hand away, knowing she had to say it first, before he did.

'You don't want me to think of you in a special way, because you don't feel the same way about me, do you? All that silly talk of marrying me someday was just kids' talk, wasn't it?'

'Of course it was kids' talk. We were only kids when we said it. It doesn't mean I don't think a lot of you, Amber, and I always will. But I think it's wrong for us to get too serious about one another right now. The timing's all wrong.'

Well, how idiotic was *that*? As if timing made any difference to when people fell in love . . . but she knew he was floundering. He wasn't the articulate Luke he had always been. He was trying not to hurt her, but he could hardly hurt her more. Every bit of her was hurting, and if this was what her gran had meant by puppy love that didn't last, then she wanted no more of it. She lashed out at him.

'Well, I'm sorry if rotten old Hitler had to start a war and make the timing all wrong for you. Perhaps we should have told him to hang on for a few years until you didn't think of me as a kid any more.'

He caught hold of her hands and held them tight.

'I don't think of you as a kid any more. That's just the trouble.'

Her heart pounded. 'What's that supposed to mean? Why should that be the trouble? I don't understand you. Don't you want me to grow up? I'm not going to be Pollyanna for ever.'

'You never were.'

She felt like stamping her feet, but if she did it would only underline the frustration she was feeling now. The *childish* frustration. She folded her arms tightly, the way she often did when she was trying to hold in her emotions. They were still standing close, but she had never felt more remote from him. The night had darkened and grown colder, matching her mood, and she couldn't see the expression in his eyes any more.

'Why don't you just come out with what you're trying to say, Luke?'

'Perhaps I should, even if you're not going to like it. It's about what I said yesterday – that I might not come back – it's no use being an ostrich about this and burying your head in the sand. And what I said about marrying you, well, that's just about as unrealistic, isn't it?'

'Is it?' Amber said in a strangled voice.

Her head was spinning now. Did he mean he didn't love her? That he had never loved her?

Luke swore beneath his breath and pulled her into his arms. She was still holding herself tightly, and it was an awkward and uncomfortable embrace. There was no romance in his voice when he spoke. Instead it was harsh, almost angry.

'Amber, if you can't face these facts then you're certainly not ready to sit at home brooding, and waiting for something that might never happen. There's a war on, in case you hadn't noticed it. People are being killed, or, at the very least, returning home wounded, some with terrible injuries that will never heal. Remember how we all felt over Mr Thomas's son, and none of us even knew him.'

'Not everybody gets wounded or killed!' she almost wept. 'How can you be so stupid as to lump everybody together like that?'

'But why should I be one of the lucky ones? Just because I've got your piece of amber to protect me, that doesn't take account of all the Jerry U-boats out there waiting to destroy our ships. I'm sure there are sailors on those bloody evil subs who have got good-luck charms from their girlfriends as well. Why shouldn't they be the ones to survive?'

'You're scaring me now,' Amber said shrilly. 'Have you got a death wish or something?'

'Of course not. I want to come home safely after the end of the war and lead a normal life again. Don't you think I'd far rather be building boats than blowing them up? But until that day comes, I refuse to have any obligations that I may never be able to fulfil.'

'You don't want me to be your girl then?' Amber said, her voice brittle.

'You'll always be my girl, and if we were both five years older I'd think differently about things. But you're only fifteen, Amber. You're not even legally old enough to get married, and you must promise me that you won't waste your life waiting for me to come home. Promise me now.'

How could she possibly promise such a thing when her heart was breaking? He was being so sensible, so much more grown-up than she was. The years between them suddenly seemed more like eons, and she was raging inside at the unfairness of it all. But he was waiting for an answer, and she knew she had to give it. You didn't send a warrior away to war without giving him everything he wanted, even if it seemed that he didn't want *her*.

'All right,' she said finally, her voice choking. 'If it's what you want, I can hardly object, can I? Don't imagine that I won't think of you and pray for you and all that stuff, though, because I will, every day. I suppose I'm still allowed to write to you now and then, or is that off limits as well?'

'Of course. We're old friends, Amber, and real friends don't ever lose touch.'

The words seemed to damn their relationship for ever, but somehow he had released her tightly folded arms and she found herself clinging to him. He kissed her just once, a sweetly chaste kiss, the kiss of a friend, and then she turned swiftly and ran inside the cottage, unable to bear it a minute longer.

Once inside, she leaned against the door she had slammed, her eyes brimming with tears, and with the sixth sense she was blessed with, Granny Pen held out her arms and Amber rushed into them, sobbing her heart out.

Finding it impossible to go straight home, Luke headed for Pendennis Hill where he and Amber and all their friends had spent so many madcap hours over the years. It was a long walk and would be an even longer walk back home, but he was in such a foul mood he hardly noticed it. He felt like yelling out loud with the worst cuss words he could think of, because he knew bloody well how much he had hurt her.

He had to get away from people, to come up here to the place they had always loved best, to try and cool off before he went home. It had been the hardest thing in his life to do what he had just done, seeing the spirit go out of Amber's beautiful eyes and knowing he was ruining her lovely romantic dreams. His too, he thought harshly, because she would never know how much he had fought against the urge to crush her to him and make love to her, to put the final seal on a special relationship that had begun so many years ago, and to make her irrevocably his. He had a lusty nature and sometimes it was hard to curb it.

But already, in the relatively short time he had been at sea, he had seen and heard about too many sorrows in marriages that had been too hasty. He had read the newspapers, giving their guarded numbers of the casualties the Allies were suffering. He had read his mother's letters, in which she had felt obliged to tell him of people he had known, boys he had been at school with, coming home maimed, or not coming home at all. He wasn't a fool, and he knew this didn't necessarily mean such a fate was in store for him, but nor did he think he was especially charmed, despite the smooth, warm feel of the piece of amber he was never without.

It all came down to the same thing. Amber was too young to be tied to any romantic dreams of him. She had to be free to make other friendships, and so did he. That didn't mean he intended being a skirt-chaser like some of the blokes on his ship. His feelings for Amber were as deep as he was sure hers were for him, but it was too soon. If the war hadn't happened . . . but it had, and for them the timing *was* all wrong, and there was nothing anybody could bloody well do to change that.

When he reached and rounded the top of the hill he stared down savagely into the inky black waters below him. The sandy beaches to his right that had once been so welcoming in the soft summer months now looked menacing with their barbed wire entanglements. The hill sloped more gently at this point, and not too far below were the caves where their old school gang had so often played and sheltered from sudden storms. In some ways it seemed like yesterday, but they had all moved on, and one or two of the older boys they knew would never be coming home again. Luke had steeled himself into making sure that no matter how long this war lasted Amber wasn't going to spend her time worrying and grieving for him.

But because he was being completely honest with himself, he knew that part of him was also relishing this chance to go away and be a hero. If it took a war to bring this chance that came once in a lifetime, then so be it. All his life he had loved boats and the sea, like his father before him. It was in his blood, and if the worst ever happened, he couldn't bear the thought of Amber mourning him.

There were widows in the town from the last war, sad, lonely women, no older than his own mother, and he would never put someone he loved through that loneliness. He may be only eighteen years old, but he thought far too much of Amber for that. He respected her, too, and one day when all this was over they could think about the future properly. She would eventually realize that this was no more than a temporary pause, and in Luke's mind it was inconceivable that they wouldn't be together, one day . . .

Amber didn't have to tell her gran what had happened. The misery was all in her eyes. She was given a hot sweet drink, as if she was in shock, which she supposed she was, and then she went to bed, nursing her badly bruised feelings. But she had to tell someone. And the more she wrote, the more defensive she became.

'I wasn't going to tell you any of this,' she wrote finally to Dolly, when she had poured it all out, her pencil stabbing at the page, 'but me and Luke are finished for good now. He doesn't want me waiting for him, so I won't. I shall flirt with the Yanks at the Forces' Club instead. That'll show him whether I'm too young or not.'

She read the words again. She had written them out of bravado, but the more she thought about it, the more she thought, why not? There wouldn't be anything serious about it, and she certainly wouldn't risk getting a bad reputation – she could just imagine what Granny Pen would have to say about that!

But a bit of teasing with some of those boys who were far from home was what the older girls at the Forces' Club did all the time, and she'd never heard of any of them coming to any harm. It was practically a duty to keep their serving boys happy. Anyway, thought Amber savagely, she'd bet her boots that if Dolly was here now, she'd be doing it – and more! She had to keep feeling defensive and aggressive too, or else she knew she'd feel more like falling apart.

At church one Sunday morning Amber heard from Luke's mother that he wouldn't be home for Christmas. He'd said he couldn't give her his exact location, just that it was a long way from home. It was a shame, Mrs Gillam said gamely, but there was a war on, and they all had to make the best of it. Amber gritted her teeth and tried to keep smiling as she heard those words yet again. The fact that there was a war on seemed to be the excuse for anything these days, for food and petrol rationing, and now they had fewer clothing coupons too. If it went on much longer, everyone would be starving and going around in rags, Amber thought dramatically.

Dolly's reply regarding Luke had been predictably decisive.

'Good for you, gel! You shouldn't waste your time

on Lukey-boy when there are all those good-looking
Yanks around. You make the most of it while you
can. I've got my eye on one of them as well. His
name's John-Joe McAlister the third – a scream, ain't
it? He said his grandfather came from Scotland, but
he's from some place in Ohio. I'm not sure where
that is, but I don't think it's anywhere near
Hollywood. Tell me everything about the ones you
meet in the Forces' Club.'

It was all just typical of Dolly, Amber thought,
she'd be off with the old and on with the new
without a second thought – although Dolly had
never been serious about a boy yet. Not like Amber
had been – and look where that had got her.

'You're not old enough to tie yourself down,'
Granny Pen had told her that night when Luke had
finished with her. 'I admire Luke for being so sensible
about it. There's time enough for you to think about
courting when you're older. Young people often have
several romances before they think of settling down.'

'I'm not thinking about settling down,' Amber
had raged. 'I just want to be special to him, that's
all, and I thought I was.'

'Have you really thought about what being in the
forces means, Amber? I'm not talking about the
glamour of the uniforms, but of being away for
months, sometimes years, on end.'

'They get leave, don't they?'

Granny Pen smiled. 'Yes, but it's not like being
in an ordinary job. You remember Mrs Bibby at my
Save for Victory club, don't you? Her son is in the

Navy and he's been away for eight months now. Sailors could be away for a year or more, depending on where their ship is sent. It's not like catching a bus home from Redruth for the weekend.'

'Eight months?' Amber echoed, hearing nothing else.

Granny Pen pressed on. 'And one of Mrs Bibby's nephews is a prisoner of war, so only the Good Lord knows when he'll be coming home again. He's got a young wife and baby too. Women have to be strong to cope with such partings, Amber. That's why I think Luke did the right thing in cooling things down between you. It doesn't mean he thinks any the less of you, my dear.'

If she was trying to scare Amber she was certainly succeeding. She heard nothing from Luke for weeks, until the card for her sixteenth birthday with Luke's hand-writing on it. Amber looked at it for a long moment, then deliberately screwed it up and threw it in the bin – and then retrieved it moments later and put it at the bottom of a drawer.

The Yanks became frequent visitors at the Forces' Club in the next months, along with many other nationalities of servicemen as well as the British. It was a place where any of them could drop in for recreation, with darts and billiards and board games on offer, and the inevitable cups of tea or coffee. The club was open every day until midnight, with the staff working on a shift system. They now had a licence to serve alcohol in the evenings, and since the local girls were often in short supply at the monthly dances, it was inevitable that fights would break out between the men from time to time.

It rarely got out of hand and nobody seemed to mind the scuffles, since it all added to the excitement of the evenings, especially if it blotted out the uglier sounds of gunfire and bombing farther along the coast. It was only when the air raids were local ones that most of them scattered to the hastily erected shelter behind the club. The rest stayed where they were, defiantly ignoring any bombardment. It had become a policy of the club that all the staff remained at their posts until the last person was out, and since that rarely happened, none of them ever left.

'You gals should be given medals after the war,' one of the GIs commented after one blisteringly loud Saturday night air raid. 'It's not only the guys at the front line who are heroes in this war.'

'We don't do anything,' Amber said, trying not to reveal how her hands were shaking as she gave him his change.

He caught her hand in his for a second. 'We've met before, haven't we?' he said. 'I thought I recognized you, although my unit has been away for a while and I've only just got back to camp here.'

Amber removed her hand from his and looked at him properly. This was the way the Yanks operated, worldly Jennie had told her, warning her to be careful. But there was something familiar about the young man in the smart uniform, his dark hair falling over his forehead, his brown eyes smiling.

'I don't think so,' she began.

'It was by the waterfront. A shower of rain had just started and you looked good and mad about something when you nearly bumped into my buddies and me.'

Amber gave a small shrug. 'Well, being good and mad, as you put it, is nothing new to me, as anyone around here will tell you. But I remember that day now. It was Will who spoke to me, but you're not Will, are you?'

He gave a solemn salute which made her giggle. 'No, ma'am. Lieutenant Gary Emerson of the United States Marines at your service.'

She giggled again, remembering clearly now the three Yanks near the craft shop on that day when she had stormed out of it. Will had been the spokesman, and the other two had been a bit shadowy behind him. Someone called Chuck – and Gary. She had hardly noticed them at the time.

'Well, I'm Amber, but you already know that.' If he hadn't remembered it from that day, her name badge on her overall would have told him who she was.

'A beautiful name for a beautiful young lady, if I may say so.'

She was suddenly nervous. She shouldn't be, because this was the usual chat-up line, as Jennie called it. They often heard something similar, and

200

not only from the Yanks. It seemed there was a universal language in chat-up lines.

'Where are your – uh – buddies tonight?' she asked, to cover her confusion.

His face changed. One minute it had been cheerful and smiling, and the next it was as though a veil had come down over it.

'Will bought it a couple of weeks ago and Chuck's still in hospital in some God-forsaken place in Wales with an unpronounceable name that must have a million letters in it.'

'What do you mean, Will bought it?' Amber said. In her heart she knew, of course she did, but some devil inside her made her want him to spell it out.

'Killed. Kaput. Is that plain enough for you, missy? Or do you want to know the gory details?'

'No, of course not! I'm sorry, Gary. I didn't mean to be insensitive.'

His face softened again. 'I'm sure you didn't, but I'd rather not talk about it. I came here to be cheered up, so what time do you finish tonight?' he went on.

'It's my late shift, so not until midnight.'

'It's nearly that now, so can I see you home? The all-clear's long gone now, but it's still a nervous time for you guys and gals, and I have transport outside.'

'Transport?' Amber said faintly.

'Sure, and I promise you'll be quite safe. I've got a young sister about your age, and I always used to watch out for her if she was out at night. I'm pretty harmless. You could ask any of my buddies.' His face twisted again, remembering.

Amber didn't know whether to be put out by the implication that she was like his young sister who needed to be escorted home at night, but she felt a rush of sympathy, since it was obvious that the memory of his two buddies was still raw.

Before she could think of a reply, her attention was caught by the ripple of agitated conversation in the room, and Jennie came rushing over to report.

'We've just heard some news, kid. The old Lannigan Hotel had a direct hit in the raid. It's been completely destroyed. Went down like a pack of cards, apparently, and everybody inside it was killed, guests and staff, the whole lot. They say it's a hell of a mess with rubble and bodies.'

Shock raced through Amber, as sharp as a knife. 'It can't be the Lannigan. Two of the girls from my class at school work there.'

She could picture them easily. They hadn't been part of her gang, but she knew them. Had known them. She was breathing heavily, finding it hard to resist the urge to vomit at the thought of all that was left of the Lannigan Hotel.

Jennie squeezed her shoulder. 'Well, they don't any more. I'm sorry, kid. I didn't know, or I wouldn't have blurted it out like that. Look, this has been a shock to you, so why don't you go on home?'

'I'll take her,' said Gary Emerson.

Out in the fresh air, the urge to vomit became worse, and if she wasn't careful Amber knew she was going to disgrace herself for ever in front of this considerate GI who was helping her into some kind of army vehicle now.

'Take long deep breaths, honey,' he advised, 'and then give me directions. The sooner you get home and into bed the better. Believe me, I know what you're going through.'

He was being so kind and gentle with her, after a minute or two she managed to whisper directions to the cottage. When they got there he helped her out of the vehicle and kept a grip on her arm until they reached the front door.

'Do you have a key?' he asked.

She looked at him stupidly. 'I don't need a key. I just open the door.'

'Sorry. I'm from New York,' he said, as if that explained everything.

He opened the door, closing it quickly behind them both to prevent the parlour light showing outside. Granny Pen was waiting up for Amber as she always did. One look at her granddaughter's ashen face, and that of the young man who was clutching her so tightly, told her that something was very wrong.

'What's happened?' she said, her knitting falling to the floor as she stood up and came quickly across to the two of them.

'She's had a bad shock, ma'am,' Gary said. 'Some hotel got destroyed in the air raid and as far as I can tell two of Amber's friends worked there.'

'The Lannigan,' Amber whispered. 'It was the Lannigan, Gran.'

She couldn't say any more as her stomach erupted, and she rushed through the cottage to heave over the kitchen sink. She was hot with humiliation at showing herself up like that, but a few minutes later she was thankful to find that the arms that were holding her didn't belong to Gary Emerson, but her gran.

'Let it all out, my dear,' Granny Pen said, as Amber began to weep. ''Tis only the two of us here now, so there's no need to be embarrassed. The young chap's gone, but he says he hopes to see you at church tomorrow morning.'

Right then Amber's horrified thoughts didn't include a stranger who had shown her such kindness even while he too was grieving. All she could think about were two girls aged sixteen who had been in her class at school, who she had known since they were all old enough to hold a pencil, and who had been as bubbly and full of life as her a few hours ago. Now they were dead. The wickedness of it all was almost too much to bear.

Chapter Twelve

Amber didn't want to go to church on Sunday. She hadn't slept for thinking about the two girls she had known for so long, and she knew that talk of the bombing of the Lannigan Hotel would be on everyone's lips. But Granny Pen insisted.

'How will it look if everyone stays away? Of course people are upset, but at times like this people should be together if only to show Hitler that we can still carry on our ordinary lives, no matter what he throws at us.'

'And how is he going to know that – or care? It wasn't your friends who were blown to bits, so who's next, I wonder?'

She shuddered, knowing that Gillam's boatyard was much nearer the docks than they were at the cottage. Luke would probably have been in as much danger of being blown up if he'd stayed at home as he was somewhere at sea.

'Now you just listen to me, Amber,' Granny Pen said. 'People can get killed running across a road. They can drop dead from heart attacks the way poor old Mr Veal did. There's no discrimination when it comes to dying, war or no war, and when your number's up, it's up.'

'Well, that's fine, coming from you! How come you didn't see it all coming in the tea leaves then! How come you can't tell us which bit of Falmouth is going to be hit next, so we can all pack our bags and go away until it's all over?'

She was in the mood for an argument, simply because she didn't know what else to do. Granny Pen sighed.

'I'll overlook that bit of nonsense, but just remember the nice young man who brought you home last night, and his two friends that you told me about. I'm sure he's upset as well, but he's getting on with things because he has to – and didn't he say he might be at church this morning?'

She could be about as subtle as a barrage balloon when she tried, thought Amber. As if the thought of seeing Gary Emerson at church was going to stop the jitters that kept rushing through her with nerve-shaking regularity. But she knew she was never going to win this argument, short of shutting herself in her bedroom, and how childish would that be!

There were several small groups of GIs at church that day. The sermon was based on forgiveness and hope. It was necessarily more emotional than usual as the vicar stressed that everyone should say a prayer for those who had lost their lives in the tragedy of the Lannigan Hotel, causing more than one woman in the congregation to be sniffing into her handkerchief. It was a great relief when they could all spill outside into the fresh air of a warm spring morning.

'There's your new friend,' said Granny Pen.

Amber looked back to the church door where the GIs were shaking hands with the vicar. Gary was among them, and she saw the vicar give his hand an extra squeeze and murmur something to him. She felt suddenly ashamed of her earlier outburst that morning. The church had been especially full today, as if to underline her gran's words that ordinary lives still carried on, despite all.

When Gary turned away from the vicar he caught sight of her. He smiled at once and came striding across the gravel.

''Morning, ma'am,' he greeted Granny Pen. 'It's good to see you again on this fine morning, and I hope you're feeling better now, Amber.'

'I am, thank you,' she said.

She supposed she was, more or less. The hymn-singing had been no less lusty than it ever was, and the vicar's final words had been uplifting, as always. She didn't know what else to say to him. They were strangers, and they were standing here like idiots now until Gary cleared his throat.

'Well, I guess I'd better go and join my buddies. We're off tomorrow morning, so I won't be seeing you at the Forces' Club for a few weeks, Amber. I hear there's some lovely country around here, but I haven't had the chance to see much of it yet. I've even heard tell of some place called the Lizard. So when I get back, I wondered if you'd care to come out for a drive with me one afternoon. That is, with your approval, ma'am,' he added to Granny Pen.

'I'd like that very much,' Amber said, before her gran could say a word.

'It's a date then,' Gary said, and he shook both their hands before moving off to join his companions.

'Well, you jumped in there pretty quickly, miss,' Granny Pen commented. 'What if I'd objected?'

Amber was defiant. 'You wouldn't though, would you? You'd have thought of it as an omen, like I did. If I promised to go for a drive with him when he comes back, then he'll be sure to come back, won't he?'

'And you're a bit of a devious little witch in disguise, aren't you?'

But her gran was smiling, and she knew she'd got the better of her – and it wasn't just for that reason that she'd accepted the invitation. She liked Gary Emerson, and what would be so wrong in going out with a well-behaved GI (with transport) on a sunny afternoon?

Two other people were approaching them now, and Amber's heart shifted uncomfortably as she saw the disapproving expression on Luke's mother's face. It implied that Amber hadn't wasted much time in forgetting Luke and getting friendly with a GI. She lifted her chin. She'd done nothing wrong, and Luke had spelled it out, loud and clear, that he didn't want her brooding over him while he was doing his bit in the navy, so she had every right to make other friends.

'That was a terrible business at the Lannigan last night,' Mrs Gillam was saying to Granny Pen once they had greeted each other. 'I gather there were only a few guests, but there was no hope for anybody inside.'

'Two girls from my class at school worked there,' Amber said jerkily, feeling she had to make Mrs Gillam look at her, which it seemed she was avoiding now. Or maybe she was imagining it, and was just being over-sensitive.

'That's very sad,' Mrs Gillam said now, her expression changing to one of sympathy. 'We always expect our old friends to be there for ever, don't we?'

Was that a dig about her and Luke as well? Amber felt her palms grow damp inside her cotton gloves. But then Mrs Gillam leaned over and kissed her cheek.

'I'm afraid we have to accept whatever comes our way in wartime, Amber dear. At least it was a blessing that none of those people in the hotel could have known what was happening. They say it was a direct hit, and that nobody could have survived for a moment.'

Amber nodded, fighting down the urge to cry. She didn't intend to burst into tears here, when there were people all around them, sharing their own versions of the terrible events of the night before. She felt stifled by it all, and thought longingly of a drive in the country at some future date, where the war and all its atrocities could be forgotten for a few hours. She gulped down the lump in her throat and said huskily to Granny Pen that she really would like to get home now.

'You know, my dear,' Granny Pen said, once they were out of the vicinity, 'I think the very best thing you could have done is to accept that kind invitation from Gary. It will give you something to look forward to. Summer can't be far away and Cornwall is never lovelier than in the summer months, especially when you are looking at it through a stranger's eyes.'

In other words, she had her gran's blessing, Amber thought, with an odd little catch in her throat. And more than that. She had a new friend, even if she wasn't going to see him for a few weeks, and the last thing she was going to do was to speculate where he and his unit might be sent to during that time.

The local newspaper announced that the disaster at the Lannigan Hotel in Falmouth was probably no more than a rogue bombing as a German plane dropped the remainder of its bombs to lighten its load before turning for home. The fact did nothing to help the relatives of those who had been killed, and there was a succession of sad funerals in the next couple of weeks.

Then in late April Winston Churchill decreed that church bells could be rung again for services or weddings. Until now, they had been silenced for the duration, and would only have been rung as a warning of invasion. Now the government had decided that such a threat was over; it was an announcement that lifted people's spirits and made them think that surely the war must be coming to an end soon.

Dolly's latest letter to Amber didn't uphold that idea as she wrote excitedly about an horrific accident in a daylight air raid near a tube station in London.

'What do you think of this for rotten bleedin' luck, Amber?' she wrote. 'A woman carrying her baby tripped and fell down a flight of steps just as she got inside the entrance. An elderly man fell on top of her (no, not like that!) and there were crowds of people rushing to get down the shelter as well and nobody could see what was happening, so they all fell on top of one another like a pack of cards, and they crushed one another to death. They said there were nearly two hundred people dead. And here's a turn-up at the end of it – the woman survived it all, but her baby died. Makes you think, don't it? Is it safer down the tube, or under the stairs, which is what Mum and me do most of the time when we can't be bothered to leave the house? It's too bleedin' smelly down the tube anyway. After a night of it, you're glad to breathe fresh air, even smoky old London air.

'I suppose it's all quiet down in the sticks now. Don't forget to tell me about the Yanks you've got there. John-Joe brought Mum and me some nylon stockings the other week, but being Mum, she put her fork straight through one of them and it laddered from top to bottom. I told her to wear it so's it looked like a seam at the back anyway, then she wouldn't have to draw it with a black eyebrow pencil. And don't ask what she was doing with a fork on her stockings!'

Amber had felt shocked at reading the awful first part of Dolly's letter, but she was laughing at the end of it. She felt obliged to tell her about the Lannigan Hotel, and the two girls they had both known, but she also told her about Gary, and that they were going on a date as soon as he came back from whatever manoeuvres he was on now. She deliberately didn't mention Luke at all. There was nothing to say about him, anyway. And she knew it was daft, but it made her feel like holding her head up high at being able to tell Dolly that she wasn't the only one who knew a Yank – and had a date.

By the middle of May, the horror of the Lannigan Hotel had faded a little, except in the minds of those who were most closely affected by it. Amber had accepted that her gran's words about sailors being away for long stretches of time had been right, because she hadn't heard from Luke for ages, and she knew he hadn't had any leave or he would surely have been to church with his parents, even if he hadn't contacted her. She still thought about him, but not nearly as much as when he first went away.

It made her feel guilty, because she didn't want her feelings for him to fade. She wanted to keep them burning as brightly as they had ever done, but it wasn't easy to do when it seemed as if they weren't reciprocated.

'You'll wear that door out if you don't stop looking at it,' Jennie remarked one evening at the Forces' Club. 'He won't come back until he's good and ready, kid – or, rather, until Jerry sees to it that he does.'

'I know,' Amber said, her head still full of Luke at that moment.

'Or maybe I spoke too soon,' Jennie added. 'That looks like your chap in the middle of that crowd coming in now.'

Amber's heart soared so much it felt ready to burst.

'*Luke,*' she breathed . . . and just as instantly she knew it wouldn't be Luke, because Jennie had never met him, and she couldn't think that Luke would come to see her here at work, instead of being somewhere on their own . . .

In any case, the tall figure separating himself from the others now wasn't wearing navy blue. He reached the counter where Amber was still experiencing a searing case of disappointment, and leaned across it to grasp both her hands in his.

'You sure are a sight for sore eyes, honey, especially after some of those I've seen recently. Give me a beer, will you? I don't care if it's warm like you Limeys seem to prefer, it'll still taste good to me.'

'You're back then,' she stammered to Gary Emerson.

What were you supposed to say next? *Did you have a good time?* Hardly. *How did it go?* You didn't know where he had been or what he had been doing. And you could hardly say you hoped everybody got back all right, because you knew very well that sometimes some of them didn't.

At her words, Gary pretended to look himself over.

'I guess I am, unless I'm a cardboard cut-out of myself, or one of those stunt doubles they have in the movies. I told you I'd be back, didn't I? We have a date, so how about next Saturday afternoon? You don't have to bring anything except your lovely self, and now I know where you live I'll pick you up and you can direct me to this Lizard place, whatever it is.'

She had to admit he was like a breath of fresh air. He breezed into the room and spoke so confidently, clearly never expecting a negative answer, and she didn't intend saying no, anyway.

'All right,' she said, her voice slightly breathless. 'But don't expect to see monsters or dinosaurs, will you? It's only the name of the area.'

'What a shame. I quite fancied rescuing a lovely lady in distress from a dinosaur. And when we get there you can tell me all about Cornwall. It seems quite a cute little place.'

Amber laughed, refusing to be affronted by his remark that Cornwall was a cute little place. She

214

supposed it was, compared with the huge map of America that she remembered from her school days. She was also aware that she was feeling better by the minute. It was like her gran always said. Life had to go on and you had to go on with it. The fact that Luke wasn't here right now didn't mean that she had to spend her days like a nun. In any case, Luke had made his opinions pretty plain the last time she had seen him. She forced herself to stop thinking about him, or comparing him with this fresh-faced GI who was making no secret of his interest.

'I'll tell you about Cornwall if you'll tell me about New York,' she said.

'It's a deal, but I can't stay much longer tonight, as I've got to get back to camp to make a report. I just wanted to check with you about Saturday.'

He drained his beer and she watched him weave his way in and out of the intake of servicemen that evening. When he reached the door he turned and waved. Jennie was hovering behind her by now.

'I see you've made a conquest, Amber. You'd better mind what you get up to on Saturday.'

'Were you listening?'

Jennie grinned. 'Just being envious, more like. He's a smasher. Just make sure you hold on to your principles, if you know what I mean,' she added with a wink. 'And if you can't be good, be careful.'

Amber felt her face go red. She wasn't naive, and she'd heard enough raucous banter among the men who came in here for a change of scene and a bit of harmless flirtation to know what Jennie was talking about. She knew that some of the girls had gone out with the GIs already and were full of the good times they had and how generous they were. Some even hinted about how far they had gone with their Yanks, or how far they were prepared to go. The other girls were all older than she was, and for the first time she felt nervous, wondering if Gary realised she was only sixteen. She was tall and well-rounded now, and she usually wore her long hair twisted up on her head for work in the canteen, which made her look older than she was. She hoped Gary wasn't going to get the wrong idea about this date . . .

For some reason she found herself picturing how Dolly would react at being invited out on a date with a handsome GI. Dolly wouldn't turn a hair, nor think twice – and there was no way that Amber was going to let Dolly get the better of her! She was going to enjoy it – and the nearer it got to Saturday, the keener she became.

When the day arrived, she had let her hair down. She had plaited it overnight in the hope that it might retain a few kinks by morning, but by the afternoon it hung down past her shoulders, as straight and glossy as ever. She wore a pretty yellow and white frock and white sandals, and the white crochet gloves that her gran had made her. The day was warm and sunny and calm, a perfect day for a drive in the country, the sort of day when it was easy to forget that there was a war on at all.

'You look a picture, Amber,' Granny Pen said when she came downstairs to wait for Gary. 'Just take care, won't you?'

In case Granny Pen was about to give her a few words of advice over how to behave with a young man, advice which was sure to make her squirm with embarrassment, Amber spoke quickly.

'It's all right, Gran. I've had all the pep talks from Jennie at the club, and I won't let you down.'

'Well, I'm not sure Jennie at the club is the right person to do a parent's or a grandparent's job,' Granny Pen said dryly, 'but I know you've been brought up to know what's right and what's wrong, my dear.'

'Trust me to remember it then,' Amber said, and turned in relief as she heard the toot of a horn outside the cottage gate. Before Gary came inside and had to listen to her gran's unsubtle warnings of how to treat a girl, she saved her embarrassment by kissing her quickly and ran outside to the waiting Jeep.

'Gee, you look fantastic today,' Gary said. 'Quite the little movie star. Have you ever thought about trying to get into pictures?'

Amber burst out laughing, her brief nervousness disappearing at such an absurd question.

'What a thought! I can't imagine myself on the silver screen. My friend Dolly's more inclined to want fame and fortune than I am. She's friendly with a GI who lives in Ohio. Is that anywhere near Hollywood?'

It was Gary who hooted with laughter now as he started up the Jeep and followed Amber's directions to drive westwards away from Falmouth and out towards the Lizard peninsula. Petrol was obviously no problem when you were a GI, Amber thought fleetingly.

'I should say not! Ohio's about as far as you can get from Hollywood – barring New York and the Eastern seaboard.'

'What's that when it's at home?' she asked, mystified.

He glanced at her, seeing how the small breeze ruffled her glorious hair, and how her blue eyes were shining with excitement, and thought he had never seen anything so lovely. He was a long way from home, and he had just spent an uncomfortable and unexpectedly dangerous few weeks on manoeuvres, and all he wanted was to spend these summer hours with a pretty girl.

'I'll tell you all about it later. We'll compare our lives, and get to know one another, and we won't mention the W word. Is it a deal?'

She twigged right away, and nodded fervently. Who wanted to spend this lovely day discussing the war? She concentrated on giving him directions. She hadn't been to the Lizard for ages now, and the last time it had been at the end of a long cycle ride with her friends, but she wasn't thinking about them today – not even a certain one of them. They reached Helston and turned left to begin the drive down the Lizard peninsula.

'Some crazy names you have around here,' Gary commented.

'I daresay you'll think we have some crazy customs too,' Amber said. 'If you'd been here a few weeks ago, you could have seen the Helston Furry Day. It's not quite as colourful as it used to be in the old days, when folk used to dance through the streets and in and out of one another's houses. They wore garlands of flowers and were led through the town by fiddlers. It's still carried on to a lesser degree, though.'

'That sure is some weird custom,' Gary said with a laugh. 'Although I guess some places in the midwest of America have some quaint old customs too. Don't ask me about them, though. Like I said, I'm a New Yorker.'

'What's it like? You said you'd tell me.'

'Well, it's nothing like this,' Gary said, as they began to travel down the Lizard, and the vast green areas opened out in front of them, thick with gorse and wild flowers and with an almost overpoweringly sweet fragrance. 'New York is all concrete and skyscrapers, except for the relief of Central Park, but it's not natural, the way this place is.'

'It is beautiful, isn't it?' Amber said, seeing it through his eyes now. 'If you like natural things, then you ought to see Kynance Cove, but when we get there we'll have to leave the Jeep and walk down. There's no other way down to it, unfortunately.'

'That's OK, honey. I'm just enjoying the afternoon out, and I hope you are too.'

She was. She felt happier than she had in a long while, and it was easy to forget the W word completely now. This place was untouched by any bad memories, and she was eager to show Gary the places she knew and loved. She didn't love *him*. That kind of feeling didn't come into it and wasn't likely to. She was just happy to be alive and out in the country in familiar surroundings.

They drove as far as they could to the area above Kynance Cove. The granite cliffs were awesome here, but there were grassy slopes where it was possible to slither, laughing, hand in hand down towards the cove. The sea crashed magnificently against the rocks, the white foam contrasting vividly with the blue of the sea and sky. Offshore was Asparagus Island and Gull Rock, both circled with spume now.

'At low tide you can walk over to Asparagus Island,' Amber said, as they paused for breath once they had reached the sandy inlet. 'There are caves here too. They've all got funny names, like the Kitchen, the Parlour, the Drawing Room and the Devil's Mouth. Then there's the Bishop's Rock and the Devil's Letter Box and Bellows, where the water is forced up through the hole with a lion's roar. It scared me to death when I first heard it. You have to go inside the Drawing Room and take a look at the colours in the rocks, too. It's supposed to be lucky to touch as many colours as you can. And am I talking too much?'

She knew she was. All of a sudden she was

nervous. She was here alone with a handsome man, who must be at least a few years older than herself, and they had seen no other walkers about on this fine afternoon. She began to wonder if she had been headstrong and foolish in suggesting Kynance Cove, because what did she really know about Gary after all?

Before he answered, he sat down on a rock and proceeded to take off his shoes and socks, and she looked at him in even more alarm.

'What are you doing?' she stuttered.

'I'm going to dip my toes in the ocean,' he said. 'It's too tempting to resist, and I bet you're itching to do the same.'

Amber began to laugh. 'Not likely. Do you know how cold it's going to be?'

'Well, I'm not suggesting dunking my entire body, just my toes, so watch!'

He rolled up his trouser legs, raced down to the edge of the sand and walked right in, then turned with a yelp and ran back out again, hopping about from one leg to the other until he got more used to the cold, then he trekked along the edge of the waves more leisurely.

'It's great. Come on in!'

Amber didn't resist any longer. She slipped out of her sandals and ran down the cove to join him, taking the hand he offered until her toes touched the freezing water and sent a shiver up through her whole body. It was still early summer, and the sun hadn't warmed up the sea sufficiently to enjoy it yet.

'We must be mad,' she gasped, as they waded along the water's edge together. 'I used to do this with my friends, but not this early in the summer.'

They didn't stay in the sea for very long. Gary produced a clean folded handkerchief and handed it to Amber to dry her feet while he rubbed his own dry in the sand and pulled on his socks and shoes.

'My girl and I used to do it too, so I guess that's what I was thinking about. But enough is enough. Let's dry these feet and get back up top and do a bit more exploring. I want to see more of this Lizard.'

'Your girl?' Amber said, as usual picking out the relevant piece of information from any conversation and ignoring the rest.

Chapter Thirteen

When they reached the top of the cliffs again, they flopped down on the grass to get their breath back, and Gary pulled out a wallet from his jacket pocket.

'I'll show you her picture,' he said. 'Her name's Greta.'

'Like Greta Garbo?' Amber said, unable to think of anything else as she looked at the very glamorous blonde girl smiling up out of the photograph.

Gary laughed. 'Hardly, although my Greta also comes from an old Swedish family. They came to the States a hundred years ago and settled there and made good. Greta's an actress too. One day she hopes to play on Broadway, but you have to do more than just live in New York to make the boards there. Show business is a tough old world, especially when girls with any looks at all think they could make it as movie stars.'

This was all going slightly over Amber's head now, having had so little to do with show business herself, and she didn't think that mentioning either her old school or the local amateur dramatic group would impress Gary too much.

He gazed at the photo for a minute longer, ran his thumb softly over the image, and then put it back in his wallet. He was a long way from home, and missing his girl – and having her photograph at least brought her that little bit nearer. Amber wondered immediately if Luke would ever have thought of doing anything like that – even if he had any photographs of her, which he didn't.

She heard Gary clear his throat, and realized she had probably been silent for too long. She jumped up and held out her hand, deliberately cheerful.

'Well, come on, you wanted to see some more of the Lizard, didn't you? If you're feeling more adventurous at some other time you could drive right down to Land's End and wave to America.'

She hoped he didn't think she was angling for another invitation, but he laughed, catching her hand and her mood as he stood up.

'That would be something, wouldn't it? And you've never told me anything about your own special someone. A pretty girl like you has got to have one. Is he away in the forces too?'

A pretty girl like her . . . Amber smiled inside at that, and then realised he wanted her to say she had a special someone. Maybe he thought she'd imagined she was falling for him, which was why he'd mentioned his Greta. He needn't worry, though, because she wasn't falling for him. It was just nice to have a friend. It was flattering, too. It made her feel good. It was almost a status symbol to have a Yank these days, she thought fleetingly, and it was such a shallow thought that she was instantly ashamed of it.

But she had her pride too, so of *course* she was going to mention her someone special. He was special to her, even if she wasn't to him.

'His name's Luke,' she said, as they clambered back into the Jeep. 'We've known each other for ever, and now he's in the navy, and I haven't heard from him for ages.'

Her face suddenly crumpled, and her eyes filled with tears. She hadn't expected this and she didn't want it. She didn't want to blubber in front of this lovely, considerate Yank who was handing her his handkerchief again. It was gritty and full of sand now, but after a few minutes she blew into it hard. While she was still wondering whether or not to hand it back to him, he told her to keep it, and then he leaned across and kissed her flushed cheek.

'You're a nice kid, Amber, and this Luke must be crazy not to keep in touch. But don't blame him too much for that, honey. It's a miracle that any correspondence gets anywhere in this war. You may not hear from him for weeks, and then you'll get a bundle of letters together, you'll see.'

'Perhaps you're right,' she said, her eyes still watery, knowing damn well that this wasn't the case. She was grateful that at least he hadn't suggested anything more sinister in the fact that she hadn't heard from Luke in ages, like his ship being torpedoed, or being captured by the enemy . . . but she would have known if anything like that had happened because his mother would have had one of those dreaded telegrams, and she would surely have told her . . .

Both lost in thoughts of their own, Gary drove the Jeep down the length of the Lizard peninsula until they reached Lizard Point, where the ocean crashed on to the rocks, and the wind almost took their voices away. Out in the sea stood the sentinel of Wolf Light, the lighthouse that was the model for so many multicoloured souvenirs made from Cornish serpentine stone and sold in local shops in Lizard Town nearby and everywhere else in Cornwall.

'They say the light is only visible for about twenty-one miles because of the curvature of the earth,' Amber told Gary. 'It's one of the few things I remember from local history lessons at school, because when I was a kid I used to think the light-house might fall off. It doesn't prevent the shipwrecks happening though. We've always had our share around the Cornish coasts, and a lot of piracy and smuggling in the old days too.'

She wished she hadn't mentioned shipwrecks, and she gave a small shiver as they left the Jeep and walked along the edge of the cliffs.

'You're cold,' he said at once. 'I think we should go and find one of those little cafés in the town and have something hot to drink. I might buy one of these cute little lighthouse models you're talking about for Greta too. She likes collecting things, and I know she's never seen anything like that.'

'She sounds very nice,' Amber said, for want of something to say.

'She is. We were thinking of getting engaged just before I was sent overseas.'

'Overseas? Oh, you mean here!'

'That's right, but it seemed foolish to rush into something when I was likely to be away for the good Lord knows how long. I know she'll wait for me though, just like I guess your boy knows you'll wait for him, although I guess you're still a bit young to be thinking of anything permanent.'

'I'm sixteen!' she said indignantly.

'And I'm twenty, and never did four years make such a difference.'

She didn't care too much for this conversation, since he evidently considered her little more than a child. It was so obvious that he was missing his Greta, and wishing even more that he was anywhere but here. Well, she didn't much want to be here, either, not with him, and she was missing somebody too.

'Gee, honey, I didn't mean to sound so gloomy, and we were in danger of getting around to the W word,' he was saying now. 'Let's go and get that hot tea and maybe a scone or two to go with it, if we're lucky, and we'll just make the most of this lovely day and not think about anything else. Is it a deal?'

'It's a deal,' Amber said solemnly.

Late that afternoon, Granny Pen had the table laid with fish paste sandwiches beneath a lace doily to keep them fresh, together with fresh-baked carrot and turnip cake, and clearly expected Gary to eat with them before he went back to camp.

'This is very good of you,' he said, 'though I didn't expect it, and you shouldn't have gone to so much trouble, ma'am.'

'When the day comes that a Cornish woman can't offer hospitality to a stranger, that's the day I shall hang up my boots,' she said spikily. 'The Jerries have taken plenty from us these past few years, but they haven't broken our spirit yet, and they never will. So sit yourself down, young man, and don't tell me you Americans haven't got good appetites, because I'm sure you're no different from the rest of us in that respect.'

He grinned. 'You sure do remind me of my grandmother, ma'am, and I say that as a great compliment. She's a game old gal too.'

Amber giggled, not sure how her gran was going to react to such a remark, and then she saw Granny Pen go a bit pink and answer with a sniff.

'I'll take that as being a good thing, then. Now let's eat, because I can't bear to think all this is going to waste. There are starving children in Africa who'd be glad of such a feast.'

Amber groaned, wondering if Gary would think this was a twee thing to say, but he winked, and said that his grandmother had always told him about the starving children in China to make him eat up his greens. They weren't so different then.

She was undecided about how much to tell Dolly about their date. On the one hand, it would raise her prestige no end if she said she had had a romantic afternoon in the country with Gary, and that he'd kissed her. Well, so he had, but only on the cheek. It was hardly what you'd call a romantic kiss, but since she hadn't wanted one, it didn't matter. It wasn't the kind of thing you told a friend like Dolly, though. Dolly would expect chapter and verse on how torrid the afternoon had been, and how she had had to beat him off to save her honour, and Dolly would have been pea-green with envy to hear about it.

In the end she exaggerated a bit, but not too much. If she made it sound as if she had forgotten all about Luke, maybe that was all to the good. Although, reading her letter back, it did seem as if it was all Gary, Gary, Gary, and it made her feel a bit uneasy, as if she was writing a story instead of reporting the things that had really happened. She certainly didn't mention blonde Greta, who looked as if she already belonged in a Hollywood picture. Why would Gary ever look at any other girl when he had her to go home to?

Amber gritted her teeth and finished her letter with a flourish, saying she wasn't sure when she'd be seeing him again, because the Yanks seemed to come and go so often on what Gary mysteriously called their missions, so she'd just have to be patient and pine.

When she read the letter back again it seemed so silly and melodramatic that she was tempted to screw it up and begin again, but then she imagined

Dolly's eyes getting wider and wider as she read it, so she quickly stuffed it in an envelope ready for posting. Let Dolly think she was having a whale of a time in her war, Amber thought grimly.

Six weeks later, when summer was at its height and the Yanks in Gary's unit had temporarily gone out of town, there were two letters from Luke on the same day. It was just as Gary had said. You never knew where letters got to these days. There would be nothing but a deafening silence for weeks, and then they would all come in a bundle. Not that two letters were exactly a bundle, but they were something to make Amber's heart thump with excitement, something to cherish, and to take upstairs to her bedroom to read in private, even though they weren't exactly love letters.

'We thought we'd bought it the other night,' he wrote, in the kind of shorthand language they all used now. 'In fact a couple of our sparks – that's electricians to you – were quite badly wounded when we got hit, but it was only a glancing blow to the ship, and luckily we were near enough to a port to put in for repairs. Naturally I can't tell you where, Amber, but they don't speak English!'

And how frustrating was *that*, Amber thought, fuming. She would love to have followed his progress on a map, but she knew he wasn't allowed to give away his position these days, presumably in case she was going to rush off and tell it to some enemy spy! She wondered where this port could be. It had to be somewhere friendly, and there weren't that many places open to them in the world now. It was a frightening thought. Maybe it was Norway. And maybe it wasn't.

She carried on reading, and her heart gave a jolt at the next bit.

'You'll be glad to know I always carry my lucky piece of amber with me. It's my talisman. I rely on it to keep me safe, and I don't fancy being fish bait just yet.'

Her face softened, her eyes glistening, her fingers running gently over the paper as if she could trace the movements of his fingers holding the pencil as he wrote the words. As if she could breathe his breath as he leaned over the letter in the dimness of the night to write to her. How could she forget, even for a moment, how much she loved him and wanted him back? If she had to wait years for him, he was the only one she had ever wanted, and she wanted him still. She realized, too, that he always mentioned the piece of amber she had given him, as if to remind her that he still carried a little piece of her with him wherever he went.

The second letter was very short. It merely said that they were off on some special course of action, and if she didn't hear from him for a while, she wasn't to worry. Like a bad penny, he'd turn up when she was least expecting him. It didn't thrill her to read this letter. It seemed to be guarded, as if he was afraid to say too much at all, and in any case, whatever this special course of action was, it was probably over and done with by now – or they were still in the middle of it. She always scanned the newspaper for any news of it, but compared with the big naval battles of the war, such as the strikes on the German battleships, there was never any mention of it.

It was as if it had vanished as surely as the *Marie Celeste*. She knew that wasn't true, of course, because she had the evidence of it here in her hands, in the two precious letters he had sent her. She put them with all the rest in her memory box, and sent up a silent prayer that this war would be over soon, and that they could all get back to living normal lives. But for now she had the consolation that Luke still thought of her. She was still his girl, no matter how many times he professed that this wasn't the right time for young girls to get serious.

Besides, she hadn't inherited her grandmother's feyness for nothing. He could pretend all he liked, but when fate had decreed that two people were meant to be together, it was unstoppable. It was a thought to lift her heart, no matter how long the parting. Even Gary Emerson knew that. He may not have a Cornishman's sense of knowing such things, but he knew it in his heart that his Greta would wait for him. Just as Amber would always wait for Luke.

Dolly was agog at reading Amber's latest letter.

'Well, blow me down with a feather,' she remarked to Jude, the girl on the market stall alongside hers.

'Who says these gels at the back of beyond are slow at coming forward?'

'Is that the one you was evacuated with?' said Jude. 'I thought she had a boy down there that you was quite sweet on as well.'

Dolly tossed her blonde curls. 'We was always going to be rivals, me and Amber, and I wasn't seriously interested in Luke, even though he was the best of a bad job among the kids in Falmouth at the time. I always thought I had a bit more gumption than her though, and I didn't see why he should fancy her over me.'

Jude gave a shrieking laugh. 'You was never a shy one, was you, gel?'

Dolly shrugged. 'If you've got it, flaunt it, my mum always says. But now this little shrinking violet's gone and got herself a Yank, so I reckon Lukeyboy's well out of the picture. If I ever go back down to the sticks, I might have another go at him myself.'

'But you ain't thinking of it, are you? What about John-Joe? Ain't he planning to take you to America and make you a movie star?'

Dolly flushed darkly. 'I found out he's bleedin' well married, and I ain't wasting my time on him no more. I'm not saying I'd ever go back to Cornwall again, but I might go one day, just to take a look around, 'specially now that my mum's talking about getting hitched to Uncle Joe. I used to get fed up with their lovey-doveying, but they're squabbling half the time now, so they might as well be bleedin' well married!'

She scowled. It had been fun when she was a kid to have all these uncles coming around. Uncle Joe, in particular, had always brought her things when he'd been courting her mum, but now they were thinking of making it legal there weren't so many little extras coming her way any more. She didn't think of herself as being particularly mercenary, but when you had been used to it for so long, you missed it when it wasn't there any more. It wouldn't be such a bad idea to get away for a while, particularly if Lukey-boy came home again.

She found it easy to overlook the fact that Luke had always been Amber's boy. If she no longer wanted him, that left the way open for Dolly – and in any case, she wasn't likely ever to let such a small consideration get in her way, she thought with a grin. All was fair in love and war.

Towards the end of 1943, more and more US troops poured into Falmouth and other Cornish coastal towns as their Advanced Amphibious Training Bases were established at St Mawes, Falmouth and Fowey. It was obvious to everyone now that a big invasion was being planned to take place along the northern French coast to push the Germans back. Nobody had any idea when it was going to happen, and it couldn't take place until everyone was certain of what they had to do and had the means and equipment to do it. But excitement in the area was rife, not least because there were so many more servicemen in the area now, and Jennie at the Forces' Club said that any girl who didn't have a GI boyfriend wasn't doing her bit for the war effort.

'If that isn't just like you,' Amber said, exasperated. 'It's a pity Dolly's not here to listen to such tripe, because she'd be sure to go along with it.'

'And you're not? Since when did you become too high and mighty to go out with a Yank? The minute your friend Gary shows up here, you're not slow on the uptake, are you, kid? Though I notice he ain't been around for a while.'

'He's on manoeuvres,' Amber said mechanically. It was the usual reply when you didn't have a clue where anybody was these days. The only certainty about this war was the sense of *un*certainty.

One thing was certain, though. Meeting Luke's parents at church recently, she had learned that there was no chance of him getting home for Christmas. Mrs Gillam was resigned to it now, but she couldn't disguise the anxiety in her eyes as she spoke of her son. Nor when she mentioned that that nice young Eddie Fielding had been killed in France. Amber felt completely shocked.

'*Eddie Fielding?*' she echoed, instantly picturing the thin, spotty youth who had been in the class above them at school, and who Dolly had amazingly been smitten with at one time. 'What was he doing in France? I thought he was working at the docks, and he surely wasn't old enough to join up.'

'None of them are old enough to be shot and killed,' Luke's mother said acidly. 'But like so many

235

young boys, they get carried away by the excitement of being soldiers, and this is the result. It's the mothers I feel sorry for.'

'And the wives and sisters and girlfriends,' Amber murmured without thinking, and was shocked again to receive a freezing look from Luke's mother.

'It seems to me too many young girls find it easy enough to forget that their boyfriends are away fighting for them,' she said.

Amber's temper flared at once. Thankfully Granny Pen was talking to some other friends, and couldn't hear how she snapped at Luke's mother.

'Well, if that's supposed to be a dig at me, Mrs Gillam, perhaps I should remind you how you insisted that I was far too young to have any romantic ideas about Luke. It's hardly my fault that the war has gone on so long, and that I've grown up in the meantime, is it? Anyway, I don't think it's going to be much consolation to Eddie Fielding's mother whether he had a girlfriend or not!'

She was more upset than she let on. It was horrible to think that school friends were being killed in this war. It was something you never even thought about. War was for proper soldiers and sailors and airmen, not for school kids. She smothered a sob in her throat as she marched across to where Granny Pen was turning to look at her now.

'Can we go home?' she said in a choked voice.

'What's happened?'

'It's Eddie Fielding from school. He's been killed in France.'

'You don't mean the young chap that Dolly went out with a few times?'

'That's the one.' And now she would have to tell Dolly next time she wrote. It would be a bit different from reporting how many more Yanks were coming into town, and who was going out with who. Suddenly it all seemed so shallow, and she wheeled around and ran back to where Luke's parents were still chatting.

'Mrs Gillam, I'm so sorry for talking to you the way I did just now. It was the shock of hearing about Eddie, that's all.'

Luke's mother had always been a kind and forgiving woman, and she kissed Amber on the cheek at once.

'My dear, we all say things we don't mean at such times, and your apology proves to me that you're growing up very fast, and not in such a bad way, either.'

If growing up fast meant the acceptance of losing more and more old friends, then she wasn't sure she wanted to know about it, Amber thought numbly, as she rejoined her gran.

'Is there any news about Luke?' Granny Pen asked quietly, tucking her hand firmly through Amber's arm.

'No,' she said, 'and before you tell me no news is good news, I always did think that was a point-less thing to say. No news is no news.'

'I wasn't going to say it. I prefer to think that when there's no news, there's always hope. You're not going to argue about that, I trust, seeing as how you're in your usual argumentative mood today?'

Amber felt her face relax a little. It wasn't fair to take out her frustration on her gran. They all had to face up to whatever fate – and war – threw at them, and more than one of Granny Pen's friends had lost a son or a nephew. War touched all of them in some way. It was just harder to accept it when you were not yet seventeen, and worrying about what might be happening to someone special.

'I'm going to be all sweetness and light from now on,' she promised, which made Granny Pen burst out laughing,

'And pigs might fly, too,' she said, but she squeezed Amber's arm to her with real affection.

If she had expected some dramatic reaction from Dolly when she reported the news about Eddie Fielding, she was disappointed. Dolly merely wrote him off in a single sentence, saying she always knew Eddie was too much of dumbbell to keep his head down. She could be really nasty sometimes, thought Amber, because Eddie had been genuinely fond of her, and he deserved more than a brush-off.

But towards the end of November she had more important things to think about than Dolly's fickleness. There was a rap on the cottage door one evening, and she opened it to find Luke standing there. Her heart thudded so fast she thought she was going to keel over, and then the glory of the moment was so intense that it didn't matter what he was expecting, or whether or not Granny Pen was hovering behind her. All she could do was to croak his name before the breath went out of her, and then she threw herself into his arms.

'Well, this is a welcome and a half,' he said with a smile in his voice. 'Are you going to let me in, or are we going to show the whole town that you're pleased to see me?'

Since there were so few other cottages around this part of town it was unlikely, but she knew at once that he was pleased with her reaction. She knew him too well to be unaware of it. She knew him as if he was the other half of her.

She drew him inside, still caught in his arms, moving as one person, until they reluctantly broke apart as he greeted Granny Pen.

'Come and sit you down, Luke, and I'll get us all a drink before Amber strangles you.'

Amber grinned sheepishly at Luke, knowing this was to give them a few minutes alone . . . a few minutes, when in reality she wanted an hour, the whole night, an entire lifetime . . . she felt her face flush, knowing the way her thoughts were going now. But she was no longer a child, and her feelings towards Luke were far from the childish ones of their schooldays. She wanted him with a woman's need. She wanted to look at him, and hold him, and never let him go again.

As if something of her own intensity was transmitting to him, his gaze wandered over her, as if he had never see her before. They were sitting several feet apart now, yet the distance between them was as nothing. She shivered, knowing his feelings were changing as swiftly as hers had done. She could sense it as surely as she breathed.

'I thought we could go for a drive up to Pendennis Hill,' he said, moments before Granny Pen came in with a tray of hot drinks. 'I've got my dad's car outside, and a bit of petrol to spare, and I've got a yen to see our old haunts again while I've got the chance. This is a special leave, Amber, since I won't be home for Christmas, so I want to make the most of it. What do you say?'

She knew he was asking for more than a drive to visit their old haunts. She knew it and accepted it and agreed to it, lovingly and joyously.

Chapter Fourteen

As soon as they decently could, they left the cottage and Amber slid into the car seat beside Luke. The night wasn't cold, but she was shivering inside with a different kind of shivering now, knowing that whatever happened tonight was going to change her for ever. She knew what making love meant, but all those stumbling words from the teachers at school, all the snide sniggering from some of the older girls at the Club, all the times that Dolly had pretended to be so sophisticated and to know all about it . . . it all meant nothing, compared with her churning excitement.

They were necessarily close together in the small car, their legs touching, their breath warming the interior and steaming up the windows, and they didn't speak as the car took them up the steep, rounded climb to the top of the hill. It was fitting that it would be here that they finally professed their love and made it real.

Luke stopped the car on a grassy patch at the top, and when he turned off the engine the silence was like a living, breathing thing. Above them the grey sentinel of Pendennis Castle seemed like a benevolent, sleeping giant. Far below the sea glittered in the pale moonlight, where dozens of ships of all shapes and sizes, grey and menacing and yet oddly protective of the harbour, formed a magnificent backdrop, as still and silent now as a film setting. It was as if the whole world was waiting tonight; there were no air raids, no enemy planes, no burning buildings, just a breathtaking silence punctuated only by their heartbeats.

'Beautiful, isn't it?' Luke said at last, and she knew that for one moment more he was seeing the flotilla below through a seaman's eyes and not as a lover. Then he turned to her. 'But not as beautiful as you. I've been waiting so long for you to grow up, Amber, and then I went away and I almost missed it.'

She didn't know how to answer that, but there was no need, because he was pulling her into his arms, and his kisses were urgent and passionate and everything she had ever wanted. He was so dear and familiar, part of her life, and yet at the same time he was a thrilling stranger she had never known before, not like this.

'God, how I want to make love to you, Amber,' he was saying huskily, his mouth against hers. 'You'll never know how much I'm fighting against it.'

'Why are you fighting against it then?' she whispered. 'Don't you think I want it too? Don't you think I've wanted it all my life?'

She didn't know where the words came from, or

242

if it was proper to say them. She revelled in the fact that he wanted her, needed her, and loved her. Nothing and nobody else mattered.

'Are you saying that you wouldn't think too badly of me . . .'

She answered by taking his hand and pressing it to her breast. If he was the older one, then she was the wiser one when it came to these special moments that were going to deepen their relationship for ever.

'I would think badly of you if you didn't make me feel that you loved me as much as I love you,' she said. 'We're not children any more, Luke. The way I feel about you has nothing to do with childish feelings. You must know that.'

She held her breath as his hand moved over her breast. She hardly knew that the buttons on her blouse had somehow become undone until his hand had slipped inside it and she felt the warmth of it against her flesh. She gave a soft sigh of pleasure and yearned against him in the confines of the small car.

'This is ridiculous,' she heard him say roughly. 'It's not the place for us to make love for the first time, either. There's a blanket in the car and the caves will shelter us. Will you come with me?'

For one second she was tempted to give him one of her throwaway answers, one of the silly, teasing retorts they had so often thrown at one another. But this was not the time or place for that, either.

'It would take an earthquake to stop me,' she said softly.

They left the car and ran along the grass to where the slope was more gentle, down to the small caves they knew of old. Amber's heart raced erratically, but she knew that moments from now Luke would be irrevocably hers, and she would have gone to the ends of the earth for this night. They slithered down the grass until the opening of the first cave was alongside them. It was dark inside, smelling faintly of dampness and seaweed where the rough seas threw up the spume and sometimes even filled the lower part of the cave. But not tonight. Tonight the sea was calm, rippling gently far below them, and Luke spread the blanket on the sandy floor of the cave and drew her down beside him.

'My lovely girl,' he said huskily, stroking her tangled hair. 'My lovely, patient, grown-up girl. Do you see what you do to me?'

He took her hand, pulling it gently down over his body, where she could feel the hardness of him. She swallowed, frightened for a moment at the sheer power in a man's body, and as if he understood he quickly removed her hand and pressed it to his lips.

'There's no need to be afraid, Amber. I would never hurt you. I only want to prove to you how much I adore you.'

For a brief moment she felt a strange sense of anger. Perversely, in this intensely pleasurable moment she wanted to shriek at him that if he adored her so much, why had he left her alone for so long? Why leave her not knowing if he was alive or dead? Why never write the letters she longed to have from him?

The moment passed as quickly as it came. There would be time for explanations later, if there were any to be made – and if she wanted to hear them. Right now, as his hands began to explore her body in a way that was completely new to her, she wasn't sure she wanted to hear them at all. He was touching her as she had never been touched before, kissing her in places she had never been kissed before, and she was responding in a way she had never known before.

'Oh Luke, my Luke,' she breathed, hardly able to bear the exquisiteness of the sensations he was arousing in her.

Then at last she felt his body heavy on hers, and the small pain as he entered her for the first time brought only the faintest of cries from deep in her throat. And then she was rising with him, riding with him, and glorying in being one with him.

A long while later, wrapped together for warmth and comfort in the blanket now, they rose reluctantly from the floor of the cave. He had murmured so many incoherent words to her in the moments after their joining, and she had whispered them back, wild, emotional words of love and forever . . . and other words from Luke, about things he had seen and done which were indelibly part of the nightmare of being at sea, at war, a man's war. They were ugly words that she didn't want to hear, but which seemed to be torn out of him in a kind of release, as important to him as that other release that had bonded them together for ever.

'I've only got three days' leave,' he said abruptly when they were finally back in the car again, and still reluctant to leave this place. 'I didn't want to tell you before, but everything is so uncertain nowadays, and I think of us as the one constant thing in this world. I needed to be sure that you feel the same, sweetheart, and I think I know it now.'

Sometimes, Amber thought, with a flash of her usual spirit, men could be the blindest people on earth. How could he *not* have known, for all these years, the way she felt about him? But then his words registered properly.

'Only three days?' she echoed. 'It's not enough time, Luke.'

'It's never enough time, but it's all I've got, so we must make the most of it, sweetheart, and I promise I'll try to write to you more often in future.'

'It doesn't matter. Well, it does, but as long as I know you're safe, I won't worry too much.'

'Of course I'll be safe. I've got my piece of amber, and I've got my *real* Amber now, haven't I?'

You always did, she thought.

'I wish I could spend every minute with you in these three days, darling, but my mother wants us to visit her cousins who were bombed out in Plymouth, so that'll take care of tomorrow.'

'I thought you meant *we* were having three days together!'

'So did I until I heard about these cousins, but I could hardly say no, could I? I'd much rather be here with you, Amber, believe me.'

246

Somehow the war had intruded on them again. The mention of Luke's mother's cousins who had been bombed out in Plymouth was enough to remind them that their brief idyll was over. Inevitably, and almost against their will, they found themselves talking about people they knew who had been killed, most recently the girls at the Lannigan Hotel and poor Eddie Fielding.

'Who ever would have put Eddie Fielding down as a hero?' Luke said. 'But they're all heroes these days, especially the poor devils fighting in France.'

'What about you? It can't be any picnic going to sea and never knowing if your ship's going to be sunk, or for the airmen being blown out of the sky.'

'No, I wouldn't say it's a picnic for any of us. But we do it because we have to, and one day soon, please God, it'll all be over, and we'll all be coming home again. Most of us, anyway,' he added.

Amber shivered, not with pleasure now, but with a sense of foreboding. She didn't like this kind of talk. She didn't like it when the newspapers bragged about sinking the German battleships. She knew everyone cheered when they heard such news, but common sense told her that at the same time the German newspapers could be bragging about sinking one of their own. One day it could be Luke's ship.

She hugged his arm. They had been sitting in the car for too long now, and their mood had grown sombre along with the coolness of the night. The earlier euphoria of their love-making had vanished for the moment and Amber didn't know how to bring it back.

'You're cold,' he said. 'Do you want to come and have some supper with us? I was supposed to ask you earlier, but it sort of got forgotten,' he said with a grin.

She didn't particularly want to sit and make conversation with his mum and dad, but the alternative was going home, and she'd prefer to go back to the cottage much later when she was sure her gran would have gone to bed, rather than risk her suspicious looks about what had been happening that evening.

So she accepted the invitation to have supper with the Gillams, and had to be content with sitting across the table from Luke and interpreting the occasional smile he gave her, which told her there was no doubt that he was remembering too.

Three days' leave was impossibly short, especially when one day was taken out of it by visiting relatives in Plymouth. Amber was shamefully jealous of these cousins who had taken Luke's precious time away from her, and impatient for him to return for the one last day of his leave. When he did, it was a wet and blustery day, with an even worse evening, and no possibility of repeating the time they had already had, and nowhere they could go to be alone. In Granny Pen's cottage, the three of them played a game of monopoly until Granny Pen decided she was going to have an early night, as the weather was playing havoc with her rheumatics.

'Don't be too late now,' she said to Amber, 'and just remember I've got good hearing, so don't be thinking I don't know how young 'uns carry on with your canoodling. You take good care of yourself, Luke, and come back safely.'

'Thank you, Granny Pen,' he said solemnly, and only once they were sure that the last creak on the stairs meant she was closing her bedroom door did they burst into laughter.

'Oh, shush,' Amber gasped. 'You heard what she said. She knows how we young 'uns carry on and she's probably putting a tumbler to the ground to catch us with our canoodling.'

'I think that only applies when you put the tumbler to a wall, but it would be a shame to disappoint the old girl, wouldn't it?' Luke whispered. 'If she's expecting canoodling, then we should give her canoodling.'

It was all they could do, and, if she was honest, for Amber it was enough to sit close to him on the old sofa, his arms around her, and snuggle up to him. To snatch an extra hour of love-making in this cottage would take away the importance of that first lovely time, when there had been such a sense of freedom in the wild place they both loved, with the sounds of the sea all around them and only the sea-birds to hear. But they could kiss and hold one another, and know that their lives were inextricably bound together, as they had always been destined to be.

*

It wasn't until he had finally left Falmouth, and gone back to his mates, and back to the sea, that Amber realized anew the enormity of her loss. They had made love, and she had had something of him that no one else had ever had. They had shared one another's bodies, and now she had no idea when she would see him again. It had happened to thousands of others, but until it happened to her she hadn't fully realized what a wrench it would be. And this was one experience she had no intention of sharing with anyone else, least of all Dolly, who would want to know every detail, and was going to hear none.

She knew the dangers of making love before marriage, but she admitted that it was something that had not occurred to her at all while she and Luke were in the cave. If the unthinkable happened, and she found she was expecting a baby, she knew the shame and scandal would be too great for Granny Pen to bear. But it didn't happen, and when her monthlies began a week later, her relief was mixed with a weird kind of guilty resentment, because this would have been something of Luke's that no one could take from her. They would have had to kill her first, she thought fiercely. As it was, there was nothing to show that they had been together, only the feelings in her heart – and the large X in her diary on the day it happened.

She wasn't going to enjoy Christmas, either, knowing that he wouldn't be coming home on leave. In fact, she set out deliberately *not* to enjoy any of it, until Granny Pen at home, and the girls at work, began to get fed up with her. As Jennie and the others hung up decorations in the Forces' Club, they turned on her angrily.

'If you can't help, at least don't stand there with that sulky look on your face,' Jennie snapped at her. 'Do you think you're the only girl in the world who won't have her boy coming home for Christmas? Think yourself lucky he's coming home at all. There's plenty that won't.'

'Here,' she went on, tossing a bundle of tinsel at Amber. 'Hang this around the tree and then I'll tell you some news to make you smile.'

'What sort of news?' Amber said sullenly, not relishing the way she was being made to feel so petulant, yet knowing she deserved it.

'We had a visit from some of the chaps at the GI base last night while you were off. They want to put on a Christmas party here for the local infants, and they're providing the food and everything.'

'Crikey, are they?' Amber said.

'Yes, and since you're doing so little work around here, you can have the job of going round the infant schools to spread the word. Perhaps it'll cheer you up.'

It cheered her already. Amber thought it was such a sweet and generous gesture from the Yanks, but having seen the way they always stopped to chat to the kids and passed on sweets and chocolate, it was no wonder the friendship was mutual. If so-called Anglo-American relations started with the children,

Amber thought, then it wasn't doing such a bad job.

It was good to get out of the club too. It wasn't fair to take it out on everybody else just because she was feeling miserable. That was just what people did, though, it wasn't peculiar to her. She vowed to make it up to Granny Pen when she went home that evening, and since she had souvenirs very much on her mind now, she stopped at Veal's Craft Shop to buy her something.

'Still working at that Forces' Club, are you?' Myra said, as if it was something immoral.

'Yep. Still stuck behind the counter here, are you?'

'It was good enough for you, as I remember, miss, so don't look down your nose at me. Were you wanting something? If not, I've got work to do.'

'How's Mrs Veal?' Amber remembered to ask. 'Is she well?'

'Well enough. Now then, tell me what you want, and if you're looking for a job, there's no vacancy.'

Amber bit back a tart reply. There was no point, and the sooner she was away from this unpleasant woman the better. On impulse she chose one of the lighthouse models that Gary had bought for his girl. If Granny Pen didn't like it, Amber could always put it in her bedroom and start her own collection.

She was glad to get out of the shop. Once, she had loved the aromatic scents of candles and herbs, but it didn't benefit from having Myra's cheap perfume added to it. Perhaps she was hoping to attract a GI for herself, Amber thought, stifling a laugh. He'd have to be wearing a blindfold first.

She was in a far happier mood by the time she had visited the infant schools and passed on the information about the Christmas party. She was greeted as some kind of divine messenger, she told Granny Pen later. The kids went wild and cheered at the prospect of having a party laid on for them by the Americans.

'It's a very generous thing for them to do,' Granny Pen agreed. 'The poor little dabs all have to grow up early in these uncertain times – and so do you older ones, too.'

'What does that mean?'

'It means it's a shame to let go of childhood before you have to, Amber. There's time enough for falling in love and settling down. There are plenty of years ahead for that.'

'Tell that to my friends at school who won't have the chance for any of it!'

'I think you know what I mean, my dear. I've heard tales about what some of the local girls and the Americans get up to. Nice and friendly they may be, but once this war is over they'll be going home to their own friends and families, and it doesn't pay to get too close.'

'Well, I wasn't getting too close to Gary, and I never intended to, either. He's got a girl of his own and he showed me her photo. He's just a friend, that's all.'

'And what of Luke? Is he still just a friend?'

Amber felt as if her blood was curdling inside her. She didn't want to remember that everyone said that Granny Pen could *see* things, with or without the tea leaves and the palm-reading. She didn't want to think that Granny Pen had the slightest notion, real or imaginary, of that one magical evening with Luke in the cave below Pendennis Hill. It was private, and it was theirs alone.

'He's my best friend,' she said defensively. 'He always has been and I hope he always will be.'

'Then if he's the one you want, you have my blessing.'

She had never spoken so frankly before, and Amber stared at her in astonishment for a moment, until Granny Pen sighed and patted her hand.

'I wasn't born yesterday, Amber love. A girl has a certain glow about her when she finds the right young man for her, and you have it every time you speak about Luke, whether you realise it or not. Just be aware that although the Americans are charming young men too, a reputation can very soon be sullied.'

Amber breathed more easily. Granny Pen wasn't referring to the certain glow she must have had when she came home that night, it was just a friendly general warning. Impulsively, she kissed her gran's leathery cheek.

'I know, and you don't need to worry about me, Gran. I think I've always known that Luke was the one for me, and before you say that sixteen – nearly seventeen – is too young to know my own mind, well, it isn't. It just *isn't*.'

She finished so fiercely that Granny Pen smiled. 'I wouldn't dare to dispute it!'

The preparations for the infants' Christmas party arranged and paid for by the Americans caused plenty of excitement in the town. Not all of the Yanks had something to celebrate, though, as word filtered through about casualties and fatalities, and at one time Amber feared that Gary had been among them. But he turned up again, like a bad penny, he said, though with a certain tightening around his jaw that hadn't been there before. Like most of them, he rarely spoke about where he had been, or how bad it had been.

There had been another letter from Luke at the beginning of December, and because they knew all forces' letter were censored before being sent home, he was guarded in the things he said. She had to read between the lines to know what his real feelings were, and how much he was missing her. He missed her even more now, he said, because of that last brief leave together – and she knew exactly what he meant by that. It also meant he was thinking of her, and remembering how close they had been, the way she remembered it, and it warmed her heart.

Dolly's letter, just before Christmas, was full of complaints.

'I'm really fed up with my mum and Uncle Joe, kissing and slurping all over the place. That's when they ain't squabbling, of course. I may come down and see you in the summer, Amber, as long as Jerry leaves us alone. A neighbour along the road from us had an unexploded bomb on her doorstep and it really put the wind up us all until the Army chaps came and disarmed it. A real dishy lot of chaps they were, too. Me and Mum made them cups of tea while the poor old biddy was having the vapours or something, and I nearly got a date with one of them.'

She didn't explain why it was only nearly, Amber thought with a grin. She thought about what Dolly said about coming down for a visit, and couldn't decide if she would welcome it or not. She couldn't say no, but time and distance had changed them both, and if they had been rivals of a sort when they were children, how much more would they be now that they were virtually grown up? She knew her gran would say it was unworthy of her, so she simply didn't reply to that part of Dolly's letter at all. If it happened it happened, and if it didn't, well, it didn't.

The Christmas party took precedence over everything at the Forces' Club that month, and even though one or two people mentioned that it would be nice to make it an annual event, the main hope was that it wouldn't be necessary because the war would soon be over and the Yanks would all have gone home by this time next year.

But there was no denying the infants' joy in having the kind of food laid on for them that few of the youngest ones had even seen before. The Americans organised games for them as well, and every child went home with a balloon and what their hosts called a bagful of goodies. It was easy to forget there was a war on at such times, and if the Jerries were also taking advantage of the special season to temporarily slow down their bombing raids, people could only offer up a heartfelt prayer of thankfulness.

'Do you think that somewhere in occupied France the German soldiers are doing this for the French kids?' Amber asked Jennie idly. The other woman snorted.

'If they are, I doubt that many French mothers would let their kids attend. The Jerries might do it to try to curry favour, but it's a different situation in France. The Yanks here are our allies, not our enemy. If the Jerries offered to put on a party for the French kids they'd probably be spat on even if they risked getting shot for it.'

Amber was shocked at her vehemence, and Jennie shrugged.

'Don't look like that, kid. My old grandad was in the first lot, and he told me a thing or two about Jerries. Not that I think our lot would be any better if it came to the point. You don't bother about manners when a bloke's pointing a rifle at your head or sticking a bayonet in your gut. It's everyone for himself then. I rarely talk about it, and I'm not mentioning it again, but take it from me, Amber, nobody behaves in a civilized way when they're fighting for their lives. These Hollywood pictures don't tell you the half of it, believe me.'

Amber hadn't expected any of this, and she wasn't

sure how it had all started, but since Jennie seemed genuinely disturbed she changed the conversation quickly. It was only later that she learned from Granny Pen that Jennie's grandad had been terribly wounded and shell-shocked in the First World War and still suffered unbearable nightmares because of it, all these years later.

It made Amber wonder uneasily about the after effects of being involved in the fighting, let alone being wounded, and if people ever really got over it. She was still thinking about it as the church bells rang out on that Christmas Day when the war had already lasted for more than four years. Every Christmas and new year that came and went, they hoped desperately that this would be the turning point, until another one came and went . . .

Chapter Fifteen

In the first few months of 1944 Amber had to accept the fact that letters from Luke were going to be sparse, if they came at all. Whenever she saw his mother she asked about him, and got the same reply: that there was no use worrying until they had something to worry about. Mrs Gillam seemed so calm about everything, fumed Amber – not that she thought Luke's mother could be so calm underneath. But such complacency didn't do much to help somebody who was only seventeen, and aching to see her sweetheart again. She longed for him with a fever of impatience she had never known before.

Then, two months after her seventeenth birthday, something happened that overshadowed everything else: Luke, the bombing raids, the floods of more and more Americans coming into the area in preparation for the Allied invasion of France. It was no secret any more that it was going to happen. The only question in everyone's mind was when.

Amber was up early on that Sunday morning in April. It was going to be a fine spring day, and there were wild daffodils pushing up in their small garden among the cabbages and carrots that took the place of other flowers now. It was so unusual for Granny Pen not to be up and about that Amber decided to take her a cup of tea in bed. She knew her gran probably wouldn't thank her for it, since she considered such a thing as being more for the upper classes who had nothing better to do with their time. She would also be horrified to think she had overslept.

Amber tapped on her bedroom door and then pushed it open. Granny Pen still lay neatly in her bed, the way she always did, in a way that was a marvel to Amber, whose bedclothes resembled more of a jumble sale by morning. She put the tea down on the little side table beside her gran's bed, and spoke teasingly.

'Come on, Granny lazybones. If you don't get a move on, it'll be time for church before you're up and dressed.'

When there was no response, Amber felt the first flicker of fear run through her. Her legs were reluctant to move as she got nearer to the bed and put out a shaking hand to touch Granny's Pen's cheek. It was cold, and there was no reaction from her at all. Amber flinched back, her heart thumping violently.

'Wake up, Granny Pen,' she croaked. 'Please wake up. Please don't be dead.'

As the word was wrenched out of her, she let out a small scream, because it was blindingly obvious that the old woman in the bed was dead. And Amber was seventeen and she didn't know what to do. Grief hadn't yet broken through her instant panic, but it would, and she knew that it would.

She felt as though time had stopped and had no meaning any more. She felt as if she stood transfixed for hours, and yet it was only seconds before she was sobbing, and backing away from the woman who had always given her such love and care, and was no longer there. In those first horrific moments, that was all she could think about. There was no supernatural sense of souls hovering, or afterlives, or angels watching over her from some ethereal nowhere. There was only a great feeling of nothingness and loss.

She turned and ran down the stairs of the cottage, still sobbing. She was breathing so hard and so fast that she felt as if she was suffocating, and she had to get outside in the fresh air because the house itself was stifling her.

Over the fence their neighbour, Mrs Phillips, was cutting one of her cabbages for Sunday dinner, and looked up in astonishment at Amber's obvious distress. The cabbage dropped from her hand as she came quickly towards the fence.

'Whatever's wrong, Amber love?'

'Can you come?' Amber gasped. 'It's Granny Pen. She's still in bed and she's not moving. She won't wake up.'

It would have taken a team of horses to drag the dreaded word from her lips again, but it was clear to Mrs Phillips what she meant.

'I'll just fetch Father,' she said quickly, 'and then we'll come and see what's what, my dear.'

She always called her husband Father, just as Mrs Veal had done, Amber thought wildly, and found herself wondering what they had called their own fathers and if they had ever got them confused. Thinking about anything, however inane, was better than knowing she had to go back upstairs, to face the truth of what had happened during the night. She felt the choking sobs rising in her throat again as the questions began to storm through her mind. When had it happened, and how long had Granny Pen lain there like that . . . and had it hurt, this dying . . . or had she simply drifted from one sleep to another?

The neighbours came around to the cottage and Mrs Phillips took Amber firmly by the arm as Father walked behind them, clearing his throat all the way.

'Now you go inside, Amber love, and put the kettle on for a hot, strong cup of tea. 'Tis always the best remedy in cases of shock, and 'tis clear that you've had one this morning. Me and Father will go upstairs and check on Granny Pen and see whether we need the doctor or the undertaker, or both.'

She said it brutally, knowing it would shake Amber, but it was best for the little maid to accept it, rather than have false hopes, she thought silently. From the sound of it, she was quite sure Granny Pen would have died in the night, and it was exactly what she and Father found when they went to see the old lady, looking as peaceful as if she was sleeping the sleep of the just.

Amber heard their heavy steps on the stairs a few minutes later, by which time she had just about managed to fill the kettle with water, spilling half of it over herself, and put it on the gas. Now she was carrying a tray of cups into the parlour and trying not to drop it with her shaking hands.

'Sit yourself down a minute, Amber, and we'll have that tea when the kettle's boiled. Meanwhile, Father will run and get the doctor.'

'Is she all right then?' Amber gasped wildly as Father left them to do his errand.

Mrs Phillips shook her head sorrowfully. 'Well, my dear, if you're asking if she's all right in this world, then she's not, but I daresay she's more than all right in the next. She'll be up in heaven right now, reading the tea leaves of the angels, I wouldn't be surprised.'

This was too much for Amber. She banged the tray of cups down on the table, rattling them so hard it was a wonder they didn't all crack.

'How stupid you are,' she raged. 'My gran's lying dead upstairs, and all you can say is that she's reading the bloody tea leaves for the angels in heaven!'

She swore without realising it, and she had never been so rude to a neighbour before, but nothing was normal any more. She registered that Mrs Phillips had delicately avoided mentioning the undertaker again, but he would have to be informed, and he would come to the cottage, all hushed-voiced and sombre-faced and black-suited, and they would bring the hated burial box into the cottage and take her gran away . . . She found herself gasping for breath, and the room jazzed in front of her eyes, and before she knew what was happening she felt Mrs Phillips thrust her head between her knees and tell her to breathe slowly and deeply.

When she had done so for a few minutes, the urge to vomit and faint had diminished, and she felt ashamed of her outburst when the woman was only doing her best for her. She sat up carefully, trying to be more calm.

'I'm sorry,' she whispered.

'Lord love you, my dear, if a body can't let rip in times of trouble, when can they? No offence taken, my love. You cuss all you want if it makes you feel better.'

It didn't, and she knew it wouldn't. But she gave Mrs Phillips a wan smile after she had fussed about making the tea, and insisted that Amber drink the hot sweet mixture. There were tea leaves floating about on top, and without warning the tears flowed again, as she imagined her gran taking the empty cup, turning it upside down, swirling the leaves about in the bottom and giving one of her mysterious prophecies. Well, Amber didn't need that now. She knew what the future held. She was totally alone in the world from now on.

'I wish Luke was here,' she whimpered against her will, and was immediately thankful that Mrs Phillips hadn't heard her since she was tidying up for the doctor's visit.

Why did people always do that, Amber wondered in a fit of pique? Didn't doctors have untidy houses as well as ordinary folk? She knew she was still thinking of anything but the reality of what lay ahead of her.

The doctor came quite soon, and went straight upstairs with Mrs Phillips. Amber knew guiltily that she was letting everyone else take over, and simply allowed them to do it. There would be time enough when she had to do the necessary things after they had taken Granny Pen away, all the sorting out to be done, the clothes, the personal possessions that were so private when a person was alive, and became public property for any prying eyes after their death. She took a shuddering breath. At least there would be no other prying eyes but hers for her gran, she thought fiercely. It was her first positive thought since early morning.

She hadn't realized she had shut her eyes tightly, as if to will all other thoughts away, until she heard the doctor's voice.

'Amber, my dear, I have to tell you that your grandmother died in her sleep sometime during the night. It must have been a peaceful passing, because there are no signs of any distress, so you should take that as a small consolation.'

Amber bit her lips hard. If she hadn't she would have fallen into what Granny Pen always called one of her contrary moods, picking on every annoying little word that wasn't absolutely accurate. People didn't *pass* anywhere. They died. And how she hated that word *should*. Nobody could tell another person how they should feel, or react, or grieve. Until it happened to you, you had no idea how you would feel, and there was no *should* about it.

And oh God, she was being so petty now, when everyone only wanted to help. She knew that. But nobody could help. This was something you had to face alone, whether you were the dying or the bereaved.

'What happens next?' she muttered, since the doctor was obviously waiting for a reply.

'I'm going to issue a death certificate,' he said briskly, 'and then I will alert the undertaker to come and attend to the body. There are certain things to be done, Amber, and then he will make arrangements to take her to the Chapel of Rest. You don't have to think about that right now,' he added, seeing her flinch. 'It's a lot to take in for a young girl. It's unfortunate that it's a Sunday and people will be at church, but I'm sure Mr Horseley will be here as soon as possible in the circumstances.'

'Well, I'm sorry to inconvenience him in having Gran die on a Sunday,' Amber heard herself snap before she could stop herself.

Mrs Phillips drew in her breath at such impertinence, which almost amounted to blasphemy, but the doctor merely patted Amber's hand.

'We can't determine the moment of our birth or our death, my dear. We leave that to the Almighty to decide.'

'Or Hitler,' Amber muttered, hardly knowing

where the words were coming from, but seemingly unable to stop them.

'Or Hitler indeed,' the doctor said, glancing at Mrs Phillips. 'Do you know if there's any brandy in the house, Mrs Phillips? I think a medicinal drop might be advisable just now.'

'In the sideboard,' Amber said mechanically. She knew where everything was kept. It was still their house, hers and her gran's. But she supposed it was *her* house now. Just hers.

She drank the bitter-tasting stuff that was thrust into her hand and let it wash down her throat, burning and rasping. Or was that just the result of so many tears? She could hear the mumble of voices between the doctor and her neighbour, and then he left, and Mrs Phillips took her cold hands in hers.

'You're not to be alone, Amber love. You're to come and have some dinner with us, and come and sleep in our cottage tonight.'

Amber looked at her. 'Why would I want to do that? I've got a bed here, and I can't leave Gran here alone.'

Even as she said it, she felt an odd sense of calm wash over her, and she knew she wasn't sending Granny Pen away to some anonymous Chapel of Rest. Not yet, anyway. This was her home, and once the undertaker had done whatever he had to do, Granny Pen was going to stay here in her own bed for at least one more night. After that, well, she would decide what to do then.

'Then I'll sleep here too,' Mrs Phillips said. 'I'll

manage perfectly well on the sofa. It's not right for a young maid like you to be alone in the house with a corpse.'

'Don't call her that! She's still my gran, and she wouldn't want to be called by such a horrible name.'

'Well, I'm sorry,' the neighbour said uncomfortably. 'But I'll still sleep here for tonight, Amber, and you'll be glad of the company, whatever you might think. As for your dear gran, she's had a long life and deserves her rest.'

Amber bit her lips hard again, thinking they would be black and blue if she didn't stop it, but knowing she would probably explode after such a daft statement. She was perfectly sure her gran hadn't wanted a permanent rest, and she wasn't ready for it any more than Amber was.

Later, Mrs Phillips told Father that she hoped the young maid wasn't going to go all weird. It happened sometimes, and it was well known that Granny Pen had had the second sight, so her granddaughter probably wasn't far behind.

The morning passed in a kind of nightmare for Amber. Her neighbour insisted that she should go next door with them to have some dinner, although it was all she could do to pick at the food when it eventually arrived. Crazy things kept floating in and out of her mind. Granny Pen would never sit down to dinner again. Granny Pen never liked to miss church the way she had done today, and now she would never be going to church on a Sunday morning again.

When Father muttered that the undertaker was coming along the road, they all went back to Amber's cottage, and suddenly it seemed as if it was full of people. The undertaker's assistant was with him, and she watched them go upstairs to her gran's bedroom, not wanting to imagine what was going on up there, nor how indignant Granny Pen would be at having certain things done to her, of which Mrs Phillips had found gruesomely necessary to inform Amber.

By the time the undertaker and his assistant came back downstairs Amber was near to hysteria. They had a strange smell about them that she couldn't identify that made her long for fresh air again. But she knew they wanted to speak to her and she made herself listen to what they had to say.

No, she didn't want Granny Pen removed just yet. This was her home, and she had a right to remain in it a while longer. But yes, they could bring the coffin and take her away in time to prepare for the burial. Until then, Amber wanted her gran to remain in her own bed.

'It's not usual, Miss Penry,' the undertaker said. 'Most folk want to be settled decently in their coffins for friends and family to come and pay their last respects.'

'Well, I don't want people to come gawping at my gran, and most folk don't want to be settled in their coffins at all,' she said shrilly. 'What's wrong with her staying in her own bed for a few days longer, anyway? Is there any objection to it?'

'Not really,' the man said uneasily. 'But let's say just for two more days at the most. By then, well, it will be time, my dear.'

Amber could still hardly take in that she was obliged to be making plans for Granny Pen's burial, but finally it was all arranged and after the undertaker and his assistant left to make the arrangements with the vicar on Amber's behalf, she looked at Mrs Phillips.

'What did he mean, that it would be time? What wasn't he telling me?'

Mrs Phillips cleared her throat delicately, trying to find the right words. It was her more practical husband who provided them.

'The weather's getting very warm already, Amber, and even though it's nothing like a hot country, I was in India during the last war, and they always buried their dead the next day because of the heat. It turns 'em, you see,' he added gruffly.

'Turns 'em?' she echoed.

He cleared his throat noisily. 'You know what happens to dead meat when it goes off? Well, we're no different from meat when we go off, see?'

For a second Amber didn't understand, and then she felt the bile rise in her throat at the picture he was painting. She scrambled to her feet, her heart beating painfully fast.

'That's *horrible*, and I wish you'd never told me.'

'Well, you would ask,' the man said. 'I didn't mean to upset you, but it's best if you realize that the undertaker knows what's best for your old gran. Now then, if you want me to do any errands, you just tell me, my dear, and my missus will stay here with you for the rest of the day.'

She tried to will the image of her gran *turning* out of her mind and concentrate on what he was saying now. Of course, there were people to be told. She couldn't go back to work until after the burial, so her employers had to know. She wished desperately that Luke was here, but he wasn't, but she knew his mother would want to know what had happened. And there was Dolly. She caught her breath on a sob, wishing so hard that Dolly was here with her no-nonsense approach to life and death and everything in between.

'I'll give you a list,' she gasped, knowing that if she didn't do something with her hands she would burst into tears again. 'There's only Jennie at the Forces' Club, and Mrs Gillam at the boatyard, and tomorrow it's very important that I send a telegram to Dolly in London.'

'You just write it out for me and I'll see that it's sent off in the morning,' Mr Phillips said. 'Do you think the little maid will come for the burying then?'

'I know she will,' said Amber, knowing no such thing, but mentally crossing her fingers and toes and everything else.

With Mr Phillips spreading the word, the news that Granny Pen had died got around the town very quickly. All afternoon and into the evening people came to the cottage, offering sympathy and gifts of flowers. Some people merely left them at the gate rather than intruding on a family's grief. As well as flowers, there was garden produce and a few bags of home-made biscuits, until Amber wondered if everyone thought she was about to starve just because her gran was dead.

She had to keep repeating the word to herself now, making it real, making it less bizarre than it had been that early morning when she had taken her gran a cup of tea. It was impossible to think that had only been this morning. It seemed a life-time ago, and yet it seemed like only a second ago. How long had it taken her to die, she wondered? Did she know, or had she simply stopped breathing in her sleep? She still couldn't get the ghoulish questions out of her mind, nor had she yet gone back up those stairs to see her gran, laid out so nicely now, according to Mrs Phillips, and looking a real picture, with all the lines in her face smoothed away.

One or two people, old friends of Granny Pen, had asked to see her, and Amber had felt obliged to allow it, even if she couldn't understand their need. Why did they do it? she raged. Why would anyone *want* to do it?

'It's to say a last goodbye,' Mrs Phillips told her, over so many endless cups of tea that Amber felt she was going to burst with it all. 'And you must do it too, Amber. Your gran would expect it, and she would want you to.'

'I can't,' Amber whispered. 'I just can't. Not now the undertaker has done those things to her.'

'She looks beautiful, like a young girl,' Mrs

Phillips went on, which was a comment that could have made Amber laugh out loud had she not felt more like weeping. 'It's important for you to touch her, Amber, and to kiss her too. It will bring to a close the lifetime you've spent with her.'

Amber listened to this in horror. Perhaps when you were old you could talk about such things without feeling the hairs on the back of your neck curl up and freeze. Perhaps you became more accepting of death when you were old and it wasn't so far away . . . and then, in an instant, she remembered all the young people who were dying in the war, even her own old school friends, and she knew how their mothers and fathers would want to hug them and kiss them for one last heartbreaking time before they were committed to the ground for ever. And she felt ashamed of her weakness.

'Have I done wrong in wanting to keep Gran here?' she said, choked.

'No, love, but I think you might ask Father to see the undertaker again tomorrow and have her removed to the Chapel of Rest quite soon. It's more dignified, and it would be what she wanted, I'm sure.'

'Before that happens, then, I must say goodbye to her properly.'

'Good girl. She'll like that.'

Amber didn't bother to comment on the fact that she spoke in the present tense, as if her gran was still here, and would be aware of the moment when Amber went to see her, and touch her, and kiss her

. . . if she could. At least she intended to try, and she had to admit that she was disbelieving that Mrs Phillips thought Granny Pen looked like a young girl again. It was something Amber couldn't imagine, never having seen her as anything but her old gran.

In the early evening, Luke's mother arrived. She took Amber into her arms without a word, until the girl had managed to stop sobbing against her shoulder.

'My poor little love, this must have been a terrible shock to you,' she said at last. 'As soon as I heard I wrote a letter to Luke, and then I came right here.'

'Thank you,' Amber whispered, thinking she would have done that herself, if only she had been left alone long enough. But it seemed that people never wanted to leave you alone when you had been bereaved.

'I'd like to say goodbye to your gran,' Mrs Gillam said, when she had accepted her cup of tea from Mrs Phillips, who told her cheerfully that until Amber felt better she was taking over as general housekeeper-cum-dogsbody. 'Will you take me to her, Amber?'

Amber took a deep breath. This was the moment, then, and if she couldn't yet do it on her own, who better to share it with than the mother of her sweetheart? She nodded and they went upstairs together, to where the sweet, sickly smell drifted out from her gran's bedroom. Mrs Gillam walked straight to the bed where Granny Pen lay, the sheets neatly covering her body now, in total repose. Luke's mother said a few soft words that Amber couldn't hear, then put her fingers to her lips and pressed them gently on to Granny Pen's cheek. She glanced back to where Amber still stood uncertainly near the door, and gave her a gentle smile.

'She never hurt you in her lifetime, Amber, and she won't hurt you now.'

As she held out her hand Amber walked slowly towards her until she was looking down at her gran's face. She didn't look like a young girl, she thought, but she didn't look creepy, either. She just looked like her gran.

Luke's mother moved quietly away from the bed until there were just the two them together, the grandmother and the young Cornish maid she had always loved as devotedly as if she was her own child. Amber knelt by her side and tentatively stroked the grey hair away from her forehead, knowing those caring eyes would never open again, and that sweet mouth would never give her words of wisdom again. But she would always remember them, she thought fiercely. She would never forget the woman who had always meant more to her than anyone else in the world. But Mrs Phillips had been right. Granny Pen had lived a long life and deserved her rest. She leaned forward and kissed the papery cheek and said her last goodbye, knowing she would never set foot in this room again while her gran remained here.

'I love you, Gran,' she whispered. 'I'll always love you.'

*

The funeral had been arranged for the following Friday. Before then, with Granny Pen now at the Chapel of Rest, Mrs Phillips had insisted that Amber should go next door and play a game of cards with Father while she sorted out her gran's bedroom and got it thoroughly aired, and took the bedding away to be washed.

Amber couldn't imagine anything stranger than wanting to play a game of cards with Father, but she did as she was told, still moving like an automaton as everything led up to the day when the final goodbyes were to be said. Her nerves were constantly on edge, and even though Mrs Phillips still insisted on sleeping with her each night, the sound of her snuffling breathing from the bed that had been Dolly's was enough to keep Amber awake for hours.

The night before the funeral Amber was especially jittery. It was a necessary ritual to get through, and there had been plenty of those in the town lately, both for young and old, but it didn't make the thought of it any easier when it was someone close to you. She was trying hard to enjoy the vegetable stew that Mrs Phillips had prepared when there was a knock at the cottage door, and she left the meal thankfully as she went to answer it.

'Thank Gawd,' said Dolly. 'It's starting to rain and I didn't fancy getting soaked as well as bleedin' well exhausted from the train journey. Are you going to let me in, gel? I need to drop this suitcase before my bleedin' arms drop off!'

Amber simply stared at her for a moment, and then they were hugging one another and weeping on one another's shoulders until Dolly shrugged her off and pushed her way into the cottage.

'I daresay you've done enough crying in the past few days,' she said, 'so I've come to cheer you up. I can always kip down in Granny Pen's old room if you've got next door in to keep you company,' she added, not missing the way Mrs Phillips was looking her up and down. 'Unless you've moved in there yourself?'

'No, I haven't,' Amber said quickly, never having thought of such a thing. 'But your old bed's still in my room, and I expect Mrs Phillips will be glad to get back home now you're here for the funeral.'

'Oh, don't worry, I'm here for more than that,' Dolly declared. 'I've come to stay.'

Chapter Sixteen

Before Dolly came back, Amber had written a long, impassioned letter to Luke, pouring out her heart to him and being far more emotional in a letter than she had ever been before. She had no idea when he would receive it, or when he would be able to reply. She knew his mother had written to tell him of Granny Pen's death, but she also needed to do it herself, to feel that bit closer to him while she wrote the words that filled her heart.

On the day of the funeral, a huge number of people had turned up to pay their own respects to a well-known figure who had been in the town for so many years. She was known to all, and even feared by some who were nervous of her powers and her second sight, whether it was real or imaginary. But whatever people thought of her, they could never ignore her, and according to Dolly that was better than being famous.

'How do you make that out?' Amber said, trying to sound interested. Glad as she had been to see Dolly, she was quickly realizing she could find nothing in common with this newly smart girl, whose hair was an even brighter shade of blonde than before, which Mrs Phillips had said darkly owed a lot to the peroxide bottle.

'Stands to reason.' Dolly sniffed. 'When you're famous, you've got something to live up to and you can soon be forgotten when somebody better comes along, like them film stars. But when you're a bit weird, people remember you.'

'You're daft,' Amber said.

'And you're still a bit weird as well. People know who you are, don't they? So that proves my point.'

'No it doesn't. They know me because I've always lived here. So are we having an argument already?' Amber said impatiently.

Dolly laughed. 'Why not? It beats moping about the place. By the way, how's Luke? Have you heard from him lately, or is that all off now?'

For one stupendous second, Amber felt like crowing that she and Luke were as close as one person now. They were soul-mates – and body-mates, she thought with a delicious little shiver – and after that evening in the cave nothing could separate them again. But then she sobered, because they were as physically separated by the war as if they were poles apart. And she didn't want to spoil the memory of that perfect evening by confiding in Dolly daydream either. She jealously guarded that memory from everyone but herself and Luke.

'I told you we weren't so close any more,' she said as coolly as she could. 'It was just a crush, that's all.'

Dolly grinned. 'So when he comes marching home again, you won't mind if I have a go at him.'

Amber felt a jolt in her stomach. 'I didn't say that!'

'Too bad, kid, but all's fair in love and war, isn't it? Anyway, I've still got to check out all these Yanks in the town. I wonder if I could get my old job back at the Forces' Club,' she said thoughtfully. 'You could put in a good word for me when you go back to work on Monday.'

'You really are planning to stay then?' Amber said, hoping she didn't sound too dismayed. A visit was one thing. Moving in for good was something else.

'For a while,' Dolly said with a shrug, 'but you know me. I get fidgety if I'm in one place for too long, so I doubt if it will be for ever.'

Praise be, thought Amber.

It was a week since Granny Pen had died, a turbulent week as far as Amber was concerned, but, as everybody kept telling her, life had to go on, and you had no choice but to go on with it. Either that or hang up your boots for good, and at seventeen it seemed a waste of a future to even think of such a thing.

Besides, Granny Pen would want her to carry on and be happy. She knew that without being told, and on the day after the funeral she and Dolly had set about going through her gran's belongings properly. It was a task she had hated to think about, but it was far better to do it with Dolly's help than with Mrs Phillips poking into Granny Pen's private things.

They planned to take the boxes of clothes to the Red Cross, knowing they would find good homes from there, what with clothes rationing and bombed-out people and all. If Dolly had had all this stuff in London, she told Amber, they would have done a roaring trade down the market among the old biddies.

For all her sharp remarks, Dolly proved to be a godsend when it came to dealing with it all in a practical way, and one of the only times Amber found herself crying was when she packed up all her gran's playing cards and suchlike, vowing never to look at them herself. Although the tears also began to flow when she finally made herself open her gran's cardboard memory box.

'What the heck's all that stuff?' Dolly said, as they sat on the bed in Granny Pen's room.

'It's things she'd saved over the years. Special things that meant a lot to her. They belong to me now, and I'm not getting rid of any of it.'

'You're welcome to it. Most of it's a lot of old tat. Who's that old geyser?' Dolly asked, pointing to a faded sepia photograph.

'I think that's my grandad. I never knew him, but Gran showed me his photo once. And this one –' she picked up another faded photo and ran her fingers lovingly over it – 'this one is my mum and dad. I told you I never knew them, either, and Gran could never bear to have them on show, but sometimes she let me have a look at them. Not for years now, though. I'd almost forgotten what they looked like.'

'You look a bit like your mother,' Dolly said, 'and I daresay you did just as well with your gran bringing you up. My mum's never been much good, and my dad never could get the better of her.'

'That's an awful thing to say, especially after your dad was killed in the war.'

Dolly shrugged. 'You probably had it better than me, with your gran doting on you. You've seen my mum, and you know what she's like, and you might as well know that we had an almighty bust-up before I came down here, which is why I packed my bags and left.'

'So that's why you came!'

Dolly glanced at her, seeing the red spots of anger on Amber's face now.

'I came because you sent me the telegram saying Granny Pen had died, idiot. It just so happened that I was on the point of jumping on a train to anywhere, what with my mum harping on at me all the time, and getting fed up with the bleedin' air raids that have started again. They call it the little blitz now because although it wasn't as bad as the first one, it's bad enough.'

She was rabbiting on because she was suddenly nervous, realizing how she had upset Amber. But that was Dolly, always saying things before she stopped to think, no matter who got upset.

She suddenly sat down heavily on the bed, glaring

at Amber, and trying to blink back the unexpected shine of tears in her eyes.

'You think I'm hard, don't you? You think I don't care that the nice old girl has popped it. Well, I do care. She was good to me. I cared about her a lot. This was the first decent home I'd lived in, what with my mum gallivanting about whenever she got the chance, and my dad too feeble to stand up to her. You were the lucky one, Amber, even without a mum and dad.'

'Crikey, if you don't stop you'll have me bawling again in a minute,' Amber said with a gulp. 'Are you serious about working at the Forces' Club, by the way?'

'Do you want me to?'

'Of course I do.' Well, what else could she say? It would be cruel to say she didn't want Dolly there, or that she was jealous of Dolly's easy chat with the Yanks, or that she would prefer Dolly to be anywhere but here!

It was easily arranged, and another pair of hands was never refused. With so many servicemen in the area now, the club was always full to bursting in the evenings and in the daytime, too, when the men wanted somewhere to go for recreation. All the talk, however guarded, was of the coming invasion plans. There was still no date mentioned, but the town rattled with the sounds of despatch riders going to and fro from the various barracks.

Within a couple of weeks, Dolly had asked to use

Granny Pen's bedroom, and although Amber was in two minds about whether or not to let her have it, it was a relief to both of them to sleep in separate rooms. Amber was fed up with hearing of Dolly's dates with any Yank who would ask her out, and she was continually fretting over the long silence from Luke.

'You really must try not to worry, my dear,' his mother told her, whenever they met at church. 'I'm sure we'll both hear from him soon.'

She said it almost as a mantra, and Amber wondered if it was to reassure herself as much as Amber. Or did older people find it easier to be patient than those who were longing to feel their sweetheart's arms around them again? Against her will, Amber knew the memory of that evening in the cave was beginning to fade, and she couldn't bear it if that happened. She wanted to keep it fresh and new, and she was superstitiously afraid that if she lost it for ever it would mean that something bad had happened to Luke. She knew that Dolly would scoff at such omens, but Dolly didn't have her Cornish intuition . . . and, anyway, it was something to hold on to.

If the town had been bristling with army and amphibious vehicles before, and the harbour almost blocked by ships, it was overwhelmed with them over the next weeks. Excitement was high in everyone's mind now, because an Allied invasion would surely put an end to it all, and they could return to normal living again. Amber hadn't seen Gary for weeks, and chose to assume that he had been sent somewhere else on manoeuvres, rather than think the worst. And then, very late one evening towards the end of May, there was a knock on the cottage door.

'Blimey, it's a bit late for visiting,' Dolly complained. 'I was just getting ready for bed, and before you start panicking, it's a bit late for any telegram boys to come knocking.'

Amber hadn't even considered such a thing, as she ran to answer it, her heart thumping, her thoughts full of Luke. It would be just like him to arrive here without any warning as he had done once before. She pulled open the door and gaped.

'It's you!'

Gary laughed easily. 'Yep, turning up again just like the bad penny. Sorry I haven't been in touch lately, honey, but you know how things are, and pretty soon our guys will be shipping out of here. Can't say when, but it'll be soon, and who knows when or if we'll be back here again?'

'Don't say that,' she said quickly, 'and for goodness' sake come inside, Gary. It's great to see you again, but I've got my reputation to think about, you know.'

She tried to smile and to speak lightly, but it was hard to hide the searing disappointment that he wasn't Luke.

'Are you sure it's OK?' he whispered in a conspiratorial manner. 'The old lady won't look down her nose at me for calling so late, will she?'

Feeling something like horror at the question,

Amber looked at him mutely. He didn't know. Of course he didn't know, and why would anybody have thought to tell him? He was one GI among hundreds in the area, and he had been away on manoeuvres, and the death of one old lady wouldn't have been important news compared with the forthcoming most daring adventure of the war so far.

'What have I said?' he asked at once, seeing her change of expression.

Dolly pushed forward at hearing the American voice.

'Who is it, Amber?'

'Say, I'm sorry,' Gary said, backing away. 'I didn't know you had company. I'll come back again another time.'

Amber pulled him inside the cottage almost savagely. 'No, please don't go, Gary. You took me unawares, that's all. Come and meet my friend Dolly, and I'll tell you all my news.'

By now Dolly was looking more than interested in the handsome young GI who had obviously taken a shine to Amber. She remembered the name from Amber's letters, and now that she saw him she decided it was no wonder that Luke Gillam was out of the picture.

'Come and have some cocoa with us,' Amber said mechanically. 'I'm afraid we've got nothing more exciting than that to offer. Dolly won't mind making it.'

Whether Dolly minded or not, Amber ignored her glare, and after a moment Dolly left them together, being sure to leave the adjoining door open so she could hear everything that went on. She didn't miss the way Gary sat close to Amber on the sofa and took her hands in his. Well, well.

'What's happened, honey?' he said quietly.

It was one thing to be gradually accepting the fact that she would never see Granny Pen again, and to get used to not having her around to scold or advise or just be there. It was a different matter when it came to telling people, to actually saying the words that Granny Pen had died. And before she knew it, she was blubbing on his shoulder, and wondering wildly just how many tears a person could possibly have inside them.

'I'm sorry,' she gasped finally, when she moved away from him, feeling foolish. 'I didn't mean that to happen, but I find it painful to actually say the words, let alone believe it. I keep expecting to come home from work and find her here, and it still gives me a little shock to know that it will never happen again.'

'You wouldn't be human if you didn't feel like that. It's a natural reaction. We've lost quite a few good buddies now, and it's hard to accept that they're not going home. I've written a few letters to relatives myself, and I know what it's like to try to make sense of it all.'

'But it doesn't make any sense, does it? Not in your case, anyway. My gran was old, and I suppose it's something you should expect, but I never did. I just thought she'd go on for ever.'

Dolly brought in three cups of cocoa and dumped them on the table.

'She needs cheering up, not having gloomy faces around her. How about if I put on a gramophone record? You could teach us to jitterbug, Gary.'

The other two looked at her as if she was mad, and she snapped at them.

'Don't look at me like that. My dad was killed too, but it didn't mean me and my mum had to stop living.'

'You're right,' Gary said. 'OK, put the record on, and we'll give it a go.'

They were both mad now, thought Amber, and there was no way she was going to get up and try to do a jitterbug, but after a few minutes of watching Dolly doing her best, she began to laugh, and when Gary put out his hand she joined in. She couldn't imagine Granny Pen objecting to this, anyway!

By the time Gary left, they were less edgy with one another, and Dolly was declaring that if Amber didn't want a date with him, she wouldn't mind!

'You needn't bother. He's got a girlfriend back home, and they're going to get engaged when he gets back for good.'

'That doesn't stop him having a bit of fun. You went out with him before, didn't you? Are you telling me you didn't have a bit of a kiss and cuddle?'

'No, we didn't. I was thinking about Luke at the time, and he was thinking about his girl. We just enjoyed one another's company, that's all, so don't try to make anything of it.'

Dolly laughed, clearly not believing a word of it. 'Well, like I said, all's fair in love and war, gel.'

On Bank Holiday Monday, the last Monday in May, the sound of German aircraft was heard shortly after midnight, and the bombers swept in across the harbour, the Carrick Roads and the docks. People who hadn't taken to the air-raid shelters stood outside their homes, watching in stunned horror as the leading planes dropped red and green flares to mark the bomb path, which Dolly called bleedin' stupid, because now the big guns knew just where to fire at them. But the planes continued relentlessly, along the seafront to Swanpool and out towards the Helford river, dropping their bombs. Amber and Dolly went outside to watch the display, and learned later from an excited Mr Phillips next door, on Home Guard duty, that an underground fuel tank at Swanpool had been hit, sending a surge of burning petrol flowing down the hillside towards the village. American soldiers and sailors awaiting embarkation joined scores of local firemen in putting out the blaze. Several houses and hotels were destroyed in the raid, bringing to mind that other one at the Lannigan Hotel, where everyone had been killed, including two schoolgirls.

It was the only talking point for days, but then, just a week later, the weirdest thing happened. For so long now, the town and harbour had been packed to capacity with troops and vehicles, naval ships, American landing craft and infantry landing craft, all awaiting the instruction to go. And then, on the morning of June 6th, they were gone. There was an almost eerie hush over the harbour as people went about their normal business that day, and gradually the news that everyone had guessed filtered through that D-Day, the Allied invasion of France, had at last begun.

'It's going to be a bit dull here now,' Dolly sulked. 'Though I suppose when they start sending casualties back the more able-bodied ones will be glad of a few hours at the club.'

'You are a pig sometimes, aren't you, Dolly? Is that all you can think about? That it'll be a bit dull around here? What about the poor devils on their way to France, and never knowing how many of them will be killed?'

'Well, we can't do anything about it, can we? We might as well stay cheerful for when they do come back. You'll be thinking about Gary, I suppose.'

'I'm thinking about all of them,' Amber retorted.

Of course she was thinking about Gary, but not only him. She was thinking more and more about Luke these days, and praying that he would come home safely. The only consolation if she didn't hear from him was that his mother wasn't getting any letters from him either. It was truly as if his ship had vanished like the *Marie Celeste*. She had thought it once before, and it still made her feel sick with unease.

*

The news that D-Day had been a stupendous success was broadcast on the wireless and filled the pages of every newspaper. At last it seemed as if the Jerries were on the run, and there were Allied victories being reported everywhere. Prayers that it would soon be over were on everyone's lips. But it was as though good news always had to be countered with bad, just as Granny Pen always said, and a week after the Allies landed on the beaches of Normandy, the Germans unleashed their most vicious weapon yet, the doodlebug.

'That's not its real name, of course,' Dolly told Amber, after a hysterical letter from her mum, 'but it makes it sound a bit less scary than the real name for it. Mum says they don't know it's coming, and then it drops without a sound and does a bleedin' lot of damage.'

It wasn't only Dolly's mum who found it scary, thought Amber. Dolly had gone a sickly colour as she finished reading the letter.

'Blimey, she's talking about getting out of London now. I hope she don't start thinking about coming down here, because it's the last thing we want, ain't it?'

'Well, she couldn't, because we don't have room,' Amber said quickly, thinking that for once she was in total agreement with Dolly. She couldn't imagine sharing the cottage with Dolly's mum, with her cheap scent and her cigarettes.

'Is that the only reason?' Dolly asked directly.

Amber gave an uneasy laugh. 'It's the main one.

And don't you think I've got enough to put up with, having you arguing with me day and night, without you and your mum going at it as well?'

'Oh well, don't let me forget that you're in charge here now, will you? You're such a snob, Amber. You don't think we're good enough for you.'

'I never said that! I've *never* said that!'

'You thought it though. You and your gran.'

Amber couldn't let this pass. 'How can you say such a thing? Don't you remember when you first came here and you had practically nothing? Who was it who took you in and made you welcome and treated you no differently from the way she treated her own granddaughter?'

She felt the choking sensation in her throat again, remembering those days when she had been un-believably jealous of Dolly daydream and her blonde curls and her blue eyes and her dainty little body. It was true that she hadn't wanted her here in the begin-ning, but Granny Pen had made her see that she was being unkind to a young girl far from home, and eventually they had become closer than peas in a pod. The eerily *same* pod, once they had discovered that they shared a birthday. How spooky was that?

'Don't let's quarrel, Dolly. I'm sure your mum wouldn't want to come to Cornwall any more than you'd want her to. I'm right about that, aren't I?'

Dolly's face relaxed in a grin. 'Darned right you are. Imagine if Uncle Joe wanted to come as well and we had to shove them both in Granny Pen's old bedroom and listen to their shenanigans every night!'

'Oh, *don't*,' Amber said, as the image of it started to make them both giggle, and then they were howling with laughter until their sides ached.

Alone in bed in her own room now, Amber lay looking up at the ceiling, thinking over what had been said. She didn't think for a minute that Dolly's mum and Uncle Joe would want to evacuate to Falmouth at a time that everybody hoped was the late stage of the war, no matter what the Jerries threw at them. It would be impossibly crowded in this little cottage. It was too crowded already.

Her heart gave a small, uncomfortable leap at the thought. It wasn't that it was too small for the two of them, it was more that they were in one another's pockets the whole time now. It was like being two sisters who bickered constantly, simply because they could never get away from one another. They lived in the same house, ate together, slept in adjoining rooms, cycled to work together, spent all day together. They were never apart. It was like being married without the fun.

There and then, Amber made up her mind. Dolly had always enjoyed working and flirting at the Forces' Club more than she did, and she had settled back into the old routine as if she had never been away. Besides, now that so many of the forces had left the area, there was sometimes little to do for the staff there. So tomorrow she would look for another job, and the one she wanted more than any other was in Veal's Craft Shop – if she could bear to put up with Myra Veal's sniping.

It was odd, but once she had made up her mind to do something positive, she had the most untroubled night's sleep since Granny Pen had died. For the first time, she felt she could sense a guardian angel keeping watch over her, and knew exactly who it would be.

'You're a glutton for punishment, aren't you?' Dolly said, when she told her of her decision. 'I thought you couldn't stand the old duck.'

'I'll just have to put up with her then, won't I? I liked working there and being surrounded by all the things they sold, and so as long as we keep out of one another's way, we'll be all right.'

'And how are you going to do that in such a poky little shop?'

'I don't *know*,' Amber said crossly, 'but I just wish you'd stop making objections and putting doubts in my mind.'

As if they weren't there already . . . not about the shop, just about Myra. But she wasn't going to be deterred. She wasn't due at the club until the afternoon, since they were still working in shifts, and she cycled into the town, marvelling at how vast the harbour looked now that so many of the landing craft and other invasion ships were gone. The weeks were moving on, summer was slipping into autumn, and in Amber's eyes Pendennis Castle had never looked so impressive in all its sunlit splendour. With a fervour that startled her, she found herself wishing with all her might that no German bombs would ever rain down on that ancient fortress. It was what they stood for, Cornwall and England and all that . . .

She was so caught up in her thoughts that she had to swerve to avoid a couple of small boys who yelled at her. They were carrying bits of shrapnel, and she thought what a strange world it was now, when twisted bits of metal had become such prizes for small boys to barter over.

She went into the craft shop, breathing in the familiar smells of pot pourri and other spicy scents. Myra immediately came through from the beaded curtain and gave a sniff when she saw it was Amber.

'Me and Mother were just talking about you the other day,' she said.

'Were you? What about?' Amber said, caught off guard.

'I've decided I want to go back to Redruth. I never did like Falmouth, and me and Mother can't live together for ever, that's for sure. So if you're fed up with your job at the Forces' Club, you're welcome to this one.'

Amber felt her heart jump. 'This is so weird,' she said. 'That's exactly why I've come to see you.'

'Well, we'd better see about it then, hadn't we? It'll take a couple of weeks to get everything settled, but the sooner the better, I say.'

Myra gave her the first grudging smile Amber had ever seen on that plain face. It didn't improve her looks, but it sealed a bargain.

Chapter Seventeen

'I still think you're mad,' Dolly told her. 'Why would you want to work in a shop like that instead of at the club? I'd be bored to death.'

Amber was tempted to echo something of Myra's feelings about her mother. Maybe it's because you and I are too much in one another's pockets, and we'll probably end up hating each other, and this is the best way of disentangling ourselves. She didn't say it, but she thought it.

'I always liked working there, and once Myra's gone I'll be more or less my own boss. I won't be just one more girl in an overall.'

Dolly glared at her. 'Suits me. I'm not sure how long I'll be staying, anyway.'

'What do you mean? You're not thinking of going back to London now the Jerries are dropping those doodlebugs, are you?' Amber was alarmed. They might not be getting on as well any more, but going back to London when she didn't have to sounded plain stupid.

'I might. I don't know. I'll see how things go.'

'Well, don't do me any favours,' Amber muttered.

'You've changed,' Dolly said.

'Well, I should hope I have, and so have you. We're not twelve years old any more, in case you hadn't noticed it.'

'Oh, I've noticed it all right. You didn't want me then, and you don't want me now. You don't want to work with me, that's for sure.'

Amber sighed. 'Why are you being like this? Can't you see that it would be better for us to be apart for at least some part of the day? We're not Siamese twins, Dolly.'

'No. Just February ones,' Dolly said. 'Oh, don't take any notice of me. I'm just fed up, that's all. I don't feel as if I belong here, and I feel it even less now that Granny Pen's gone. She sort of held us together, didn't she, gel?'

'Well, if we're being honest with one another, I suppose she did.'

Dolly sat back on the sofa, her arms folded. 'So when are you starting back at the craft shop then?'

It took a few weeks before it was all arranged. For Mrs Veal, the initial trauma over her husband's death had faded and she was glad to be back in her own home again.

'It's a sad thing to be glad to see the back of your own daughter, Amber,' Mrs Veal commented, when things were finally back the way they used to be. 'But I swear that I'd far rather see your pretty face than Myra's in the shop any day.'

'I'd far rather be here too,' Amber told her. 'I enjoyed working at the Forces' Club, but sometimes the stories the men had to tell were pretty harrowing, and they always wanted someone to listen to them. You couldn't say no, considering what they had been through.'

Mrs Veal nodded sympathetically. 'Young maids like you shouldn't have to hear such things, my dear. I'm sure your gran felt the same, caring about you the way she did.'

'Maybe not, but if they have to go through it all, you couldn't turn away and show your disgust, could you?'

To her surprise the shopkeeper gave her a small hug.

'I wonder if your gran knew how lucky she was to have you, Amber.'

'I think we were very lucky to have each other,' Amber said, feeling her face go hot, and thankful that the shop door bell tinkled before they started getting too mushy. But in any case it was time for Mrs Veal to go upstairs for her regular afternoon nap. She often stayed there, leaving Amber to deal with any customers, and to close the shop at the end of the day.

It was a fairly quiet afternoon, but towards the end of it Amber turned with a smile to see Luke's mother enter the shop, and then her smile quickly faded as she saw the look on Mrs Gillam's face.

'What is it?' she whispered.

It was a moment when she felt as if the whole

world was closing in on her. The exotic scents inside the shop seemed to be suddenly intensified. The semi-precious jewels and coloured stones in the ornaments on the shelves seemed to burn brightly, dazzling her. She seemed more intensely aware of everything, the clock on the wall that said it was half past four, the calendar that said it was the last day in October. She didn't yet know what was wrong, except that instinct, certainty, intuition, second sight, superstition . . . everything Cornish within her was telling her that something was very, very wrong, or why was Mrs Gillam here, looking distraught, knowing Amber was back at the craft shop again and seeking her out?

The woman spoke quickly, her voice higher than usual. 'There's been a telegram, Amber. Luke's ship has been sunk. His father has been trying to gather as much information as possible, but I couldn't delay coming to see you any longer. It's feared that most if not all of the crew have been drowned, my dear.'

'*No!*' The long animal cry was wrenched out of her, as she clutched Mrs Gillam's arm, digging her fingernails into the flesh and not noticing it. 'Did the telegram say he was drowned? Did it *say* so?'

She didn't know why it was so important to know the exact words, to see his name, which would eventually be listed publicly among the dead. She *wouldn't* believe it until she saw it.

Mrs Gillam pulled the crumpled yellow envelope out of her pocket. For a moment Amber was tempted to snatch it out of her hand, tear it up and throw away the pieces. If she didn't see the words, it hadn't happened. It wouldn't be real. But Mrs Gillam was already taking the piece of paper out of the envelope with shaking hands and telling her to read it.

We regret to inform you . . . Her heart jolted so painfully it felt near to bursting. Her eyes were blurred with unshed tears, but her voice was stormy.

'It says "missing, believed drowned". It doesn't say it's true. It only says "missing, believed drowned". That doesn't mean he's anything but missing. People are found safe all the time when they've been reported missing. How can you write him off so easily!'

'Of course I haven't written him off, Amber. Please, my dear, try to calm yourself.'

'I can't.' She thrust the telegram back at Luke's mother. 'I won't believe it unless it's made official, and I wouldn't have thought you would, either. Or are you already planning his memorial service?'

It was hard to say who was the more angry now, Amber, whose only way of dealing with this news was to rant and rave, or Luke's mother, who couldn't believe that this girl she liked so much was reacting in such a cruel way.

'How can you even think such a thing, let alone say it? I thought better of you, Amber. I thought you would want to know about Luke as soon as possible, and pray for him the way we all are, but I wish I'd never come to tell you now.'

As she turned to go, Amber caught at her arm again, almost convulsed with shame and embarrassment.

'I'm so sorry, truly I am. I didn't mean any of it.

I'm just so upset that I can't think straight. But I can't believe anything bad has happened to Luke, Mrs Gillam. I know he's safe. I *know* he'll come home.'

His mother's throat worked as she tried to control her own emotions.

'Then I just wish I had your faith, my dear,' she said quietly, and turned to walk out of the shop before she said anything more.

Amber immediately turned the shop sign to Closed. What did it matter if there was still an hour to go before the proper closing time? How could she deal with people wanting mementoes to give to loved ones, when her own . . . her own beloved Luke . . .

She didn't know what to do. To have this happen so soon after her gran was just too cruel. It couldn't be real. She couldn't go home yet, and Mrs Veal would still be sleeping upstairs. She needed something to occupy herself, and she began feverishly tidying the shelves, dusting where there was no need, allowing her fingers to touch and caress the gleaming, polished stones she always loved to hold. Caressing a similar piece of amber to the one she had given Luke, to keep him safe always. Clutching it tight to her heart, as if somehow she could transmit the magical powers of it to him and make him safe.

She remembered how some of the servicemen called those who were drowned at sea 'fish bait'. It was horrible, and yet she remembered how the girls at the club had laughed along with them, knowing they didn't mean to hurt, and that it was simply their way of letting off steam after some of the sights they had seen, some of the ordeals they had been through.

She couldn't bear to think of it now, and yet she couldn't *stop* thinking about it while her hated imagination got the better of her, picturing Luke's face as he sank lifelessly to the bottom of the sea. She heard herself moaning as if with a real physical pain, and she felt as if all her bones were turning to jelly as she sank in a crumpled heap on to the floor of the shop, weeping uncontrollably.

She hardly noticed the rustle of the bead curtain until Mrs Veal was kneeling down beside her, rocking her in her arms.

'There now, Amber love, did I upset you so with that talk of your gran? I didn't mean to, love, but sometimes it's better to talk about them than to push them out of our minds.'

Amber looked at her blankly, hardly able to take in what she was saying, and then she slowly got to her feet, feeling like a very old woman, with Mrs Veal still holding on to her.

'It's not you,' she stuttered. 'It's Luke. His mother came into the shop a while ago. She's had a telegram.'

She didn't need to say any more. It was becoming a horrible ritual these days, for people to comfort one another after the delivery of a telegram.

'Drowned, was he, love?' Mrs Veal said sadly, her arms still tightly around Amber as if she was afraid the girl would fall over again once she let her go. But Amber shook her away.

'No, he wasn't drowned. He's missing, but he's not drowned. They'll find him, I know they will. I gave him a piece of amber to keep him safe. They say it protects sailors – but you knew that, didn't you?'

She was babbling now as Mrs Veal steered her into the back room and poured her a tot of brandy. Did everyone keep a bottle of the stuff for this kind of emergency nowadays? thought Amber wildly. She drank it dutifully, hardly noticing the taste, and trying even more not to notice the pitying look in Mrs Veal's eyes that said here was a girl valiantly trying to believe her boy was safe, when it was clearly not going to be the case. But if you didn't have hope, what was there left? And at seventeen, Amber was still young enough to believe in miracles, however unlikely they may seem. And she wasn't going to let anyone take away that hope. She wished she really had been blessed with her gran's second sight, or her weird way of knowing for certain when things were bad, but instead she just had hope, and she was going to cling on to it for ever. Or until things proved to be hopeless.

She couldn't get the word out of her mind, and the craziest thought swept through her at that instant. If – and when – Luke came safely home and when they got married and had children the first girl would be called Hope. It was a kind of promise that she floated up on the ether, because God surely wouldn't deny it.

'I'm all right, Mrs Veal. It was the shock, coming

so soon after my gran,' she said shakily a little while later. It wasn't that soon, but it felt like it. It had brought back all the turbulent emotions she had felt when she discovered Granny Pen lying so still in her bed on that Sunday morning, but she was oddly calmer now, and still ashamed of her outburst to Luke's mother.

'Then as I see that you've closed up the shop for the day, my love, you go on home whenever you're ready and get a good night's sleep.'

She wasn't going home, but Mrs Veal didn't need to know that. Firstly, she was going to go to the church to say a silent prayer for Luke's safe home-coming. And then she was going to see his mother again, needing to be around other people who loved him. And to apologize for her earlier outburst.

She bent low over the handlebars of her bicycle, not wanting to talk to anyone she knew, nor to let anyone see how agitated she still was despite her resolutions. The interior of the church gave her a small comfort as it always did, but it was cold and lifeless without the usual Sunday congregation, and she was glad to get outside and on her way to the boatyard. She had expected it to be closed, but she could see Luke's father working away, planing down a plank of wood as if his life depended on it. She knew at once that it would be his way of dealing with the news, the same as Luke's would be if he was here. They both loved the sea and everything that floated. In those halcyon pre-war days, what neither of them could have foreseen was that one of those hideous German U-boats, the silent killers beneath the waves, would have undoubtedly sunk the *Tigress*.

On an impulse she dropped her bicycle, and as she did so Mick Gillam looked up and saw her. The pain was etched on his face, and without a word he opened his arms to Amber and she ran into them and was held tight.

'I need to talk to Mrs Gillam,' she said, when she could catch her breath. 'I was so rude to her before.'

'Go on inside the house while I finish up here, Amber. I daresay she'll want you to have a bite to eat with us, and it's good to have your company right now.'

Amber wasn't sure she could eat anything, or that Mrs Gillam could possibly be thinking about cooking a meal, but there was a succulent smell coming through the open kitchen door, so Mrs Gillam probably had her own way of dealing with things too.

'Can I come in, Mrs Gillam?' she said awkwardly. 'I want to say I'm truly sorry for the way I behaved earlier.'

'There's no need for apologies, my dear. No need at all, but since Mick and me don't seem to know what to say to one another, you can stay and share these sausages with us. The butcher saved me some, and they look really tasty, so I'm making them into a toad-in-the-hole. It's Luke's favourite.'

Her voice wavered slightly as she finished, and

Amber got the feeling that she had to keep saying his name as much as possible. She understood that so well. It echoed exactly the feelings in her heart. Keep saying his name and he won't be dead. Any minute now he'll walk right through that open door. She swallowed, because of course he wouldn't, but she knew she had been right to come here, because the three of them needed each other now.

'I envy you so much, Amber,' Luke's mother said suddenly.

'Do you? Why?' she said, startled.

'You have the belief of youth, and rightly so. If anything in the world can bring Luke back to us, it's your blind faith. And you must think I'm talking nonsense now.'

'Of course I don't. I always thought you were a very wise lady.' She looked down at her hands, clenched together in her lap. 'I never knew my mother, but if I had I would have liked her to be someone like you.'

The words were out before she had time to think, and she felt horribly embarrassed at having said them.

'Bless you, Amber,' Mrs Gillam said, looking away quickly, as if she was embarrassed too.

Amber found herself thinking, that if and when Luke came home, and they eventually got married, then this kind-faced woman would be her mother-in-law. She wondered if Mrs Gillam ever thought about it too, but right now certainly wasn't the time to start fantasizing about such things.

It was a strained little meal that evening. Luke's father didn't say very much, and his mother had become over-bright, as if to compensate. In the end, Amber was glad to get away and cycle home in the twilight, knowing the ordeal that lay ahead of her, when she had to tell Dolly what had happened.

She still couldn't face going home and she avoided the laughing soldiers spilling out from the Forces' Club, along with several of the girls who were finishing their shift. The lure of Pendennis Castle seemed to draw her like a magnet as she turned her bicycle wheels towards the curving slope to the top of the hill, and she paused there to gaze down at the darkening waters far below.

What had it been like, somewhere out there in the vast ocean? The small, insidious little voice whispered inside her head and she couldn't rid herself of it. Did it happen in daylight or in the dark of night? Had the crew of the *Tigress* been unaware of what was about to happen when a U-boat's torpedo sped silently towards them beneath the waves and struck the mortal blow? Or had they seen it coming, expected it, waited in horror as the tube-like shape of the lethal, disgusting thing aimed directly at their own craft, hell-bent on its killing spree?

And then what? Amber could almost hear the tearing of metal, the splintering, the sweating, terrifying realization that the ship couldn't be saved, and that few, if any, of the crew were going to be saved either. She shuddered violently, wishing she didn't have a such a vivid imagination that could tear her apart like this. Wishing she didn't feel this wild, awful urge to imagine Luke, floating, foundering, drowning . . . and willing him to hold on to the little piece of amber he always carried, to hold on to *her*, to their dream, their future . . .

'I thought it was you!' she heard a familiar voice yell, together with the sound of bicycle wheels slewing to a halt beside her. 'What the dickens are you doing up here, Amber?'

The shock of hearing Dolly's voice made her flinch even more violently. Amber almost hated her for breaking the spell, no matter how dire it was. For those moments, she had been with Luke in spirit, and now the feelings were shattered.

But Dolly wasn't as insensitive as she might have thought. She came nearer, still half astride her bike, and looked at Amber apprehensively.

'What's happened now? Not more bad news, is it? Whatever it is, it's too bleedin' chilly to stand around up here all night. Let's get on home and warm up last night's leftover soup. There's not much else in the house.'

'I've already eaten,' Amber mumbled, still wondering how she could have forced the food down. 'I went to Luke's house and had a meal with his parents.'

'Did you now?' Dolly said, not yet understanding. 'That's a turn-up, ain't it? Does this mean it's all on again with you and Lukey-boy?'

'I wish you'd stop calling him by that stupid name,' Amber lashed out. 'It's so feeble and childish, and, anyway, he's – he's –'

She couldn't say it. Her throat was choked with tears, but at last Dolly realized something was badly wrong. She flung her bike down and came close to Amber, gripping her shoulders.

'You ain't telling me he's bought it, are you, gel?' she said hoarsely.

'*No!*' Amber said, shaking her off. She wouldn't allow those words to be said or believed for a moment. 'His ship has been sunk and his mother's had a telegram to say he's missing. But he's not drowned. He's *not*. I won't let him be drowned.'

'Blimey, kid, don't take on so,' Dolly said, alarmed at her vehemence, and thinking her mind must have turned.

Amber was trying hard to convince herself that if she said it enough, it would be true. She closed her eyes for a moment and simply let the tears course down her cheeks, ignoring the salt sting on them as the wind blew in from the sea.

'Let's go home, Amber,' Dolly said quietly. 'I know you want to be here where you can look out to sea and imagine you can will Luke to come back safely. But you can do that just as well at home. You can go to bed and say a private little prayer for him, or pray all night if you think it will do any good. Let's just go home and do it.'

Amber gave her a twisted smile, a bit startled at such understanding, even if she wasn't too sure how

309

much praying Dolly ever did. It wouldn't last, of course, but it was nice to hear it, however briefly.

'All right. And if you were afraid I was planning to throw myself over the edge to join him, you needn't worry. I'm not that stupid.'

'I never thought you were. Just weird,' Dolly said.

The news that Luke Gillam was missing, believed drowned, was soon common knowledge. His parents still went to church on Sundays and held their heads up high, and Amber tried to follow their example. Naturally, they were the ones who people sympathized with, for no one had any idea that two old sparring school friends had become lovers. Amber was feverishly glad that nobody knew, but it also left her feeling more and more isolated. She grieved for Luke as deeply as she grieved for her gran, but not even to Dolly was she going to confide how close they had been for that one brief, beautiful evening. *Especially* not to Dolly, who would probably blab about it to anyone who would listen.

It was ironic that although everyone was weary of war, people were feeling more hopeful about the end now, despite the concentrated attacks of doodle-bugs on London and the south-east. News from farther abroad continued to be better. The Allies were gaining ground wherever they fought, and it would soon be all over. If another Christmas had to come and go, they would welcome in the new year, sure that they had definitely turned the corner and 1945 would see the end of it all.

As far as Amber was concerned, such optimism was like a bitter taste in her mouth. Of course she wanted it to be over. She wanted the world to go back to the way it was before Hitler invaded Poland. She wanted Dolly to go back home where she belonged, even though they were rubbing along slightly better now. She wanted Granny Pen to be there every time she went back to the cottage. Most of all, she wanted Luke back. The distant dream of herself in a long white dress, marrying her sweetheart and eventually having their babies, was simply that. A dream, and nothing more. And everyone knew that dreams rarely came true.

It was hard to say her prayers every night, and to wonder if they would ever be answered. Or to imagine that the prayers of one girl were even going to be heeded, when the whole world seemed to be praying and hoping for the same thing.

Dolly came home from the club one evening, her face a sickly white.

'I don't know how to tell you this, Amber,' she said uneasily, 'but some of the Yanks are back, and they told us that your friend Gary was wounded recently. He ain't dead,' she added hastily, seeing Amber's horrified expression, 'but his mates say he had his arm shot off and he's already been sent straight back to America from France, so there was no chance of seeing him to say goodbye.'

Amber was numb with this new shock. On top of the lack of any definite information about Luke, it truly felt as if the whole world was closing in on her.

'I'm beginning to think I'm a jinx,' she stuttered. 'Those girls we knew at school, then your Eddie, now Gary – and Luke's still missing.'

Dolly shifted uncomfortably. 'That's crazy talk. We all know you're a bit weird, but you're not a jinx. Mind you, I think you're believing in miracles if you think Luke's still out there somewhere. You've got to be realistic, gel. If any of the crew of that ship had been saved, we'd have heard about it by now.'

'Well, I do believe in miracles,' Amber said stubbornly. 'I'm really sad to hear about Gary, but he's still alive, isn't he? And so is Luke. Until I hear anything to the contrary, I'll go on believing it rather than give up on him.'

'You really do care for him, don't you?' Dolly challenged her. 'I thought you'd changed your mind about that.'

'Well, I haven't. And if you thought that, then you don't know me at all.'

She flounced away before Dolly could see how close she was to breaking down completely. This news about Gary had been the final shaker. She didn't want to imagine the shock on the face of his girlfriend, Greta, when she saw him again. She didn't want to wonder about Greta's reaction when she realized he was disabled now, and no longer the strong young man who had gone away to war. She didn't want to think about her own reactions should her circumstances ever be similar, because she just didn't know how strong and resilient she would be. Nobody did, until it happened to them.

Chapter Eighteen

Luke's father Mick had been in the boat-building business all his life, as had his father before him. The prestige of Gillam's boatyard was well known in circles far beyond Falmouth, and Mick had many contacts all around the country, especially among well-heeled folk who considered a boat a plaything and came to him when they wanted the best.

He needed those contacts now, and he made many urgent telephone calls over the next days and weeks, trying to get more information about the sinking of the *Tigress*. These days so much information was kept hush-hush on strict government orders, and it wasn't even being leaked as to exactly where it had happened until he managed to get hold of one Lord Binkerton at the Admiralty.

'Binky,' Mick said, cutting across any thoughts of formality, however high up the man was in diplomatic and naval circles. 'It's Mick Gillam here, and I'm in desperate need of a favour.'

'Are you, old boy?' came the jovial voice. 'It's good to hear from you again, so what can I do for you?'

'I don't know whether you can do anything, but you're the best person I can think of to try. It's about the *Tigress*.'

'Oh yes?'

Mick didn't miss the change in the man's tone, and he groaned inwardly. These naval bods could be as tight as a duck's arse, he thought inelegantly, but there was too much at stake here to take offence at any rebuff that might be coming. It was his son's life.

'Luke was a crew member,' he said bluntly.

'Ah.' There was silence from the other end, and Mick could imagine that the man was dealing with a bit of conscience. On the one hand, Binky knew Luke and had always made a fuss of the boy when he was a small child. On the other, apart from the initial news that the *Tigress* had been sunk, there had been an obligatory silence in high places about it, as there was about all such events until the facts were properly assessed and released to the public. But Mick wasn't just the public. He was a father anxious for news of his son.

'Binky?' he said at last, when the silence seemed to be going on too long.

'Look, old boy, you know what red tape is like, and they'd have my guts for garters if I gave out too much information too soon.'

Mick ignored the incongruity of the words said in that so-precise Oxford English accent.

'But?' he persisted, sensing that he was going to get something, however little it was.

'It's going to be released soon that the *Tigress* sank

in the Med, and strictly between ourselves, Mick – you do understand that this is *strictly* between ourselves and your lovely Hester – there have been reports of some survivors being picked up and being taken to Alexandria. It hasn't been confirmed yet, and I don't want to give you false hopes, but as soon as I hear any more and I'm able to release it, I'll be in touch. I can't give you any more than that, Mick, old friend.'

'It's more than enough for now,' Mick said, almost dizzy with relief. 'And, of course, this will go no further than this house.'

'Then I'll be in touch.'

The line went dead, and Mick sank back on the chair in the passageway, waves of nausea sweeping through him. Relief that there was a chance that Luke might be among the survivors was almost as great a shock as the news of the sinking had been. But a different kind of shock, of course. A euphoric kind of shock. He savoured it for a moment longer before he went to find his wife and swear her to the same secrecy he had promised Binky.

Predictably, she clung to him and wept.

'I wish I could tell Amber,' she said shakily. 'The poor girl's frantic.'

'You can't. You know that, don't you, Hester? Until the news is released officially, Binky's trusted us with it. We must just continue to pray that it's true, my dear, and that Luke is one of the lucky survivors.'

'I can't bear to think of him in that way, even though it's what I want more than anything. But he's just a boy, Mick. Our boy.'

'I know,' he said, holding her close. 'But I know that Binky will let us have news as soon as possible. He'll know how anxious we are.'

Right now Mick didn't want to reveal his unease at what kind of state those survivors might have been in when they had been picked up. If they had been in the sea for a long time and swallowed a lot of water, there could be any number of infections from the flotsam floating about after a torpedo strike. They would certainly have been injured, some of them badly. They could have ended up with smashed limbs, swallowed engine oil, suffered irreparable brain damage . . .

Mick shook the terrors out of his mind. As far as he knew the Med didn't have sharks or the worst evils of the deep, and he deliberately obliterated such scenarios from his head, and set about cheering up his wife instead.

There was no knowing how long it would be before Lord Binkerton telephoned him with whatever news he was permitted to tell, and Mick knew it was going to be difficult not to let on to friends that there was a glimmer of hope. It was even harder when folk still offered them sympathy, clearly assuming the worst had happened, and that they wouldn't see Luke home again. The hardest of all was seeing Amber Penry at church the following Sunday morning.

'Is there any news?' she said at once, as soon as she could break away from the congregation milling outside in the thin wintry sunshine, as they always did, and walk straight across to the Gillams.

'Not yet,' Hester said. 'But you know what they say. As long as there's life, there's hope. We don't give up hoping, do we, Amber?'

'I'll never give up,' Amber said. She hesitated, not sure whether to go on or not, but then decided to say it, however peculiar they thought her. 'I dreamed about him last night. He was smiling and I'm sure it was a good sign. An omen. You know how my gran set such a store by omens, Mrs Gillam.'

'Then I'm sure it was a good one, my dear,' Hester said in a strained voice, and turned away quickly, before she was tempted into saying any more. She was bound by secrecy not to say another word until Lord Binkerton phoned them, but it was very hard not to confide in this girl who obviously thought such a lot of her son.

Dolly caught up with them in time to hear Amber's last words.

'She'll really think you're potty now, and you've probably upset her too, saying you'd dreamed about Luke and saw him smiling.'

'No she won't. She'll understand. It's something that Cornish people do,' Amber added pointedly.

'Is that another dig at me?'

'Well, let's face it, you're not Cornish, are you? And I'm blowed if I understand some of the things you say!'

317

She clamped her lips together after that, and for once Dolly took the hint. It wasn't the time or place to be arguing, and they collected their bikes and cycled home in an uneasy silence.

'I'm definitely thinking of leaving this dump,' Dolly announced when they reached the cottage.

Amber didn't take her seriously. She gave an exaggerated sigh.

'We've had this conversation before, and you know it would be madness to go back when the Jerries are still dropping those terrible doodlebugs.'

'I'm not talking about London. In my mum's last letter she said Uncle Joe's got a brother in Norfolk and they're probably going to pack up and go there in a couple of weeks. I could go with them.'

'You'd be bored in less than a week. What would you do in Norfolk!'

'Same as I do here. Get a job. Find a bloke. *I* don't know. But I'm as bored as hell here anyway, so I might as well clear off.'

Amber realized she was serious now. 'Dolly, please don't go like this.'

'Why not? It was only Granny Pen who was holding us together, we both know that. Anyway, I only said I'm *thinking* about it.'

Amber decided not to argue. She had too many other things to worry about without risking a real, rip-roaring row with Dolly. She didn't quite know what she thought about Dolly leaving, anyway. Part of her would find it was a relief not to have her around, forever nosing and poking into Amber's things, and another part knew she would miss her dreadfully. Dolly had been part of her life for years now, and the cottage would be empty without her. It occurred to Amber that she had never been alone in her life before. Granny Pen had always been there, and even in those few days before Dolly returned after Granny Pen died, the next door neighbours had never left her alone to brood.

On the other hand, she was almost eighteen years old now, and young men and women, younger than herself, had been brave and independent and reckless enough to go away to fight in the war and never come back. It always came back to that fact and made any little personal problems insignificant. She shivered, because never in her life could she consider Luke being missing as an insignificant problem. Not when it consumed her thoughts every second of the day, filling her dreams at night, and sometimes her nightmares too.

'I don't want to quarrel with you, Amber,' Dolly said suddenly. 'And wherever we are, we'll always be sort of twins, won't we?'

'Of course we will,' Amber said, ready to be generous at once. She didn't want to quarrel, either.

'I probably will go to Norfolk,' Dolly said as a passing thought. 'I'll wait until we get news of Lukey-boy first, though. I wouldn't want to leave you in the lurch, not knowing what's happened to him. Anyway,' she added cheekily, 'I'm sure he'll be back, safe and sound, and when he is, I told you I was going to have a pop at him, seeing as how you'd gone off him. Or was that all pie in the sky?'

'Something like that,' Amber muttered.

A week later the telephone call that Mick Gillam was waiting for came soon after midnight. He struggled out of bed and padded downstairs to the telephone in the hall, thankful that Hester was still asleep. He knew just what was meant by having his heart in his mouth now. His heart, and everything else . . . and whatever he was going to hear, he needed these few moments alone.

'Binky,' he said hoarsely, in answer to the familiar tones. 'Do you have some news?'

'Yes, and it's better than we might have hoped, Mick. Your boy *was* one of those picked up off the coast of Alexandria. He was taken to hospital there and is still under their care. He suffered some quite severe head injuries, and he also has problems with his hearing after the blast, together with some loss of memory. He came off better than some of them, though. There were about a dozen survivors all told and four of them had every stitch of clothing blown off their bodies in the explosion and were badly burned. Luke wasn't one of them, Mick, but they'll be keeping him in hospital a while longer until he regains more of his memory and until they can decide how bad this hearing loss is. These Egyptian wallahs won't discharge him until they're satisfied with his condition, I'll say that for them. Once they've done that, he'll be repatriated.'

'You mean he could be permanently deaf?' Mick said, hardly taking in anything else but the fact that Luke was alive, and knowing what a small price this was to pay compared with the injuries of some of his mates. And knowing, too, that Binky had kept on talking to give him time to recover from the news.

'I don't know, old man. But you know as well as I do that his days in the navy may well be over after this, although I don't imagine that will be too much hardship for you and Hester to bear, knowing that he did his honourable duty.'

Mick was too choked now to make a proper reply. 'Then I'll just say thank you from the bottom of my heart for all you've done, Binky.'

'Glad to help, Mick, and you'll be getting the news officially very soon. Now go and have a good night's sleep.'

The line went dead, and Mick replaced the receiver carefully, as if it was something precious, resisting the urge to smash it down and go rushing upstairs to shout the news to Hester. He realized how much he was shaking, and he had never felt less of a man than he did right now. He leaned against the wall for a few moments, fighting down the nausea of blessed relief, until he heard his wife's soft voice behind him.

'Mick, my dear . . .'

He turned swiftly, and was caught in her arms.

'It's all right,' he managed to say. 'It's all right. He's alive, and it's as good as we can expect, and he'll be coming home to us eventually.'

He couldn't say any more, and then they were sobbing in one another's arms, and he no longer felt less of a man for doing so. He realized Hester must have caught the gist of his telephone conversation and known that it wasn't the news they had been dreading. It took a while for them to recover and talk sensibly, and for Mick to relate all that Binky had told him. By then they were sitting in their kitchen, drinking hot cocoa laced with brandy and some of their precious sugar ration.

'No matter what you say, Mick, I shall let Amber know what we've heard now,' Hester said determinedly. 'I won't leave her in a kind of limbo until we get the official confirmation. It's not fair on her.'

'I won't object to it, my dear, and I must admit there were times when I found myself wishing I had her kind of blind faith. Sometimes I never dared to hope,' he said shakily, 'and we're not entirely out of the woods yet. Head injuries can be serious, and if his hearing has gone completely, I'm not sure how he'll cope.'

'He'll cope the way thousands of others have coped, my love. And it could have been so much worse. Think of his companions who were badly burned, and will presumably be scarred for life. At least Luke was spared that. And now I'm going to bed to offer up a heartfelt prayer of thanks for sending our son back to us. Whatever his injuries, Luke will always be whole to God, and to us.'

Mick's heart was full of the emotion he felt unable to express as he watched her go, so much more dignified than he was. Perhaps in the end women were the strong ones after all.

Hester had always thought so, and she was still thinking it when she went to the craft shop on the quay early the next morning. She had a message that was far too important to delay, and even though Amber had dread in her eyes when she saw who entered the shop, the girl's face relaxed into a look of almost indescribable beauty when she saw Luke's mother smile. No wonder her son loved this beautiful young Cornish girl, Hester thought fleetingly. Who could help it?

'He's alive, isn't he?' Amber said breathlessly. 'If he comes home maimed or limbless, none of it matters just as long as he's alive.'

Hester took the girl's hands in hers.

'It's nothing like that, my dear. He has some head injuries and some loss of memory and hearing, but until we hear more official news, we must continue to pray that his recovery will be complete.'

'Where is he?' Amber stuttered. 'Can I see him?'

Hester shook her head. 'Hold on a moment, Amber. You had better hear the whole story, and I must warn you that we've not had official confirmation as yet, but Luke's father knows people in high places, and we're assured that it's the truth. He's in hospital in Alexandria in Egypt, and he may be there for some while yet. We'll try to get a message through to the hospital as soon as possible to give them as many details about Luke as we can to help them assist in jogging his memory.'

'You mean he may have forgotten me?' Amber said in a cracked voice, trying to ignore the overpowering feeling of horror that such a thing could happen.

'I'm sure he won't have done that,' Hester said quickly. 'The important memories in a person's life go too deep to lose completely.'

She didn't really know if it was true. She wasn't a medical person, but she needed to reassure this lovely girl as much as possible. And later that day she intended to visit their family doctor to find out as much as she could about Luke's condition and what the future might hold for him.

Her eyes blurred for a moment and then she felt Amber's quick kiss on her cheek. 'I know he'll come through this, Mrs Gillam. He had the piece of amber I gave him to keep him safe, and it worked, didn't it? As long as he believed in it as much as I did, then it worked.'

He also had a very special piece of Amber, she thought tremulously. He had had all of her, and she of him. Whatever else had gone from Luke's memory, she was certain he couldn't have forgotten that. She couldn't *bear* for him to have forgotten all that they meant to one another.

She was aware that Luke's mother was looking at her a bit oddly now, and she almost wished she hadn't said that about the amber. People had always thought her gran was a bit peculiar, and she didn't want people thinking the same about her, especially not Luke's mother. On the other hand, she thought fiercely, *she* knew there was nothing peculiar about Granny Pen, and that she had been the dearest, most loving grandmother any girl could ever have wanted. She swallowed hard, before she got too emotional for comfort.

Besides, people were out and about in the town now, and it wouldn't look good for the Penry girl to be wallowing in misery so early in the day. Even as she thought it, the shop doorbell tinkled as a customer came inside to browse, and Mrs Gillam pressed Amber's hand.

'Keep the news to yourself for now, dear,' she said quietly, 'and come for your supper tonight. It'll save your inquisitive little friend from asking too many questions,' she added.

She was right about that, Amber thought, as she turned to see what the customer wanted. Dolly would want to know everything in detail, and, as yet, Amber didn't intend telling her a single thing. It was too precious a secret, and besides, what did she really know except that Luke was safe? But wasn't that enough? It was incredibly, fantastically *more* than enough for now, and she startled the customer by turning a beaming smile on her and saying what a wonderful day it was, without even noticing that the woman had only come inside the shop out of the rain.

'I don't know why you always want to be over there,' Dolly grumbled when Amber popped into the

Forces' Club at midday to let her know she wouldn't be home for supper that evening. 'It must be bleedin' dreary for the three of you. Why don't you come to the dance at the club this evening and have some fun?'

'I didn't know there was a dance this evening, and in any case I like being with the Gillams. It makes me feel closer to Luke. And before you say anything else, yes, he is still my boy, so you can just keep your hands off, Dolly daydream.'

Dolly stared. 'Well, I must say you sound pretty perky considering you don't even know if he's fish bait or not yet. Or have you heard something that you're not telling me?'

She gave Amber a deeply suspicious look, and it was oh so tempting to shout from the rooftops that *yes*, she had heard something! *Yes*, Luke was safe, and in hospital in some far-off country, and would surely be coming home soon . . . but she managed to keep quiet about all of it, and to speak tensely.

'I've got to sound perky or go under, haven't I? You enjoy the dance and if you don't bother about me, I won't bother about what time you get home, either! We don't have to live in one another's pockets, do we?'

It was the truest thing she had ever said, Amber thought, cycling back to the shop to have her midday sandwich and cup of tea, and keeping her head down against the rain that seemed to be settling in for the day. The entire bay was covered in a heavy mist, and the ships had become fearsome, shadowy shapes, like monstrous ghosts rising out of the water. Almost imperceptibly, the town too had become shrouded in a grey gloom, and it was impossible to see Pendennis Castle any more.

Amber shivered. She hated it when it was like this, as if the sun no longer looked favourably on this most beautiful county, and as if they were physically cut off from the rest of England like the peninsula they were. It wouldn't last, of course, and in the magical way it had, the mist would lift as surely and suddenly as it had appeared, but when it descended it always gave Amber a strange and uncomfortable feeling of isolation.

She reached the shop again with a feeling of relief, threw down her bicycle and went inside, putting on all the lights before going to the back room to eat her snack and put on the kettle. It was foolish to have such fears, but they were like demons inside her head. She hated to be in the dark, but she hated it even more when the heavens seemed to close in on the earth and there was nothing that anyone could do about it. How much worse it must be for those ships at sea to encounter such a phenomenon, and she instantly wished she had never thought it.

But Luke wasn't in danger of such terrors now. He was safe in a foreign hospital. Without thinking, she reached into the basket of semi-precious gems on the shop counter for a piece of amber similar to the one she had given him. She clutched the amber in her palm, feeling its warmth seeping into her, and imagining, whether true or false, that its healing strength was restoring her. She told herself severely what an idiot she was being. Even so, she knew she would never feel totally at ease again until Luke came home.

By the middle of the afternoon the sun came out with a brilliance that was startling, as if to compensate for the greyness of the morning. Ships resumed their normal forms in the bay, the countryside became green and verdant again, and Pendennis Castle reigned supreme over the town of Falmouth.

'It's always amazing, isn't it, my dear?' an afternoon customer remarked to Amber. 'One minute it seems we're in the doldrums, cut off from the world, and the next we're in God's own country again.'

'That's right,' Amber said with a smile, thinking she couldn't have put it better herself. By now she was willing the afternoon away, eager to be with Luke's family again and to hear if there was any more news. It was pointless to be so impatient, but when you were young and in love it was impossible to be otherwise.

'You'll be the little Penry maid, won't you?' the customer said, as if only just realizing it. 'How are you getting along on your own now that your gran's gone to her Maker? I never knew her to speak to, but I knew of her reputation in the town.'

Amber tried not to wince, unsure if this was supposed to be a criticism of her gran or not. If it was, she didn't want to hear it.

'I miss her, of course,' she said simply. 'But I'm

not entirely alone. The evacuee girl from London who came to live with us is still staying with me.'

The woman sniffed. 'That'll be the one who came to church with the two of you then. A bit of a flighty one, I always thought.'

'Dolly's all right,' Amber said, defending her. 'She had to go back to London for a while, but as soon as she heard Granny Pen had died she came back to keep me company. That's being a good friend, isn't it?'

'Well, if you say so, my dear. Look, I don't think I want anything today, so I'll be getting along now.'

Amber watched her go, wondering what she'd come in for in the first place, unless it was just for a bit of idle gossip. Well, she didn't get much out of her, not about Granny Pen, nor about Dolly. And Dolly *had* been a good friend to come back to Falmouth after Granny Pen died, she thought, even if they did get on one another's nerves at the drop of a pensioner's hat.

It was odd. When they first met, they were so different, and there was such great antagonism between them, but once they had got over that they became firm friends. Somehow, perhaps because of growing up, that special closeness, that feeling of sistership because they shared the same birthday, had gradually disappeared. They had to face the fact that they were different people now. There was still a bond between them, but bonds had a habit of breaking, however sad it seemed.

The sudden thought that it could be the same

when Luke came home again was something Amber refused to consider. Theirs was a bond that went far deeper. She believed it totally. She believed it in the way she could always visualize his face before she went to sleep at night. She could instantly remember the sensual touch of his hands and the way he kissed her, whether in tenderness or in passion. She would never lose the memory of the feelings he had awoken in her in the exquisite moments when his body had become part of hers and they shared the intimacy that was theirs alone. Nothing and nobody could take that away.

The tedium of the afternoon with so few people coming into the shop took away much of the euphoria that had lasted for those few blissful moments of remembering. By the time she closed the shop that day she wanted nothing more than to get away from it and to be with Luke's family. She almost forgot to lock the premises, and that would never do. She was entrusted to care for Mrs Veal's business now, in a way she would never have expected at so young an age.

It was true, everyone nowadays did have to grow up far quicker than they would have done in peacetime. Young men lied about their age in order to go to war and fight. Because of the uncertainties of the times, young women who married their sweethearts when they were hardly out of school became widows before they had really known what it was like to be a bride. School friends were bombed and killed . . . It was desperately sad, all of it, and if she didn't stop brooding like this, she was going to be no fit company for Luke's parents that evening, Amber told herself angrily. Her moods seemed to swing from elation to despair, and it wasn't going to help anybody. Determinedly, she put on a bright face as she cycled into the boatyard and knocked on the Gillams' front door.

Chapter Nineteen

Hester Gillam looked more flushed and tearful than when she had gone to the craft shop that morning. Amber's heart gave an uncomfortable leap when she saw her. Crazy thoughts tore through her head. Surely God hadn't deserted them after all? But why should God spare one young man among so many thousands, just because a young, foolishly in love Cornish maid wanted it so badly? She could hardly think straight, but she couldn't continue standing there like a dummy.

'What's happened?' Amber said hoarsely, in a voice that was hardly her own.

Hester's voice was just as unreal. 'I'm sorry if I frightened you, Amber. You caught me at a very bad moment, I'm afraid. Every now and then it all washes over me – how very lucky we are, and how terrible it must be for all those other families who don't yet know if their boys are alive or drowned.'

Amber's relief was tinged with an unreasonable resentment that she had been scared almost witless for nothing. Yet couldn't she understand Mrs

Gillam's feelings so well? They exactly matched her own wayward moods.

'Have you heard anything else, then?' she asked, trying to sound normal.

'Nothing yet,' Hester said. 'It seems that all we can do is wait. My husband makes constant calls to his friend, but there's a limit to how much we can be told, even about our own son.'

There was no mistaking the slight bitterness in her voice now, and Amber was instantly sympathetic. It must be just as bad for Luke's parents – but in a different way – as it was for her. They all loved him and wanted him home. If nothing else, he must know how much he was loved, she thought fleetingly, willing the thoughts to him across the miles.

'But we're not going to spend the evening being miserable, are we?' Mrs Gillam said, her voice changing. 'It's not what Luke would want.'

People said that, didn't they? But how did she know if it was what Luke would want? How could any of them know what Luke wanted right now, or how he was feeling, or how seriously he was really hurt? How could any of them know what went on in another person's head? How could Mrs Gillam know that her son and the girl she welcomed into her home were lovers? Would she look down on Amber if she knew? Would she feel ashamed of her son for giving in to lust?

Unanswered questions crowded in on her, and Amber flinched as the ugly word came into her head.

It wasn't lust . . . it was so much more . . . it was lust and love and passion and the ultimate closeness between a man and a woman. It was the fulfilment of something that had been there since childhood, if only they hadn't been too immature to see it. But perhaps everything had its right time, just as the seasons changed and children grew into adulthood. And this had been their time, their one precious time.

'Are you all right, my dear?' Hester asked. 'You look quite flushed.'

'I'm fine. I was just in a hurry to get here,' Amber said, floundering a little. 'It's good to be together, isn't it?'

Hester smiled, seeing far more than Amber imagined. She knew love when she saw it, and she felt a great tenderness towards this lovely girl who loved her son, who, she never had any doubt, loved Amber in return.

'Then why don't we think about getting some supper together? I'm sure you're hungry, and my cottage pie won't wait for ever to be eaten.'

Amber had never felt less like eating, and by the time the meal was ready she was even more sure she wouldn't be able to get anything down. Although Hester chided her, she pushed her plate away, apologizing for the fact that the food would be wasted, when it was such a sin to waste anything these days. Even before food rationing had taken such a grip on the country, Granny Pen used to say sternly that there were starving children in Africa who'd be glad of good, wholesome Cornish food. The words were only changed occasionally to accommodate starving children in India . . . or China . . . Amber swallowed, remembering.

Even though the Gillams were determined to be as normal as possible, it was a strange evening, reflected Amber later, as she left the boatyard to cycle home. Strange, and cosy at the same time. After supper they played cards for a while, and sometimes they chatted quite animatedly. At other times one of them would lapse into silence, while the other two unconsciously tried to compensate by talking more loudly, more brightly. And all the time, Amber knew that there could be only one thing on all their minds – how badly wounded Luke really was, and when he would be coming home again.

She had to pass the Forces' Club on her way home, and although it was in its obligatory blackout darkness, she could hear the sounds of raucous music and wild laughter coming from the hall. For a moment she both hated and envied those inside. Hated them because they had no worries, and envied them because they had the ability to enjoy themselves, no matter what happened. Dolly would be one of them, So little seemed to affect her deeply, not her father's death, nor the way her mum carried on with men. It must be less of a strain on the nerves to be so uncaring, even if it was all a front, but Amber knew she could never be that way.

The door to the club opened for a moment and several people came outside, laughing together. She saw a girl and a soldier, their arms wrapped tightly around one another, before they disappeared into the darkness. Amber wondered briefly about them, and how their evening would end. Would they chastely kiss goodnight at her door? Or find some secret and secluded spot to make love? She ached for Luke at that moment, longing for his arms around her and his kiss on her lips. Longing for the world to be normal again.

She heard someone hiss her name, and realized there was someone else standing in the dimness of the doorway.

'Are you coming in or not, Amber? It's bleedin' cold standing here like a flamin' doorman,' said Dolly's familiar voice.

'I'm on my way home.'

'Well, you can come in and have one dance, can't you? Don't be such a stick-in-the-mud. Luke won't kill you for enjoying yourself, and I won't tell him if you won't!'

Dolly was getting impatient, and on an impulse Amber thought why not? It wasn't being disloyal to Luke to take a look inside, even if she had no intention of dancing. But once inside the club, when she heard the music and saw how the remaining Yanks in the area were teaching the local girls to jitterbug, her feet began to itch. It looked like fun, and it seemed such a long time since she had had any fun. None of the Yanks here tonight were the ones she remembered. They came and went as their orders dictated, and apart from the local girls she recognized and the staff at the club, it was almost as good as being anonymous, being among strangers.

'Come on, Amber,' Dolly shrieked. 'Show 'em your stuff!'

Before she knew what was happening, a GI had grabbed Amber's hand and pulled her out on to the dance floor. She didn't know how to jitterbug properly, but in the crush of people it hardly mattered. All any of them wanted was to be caught up in the music and the excitement, and not to think about tomorrow. Such excitement was infectious, and, hardly knowing how it happened, it made her feel alive again.

'Your cockney friend's quite a gal, ain't she?' the GI said, when she had been whirled around the floor a few times. 'I ain't seen you here before, though. Are you local or from out of town?'

Amber wanted to giggle. The dancing was fast and furious and it was already making her dizzy. Her head felt as if it belonged to someone else. The GI had just asked a friendly question, and yet all she could think was how absurd it was, when her accent must tell him she had lived here all her life. He'd labelled Dolly right enough, even if all Londoners were cockneys to the Yanks.

Anyway, he must be very stupid, she bridled next, if he couldn't recognize a Cornish girl when he saw one! A *Falmouth* girl!

Then she saw what a nice smile he had, and she sobered at once. It was a bit patronizing to think like that about a stranger in their midst who was merely trying to be sociable.

'Oh, I'm very local, *extremely* local,' she exaggerated unnecessarily, while wondering if this dizziness was quite normal, and hoping she wasn't going to throw up all over him, or faint away on the spot. She had been so full of tension lately, worrying about Luke. It was hard to relax, and it was far too long since she had eaten, other than picking aimlessly at Mrs Gillam's cottage pie. Whirling around the dance floor like this certainly wasn't doing her insides any good at all.

'Say, do you want to go outside for some fresh air?' her dance partner said anxiously a while later. 'You do look kinda green. You should take more water with it, honey.'

She didn't know what he meant by that, but she was too keen to get out of the crowd to take much notice of the fact that Dolly was now shrieking with laughter and yelling after her to go for it, gel, whatever that was supposed to mean.

Once outside, she took a few deep breaths to try to keep down the nausea, and she felt the earth and sky swirl in front of her. This was it, then. She was about to disgrace herself, and Granny Pen's granddaughter would be branded for ever as a girl who couldn't control herself.

'It was very hot in there,' the GI said sympathetically. 'You should go home and sleep it off, honey. Your folks won't want to see you in this state.'

Amber realized that of course he thought she must have been *drinking*, and it was so ludicrous that she managed a croaking laugh.

'Thanks for your help,' she muttered, 'but I'll manage all right now. It's not far to the cottage where I live and I've got my bike.'

'And you'll probably come right off it,' she was told firmly. 'You'll allow Amber to take you home and see you safely indoors. No arguments now. Your father wouldn't thank me if I let you come to any harm.'

She looked at him mutely. He was being kind, but she didn't know him, nor did she know if she could trust him. Would it be wise to tell him that her father was dead, and that there would be nobody home at the cottage? She gave up thinking, as the nausea threatened to overwhelm her again.

'All right, then let's go,' she said. 'I really do need to go home.'

He took the bicycle from her, holding it with one hand, and tucking her arm in his with the other. She didn't object, feeling as though she would fall down without some support. She was weak with hunger and anxiety, and she began to wonder just what was wrong with a young, healthy girl of not-yet-eighteen who was dragging her feet now as if she was an old woman. Even Granny Pen had been far more sprightly than Amber felt now. For some reason her gran's name kept rushing into her head tonight. Maybe she was warning her to be careful, to keep her head, and not let herself be seduced by a handsome young American . . .

'You can trust me, you know,' this handsome young American said, when she had been silent for a while, and just as if he could read her mind. 'The name's Bart Durham, short for Bartholomew, and I've got a wife and daughter back home in Colorado who trust me too. All I want to do is see you safely home, kid.'

Amber was instantly ashamed of her earlier thoughts. She must have seemed so very ungracious, and half of it was due to Dolly's stupid remarks, she thought angrily, always getting things wrong, assuming Amber was going to be fair game for a bit of slap and tickle with a Yank, and act as flighty as herself.

'I'm sorry. It's just that I was brought up to be cautious,' she mumbled.

Bart squeezed her arm against his. 'Then your folks did a good job of raising you, Amber. It's a very cute name, by the way. That is your name, isn't it? I believe it's what your friend called you. You're not sisters, are you? You don't look alike.'

'Dolly lives with me – with us. She came to Falmouth as an evacuee at the beginning of the war, and we're *sort* of like sisters now,' she said awkwardly, not really knowing why she was giving him this potted bit of information, but having to say something. She was desperate to be home, to get something to eat to stop the gnawing in her stomach and to fall into bed. She wished she'd never been tempted to stop at the Forces' Club at all. It wasn't that she felt disloyal to Luke by having a dance, she reminded herself, because nothing could have been more innocent, but she wished she'd gone straight home all the same.

She felt even weaker with relief when they

reached the cottage. It was all in darkness, but that was nothing unusual, since they never let a chink of light show outside the house. Air raids had virtually stopped here now; the Jerries were all concentrating on London and the south-east with their evil new V-bombs. Blackout orders were still in force in most places, although some had relaxed them, even in parts of London, but it would be an easy way of explaining the darkness, if she felt she had to, and why the place looked deserted. She prayed that she wouldn't have to. Feeling jittery now, she didn't want to have to invite Bart Durham inside, and she really, really hoped he wouldn't expect it.

He obviously felt more at ease than Amber did, because he released her arm at the gate of the cottage and handed her bicycle to her.

'I'll just wait here until I see you safely indoors, Amber, and then I have to get back and collect my buddies. It was good knowing you, honey.'

She hardly knew what to say to that, so she muttered something appropriate, and then she fled up the garden path, dropping her bike outside the house and going inside quickly. She leaned against the door, feeling her heart hammer much too fast. It must be due to the lack of food, she told herself, but whatever it was, she didn't like the feeling of not being in control of herself this way. Nor did she like the feeling of foolishness at thinking a kind stranger was going to take advantage of her. She wasn't some simpering Victorian virgin, she thought angrily. She wasn't a virgin at all.

She went straight to the kitchen, made herself a spam sandwich and ate it hungrily. Then she made another one and wolfed that down too. She was going to be no good to Luke or anybody else if she turned into a walking skeleton before he came home. She blotted out all other thoughts and went to bed, her head thumping violently.

She awoke late the following morning, washed and dressed hurriedly before having a hasty breakfast, and yelled out to Dolly that she was going to work. There was no reply, and, fuming, she ran back upstairs, rapped on Dolly's door and opened it without waiting for an answer.

She stared at the empty room and the unruffled bed. She realized that since Dolly normally made enough noise to waken the dead, it was impossible that she had already dressed and gone out. Besides, she never made her bed before she left for work, because she was always in such an almighty hurry. And this bed definitely hadn't been slept in.

Amber's heart began to beat uncomfortably fast. Combined with the headache that hadn't gone away and threatened to become a corker, she didn't know what to do or to think, and it took a few minutes for her brain to work logically. If Dolly hadn't come home last night, then she must have been somewhere else, and been with someone else. But Dolly wasn't in the habit of making many friends among those she often called the country hicks, and the last time Amber had seen her she had had her arms wrapped around a Yank and was shrieking like a banshee to Amber to go for it, gel.

Amber shivered. If Dolly meant what she thought she meant, it was more than likely that Dolly had gone for it herself . . . and anyone with half a brain could see what that meant. Amber had just never expected her to stay out all night. She had never been so rash before, and she was still trying not to think of the alternative – that something bad had happened to Dolly. There had been plenty of drink flowing at the Forces' Club last night. She had smelled it strongly on Dolly's breath, and on the Yanks' breaths too. Everyone had been set on having a good time . . . but Dolly hadn't come home, and there was no knowing what might have happened to her.

'Stop it,' Amber said out loud to herself. 'There's probably a perfectly reasonable explanation, and Dolly's not the type to fall into the harbour after having too much to drink, or anything so daft.'

It sounded reasonable enough when she said it aloud, but just as quickly she knew it wasn't daft at all, and that it could be the truth. There was only one way to find out. Dolly should have started her morning shift by now, and Amber would just have to go to the club and find out if she'd turned up. She felt responsible for her in a way she had never intended or wanted. She wasn't her pseudo-sister's keeper, she thought, in an attempt to be flippant. But if anything had happened to Dolly, she knew she would be devastated all the same. They had come too far for her to feel completely detached, however much Dolly irritated her.

Once she was ready to leave the cottage she pedalled down to the Forces' Club. The first thing she saw was Dolly's bicycle among the others propped up outside. It didn't mean a thing, because Dolly would have cycled there last night, anyway. She pushed open the door and looked inside. Jennie, the supervisor, saw her at once and called out cheerfully that she hoped she had less of a sore head than her friend this morning.

At that moment Dolly appeared from a back room, looking deathly pale and heavy eyed. She perked up slightly when she saw Amber, and then clamped her hands to her mouth again.

'I can't talk now,' she said hoarsely. 'I ain't been off the bleedin' lav all morning, what with the squits and the puking. We'll compare notes tonight, gel.'

She managed to give a wink before she fled, and Jennie sniffed.

'Some night she must have had. I hope yours was better, Amber.'

'I went home and went to bed,' Amber snapped.

'Well, that's what I mean.'

Amber turned on her heels, her cheeks burning, banging the door behind her. The damn nerve of the woman, implying that she was doing anything other than sleeping in her own bed – and on her own, too! She supposed it was all round the club that she'd left there last night with Bart Durham, she thought, seething. She'd have something to say to Dolly that evening if she was spreading false rumours about her and a Yank, however nice he was, when he had a wife and daughter back home in Colorado.

By the middle of the day she had calmed down a little, although her headache still raged, and she was in no mood to be teased about what she had or hadn't got up to. Dolly could be like a red rag to a bull when she wanted to find out something, and what she couldn't find out, she was just as likely to invent.

The one bit of good news during the afternoon – the one bit of wonderful, spectacularly good news – was when Luke's mother called in to tell her the news about Luke was now confirmed and official. They had had a telegram to say that he was safe and in hospital, and Mick Gillam was pulling every string he knew to contact the hospital that evening to find out when they could have Luke home. It was the brightest spot in the entire day.

She reached home after work to find Dolly lolling on the sofa. She hadn't done anything about preparing an evening meal, which was the first thing they had agreed upon, depending on who was home first. Amber was in no mood to be tolerant. She felt her temper rising, because just like Granny Pen she believed that people who lived together should be sharing the tasks. This was her cottage now and Dolly was the lodger, who should do her share . . .

'I suppose the food will cook itself then, will it?' Amber snapped.

Dolly scowled. From the pallor in her cheeks, Amber guessed that her head was still far from feeling normal either. But it was no excuse.

She snapped back at Amber. 'What's got up your nose today? I thought you'd have been all sweetness and light after going off with that horny Yank last night. It didn't take you long to forget Lukey-boy, did it?' she added with a sneer.

Amber clenched her hands together. 'Sometimes you can be so *stupid*, Dolly. If you think I could forget Luke for one minute, it just shows that you don't know the first thing about the way I feel. And I didn't *go off* with Bart last night in the way you seem to think. He just saw me home, that's all. It was all perfectly innocent, not that it's any of your business. Besides, you're the one who didn't come home last night, so don't think everyone's as big a tart as you are.'

She was gabbling far too fast, defending herself when she knew perfectly well there was no need for it.

Dolly sat bolt upright, and the next minute she was on her feet, her hands on her hips, her eyes practically spitting fire as they confronted one another.

'What the bleedin' hell do you mean by calling me a tart? You always think yourself so bloody superior to me, don't you? Just because I know how to have a good time, don't pretend that you ain't thought about doing the same, Miss High-and-mighty.'

346

'Having a good time doesn't have to involve getting a bad reputation, which is the way you'll end up,' Amber shouted.

'Oh yes? Well, I ain't got much else to think about in this dreary hole, have I? You never wanted me here, and God knows why I stay.'

'Why don't you go, then? I'm sure your mother can find another *Uncle Joe* for you, with all her dubious connections,' Amber said insultingly.

This was too much for Dolly. She lunged forward, grabbing Amber's long hair and pulling it hard. Amber screamed, retaliating at once, yanking and twisting Dolly's blonde curls and making her yell with pain, and then they were hitting, scratching and punching, digging their fingernails into one another's skin, losing their balance and sprawling in an ungainly heap on the floor. They were shrieking at one another like fishwives until Amber finally got the better of Dolly. She straddled her, forcing her arms back on the floor, her own chest heaving with fury over what was happening. But Dolly wasn't done with her yet.

'You think you're so bleedin' clever, don't you?' she screamed. 'But I don't think you're as prissy as you make out. I saw the way you was dancing with Bart what's-his-name last night, and I saw the way he had his hands all over you when you left the club. You was hot for it, bitch, just as I was, and don't tell me you ain't never done it, because I just don't believe you!'

'What do you mean?' Amber snapped.

'What do you think I mean? Don't act dumb with me, Amber Penry,' Dolly yelled right in her face, while still trying to get her arms out of Amber's fierce grip. 'I'm bloody well sure you've *done* it, same as me, and what do you think Lukey-boy's going to say about that when he finds out he's got soiled goods?'

If Amber had been flushed before, she felt as if her whole face was on fire now. Of course she had *done* it, as Dolly put it so crudely, but it wasn't any nasty bit of fumbling in a dark corner or in the back of a Jeep . . . it had been one beautiful, wonderful experience with the man she loved, and Dolly Nash had effectively ruined that lovely memory, the way she ruined everything.

She released Dolly with a suddenness that took them both by surprise, and then Dolly was rubbing her sore arms and looking up at Amber with narrowed eyes.

'Well now, country girl, it don't take a genius to see that I was right. Your face gives you away, so now I reckon you ain't going to say anything when Lukey-boy comes home and I have a go at him myself, are you? Not if you don't want him to know how you've been playing around with the Yanks while he's been at sea.'

'You disgust me,' Amber said, her voice harsh and shaking. She got up from the floor, feeling dirty and ashamed. 'I have *never* played around with any Yank, and Bart was a perfect gentleman last night when I wasn't feeling well. You were the one who never came home, and God knows what you were up to. *He* knows, but I don't want to know about your grubby little goings-on. I don't want to talk to you or look at you.'

'Suits me,' Dolly snapped. 'Until I decide what I'm going to do, I'll keep me own rations and do me own cooking, then, as long as I'm allowed to use your pots and pans. Will that please your ladyship?'

Amber bit her lips hard. She couldn't help thinking how Granny Pen would have hated all this, and how sad and horrified she would be at the way her two girls were tearing one another apart. Granny Pen had been fond of Dolly, even if she hadn't been one of her own.

'*Well?*' Dolly demanded in the small silence. 'Is that what you want?'

One of them had to be magnanimous and break this deadlock. It wasn't backing down. It was being grown-up and sensible. Amber took a deep breath.

'No, it's not what I want. While we're still living in the same house I want us to be civilized. We may not like each other very much right now, but we've shared a lot of years together, Dolly, and I don't want it to end like this.'

Dolly didn't say anything for a minute and then she shrugged.

'I'd better start the supper then,' she said.

It was impossible to think that everything was going to be back to normal after that. Too many hurtful things had been said, too many accusations had been

349

thrown on both sides. Each of them knew they were only marking time, being forcibly polite to one another, waiting, waiting . . .

What exactly were they waiting for? Amber wondered. Waiting for the war to end, like everyone else, as it dragged inexorably on towards another Christmas. Waiting for Luke to come home, with the worry over his injuries, and now the added tension of what Dolly had said, and knowing she would do exactly what she had threatened. She would have a go at Luke herself, and if Amber objected, she would tell Luke that his whiter-than-white girlfriend had been playing around with the Yanks while he had been at sea. Amber had no doubt she would do as she said.

It seemed to prove something Amber should have seen a long time ago, ever since Dolly first came to the cottage, a thin miserable little girl with blonde curls and big blue eyes, who she had never realized could be so calculating. Wanting to fit in, wanting to be friends, wanting Amber's friends, wanting Amber's gran, wanting everything that Amber had.

Dolly was acquisitive, wanting what everyone else had, and now she wanted Luke. It probably wasn't even that she wanted him for any other reason but that he was Amber's boy. And she would never have him, Amber vowed savagely.

Chapter Twenty

It was clear to everyone now that the Allies were winning the war. The big question was not when, but how soon? Rommel had committed suicide in October, and if that wasn't an indication of how desperate the enemy was getting, they didn't know what was, said the local sages. All the Allied fronts reported victories in pushing back the enemy and gaining ground. At home, the fact that the Home Guard had been stood down gave everybody fresh hope that the final victory couldn't be very far away now.

As far as Amber Penry was concerned, she was just desperate to know whether or not Luke would be home before Christmas, for this was one that she especially wanted to share with him. In her saner moments, she brushed aside all thoughts of Dolly Nash's silly threats, because she knew that Luke loved her and wouldn't pay any attention to evil gossip. All the same, she wouldn't feel completely secure until he was home again and she could see for herself.

The Gillams were well known in the town, and the news that their son was one of the survivors from the *Tigress* had quickly spread. At church on the Sunday after the account appeared in the local newspaper, the vicar made a special point of remembering Luke and giving thanks to the Almighty for having spared him. After the service, friends and acquaintances congratulated Mick and Hester as if it was they who had done something marvellous. There were small groups around the couple on that crisp December morning, wanting to know the details, and where Luke was right now, and Amber felt totally detached from it all.

Luke wasn't her relative, and they weren't married or officially engaged, or even walking out together as far as most people knew. She had no rights to any warm words from well-wishers, the way his parents had rights. She had no claim on him, other than what they both knew in their hearts – and as yet she had no idea if Luke's hazy memory would even permit him to remember how close they had been.

Hester Gillam caught sight of Amber, standing awkwardly by the church gate and waiting for her friend Dolly to catch up with her – when she could tear herself away from the group of young servicemen she was talking to. Ever since that fateful night following the dance at the Forces' Club, they had kept their distance as much as possible, but as if by tacit consent they kept up the semblance of friendship as far as outsiders were concerned.

'There's no need to look so anxious, Amber,' Hester told her quietly. 'As soon as we hear when they'll be sending Luke home, you'll be the first to know, and you know you can call at the house any time you like. I realize it must seem as if we're getting all the limelight here today, my dear, but it's hardly the kind of limelight we would have chosen, I assure you.'

'Of course it's not,' Amber said hurriedly, wondering just how petulant she had appeared. 'I do understand, Mrs Gillam, and of course I'm glad that people are so pleased for you.'

'But you're feeling left out.'

'I know I shouldn't be, but yes, if I'm honest, that's exactly how I feel. I know it's silly but I can't help it.'

'It's not silly at all. Luke is lucky to be loved by so many people.'

It was hardly as personal as hearing her say that Luke was lucky to have a girl like Amber to love him, but she had to be content with that, knowing there were other people around, and that Dolly was tripping her way towards them now.

'I'm *really* looking forward to having Luke home again, Mrs Gillam,' Dolly told Hester, gushing. 'I can't wait to hear the tales he'll have to tell about his time at sea. He must have been so brave.'

Amber couldn't believe her gall, insinuating herself into the conversation, and pushing herself forward as if she was the girl Luke would be coming home to see.

Hester gave a slight smile. 'I doubt that Luke will be anxious to say very much about those times, Dolly. As for being brave, it goes without saying that they're all brave. War makes men out of boys.'

She moved away to join her husband, and Dolly scowled, not missing the fact that she had been put in her place.

'Well, that was a pretty senseless thing to say, wasn't it?' Amber said coldly. 'Do you really think all that gush cut any ice with his mother?'

'I don't give a monkey's. It's not his mother I'm interested in.'

She blew a mocking kiss towards Amber and strolled off. If ever Dolly was showing her true colours, Amber seethed, she was doing it now all right. It was a pity nobody else could see beyond the sugary prettiness.

It was impossible for Amber to keep away from the boatyard in the next couple of weeks. The news from Alexandria was frustratingly slow, and having studied an old map of the area, and seen just how far away the Egyptian port was, Amber realized how long it would be before Luke came home, even when he was fit enough to do so. The trouble was, the longer it took, the more afraid she was over the extent of his injuries, and what the authorities weren't telling his family.

The day finally came when Hester Gillam greeted her with a smile and a hug that was more effusive than usual.

'We've had positive news at last, Amber. Luke's

head injuries were quite worrying, I understand, but his memory has returned, and the deafness was only temporary. He'll recover completely, and he'll be due for an honourable discharge, which means his days at sea are over. Officially, that is. I can't imagine he'll stay away from boats and the sea for ever, knowing how he and his father have always been so besotted by it!'

She was the one talking over-fast now, Amber thought, as if she couldn't get the eager words out quickly enough. There were tears in her eyes, too, and impulsively Amber hugged her back.

'It's wonderful news, Mrs Gillam, and I can't tell you how thrilled I am to hear it! Will he be home for Christmas then?'

She willed the woman to say yes, but her heart sank as she saw the smile slip a little on Hester's face. She shook her head.

'I don't think so. They want to keep him in Alexandria a little while longer, and then there's the voyage home to be arranged, and he'll be sent straight to a naval hospital to assess his progress before they finally discharge him.'

'But that could take weeks!' Amber said, the excitement disappearing fast.

'I know, but we just have to be patient, and be thankful that at least he was one of the lucky ones. There were so very few of them, dear.'

Amber nodded, ashamed of her outburst. 'I can write to him now though, can't I? I want to let him know – well, just, things,' she finished lamely.

'Of course you can. I'm going to write to him tonight myself. I know he'll be glad to get letters from home, but I'm sure the one he'll be looking out for will be the one from you.'

Amber blushed, knowing she had made her feelings too plain, but glad that Hester seemed to see nothing odd in it. She went home to the cottage with a piece of paper with the precious address in her pocket, determined that very night she was going to write to Luke, and she wasn't going to hold her feelings back.

'So what's the latest?' Dolly asked her when they met at the cottage that evening. 'Is Lukey-boy coming home for Christmas?'

'For goodness' sake, stop calling him that,' Amber said, nettled at once. 'No, he won't be home for Christmas, but he'll be home eventually, and all in one piece, thank the Lord. They'll send him to a naval hospital in England once the Egyptian doctors have finished with him.'

'That's if he wants to come back to England,' Dolly said slyly.

'Don't be daft. Why wouldn't he?'

'Well, I daresay he's had a pretty cushy time with all those luscious, dark-skinned little nurses looking after him and attending to his every need, if you know what I mean.'

'I hardly think I'd call having his ship torpedoed and sunk and being badly injured as having a cushy time!'

356

'Maybe not, but all the attention he got would have made up for it. Those Egyptian girls would be sure to make a fuss of a handsome bloke like our Lukey-boy. I'm told they go for white-skinned boys.'

Amber glared at her. 'If that's supposed make me jealous, you're wasting your time. Can't you just be glad that he's safe, and that he's coming home?'

'Oh, I'm glad all right. I can't wait,' Dolly said, with a platinum smile that was supposed to hide the barb.

'Sometimes, Dolly, you make me sick,' Amber told her, and went straight upstairs to her bedroom and slammed the door behind her.

Immediately she'd done it, she clenched her hands tightly. This wasn't right. This was her home, and she shouldn't feel she had to come upstairs and hide herself away to avoid Dolly's vicious little insinuations. She hadn't even thought about the doctors and nurses who would be tending Luke. All she had felt was gratitude that they were making him whole again. Now Dolly had managed to spoil all that. She never seemed to hold on to a boy of her own for very long, and now she was making it her business to make Amber's faith in Luke waver. They used to be such friends, Amber thought, with a stab of regret, but all that was changed now.

'Oh, damn and blast her,' she muttered out loud. 'I'm not going to think about her any more. There are more important things to think about.'

She went to the small bureau that had once been her gran's and now had pride of place in her bedroom to fetch writing paper and envelopes. She kept a photo of Granny Pen on top of the bureau, and she looked at it ruefully.

'You'd hate all this, wouldn't you, Gran?' she said softly. 'We never had any fights when you were around, did we?'

Well, they certainly did, she remembered wryly, but they were childish fights, and never anything like this. If this was what happened when you grew up, then it would be better to remain children all your life, she thought fervently, while knowing that it could never be.

'I'll make an effort if she will, Gran,' she said to the photo, and the next minute she jumped as she heard Dolly's mocking voice outside her door.

'Talking to yourself again, gel? That's the first sign of going mad, in case you don't know it. Though I reckon you must be in the final stages by now!'

Her laughter echoed through the cottage and then Amber heard the front door bang as Dolly went out for the evening. Up to more devil tricks, perhaps . . .

She wrote Luke's name and address on an envelope, propping it up in front of her where she could see it, and revelling in the fact that it was going to reach him across the miles of land and sea, and that he would recognize her handwriting at once, because he had known it all his life.

She began the letter, but it was more difficult than she expected. Somehow she was no longer in the mood for saying all that she wanted to say. She had imagined it would be so easy to write from her heart, to spill out all the love she had for him, and to tell him how much she was longing to see him again. But somehow the words wouldn't come, and the letter ended up as a few stilted sentences, and it was nothing like the way she had wanted it to be. She read it over, trying to see it through his eyes, and knew it wasn't right. It just wasn't right.

'Dear Luke,' she read,

'Your mum and dad have been keeping me up to date with all that's been happening, and I'm so relieved to know that you're going to be all right, and will be coming home soon. It's a shame that you won't be home for Christmas, but all the signs are that 1945 is going to be a good year for all of us and that this war will be over for good. We all miss you.'

She squirmed as she read those words. Who were all these people who were missing him, for pity's sake? She didn't care about any of them, and it wasn't a personal enough message when what she really meant to say was that *she* missed him, that *she* was the one waiting for him. She screwed up the letter and threw it in her wastebin, and tried again. But it was no good. She would leave it until later, maybe until tomorrow, when she could think more clearly.

It was weird and depressing and frustrating, because she had always felt she could say anything to Luke, and now, when she wanted to say the most important things of all, the words failed her.

She felt restless with the need to do something other than staying up here in her bedroom, or listening to the wireless or reading a book. She glanced at her clock. It was still quite early on a fine December evening, and she decided to go for a cycle ride up to Pendennis Castle. Maybe being in some of the favourite places where she and Luke had gone so often, as children and as lovers, would dispel this strange feeling of unease, at a time when she should be so happy.

As always, the fresh clean air did much to dispel the uneasy feelings and helped her to think more clearly. Instead of the negative feelings about how long it would be before Luke would be coming home, she began to feel more cheerful, more alive. It was going to happen, and they would be together again as they were always meant to be, and life would be wonderful. The awful war years would be behind them and they could think of a shared future. Her heart gave a little flip of joy, imagining the day when she would walk down the aisle of the church on Luke's arm, dressed in white, a filmy veil over her face, a bouquet of roses in her hand. Then they would be together for ever . . . for better or worse. But it would only be for the better, Amber thought positively.

Good things were happening already. The hated barbed wire along the beaches had long been removed, and the ships of war that had filled the harbour were fewer now, and there were other craft bobbing about, regular craft, the ferries and fishing boats that busily plied their trade for people with more important things on their minds than the business of war. Things like living, and loving, and raising children who were no longer under the threat of an invasion.

She smiled at herself, wondering where all this philosophizing was coming from in a nearly eighteen-year-old. Everybody said it was one effect of the war, making people older before their time, making soldiers and sailors and airmen out of schoolboys, making widows out of young brides . . . Amber felt her smile waver, and she wished these black thoughts hadn't entered her mind again just when she was beginning to feel more hopeful about the future.

She had been out for more than an hour now and the light was starting to fade, but since she knew every inch of the highways and byways of the town she had no worries about getting home safely. All the same, there was a chill in the air, another reminder that Christmas wasn't so very far away. Amber forced herself to think that even if Luke wouldn't be home for Christmas, there was another new year just around the corner, and this was definitely the one that everyone said would bring all their men home.

She was feeling decidedly calmer when she reached the cottage, her normal bubbling self returning fast. She turned on the wireless, her spirits lifting still more as she heard the rhythmic sounds of Victor Sylvester's dance music drifting out into the room, instead of the constant war news.

She hummed to the music as she dashed upstairs to her bedroom to hang up her coat, and then she stood very still. At first glance nothing was amiss, and there was no reason to think anyone had been here. Dolly was out, and although nobody locked their doors in this area, burglars wouldn't find anything much to steal here. All the same, there was something . . .

Amber closed her eyes tight, as if by shutting out her surroundings her senses would tell her whatever it was that was wrong. Granny Pen always said that all the senses became more alert in total darkness. It drifted into her nostrils then . . . the pungent, sickly sweet scent of Dolly's perfume.

Amber's eyes opened swiftly, knowing Dolly had been back, knowing she had been in here, in Amber's sanctuary. They had long ago agreed not to invade one another's privacy unless invited, but Dolly had been here for some reason . . .

She looked quickly around the room. Nothing seemed to be disturbed. No drawers had been left half open. The cupboard where Amber kept her precious memory box was still closed. It didn't seem as if the wastebin had been rummaged through. There was just one thing. Amber's heart began to beat painfully fast as she went towards the bureau. The envelope with Luke's address on it, ready for her to send him a letter, had been propped upright when she'd left the cottage, giving her a warm feeling by just knowing she could contact him there. Now the envelope lay flat on the bureau.

In an instant, Amber knew what had happened. Dolly had been here, copied out Luke's address in the Egyptian hospital, and planned to write to him herself. Maybe she had already done so, and there was little doubt about what poison she was going to tell him. Amber's shock turned to rage.

The little bitch wasn't going to get away with it. She turned and ran downstairs, not bothering to turn off the wireless, even if it used up the whole accumulator. What did such things matter? She leaped on her bike again, regardless of the fact that it was colder now, and that she wasn't wearing a coat. She tore through the streets towards the Forces' Club. Dolly didn't have a shift to do, but Amber was sure she'd find her there, toadying up to whoever would buy her a drink or ask her for a dance. At that moment Amber hated her with a vengeance.

She flung down her bike and went inside. Sure enough there was Dolly, giggling and smirking with a couple of soldiers, and Amber saw red. She marched over to Dolly, grabbed her by the hair and yelled in her ear.

'You think you're very clever don't you, bitch? Well, it's the last time you go into my room, because I'm having a lock put on it to keep you out. And the sooner you go back to whatever hole you climbed out of, the better.'

Dolly was gasping with pain now as Amber yanked at her blonde hair, but some semblance of sanity must have told her not to retaliate. Her blue eyes filled with tears, and she was blubbering like a baby.

'I'm really sorry, Amber! I didn't mean to pry, honest. I just wanted to find my comb that you borrowed and forgot to give me back.'

She said it loudly enough and yet still whiningly enough for everyone around them to hear and to gain maximum sympathy for herself. The soldiers prised Amber's fingers away from Dolly's head, which she began to rub gingerly, while those around them looked at Amber in disgust at making such an unprovoked attack on her friend.

Amber couldn't believe it. She had come here full of righteous indignation, and somehow she was turning into the bad guy! She was probably the only one who noticed the calculating look of triumph in Dolly's eyes, because nobody else knew what had gone on before. Hearing the muttering voices around her, clearly murmuring that Amber Penry was as mad as her grandmother, she turned and flounced out the way she had come, holding her head as high as possible, her eyes stinging with tears. Knowing she had made a fool of herself didn't help her feelings one bit, nor did the realization that now that she had Luke's hospital address Dolly was certainly going to spread her vicious lies to him, if she hadn't done so already.

She rode back home hardly seeing where she was going, since her eyes were smarting so much. Why couldn't she have waited instead of rushing into things the way she always did? But now she intended to write to Luke immediately and get her own letter in the post, and she was in no mood to hold back on her feelings, including the fact that she hoped Dolly would soon be leaving for Norfolk with her family, the way she kept hinting. There was nothing wrong in telling him that!

She went to bed early, not wanting to be around when Dolly came home. She heard her, though, banging doors and singing tunelessly, obviously intending to annoy her even more. Amber didn't bite. She lay tensely in her bed, wondering if her bedroom door would burst open next and Dolly would start crowing over her again.

It never happened, and eventually she relaxed and fell asleep, and when she got up the next morning, Dolly had already gone out. By the time they met again that evening, the atmosphere between them was icy, and the news they had to tell one another was delivered in as distant a way as possible.

'I'm going to the Gillams' for Christmas Day,' Amber announced, having had the invitation from Hester that afternoon.

'I'm going home for Christmas,' Dolly said, 'so we won't have to pretend to like one another, will we?'

Despite her relief, Amber felt a sense of misery wash over her. What had happened to all the friendship they had shared over the years – the giggles, the secrets, the childhood indiscretions, the cosy sense of being 'us against the world'?

'Dolly, don't let's be like this,' she said.

'Well, you started it, coming down to the Club last night and making such a show of yourself!'

'I *know*. But it wasn't me who was snooping about in somebody else's room, was it? And don't deny it. I could smell that awful scent you wear. I had to open the window to get rid of it; the room practically needed fumigating!'

Dolly glared at her, and then her lips twitched. 'You've got as big a bleedin' nose as Granny Pen used to have, ain't yer?' she said in an exaggerated way. 'I could never hide anything from her, either. Anyway, what did you have in there that was so bleedin' precious? I only wanted me comb back, and you can't deny that you'd borrowed it.'

Grudgingly, Amber wondered if she'd been wrong after all. It was true that she had forgotten to return Dolly's comb, which she was forever fussing about, and the envelope with Luke's address on it *could* just have fallen down. Perhaps she had even left it that way herself. There was still Dolly's determination to pursue Luke for herself, though, and the lies she intended telling him . . .

'So are we going to act like this from now on?' Dolly said, pushing the advantage as she saw Amber wavering. 'I'm fed up with the silent treatment, not that you were exactly silent last night, were you? Your temper don't improve with age, does it, gel?'

'Neither does yours. But I don't suppose Granny Pen would want us to be at each other's throats all the time. And you're definitely going home for Christmas?'

Dolly shrugged. 'Said so, didn't I? I never say what I don't mean.'

Such a comment could well be double-edged, but Amber had to admit that Dolly was a better friend than an enemy, and if they had to live together they just had to compromise. And who knew? Once Dolly went back to London for Christmas, perhaps she'd decide to stay . . . or at least make plans for moving to Norfolk with her mum and Uncle Joe . . .

'All right. Let's forget it,' she said at last.

'Ain't you going to say sorry for making such a fuss last night and nearly tearing my hair out, then?' Dolly taunted.

Amber gave a short, brittle laugh. 'Don't push it, Dolly.'

She never did get around to asking someone to put a lock on her bedroom door, hoping that it was enough of a gesture to Dolly that she trusted her . . . even if she didn't, not entirely. Both of them were glad when Christmas was only days away, and Dolly packed up her things and left for London. Maybe when she returned they would be able to feel more comfortable with one another, thought Amber.

By then she had had a garbled letter from Luke. She had scooped it up from the front doormat one morning, her heart leaping as she saw his handwriting on the envelope, thankful that Dolly wasn't there to ask who her letter was from. She took the letter to the outside lav in the yard so that she wouldn't be disturbed. The fact that his handwriting was far less firm than usual made her mouth tremble before she ripped the envelope open to read what Luke had written.

'My dear Amber,' she read, glorying in that one little word *My*. He remembered that she was his Amber, his girl.

'Sorry I haven't been in touch before, but the old head took a hell of a battering, and I lost some days or weeks without knowing what really happened. This meant that when I recovered my memory it was just as painful to learn about it all as when it first happened. I was luckier than a lot of my mates, and I know my mother has put you in the picture about what happened to the old *Tigress* and to me. It will have been a shock to you – and to me, believe me! I was starting to think I had a charmed life, what with the piece of amber you gave me and everything.

'I've still got it, by the way, although God knows how it remained in my pocket. The nurses seemed to think it was something special. They put it on my bedside locker so that I saw it every time I opened my eyes, hoping it would trigger my memory. I suppose it did, though for days I kept looking at it and frowning when the memories wouldn't come, and that only made the head pains worse. I'm only telling you all this so that you won't think I'm being odd if I go away to be on my own sometimes when I get home. When the head pains come, I don't want to be around anybody. The nurses here are wonderful and they understand this, but I can't expect everybody to do so. I don't know yet when I'll be coming home, anyway, as they're sending me to some naval hospital when I leave here, but, even if I'm still a bit battered and bruised, with any luck I'll be home in time for your birthday. You see, I remember that!'

He finished by sending her love and saying he looked forward to seeing her soon, but by then Amber's eyes were filled with tears and her throat was choked with the effort of not crying out loud. She knew it wasn't only the realization that he was far from being the old Luke yet. It was shameful jealousy, raw and sharp, that these nurses who had cared for him – the nurses Dolly had referred to slyly as luscious dark-skinned Egyptian girls who were partial to white-skinned boys – obviously knew this Luke far better than she did now. They had sensed that his precious piece of amber was special, yet it had taken him days or weeks to remember it – or her.

The sudden banging on the door of the lav made her jump.

'What the bleedin' hell are you doing in there, Amber? You're not the only one in need of a pee in the morning! Hurry up before I water the cabbages instead.'

Amber thrust the letter back in its envelope and slid it deep inside her pocket. There was no way she was going to let it out of her possession, especially for Dolly to find and gawp over. She opened the door of the lav, and was almost knocked over as Dolly rushed in, still grumbling.

Before she came out again, Amber was already on her way to work, red-eyed and heart-sore at all that had happened to her sweetheart, and wondering for the first time just how changed he was going to be when he came home again.

Chapter Twenty-one

Mrs Veal went away to spend Christmas with her sister and wouldn't be back in Falmouth until the beginning of the new year. She had become more melancholy of late, often commenting that she wondered why she stayed in Falmouth at all now that Father had gone, leaving her with so little interest in the shop. Amber spent Christmas with the Gillams, which was the next best thing to having Luke home, and by then they had heard the welcome news that he would be arriving at a naval hospital in Portsmouth in early January and, if all went well, he would be home for good before the end of the month.

'That's wonderful news. He said he hoped to be home in time for my birthday,' Amber said joyfully, 'although I haven't heard much from him lately.'

She tried not to sound petulant, but Hester told her that they had only had a brief letter from him too, wishing them a happy Christmas and sending his regards to Amber through his parents. It didn't sound like the words of a lover, but she steadfastly refused to have any bad omens about it, or to wonder if Dolly had really sent him a letter filling his head with lies over what Amber had been up to with the Yanks. In any case, she had too much pride to ask her. There was still a certain amount of tension between the girls, but at least Amber was positive there had been no letter back for Dolly, because Amber made a point of always being downstairs when the postman came. It hadn't been that long, she kept telling herself, even though his parents had had that one letter from him at Christmas and she hadn't.

All the newspapers were full of such optimism now, detailing the victories, large and small, that the Allies were achieving. No matter how happy the Christmas festivities, the talk inevitably turned to some aspect of the war – or the peace.

Almost for the first time, Amber began to wonder what it would be like to live in peacetime again. She had been a child when the war began, but she was a woman now. She was young and in love, and impatient for her lover to come home, and she didn't care if she was seeing the future through rose-coloured glasses. It was Luke's serious-minded father who pointed out a different side to it all, and Mick was quite adamant that there would be a period of adjustment for everyone.

'How can it be otherwise when people have been away from their loved ones for so long? And I'm not just talking about Luke, nor making this a personal observation. But think of the past five years. We've all been caught up in it, whether we went to war, or stayed at home. Our lives have changed, along with rationing and blackouts and heartbreak. Like every other town, we've been overtaken with military personnel. The Yanks have mostly come and gone, but we've all become used to a very different way of life from our ordinary peacetime routines. We're all different people now.'

'For heaven's sake, Mick, I think you'd better change the subject,' Hester said. 'It's not very festive for Christmas evening, and you're scaring Amber.'

'He's not scaring me, Mrs Gillam, but he's making me see things from a different viewpoint,' she admitted.

Mick nodded approvingly. 'You're an intelligent young girl, Amber, and you know as well as the rest of us that there's been tragedy as well as excitement, joyful reunions for some and dreaded telegrams for others. We've experienced it ourselves, and so has every other family. In fact, I doubt that there's one family in Cornwall that hasn't been touched by the war in one way or another.'

'Now that's quite enough for one night,' Hester said firmly. 'Why don't we all have a game of cards and remember that this is supposed to be a joyful occasion, too? I don't want Amber going home feeling upset and gloomy.' She glanced at the girl, seeing her downcast face. 'In fact, instead of going back to an empty cottage, why don't you stay the night, Amber? I don't know why I haven't thought of it before. Luke's bed is always made up, but it's up to you, of course, my dear.'

The offer took Amber by surprise, but she was never going to refuse, and a couple of hours later when they had played cards until they were dizzy, drunk endless cups of cocoa and eaten final thinly filled mince pies, she was shown into the bedroom that was Luke's, wearing a borrowed nightdress from his mother. Minutes later she was sliding beneath the cool covers of Luke's bed.

It was something she had never dared to think about, and she wondered if Hester had had any idea how she would feel. How rapturous and poignant the moment when she breathed in the freshness of the cotton sheets and curled her arms around Luke's pillow, resting her cheek against it and caressing its softness, knowing this was where his head usually rested. She wished with all her heart that it was Luke that she held so close to her, and she tried to transmit her thoughts and her love across the miles to wherever he was right now.

Dolly came back from London a few days after Christmas in a sullen mood, saying very little about the time she had spent with her mother and Uncle Joe, which to Amber meant that it hadn't gone well. In any case, Dolly was more interested in the New Year's Eve celebrations which were to be held at the Forces' Club.

'You're coming with me, aren't you?' she asked. 'You don't want to be sitting alone at home on New Year's Eve.'

It dawned on Amber that she was offering a grudging hand of friendship, and she wondered again what had gone on at home. And, even more, what was going on in that devious little mind of Dolly's. She didn't trust her and never would. Her first instincts about Dolly, all those years ago, had been the right ones. But they had once been such friends, almost sisters, and she couldn't abandon those memories entirely.

'Do you want me to come with you?' she asked, not giving an inch yet.

'I wouldn't bleedin' well ask you if I didn't want you, would I?' Dolly said, back on form.

'As long as you don't try to fix me up with some chap.'

'Would I?' Dolly said with a smirk. 'Anyway, I know you're still holding a torch for Lukey-boy,' she added, well into the habit of Hollywood slang now.

'I haven't been making any secret of it. Anyway, I slept in his bed on Christmas night.' She said it casually, and she couldn't have had a better reaction if she'd given Dolly an electric shock.

'You *what*? You saucy cow!' she shrieked, and then she saw Amber's smile widen, and of course she realized that Luke hadn't been there, and nor was he likely to have been sharing his bed with Amber in his parents' house.

'You're having me on, aren't you?'

'No, I'm not. It was very late when we'd finished playing cards on Christmas night, and Mrs Gillam said I could stay the night. So I slept in Luke's bed.'

God, it gave her such an enormous thrill, just saying the words. She had said them so many times to herself, and every time the sensations inside her were the same. *I slept in Luke's bed.* The only thing missing was Luke . . . *my darling Luke.*

'I bet you wished he was there too,' Dolly said slyly. 'I bet you were imagining all sorts of things.'

'Well, since you can't get inside my head, you'll never know, will you?'

Dolly giggled. 'Come on, gel, where Luke is concerned it wasn't inside your head that you was thinking about. Inside your knickers, more like!'

Amber didn't deign to answer that, nor to let her know how very near the truth she was. Of course she had been imagining Luke being with her, not in the crude way that Dolly was implying, but in a repeat of that wonderful first time in the cave, when they had been everything to one another. The memory of that one night could still jolt her when she least expected it, sending an exquisite rush of pleasure through her entire body. But Dolly wasn't going to know about that, either.

'Well, I'll think about the New Year's Eve dance at the club,' she said abruptly, since Dolly was still waiting for an answer. 'Now I've got better things to do than to stand here gossiping.'

She turned and pointedly went upstairs to her bedroom, closing the door behind her. What she had to do was to write to Luke, which she continued to do even if she hadn't heard from him, trying to make her letters bright and cheerful, and sending them to the new navel hospital address in Portsmouth. By the time he arrived there, he'd have her letters waiting for him.

She wasn't particularly looking forward to a dance on New Year's Eve. It would be even more exuberant this year, with everyone anticipating that peace was just around the corner, and people would let their hair down even more than usual. Dolly would be egging Amber on to do the same.

She was still suspicious of this sudden offer of friendship, but when they arrived on that chilly night the hall was full of bunting and balloons and excited chatter and she couldn't help but be drawn into it. She wasn't an old fuddy-duddy, unwilling to join in the fun just because her boy wasn't home yet. Neither were plenty of others, and there seemed to be more than enough servicemen in the club to go around. One of them grabbed her round the waist and pulled her on to the dance floor as soon as the band struck up a lively tune.

'I've been waiting a long time for this, sweetheart,' he yelled in her ear as he whirled her around.

'Have you?' she said. She knew who he was, even if she hadn't taken much notice of him at first. His name was Philip Slade, one of the old school crowd, much taller and broader now, and sporting a thin moustache that was meant to make him look dashing but only succeeded in making him look like a spiv. He was grinning down at her now with a lusty look in his eyes.

'Ever since Dolly said you'd had a pash on me for a long time I knew this was my night, especially with old Luke out of the picture.'

'What the hell are you talking about?' She was held far too tightly in his arms, and his hands seemed to be roaming far too familiarly over her rear, and there were too many other couples all pressing in on them now to break away.

He clutched her even tighter. 'Oh come on, you're not that dumb. You've had your fun with the Yanks, but now they've gone it's time to give the home-grown heroes a chance.'

She tried desperately to wrench out of his embrace, scarlet-faced at his insinuations, but he held on to her like a leech.

'Dolly said I'd had a pash on you for a long time?' she blurted out furiously.

He laughed more boldly. 'That's right, so don't try to deny it.'

'I *do* bloody well deny it,' she snapped tearfully, realizing that people were looking their way now, and sensing that a scene was about to erupt. 'There's never been anybody for me but Luke, and Dolly's a liar and a pig for saying such things.'

'Well, that's not what she says,' he went on, his voice uglier now. 'So why not smile for the camera, sweet pants?'

Too late, Amber saw a roaming photographer heading their way, intent on getting candid New Year's Eve snaps for the local newspaper, and the next minute a flash went off in front of her eyes as

Philip Slade fastened himself to her and planted a kiss on her cheek.

'That'll be a good one for the local gossips,' he sniggered.

Amber was finally free of him, giving him a push that sent him staggering into the crowd and left him hollering. She didn't care. It was like a nightmare, and she knew exactly who had started it, and the reason behind it. It was as if a bad film was unfolding in front of her eyes, in which she was coming off as the local tart.

She knew she was getting things out of all proportion, but all she could think was that even though the photo may be only one of many in the newspaper to celebrate New Year's Eve, the Gillams would see it. And it would be the very one that Dolly would almost certainly cut out and send to Luke. As the Yanks would have said, she had been stitched up, made a Patsy . . . She couldn't get the ridiculous phrases out of her head, and she was almost weeping as she forced her way through the dancers and out of the door into the cool December night.

She didn't realize Dolly was close behind her until she grabbed her arm.

'Where do you think you're going, you idiot? It was only a bit of fun, and Phil was more than ready to believe that you always had a secret pash on him.'

'Well, you know very well that I didn't,' Amber yelled. 'What do you think Luke's parents are going to think if that photo appears in the newspaper? I'm sure that was all part of your nasty little plan!'

'Bloody hell, Amber, you don't think much of me, do you?'

'Are you going to deny it then?' Amber demanded.

There was silence for a minute and then Dolly shrugged. 'Why should I? You've got a pretty low opinion of me, anyway.'

'So this sudden burst of friendship was all in aid of getting a stupid photo of me and that oaf Philip Slade, was it?'

She could hear the smile in Dolly's voice now, which didn't endear her one bit. 'Well, it worked, didn't it, gel?'

Amber turned on her heel. 'The sooner you get out of my house and get back where you belong the better. I can't bear to look at you any more.'

'That goes for me as well, you stuck-up twerp,' Dolly yelled after her, causing a group of late-comers to the dance to tut-tut at such goings-on at an evening of celebration.

Amber tore away from the club, knowing her face must be flaming. She hardly knew where she was going or how far she had gone, but her footsteps inevitably took her up Pendennis Hill. She saw none of the beautiful moonlit panorama spread out far below her, nor the gentle rush of the sea against the cliffs, seeing and hearing nothing but the treachery of Dolly Nash. She was sick with embarrassment over what had happened, and even more so at the way the friendship between herself and Dolly had finally disintegrated. There was no going back now to the way things had been. She wanted Dolly out of the cottage and out of her life, no matter what she returned to in London. As the thought raged through her mind, she burst into noisy tears, because it should never have ended like this. Granny Pen would be horrified if she knew all that had gone on.

She probably *did* know it, of course. The earthly body might be gone, but Amber was perfectly sure that somehow Granny Pen would know. Somewhere, in some other form, she would *know*, and just as surely as she thought it, a gradual sense of calm washed over Amber, because she had done nothing wrong. She had never betrayed the great love of her life for a single instant, not in thought or deed, and Granny Pen would know that and approve of it.

It was Dolly who had organized the photographer to be around just when that slimy Philip Slade had her in his clutches. It was Dolly who was calculating enough to try to worm her way into Luke's affections, when anybody with half an eye could see that he and Amber were made for one another. Always had been, and always would be.

She almost leaped out of her skin when she heard somebody whisper her name in a hoarse voice. Surely she hadn't conjured Granny Pen up out of some great beyond, had she? It was one thing to be deliciously sure of her gran dealing out the cards and doing tea-leaf readings for the angels in that other benevolent life, looking down on her granddaughter and protecting her from harm. It was quite another to be confronted with ghostly voices in the dark of night. But since Granny Pen always said it was better to face your demons than to hide from them, she whirled around. How could she ever think Granny Pen was a demon, anyway . . . ?

'I followed you all the way up here,' Dolly wheezed painfully. 'I've got a bleedin' stitch in my side now, thanks to you. What you going to do, throw yourself over the cliffs?'

'Of course not. What do you want, anyway?' Amber snapped, fractionally relieved to find the voice belonged to Dolly and not to some spectre.

Dolly took a deep, ragged breath. 'I want to say I'm sorry. It was a bloody stupid thing to do, but I didn't expect you to get in such a state about it. I've had words with that newspaper chap as well and told him if he puts that picture of you and Philip Slade in the paper I'll find him and kick him where it hurts. Mind you, I had to blackmail him as well by saying that as long as the picture doesn't appear I'll go to the flicks with him one night. He agreed, so you needn't worry about Lukey-boy seeing it.'

She was wheezing even more by the time she finished, and she swayed so alarmingly for a minute that Amber had to catch hold of her to stop her falling.

'Are you telling me the truth?' she said.

Dolly sighed. 'God Almighty, I know when I'm beaten, kid, and I don't really want to go back to London with you feeling that badly about me.'

'You *are* going, then?'

Amber began to think that this was the most bizarre conversation in the most bizarre place she'd ever had. Dolly nodded.

'I think it's best, don't you? I miss my mum, God help me, and she needs somebody to take care of her, what with Uncle Joe and his roving eyes.'

So that was the problem then. Amber didn't know what to say. Here they were, standing like idiots, not knowing what to do next. Did they hug and say it had been nice knowing each other? It hadn't always been, but there were plenty of times when they had been truly closer than sisters.

Moments later, as if to remind them what this night was all about, the church bells suddenly began to ring out the start of a new year. They could hear them far below in the town, and because they were up high on Pendennis Hill they could hear the sounds of other bells from far away, as if the whole county was in celebration.

'I'm going to make a new year's resolution to be good,' Dolly declared after a moment. 'What do you think?'

'I think pigs might fly,' Amber said, and then they were spontaneously hugging one another, laughing and crying and saying sorry for everything, and vowing undying friendship. It wouldn't last, but it was good while it did.

'Let's go home,' Amber said huskily. 'I've had enough emotion for one night and all I want is to fall into bed.'

They linked arms, and began the long walk back

to the cottage. The bells were still ringing, filling the air with sound, and replacing the need for words.

If peace hadn't come to the world yet, at least there was an uneasy and unspoken peace in the Penry cottage. They went their separate ways to work each day, and took it in turns to cook the evening meal. The local newspaper appeared with photos of the Forces' Club dance and other celebrations, but Amber's wasn't among them. Dolly fulfilled her obligation and went to the cinema with the photographer. All the time Amber felt as if she was waiting, holding her breath for the time when Luke would come home.

A letter arrived from him a week later. She was almost afraid to read it, still not knowing whether Dolly had ever written to him with one of her snide remarks. But she could have wept at the contents.

'I know I've been a bad letter writer, Amber, but for a time I didn't know what was happening to me. My hearing and memory loss made me very unbalanced, but they've returned to normal now. I didn't want to come back to you feeling like half a man, but I know I'm one of the lucky ones, and now I can't wait to get out of this place. The doctors and nurses have a hell of hard job to do, but I've had enough of hospitals. I want to get back to normal, doing the ordinary things that people do. For a time I even felt guilty that I was going to be discharged from the navy before the war ended, but I no longer feel like that. I know I did my bit, and now I can't wait to get home to see my girl. We've got a lot of time to make up, sweetheart.'

She hugged the letter to her heart, knowing that his feelings hadn't changed, any more than hers had. It was such an honest and uninhibited letter, and she was sure that he couldn't have heard anything bad from Dolly, or he wouldn't have written in that way to her. She was filled with renewed love and hope for the future.

His parents, too, had had a letter from him, but theirs was full of his plans for the boatyard once the war was over when Luke and his father could get back to doing what they loved best. Amber felt momentarily envious of the closeness of their family life, knowing she had no one. But hopefully, in time, she would be part of that family too. She crossed her fingers as she thought it, because it didn't do to tempt fate, no matter how much in love she was.

So far Dolly hadn't said anything more about going back to London, and it was a subject that was left unspoken between them. Once she did, Amber would be alone again, and she was torn between relief at having no more tension between them, and knowing she would feel unbearably lonely in the cottage. She couldn't ignore the years they had been together, all the fights and the tantrums, the friendship and the shared secrets too. Dolly would always be a part of her life, no matter how much she tried to deny it.

Luke's mother came into the craft shop at the end of January, glowing with excitement, and

Amber's heart leaped, knowing what she was going to say.

'We had a phone call from Luke last night, Amber. It was marvellous to actually hear his voice, and he sounded so close he might almost have been in the room with us.'

She was about to say more, but before she could do so she burst into tears. Amber was so embarrassed she didn't know what to do, and then Hester was sniffing and smiling and calling herself all kinds of a fool for getting so soppy.

'Though I think any mother can be forgiven for feeling soppy when she knows her son is coming home.'

'When?' Amber almost croaked.

Hester gave her a crooked smile, dabbing her eyes with a hanky and swallowing hard.

'In three days' time. I can hardly believe it. I feel like turning the house upside down and giving it a good spring clean, but Mick says I'm not to be so foolish, or I'll be too exhausted to enjoy it when he comes home!'

Amber laughed unsteadily, as emotional as Hester. 'I'm sure he's right, but I know just what you mean.'

'And you'll come to supper with us that evening, won't you, Amber?'

Even though the invitation was bringing her into the circle, she felt a weird sense of reluctance. 'I don't know. Should I? I know I'm longing to see Luke, but perhaps he should spend a little time with you first of all. I don't want to impose.'

Nor did she want to spend those first moments with Luke in the company of his parents, but she could hardly say as much. She wanted him all to herself. She wanted him so much, and perhaps until this very moment when she knew the time had come so close she had never realized quite how much.

'Well, you know the invitation stands, my dear, and I'm not sure it's just us that he's most eager to see.'

She leaned forward and kissed Amber on the cheek. It was the most significant way of letting her know that this was her son's girl, and she had her full approval.

By the time Amber got home that evening, she was in a high state of nervous excitement. In three days' time, Luke would be home, and their lives would revert to the way they had been before. And yet she knew they would never be the same again. They had both grown, mentally and physically, in the years since they had argued and teased one another as children. They had been through a war – and it still wasn't over – seen and experienced things they should never have seen, and they were different people now. She had never realized the truth of Mick Gillam's words more. The love was still there, but it was no longer the childish love of those halcyon schooldays. It was a stronger, more mature love, but it was a love that they had to get to know all over again.

'You're mad to get so worried!' Dolly told her. 'All this time you couldn't wait for him to come home, and now you're having the collywobbles about it.'

'Thanks for putting it so well,' Amber muttered. 'I'm just afraid that we'll look at one another and see two different people.'

'Why should you? It's not as if he's been away for years, is it? He hasn't been shut away in one of those awful POW camps. He's probably been living the life of Riley in those army hospitals, waited on hand and foot by the nurses.'

Amber didn't take the bait as she would once have done. Luke had told her he loved her, and no matter how many caring and attractive nurses had tended him, she was sure of that love, just as she was sure of hers for him. It wasn't that. She didn't know what it was, but the uneasiness inside her wouldn't go away, just when she had expected to be filled with joy and excitement. She wished desperately that Granny Pen was here to explain the mixture of emotions inside her. Her gran would be wise enough to know why she was feeling the way she did, but Granny Pen wasn't here and never would be again.

The unease persisted for the next few days. If anything it gathered momentum so that she could hardly eat or sleep, and Dolly became increasingly impatient with her. On the day Luke was due home she was all fingers and thumbs at work as she dealt with customers. By the end of the afternoon Mrs Veal told her to go home early as she wasn't doing much good in the shop.

'And for goodness' sake go and have supper with the family like you've been invited. How do you think Luke will feel if you don't turn up to see him? Go and make yourself pretty for your young man, and be happy that his parents want you to share in their happiness, my dear.'

'I am happy,' Amber said, 'I just haven't made up my mind what to do yet. But I'll do as you say and go home.'

She cycled home in the late afternoon, wondering what time Luke was coming home. His mother didn't know for certain. He could even be home now. The more she thought about it, the more jittery Amber became.

The cottage was silent as usual when she went inside. Dolly wouldn't be home from the club for an hour or more yet, and she decided to turn on the wireless to have some company. That was when she saw the letter propped up against it. She ripped it open, knowing it was Dolly's handwriting. What now?

'By the time you read this, I'll be gone,' Dolly had written. 'It seemed like the best time to go, before Lukey-boy came home, and I didn't want to make a big fuss about saying goodbye. We had some good times, Amber, and some bad ones too. I'm not likely to forget you, but it's time I went back where I belong, and I decided to leave while you were at work. I never did write to Luke and I wanted to be sure and tell you that. I was tempted to, mind, but in the end I never did it and that's the God's honest truth. He'd never have looked at me while you were around, anyway. You were always his girl – a proper little Cornish maid, as Granny Pen used to say. I'm not likely to forget her either. If I ever did the right thing instead of the wrong one, it was due to her, so you can thank her for that. Anyway, you won't want me hanging around like a spare part when Luke comes home, will you? Have a good life, Amber, and if you feel like writing to me now and then, you'll know where I am. And you'd better invite me to the wedding, or I'll have something to say about it.

'Your friend, and soul sister,
Dolly'

Amber's heart was banging in her chest by the time she finished reading the letter. She wasn't sure she believed that Dolly had really gone, and then she was rushing upstairs and into Dolly's bedroom, wrenching open cupboards and drawers. There was nothing of hers left, no clothes, no make-up, no screwed up bits of paper, no books, no odd shoes lurking beneath the bed, no chaos. It was as if she had never been here at all.

The next moment Amber was in floods of tears. It was all so final. It was like an unexpected death, with no chance to say goodbye or to make amends for the wrongs that had gone before. No matter who had done them, or how small, there was always recompense to be made, regrets to express, undying love to avow . . .

She took a deep, shuddering breath, knowing how

foolish she was being. This was what they both wanted, wasn't it? It was something that was inevitable. They had met so unwillingly, and gone through a short lifetime of emotions together, but now it had ended, as all things came to an end. And Amber was finally alone.

How long she sat on Dolly's bed, she didn't know. She had clenched her hands together for so long, she had dug her fingernails into her palms by the time she heard the footsteps on the gravel outside, and then the click of the door latch as somebody opened it. Nobody locked their doors around here; it must be Dolly, of course, and for a wild moment a mixture of new emotions ran through her. Dolly wasn't leaving her after all, and they could finally be grown up about all this and be the friends and sisters they'd always wanted to be. And then . . . how dare Dolly scare her with that daft letter, when she hadn't gone back to London, and if this wasn't just like her . . . she had always fancied herself as a bit of an actress, and she had played this particular part very well!

'Is anybody home?' she heard a familiar male voice call out.

If her heart had been pounding before, it was ready to burst now, but this would be the very worst time, when she knew so well who the owner of the voice would be. She leaped off the bed and abandoned all the memories that could stay stored away in her mind as she flew down the stairs and into Luke's waiting arms.

'Well, that's the best greeting I've had yet,' Luke said, when they had finally broken away, but with their arms still tightly entwined around one another.

'Are you expecting any more?' Amber said, tongue-tied for a moment from the unbridled passion in that spectacular kiss.

'I don't want any more. I only want my girl. I've missed you so much, and those weeks when I lost my memory were the worst, but whatever else I forgot, it was never you, Amber. You were like a golden light at the end of a tunnel and I knew I was always going to reach you.'

'Oh,' she said softly. 'That's so lovely, it's almost worthy of Granny Pen.'

'*You're* worthy of Granny Pen, my darling. You've grown up so beautiful and she'd be very proud of you. I want to keep looking at you and touching you to remind myself how beautiful and how real you are. You're no longer just in my dreams, but you're right here in my arms.'

For a moment she was embarrassed at how intensely he was looking at her now. It was as if he was looking into her soul, at everything she had been or done while he was away, and just as instantly she knew she had nothing to fear. He was the one who had been through so much, but the weeks of recuperation had evidently done their work, and he seemed as strong and whole as he ever was. She felt the gentle touch of his hand against her breast, sending the old, familiar tingling sensations through her, and since she couldn't be unaware of his growing passion, she had to ask.

'Luke, are you sure – are you quite recovered?' she asked tentatively. 'Your memory and your hearing – and the physical wounds?'

He gave his old remembered smile. 'The day I forget how to make love to my girl and can't hear the sweet music of her voice will be a long day coming, sweetheart. Anything else has long since recovered. We've got a lifetime ahead of us to talk and I know you'll want to know what happened to me, but right now there's only one thing I want to do to make my homecoming complete – providing there's no one else in the house.'

He couldn't make his intentions more plain – nor could they be more reciprocated.

'There's no one but the two of us, Luke,' Amber whispered.

It wasn't the done thing for the girl to take the initiative, but for a brief moment she had seen a question in his eyes. Did he think for one instant that she didn't want them to be lovers once more, that she hadn't been waiting all her life for them to be together in the way God meant true soulmates to be? As she stood up she caught his hand and they moved towards the stairs, arms still wrapped around one another.

'There's one more thing I've got to ask you, Amber,' he said gravely.

She paused, wondering even now if she should have waited, been less eager, but it wasn't in her nature and he knew that only too well. He turned her into him, his hands cupping her face, and everything she wanted to see was in his eyes, and she knew she needn't have worried.

'Please say you'll marry me as soon as possible, because I don't think I can bear to wait a second longer than necessary to have you with me for always.'

Her answer was in the kiss she gave him, and, from somewhere in the ether, Amber thought she could imagine a faint sense of a certain Granny Pen breaking off from her angelic card-reading to give them her blessing. The moment vanished as quickly as it came, and any such unworldly thoughts were far from Amber's mind in the joy of this special night when Luke would become finally and totally hers.